My Lo

# ZEBRA

## INSPIRED BY THE LIFE OF ATHOL WALLACE

You are my little treasure.

Jill Wallace

Love you to pieces

Always

your other sister,

Jill

xxx

TSOTSI
PUBLICATIONS

ZEBRA

by Jill Wallace



Paperback ISBN: 978-0-9997768-3-4

First edition

Published by Tsotsi Publications

www.jillwallace.com

## CONTENTS

*Dedicated to Terry D. Wallace*
*and Lesley R. Wallace Kimball*
*with love. xx*

# SOUTHERN AFRICA

## THE SETTING FOR ZEBRA

*Map by South African artist Veronica Prins*

# 1

## LITTLE BOY WHO NEVER CRIES

*Champagne Castle Hotel, Drakensberg Mountains,*
*South Africa, 1954*

JOCK WAS FREE. He lifted his face to the sun, closed his eyes and breathed in the non-smoky, non-soapy air. His plan was to climb the leafiest tree and stay there in peace as long as he could.

Being four years old was a tough business. He didn't need a team of babysitters. He needed to help his dad. Sitting quietly between branches and leaves would help him figure out how to make himself useful. Dad kept useful people close to him.

Aha! The perfect liquid amber tree. He wrapped his arms as far as they'd go around the hefty trunk, hugging it with his cheek flattened on the rough bark, and inhaling its rich woody smell. Yes. This was the one. His *takkie* found a knot in the trunk that was high enough to help hoist him up, and he moved nimbly into the camouflage of intricate branches and thick leaves.

Baboons barked. Their chattering sounds were louder than usual. Jock squinted through the foliage. The primates strutted back and forth on top of the small hill in front of the towering

Matterhorn mountain. Two baboons cartwheeled gaily. Showing off, his dad said, was their way to scare off troops from across the valley who wanted to steal their home.

They were so noisy, one of the smaller ones on the sidelines stuck his fingers in his ears. Jock laughed. They were so human-like. He'd love to play with them, but Dad said he was to stay far away because their mouths could open so wide, they could easily bite his four-year-old head off. Jock had laughed heartily until he saw his dad was serious. Serious meant trouble.

Oh, no! They were disappearing over the lip of the *koptjie.* He couldn't see them anymore. Well, he'd just climb up the hill and watch from the top. But Dad said ...

He climbed higher into the tree and found a perfect spot. At least he could listen and imagine.

There was so much barking. Sometimes they sounded like dogs.

Then he heard a cry. It was a high-pitched sound of agony and broke Jock's small heart. It was coming from over the hill. But Dad said ...

The sound again, pitiful. Jock pushed the sight of his dad's face from his mind, slithered down the tree, and pumped his legs with all his might up the hill.

As he peeped over the ridge, his eyes were bigger than his bravery. Dad was right. Trouble.

CONSTANCE the laundry mistress reveled in her generous folds. She had more flesh on her bones than she had bones. Constance was a woman of substance, a supreme nurturer and in charge of this busy hotel laundry.

The laundry had three cylindrical stoves on which the irons leaned, always hot and ready. She and her female staff stoked and stroked all day and into the night in high season, so they could produce the whitest, most well-ironed sheets and pillowcases, tablecloths and serviettes in all of the Drakensberg.

Against the walls of the large room were cast-iron sinks and scrubbing boards. Bars of olive green, Sunlight soap, were everywhere. No excuse for dirt.

Constance wasn't sorry to see the backsides of her last employers leave the hotel property. The new bosses were a young family with a small boy. She'd had very little interaction with them since their arrival two weeks earlier when all the staff lined up to greet these new owners.

Shortly afterwards, Nicholas, the Zulu voice of authority, gathered heads of all the departments together. Eteemot represented the outside boys; Constance the laundry girls; Billy Pillay the wine stewards.

"Know your place and you'll keep your jobs. They've never run a hotel before. Most important part of your job is training them. But they must never know. After you've shown them how and they make you do what you've just taught them, praise them for their good idea. But be smart because they are smart. Your livelihood depends on how well you teach them without them realizing it. If they don't do a good job, we won't have jobs."

"Eich" was said by many in sheer exasperation of having to teach white folks their jobs. Again. But the alternative, losing their positions, was too awful to imagine, so they went off to share Nicholas's ground rules with their staff.

What Nicholas said was done. Nicholas was the law.

The parents were so busy with their new business, they had no notion of what to do with their young one. Nicholas suggested the laundry building might be the safest place for him till they could come up with a better solution. Only one door in and one door out. The *umtwana* couldn't go anywhere. Nicholas gently suggested Constance's added responsibility should be rewarded, and Inkosi, as their new chief was respectfully called, was quick to oblige.

So Constance took on the responsibility. When her staff went outside to hang the washing on the many lines, she dangled the fear of the ancestors over their heads to make sure the boy didn't sneak out. He was sturdy and quick. She could tell by the looks of him he was a determined little thing. She could not afford to be in poor favor with Nicholas. Besides, it took a mountain of chocolate to sustain her voluptuous folds, and the additional Cadburys were contributing nicely.

Constance ruled with chatter. She ignited it and encouraged it. As long as her ladies were talking and doing their jobs, they didn't know how hard they were working.

An introverted laundry woman, welcomed under Constance's hot, soapy umbrella, was in less than a week airing her own dirty laundry for all to ponder, sympathize with and advise upon.

The umtwana spent most of the time with his hands over his ears. Every now and then Constance would feel the need to engulf him in her strong arms, and he resisted like a shrew fighting off a snake. Constance was undeterred and repeated the performance every couple of hours. He didn't talk much, but his expressive face told its own story.

It was time. She left her ladies chattering and swept off to wrap her arms around her charge, thoughts of a slab of Cadbury's fruit and nut making her mouth water.

She felt a niggle when he wasn't found sitting with his back to the door, hoping for the chance for a quick getaway. She took a look around her turf and saw an open window behind one of the empty sinks.

Constance's internal thermometer—always topping the red —plummeted to six degrees Celsius. She began to shiver.

Easy for a boy to climb onto that sink and out of the window.

The high-pitched keening sound that emitted from her mouth summed up the fear and panic that surged through her body.

"Umtwana's gone," she shouted, and it cut through the noise and created a rare silence that hovered ominously in the smoky, stifling heat. The severity of those words caused a paralysis in that laundry for five long seconds.

When Constance moved, fervent activity followed. Ladies abandoned washboards and irons and searched inside laundry baskets and in cupboards, then spilled outside onto the green grass, weaving between wash lines to inspect surrounding bushes and trees.

Constance shouted to her staff. "Go! Find him. I must tell Nicholas."

Constance had a sudden image of bars of Cadbury's being snatched from her as she ran, apron flying. She had no idea she could work up such a speed.

"Why is there a wasp in your bosom before lunch, Constance?" Nicholas's voice boomed.

She stopped short, and the notion of confessing the loss of "Little Boy Who Never Cries," as the waiters called him, sent fear-spears through her chest.

Nicholas glanced down at her apron. "I see your babysitting allows you extra sweeties."

Guilt replaced the fear-spears as she looked down and saw the telltale shiny gold wrapper of her chocolate peeping out of her pocket.

She felt herself start to wobble from her legs up to her tummy, and she burst into body-shaking sobs and cried like she hadn't since she'd been orphaned at seven. She heaved, blubbered and sniffed until the fear-spears pierced again during a deep breath and she was reminded of why she'd sought out Nicholas.

Nicholas hastily led her mucus-covered self away from prying eyes and flapping ears.

"Tell me everything," he demanded.

And she did, in staccato sentences between sobs. "Little Boy Who Never Cries is gone from my laundry! Lose my job. No more work for my ladies either. New bosses. My Cadbury's ..." And then the wail took over and the tears flowed in earnest again.

Nicholas's voice was firm and quite scary, really. "You stop that now! Snot and tears will not bring him back. Call your ladies to the kitchen back door. Get word to Eteemot to bring ten outside boys. We will start the search—properly and in an orderly fashion so we know all the ground has been covered. NOW, Constance. Get your big self into gear!"

Those harsh words rendered her hard-earned confidence nothing but *putu pap*, and she was a frightened girl once more.

Nicholas pushed her in the direction she needed to go, and she went. Dispatching messages and gathering her ladies, she shepherded them outside the kitchen's back door.

In two years, she'd risen like a bar of Sunlight soap to the top of the sink to become head of the laundry. Without it, she had nothing. The kraal down the valley was her home, the only one she'd known since she was a girl. She couldn't justify living there without a job.

She'd lost a boy, and her life was over. Her temperature plummeted again, and she shivered as she heard herself wail. Laundry ladies gathered around her with pats and rubs and comforting Zulu words.

When they were all assembled outside the back door of the kitchen, Nicholas appeared and stood facing the small crowd he'd summoned.

Nicholas spoke Zulu to the assembled employees. The Indian waiters understood the language because they had to.

White men did not need to learn an African language. They were the bosses and the brown and black men, their servants. It was these servants' mission to understand their boss, not the other way around. It was the way things were done. There were no grander expectations.

Nicholas was a big Zulu, both in size and in presence. He was broad in knowledge and in fairness. But he scared the manure out of all of them.

"Umtwana is missing. The boss does not know. Nobody must know, especially not the boss. This lost boy is our secret. Find him, send word to me, but stay with him. He's fast."

Nicholas looked into the eyes of each man and woman who stood before him, and under his glare, each shrunk at least two inches, just the way he expected.

"Three outside men to the quarry—inspect every square inch. Five outside boys—down toward the stables. Pick up the horse boys on your way to help you search farther. Go wide and up, toward the mountains. The last two of you, go through the gum trees. Check where the rinkhals live and speak nicely to the ancestors as you go, because if the boy is there ..." Nicholas let the severity of that potential discovery linger in the ominous air.

Ten strapping Zulus peeled off to do as instructed.

"Constance, take all five bedroom-boys and search every *rondavel. Go!"*

"Ladies of Laundry, check each and every square inch of the bowling green, the swimming pool, verandas, inside the dog kennels—he's been there before—the tennis courts. Look up the trees and inside the bushes. All around the outside of the hotel." Ladies scattered.

"Scullery boys, check inside the walk-in pantry, even the freezer. Then every square inch of the main hotel. Under couches. Behind chairs. Bars. Lounges. Game Room. Dining room—and quickly before I ring the bell for children's lunch.

Anyone asks, you tell them you're looking for dirty glasses. Even Inkosi. You tell him the same."

"Yebo," the two said in unison and disappeared.

With his posse dispatched, big Nicholas pulled the lapels of his smart jacket down, straightened his thin black tie and walked into the kitchen, which was in a pre-lunch flurry.

David Walsh, the missing umtwana's father, smiled, and Nicholas flashed one of his finest and bowed slightly. "Inkosi."

"You were having a meeting?" David asked.

"Indeed, Inkosi. Making sure all parts of the whole make you proud of your new undertaking."

"Well." David smiled. "I certainly would have trouble knowing what comes next without you. We had no official handover from the last owners."

"Your know-how will come, Inkosi. Until then it is my delight to assist in the process." Nicholas bowed again.

David said, "Nicholas, I've never worked so closely with Zulus. You are an exceptionally courteous people. I know looking away from me is a sign of your respect, but I'm a man who likes to look into another man's eyes. One can find truth there ... or not."

Nicholas and David looked each other in the eyes until they both nodded. David was satisfied. Nicholas was guilty as hell and felt bad, in this case, that he'd mastered not letting another read what was behind his eyes.

David continued, "So much to learn, it's overwhelming. Thank goodness you found a safe place for Jock for the time being."

Nicholas felt a surge of dread and feigned an excuse to look inside the fridge so he could avoid those frank eyes of his new boss. He put on his calm face as he and Inkosi watched the pre-lunch organized-chaos: Thabo, the always-smiling head chef, effectively directed while assistant chefs executed. Waiters came and went through swing doors to the dining room, preparing for the lunch onslaught.

Inkosi said, "Nicholas, you have the authority of General Montgomery and the size and wisdom of Winston Churchill," and he looked to Nicholas for a response. Having no clue what was expected of him, Nicholas smiled and nodded what could have been thanks.

Inkosi continued as if thinking aloud: "One is so spoiled in the city. You switch on the light and think nothing of it. You run hot water without thought. Here, light only comes on if the weir is not jammed and the water flow is adequate to start the generator. If there's no light, you have to find out why—remove dead frogs or snakes blocking the weir, repair the generator, and start again. Wood must be constantly chopped and dried for fires, which have to be stoked to provide excellent food, many hot showers and clean linens. Adequate paraffin must be hauled up the mountain to keep our fridges and deep freezes cool. Cows must be fed so they can be milked so the separator can be wound by two men to get the cream for the pudding tonight. Nothing just happens. It's constant forward planning and massive manpower, all to make everything seem effortless to our guests."

"It is so, Inkosi." Nicholas turned to David. "It is time for me to ring the children's bell for lunch. All is prepared."

Inkosi nodded, and Nicholas was relieved to get out of the kitchen. He wandered the grounds ringing his tinkling silver bell through the rondavels, through the main hotel and across the sprawling property so not a guest-child at Champagne Castle Hotel would have an excuse to miss their call to lunch. Where was the umtwana? His stomach did a flip.

As his bell tinkled, Nicholas checked in with passing search members. There was no need for conversation, just eye contact and a slight shake of the head.

Nicholas, who was not one to worry, began to do so. Yes, he was in good favor as his boss's only link to understanding the hotel business. But Nicholas knew his worth could disappear in a flash when the boss found out his only son was gone. It was Nicholas who'd recommended the child be left in Constance's care, so it was indeed he who lost the child. If the boy was never found, if he was maimed or if he was dead, Nicholas would be blamed. And rightly so. This couple relied on his advice.

Nicholas talked seriously to the ancestors. Though he smiled and waved at the excited white children, thoughts of Mrs. Inkosi finding out her only son was missing had unfamiliar panic nipping at his ankles.

The full force of the barrage of excited children on holiday entered the dining room. His waitstaff were ready to serve kids and impress mothers and fathers who tagged along. All looked as it should. No one could tell Nicholas was experiencing his first bout of fear since ... since he became important.

Nicholas glanced at the clock. An hour and a half since they'd found umtwana gone. It took only seconds for anyone—let alone a helpless child—in these mountains to lose their way, lose their consciousness, lose their limbs or lose their life. Venomous snakes. Wild animals. Deadly spiders. Primal baboons. Crevices. Streams. Waterfalls. Dizzying heights.

He was staring out of the dining room discussing these issues with the ancestors when he saw a horse on the gallop toward the hotel. News. His knees buckled ever so slightly.

The horse was closer, and he could make out a bundle in a horse blanket in front of the young horse boy. A bundle, not a boy? His *Gollaga-inja* knees buckled again. Another quarter of an inch and they would have taken his big-self down in his own dining room.

Recovering, he found his most reliable waiter and whispered to him to take charge. In the kitchen, Inkosi was safely oblivious and thoroughly involved in the shuttling of children's fare. Nicholas hightailed it out of the back door, and closing it behind him, he lifted his head to the ancestors in feverish prayer.

The horse boy's face was hard to read from this distance. He steadied a bundle—too big for just a umtwana—between surprisingly strong arms that held the reins.

Why was there was no young boy sitting up straight, excited out of his wits by his first horse gallop?

Perhaps the boy was in pieces inside the bundle.

*Gollaga-inja!* No! NO!

His secret searchers had also spotted the galloping horse and were gathering for news.

At last, but yet too soon, Papin the horse boy brought the giant mare to a stop right in front of Nicholas. But where was this boy's famous smile? The one that split his face so easily with pleasure? NO!

Papin swung his leg over and dropped to the ground with the big bundle in his arms and laid it gently down.

A squirm and a once-white, small face with big eyes popped out, covered in dirt and blood.

Praise the ancestors! Nicholas had never known such relief. He reached down to pick him up, but the boy pulled away, shouting in panic, "Not me. Him!" as he pointed to the fur-and-blood form lying inside the blanket.

A medium-size, medium-colored dog had a mass of blood where his rear extremities should have been. His leg was missing too.

"Help," the boy cried, imploring Nicholas with those big eyes.

And the back door opened with a whoosh.

Nicholas felt Inkosi before he saw him. There was absolute silence around him as everyone froze in fear.

"Dad," the boy called "Help! Puppy is broken."

In seconds, Inkosi picked up his son for a quick investigation, noticed his one shoe-less foot, and put him down, Then, much more gently, he lifted the dog by the scruff of its neck to inspect it.

"We need axle grease. Quickly, to the workshop." Inkosi took charge, and Nicholas sent one of the outside boys ahead with towels and another in search of the grease.

"I need to know exactly what happened once we've all calmed down," said Inkosi to Nicholas, who was grateful there was no time for words and less still for looking into a man's eyes.

Once inside, Inkosi gently laid down the dog on the towel-covered workbench, picked up Umtwana and plonked him near the dog. He looked at his son. "You okay, Jock?"

The boy nodded, his eyes never leaving the mangled mutt.

When Eteemot presented the axel grease in a mighty tin, Inkosi cupped a big handful, then very, very gently plastered the dog's backside with it. The mutt whimpered softly, and Umtwana's eyes were painfully sad as he softly stroked the dog's snout.

Done, Inkosi wiped his bloodied, greasy hands on a towel. The boy looked up at his father with adoration and faith. A thousand words were spoken in that look, and Nicholas wished he'd had a son. This umtwana believed his dad could fix anything. Even this dying dog.

Nicholas leaned in. The weak little mutt was barely breathing. What hope did it have? It was missing half of its behind and a leg.

"Inkosi? This dog was born with three legs ... or its leg was taken by a baboon long before his bum was taken today."

Their three heads converged on the dog's rear. When he and Inkosi nodded their confirmation, so too the boy's head went up and down as he grinned.

"Good. Good. Then he stands more of a chance. Axle grease

should kill any germs and seal and heal the flesh, if we can just get the dog through his shock. Nicholas, get me milk, sugar and a dropper from one of the first aid kits. Get a couple of tots of brandy from the wine steward on your own authority."

Inkosi was unquestionably in charge.

Nicholas left to do what was needed, all the while dreading to see Inkosi's faith in him lost when the truth came out. This was no doubt his last day. He felt sad. He liked Inkosi, and this little umtwana was quietly worming his way into his heart. The thought of dealing with a lamenting Constance as they trudged down the mountain road in search of new jobs was a fate worse than death.

On his way to the workshop, Nicholas found the anxious horse boy and asked him for details of the rescue. He'd better know the full story before he was called upon to deliver it.

Back in the workshop, Nicholas filled a dropper of the hastily prepared *muti,* and standing next to the boy, he lifted the floppy little head and eased the dropper into the dog's mouth, squeezing it in little bursts. At first, the liquid dripped out the side of its mouth. But Nicholas persisted. He felt the boy's eyes studying his every move.

The softest little murmur came from the dog, and the boy's face lit up.

His father's voice was soft and kind. "Don't get your hopes up, Jock. He's been badly bitten."

Nicholas said, "I heard baboons at the bottom of the Matterhorn earlier. Their barks and chatter happen sometimes. Never a need for concern."

"Don't tell the dog that. They really did a number on the little mite."

Nicholas thanked the ancestors' baboons for not doing to the boy what they'd done to the dog. Just then, he felt a tug at the end of the dropper.

In a minute, he pulled it out slowly. Empty. He drew in more mixture from the bowl and gave the dropper to the boy.

He covered the small hand with his own and guided it to the mutt's mouth. He helped the umtwana squeeze just the right amount of liquid into the dog's mouth, and when, once again, the dog's natural suckling inclination kicked in, the boy's face lit up with pleasure.

Inkosi ordered an old sheet and blanket, and Constance brought them in—still quivering.

Inkosi tore the sheet into strips. He bound the dog's rear end to ensure the whole area remained covered in grease. Then he swaddled the dog in the blanket and carried it into the kitchen with Umtwana following closely and Nicholas behind them.

Inkosi made room in the corner of the scullery for the boy to sit, and once he was down on the cool slate, his father placed the limp dog in the blanket between his son's legs. Nicholas handed him the full dropper, and the boy smiled his thanks and did as he'd been shown.

Inkosi, his clothes covered in dog's blood and grease, called for Nicholas to follow him into the big walk-in pantry. Inkosi closed the door.

Nicholas looked around, and all of his senses came alive. The smell of flowers standing in a bucket, freshly picked to replace almost tired ones on the tables before dinner ... pungent, picked garlic hanging upside down in a dark corner of the pantry, rosemary, chives ... perhaps it was the last time he'd see and smell all that was so wonderfully familiar.

"Nicholas. What happened?"

"It's my fault, Inkosi."

"Just tell me."

Nicholas was not used to quiet, civil conversation where anger lurked. He found it to be more frightening than being beaten with ugly and insulting words. Nicholas had never been frightened. Of anything. Before today.

"Inkosi, he was in the laundry, then he wasn't. The girls found an open window above an empty sink. It's very hot in there, Inkosi, but the girls know one of their jobs is to protect Umtwana and would not normally open a window unless they are working in front of that sink. I plan on finding out who is responsible, Inkosi."

Nicholas braced himself for the onslaught of abuse and reminders of his incompetency.

When they never came, he spread his legs to firm his stance against the new knee- buckling sensation this ordeal had uncovered and mustered every steel nerve in his body for the courage to look into the eyes of his new boss.

He took a deep breath and looked in the eyes of Inkosi, ready to take what he deserved.

He couldn't believe the look on his boss's face.

It was genuine grace.

"Nicholas, it's thanks to your exceptional organization, dispatch and follow-through that this little rascal was found at all. Nobody is to blame. It was an inadequate place to hole up a four-year-old. Renee and I should have known better. The responsibility on Constance was far too great. It's smelly in there. If I were Jock, I would have hightailed it out of that hot laundry first chance I got."

"Thank you, Inkosi," was as much as Nicholas could manage with tears threatening. He was a middle-aged man who men and women feared! What did he know of tears?

"Nicholas, I am of British heritage. Stiff upper lip, you know. Men don't hug men. Men don't cry. Men are stoic. But I'll tell you this. I'm a man ready to break good old British tradition, and all because of you. Thank you for finding my son."

They stood, these manly men, avoiding each other's eyes

because they were both grateful and embarrassed by the extent of their indebtedness.

"How many people were involved in the hunt?" asked David.

"Thirty or so, Inkosi," Nicholas replied.

"What can I give the staff as a thank-you, Nicholas?"

"Beer, Inkosi. They love Castle Lager."

"So it shall be. How did the horse boy find him?"

Nicholas was relieved he had the answer. "He took Beauty and wove back and forth, back and forth up the small hill in front of the Matterhorn, Inkosi. Once he got over the lip of that hill, he found the umtwana cradling the dog and hiding behind a bush. He must have followed the sound of the dog's cries and then not wanted to leave him to get help. He would never have heard us calling for him or seen the flurry of our search from where he was, Inkosi. Thank the ancestors the baboons had retreated, but they were still noisy and would have drowned out our cries to call him home. Papin, the horse boy, said the umtwana had wrapped his body around the dog to try and stop the bleeding. I think that helped to keep it alive."

David cleared his throat. "Tell me about the young horse boy, please, Nicholas. Then bring him to see me."

DAVID LOOKED DOWN at his son and reckoned the dog would be smothered by love long before the angry baboon bite healed.

Thank God Nicholas had spared Renee the agony of a missing child. And him.

Little bugger. David reached down and pushed a dark curl off his son's forehead, more roughly than intended, and said, "How the hell can I see if there's anything wrong with your head when it's all bloodied up? Go wash your face."

While Jock was gone, David reexamined the young dog. *He's as strong as the kid who found him.*

Jock was back, sitting next to the dog. The mutt even opened his eyes when the little bugger returned. David smiled.

"What shall I call him, Dad?"

"Well, since he's only got three legs, how about Tripod?" David demonstrated with three middle fingers.

Jock's wet head nodded vigorously as he smiled.

Next to Nicholas, the rider of the horse stood before him. Tall and shy.

"Papin?" asked David.

The boy stepped forward. "Inkosi." He kept his eyes averted.

"How many years do you have, Papin?" David spoke in very basic Zulu.

"I have nine years, Inkosi," said Papin.

"I hear you lost your mother when you were just two years old." David spoke softly.

"I did," said the boy, his head hanging low.

"I am so sorry, Papin. That's hard for a small boy." David had run out of Zulu vocabulary and switched to English. "Nine? That's a good age to earn a better wage. Today... Nicholas, what's the word for a naughty boy?"

"Perhaps *Tsotsi,* Inkosi? But that's more like a little devil," said Nicholas apprehensively.

"That's perfect! Tsotsi it is! Papin, today you saved this tsotsi!" David roughly ruffled the unharmed, wet head of his son.

The father's harsh-sounding way with his own boy made Papin look directly at him. Then quickly away.

"Papin, look at me. Perhaps you would keep an eye on this boy of mine for me?"

The boy did so, albeit tentatively, since it was impolite practice for Zulu people. The boy cocked his head, trying to understand what David meant by the last statement.

"Your father, Sponon, does a wonderful job tending our cattle. He says you are an excellent horse boy, but you must learn patience."

"It is so, Inkosi," Papin said softly, clearly ashamed of his shortcomings but too afraid to look away.

"I can help. This tsotsi needs an expert who understands these mountains. One who can teach a small boy how to look after himself. This tsotsi needs Papin."

Papin looked directly at David, his face serious.

And then Papin's eyes grew as big as a pair of full moons after too much native beer.

"So, Inkosi. This will be *my* tsotsi to teach?" Papin asked.

"Yes. You'll earn more for each year he grows. As you manage to turn a *tsotsi* into a boy and then a man, you will get all the training you'll need to be the most patient man in Zululand. You will make your father proud!"

Papin's smile was big enough to power up the hotel generator. He looked down at his new charge, and though he spoke in Zulu, he demonstrated. "Take off the one takkie you have left. You don't need shoes when you are with me. I will carry your dog."

David watched as Jock hastily took off his shoe and Papin extended his hand and said simply, "Come, Tsotsi."

As he watched the Zulu holding the dog wrapped in the soft blanket leave the kitchen, followed by his barefooted son, David felt immense relief. A sensation he hadn't felt since his wife, Renee, Jock and he, three up on the bench seat of their old Chevy, drove 6,000 feet above sea level toward their new adventure at Champagne Castle Hotel.

But David's relief was short-lived as realism wormed its way back in. He'd been a lone signaler in a world war. Life was fraught with challenges and the unexpected. Best he enjoyed this moment, because who knew what life would deliver next?

2

# AFRICA'S CURSE

*South West Africa/Angola, 1977*

RIDING SHOTGUN, Lieut glanced past a pair of brown, hairless legs, to the man—rather, the boy—at the wheel. He watched his corporal, nineteen-year-old Cairns, slow-dancing with the massive steering wheel, tongue out, like he was using his first pair of scissors. A Polaroid of a shy-looking blondish girl was tucked into the driver's seat's visor.

The sturdy army truck roared, revved, burped and bumped forward on the "road," which was in fact a rugged path with fewer rocky outcrops than the rest of the arid, unforgiving terrain.

Between him and Cairns, Boesman—his team's Bushman tracker—stood, balancing expertly using his gnarly, bare, terrain-conditioned toes as stabilizers, gripping the edge of the worn leather bench seat.

Lieut looked up, past the brown legs, the loincloth with deer-skin waistband, beyond the naked, protruding belly, to Boes-man's head, which poked through the "sunroof." A turtle standing on hind legs. Lieut smiled as genuine affection washed over him.

With two wars going at the same time—the Bush Wars and the Border War—as soon as you left the safety of camp, you were in a war zone. Boesman was their eyes and ears and their sixth sense. Lieut wondered if his guys had any idea how much more perilous each minute of their mission would be without him.

Lieut's brief, as usual, was to catch and kill notorious terrorist Lwazi. But the elusive bastard was hard to track, except when he deliberately left an impression. Each of their days was based on the most recently extorted intelligence from Lwazi's path of destruction.

*Here we go again.*

He turned to let the hot desert wind from the open window slap his face. The quick glimpse of a small herd of springbok was further evidence of the devastating drought. The slender, long-legged antelope bunched together skittishly. There were too few to protect each other. There was none of their usual "pronking" or jumping straight-legged six and a half feet into the air. Drought forced the scrawny springbok to merely amble in a tight bunch, parched skin stretched across bones like pelts across chunks of hollow trunks to make drums. Sadness overwhelmed him.

*Nature is cruel. So is war.*

"Yissis, Lieut. You sound like a philosopher or something, man," said Cairns, his tongue pointing in the direction intended for the brute Bedford truck as he fought to conquer the oversize steering wheel with a will of its own.

Lieut looked at Cairns like he'd crawled out of a hole. He'd spoken aloud?

He forced himself to buck the hell up by looking beyond the sparse, sandy nothingness and into the earth, up to the sun, searching for animals, insects or any of nature's hidden surprises.

Her peculiar marvels burrowed and buried from the relentless sun, fighting for a slither of shade. You just had to know how and where to look for her treasures to be able to appreciate them. A bed of scorpions, too big in number to fit under all the shade of a boulder, allowed a few sand-colored pinchers to catch the sun's light.

"Cairns, did you know scorpions have up to ten sets of eyes?"

"Like Cathy, my girl. She catches me doing all sorts of shit, Lieut."

Lieut chuckled, and a few miles later, in an odd-angled, leafless tree, he saw an eleven-foot gray and brown snake draped between thorns, warming cold blood in the relentless South West African sun.

"Hey, Lieut! Is that a big freaking snake in that tree?"

"Yes. A black mamba. Probably three meters long."

"It can't be a black mamba. It's not black."

"Cairns, stop the truck and go have a good look in its mouth."

Cairn's foot slipped off the gas, mistaking conversation for command.

Seeing Lieut's grin, Cairns laughed in relief, and the Bedford roared.

"You'd find the inside of that mouth as black as pitch and holding twenty drops of venom per fang. You and I only need two drops to look forward to fifteen hours of excruciating death."

Still studying the massive snake, Lieut continued: "Look at it ... one of the few fat things in this semi-desert. It doesn't have to use its speed of sixteen kilometers an hour for prey. It can just hang around and grow fat on slow, thirsty mice. Poor little buggers."

*Nature's not for sissies, and neither is war.* Lieut's thoughts turned to Drought and her vicious favoring of the strong: the mostly lone-hunting cheetah easily outrunning a thirsty springbok, a young bush buck's frantic search for water overtaking its instinctive caution for predators and becoming easy prey for a low-crawling leopard or crocodile at a sparse water hole.

These animal scenarios were as vivid as if they'd presented their desolate pantomime to Lieut on a giant drive-in screen.

Storing nature's scenes was an excellent means of escape. One he'd been practicing for many, many years.

A cloud of dust swallowed the cab as the sturdy Bedford hit an outcrop of rock camouflaged by tufts of dry grass and sand. Lieut's bum lifted up weightlessly, then crashed down hard on the leather seat.

His gaze went first to the knotted brown toes. But like ancient, determined branches forced to curl or die, Boesman's digits still clutched the casing between him and Cairns.

"He's okay," thought Lieut as the Bushman shouted his peculiar clicking noises into the wind, expressive brown hands punching the air above the truck.

Lieut chuckled. Talking to oneself was not only his burden to bear but also Boesman's.

Lieut cupped his hand and yelled upwards, "Sorry, Boesman," and a wrinkled hand came down and patted Lieut on the head, like he was an obedient dog. He felt his cheeks bunch with pleasure.

Every time the "road" challenged the Bedford, Lieut heard muffled "Whooooas" pushing through the closed Perspex window to the back of the truck. He could imagine his boys' bodies lifting up and staying suspended in the air for a millisecond before slamming down hard onto wooden benches. Ow! He imagined them rubbing new bruises on not-so-new tailbones as cursing and moaning pulsed into the front of the cab.

Like any good caretaker, Lieut cocked his head to listen to the laments of each and then relaxed. All seven at the back were accounted for.

The next outcrop came too soon, and the truck stalled. Cairns swore and jumped out in a flash. His head quickly disappeared under the dust-encrusted khaki hood.

Muffled bitching from the back and the incessant clicking of the bushman with the bird's-eye view became background noise as Lieut's eagle eyes found an unusually large pride of lions about a hundred yards away.

The Bedford had stalled in a prime spot for viewing. If only they were on safari and he could immerse himself into nature's brilliant performance. But this was a war zone. At least four fifths of his senses had to remain on high alert. Bugger! Thirty or so of the glorious beasts, all sizes and ages, blended beige and gold into a ledge of low-hanging rocks dotted with long, wild grass.

Being gifted with this rare sight, Lieut's chest was unexpectedly filled with gratitude.

After a few seconds, he recognized the lions had made him aware he *could* still feel. Now *that* was something.

War and man's shenanigans were of no interest to the lions. Man's noise had been part of their existence for too long to deter nature's necessary course.

Some big cats stretched languidly, increasing their already incredible length. A cub suffered a necessary bath from her mother's slow tongue, and a few teenage lions played rambunctiously. Others dotted the rocks in a Sphinx-like tableau. Bloody remains of their easy-prey buffet spread across the rocks and spilled over onto the long, dry grass, crushing it. The mutilated carcass was nothing but an occasional black and white stripe dotted here and there. A zebra. *Poor thirsty bugger had no chance at all.*

*Zebra.* A thousand Technicolor images and full sensory overload flooded his head but left disappointment souring his tongue, and Lieut was relieved when a cackle of insane laughter brought him to.

A clan of mottled hyenas stood on skinny legs overlooking the big cats' picnic, laughing and waiting. When the pride was too sleepy and too full to care, the cackle would swarm in on the carcass and crunch the bones with mighty jaws until they'd had their fill. Then nature's undertakers—the vultures—would swoop in and peck away relentlessly, and finally the insects, ants, termites and spiders would consume every morsel till the dry earth left no signs of the zebra's demise. Only grass flattened by massive bodies would mark for days where the lions had feasted.

A humongous male lion yawned, a sound so loud, it made the Bedford shake. Lieut imagined the mighty beast's distended stomach pulling down heavy eyelids, begging for a post-feast sleep.

Then the lion used his five-hundred-pound bulk to bash a less ferocious half-brother out of the way to claim the last remaining prize: the sparse shade of the only thorn tree for many a hectare.

The driver's door pulled open, and Cairns's grin confirmed his mechanical prowess. He jumped back in and powered up the metal beast, touched the photo of his cutie and used his whole upper body to tango with the steering wheel and urge the brute forward.

He looked to Lieut like a little kid driving a tractor, but gobbled up by the army straight out of school, Cairns was nearly at the end of his two-year military stint. Like all of the boys of his time, there was no alternative to being thrust into his country's war as soon as he matriculated.

When the army called, whether you were getting married or

your mother was dying, you reported for duty or you went to jail. And after your two mandatory years, your career could still be interrupted at any time. The government owned you. Though your company "held your position," in the three or four months you were away on army duty, your once-indispensable business cog had been replaced and forced to turn without you, in the inevitable wheels of progress.

*Now that would successfully screw up a career and a marriage—and all for a whopping nine cents a day and no benefits.*

He mentally slapped himself and thought of the nine men under his command. He owed them his freshest eyes and his sharpest awareness. *Don't let resentment screw it up. Focus. Keep them safe.*

A huge dip in the uneven road caused another collective complaint from the top and back of the cab in three languages. "Cairns, I hope you are not considering driving for a living after this, because you stink at it," said Lieut. Then he grinned at the youngster. "But—God help us—you stink less than the girls in the back, so keep up the good work. Let's go!"

Cairns's grin was replaced by his navigating tongue a mile later.

"This desolate part of the country is the second enemy we're fighting," Lieut said.

"Shit, Lieut. It's like steering a Boer bull by the horns."

"Just keep your eyes on the dirt we call a road." Lieut pointed to the visor. "That your girl?"

"Yes. Cathy." Cairns grinned. "Been my girl since middle of high school. I'll marry her one day."

"Stay safe for her. Drought to animals is like war to humans. It separates the hardy from the weak. Be sure to be hardy, Cairns, so you can go home to your girl in one piece."

A noise his ears were tuned for came from above, and Lieut's palm went up to silence Cairns's smart retort. He craned his neck up to Boesman, whose hands painted a thousand pictures and clicks like jolts of electricity zinged from his mouth. And then came the bash on the metal roof.

"STOP!" shouted Lieut, and Cairns's quick brake-pump created a domino effect.

As "Whoooooas" erupted from the back, Lieut felt a cold shiver wrack his frame.

It had begun. His team was about to sample their first bitter taste of war.

# 3

## ZEBRA

*Drakensberg Mountains, South Africa, 1958*

JOCK SAT ALONE on his and Papin's favorite spot, an eight-foot-wide, six-foot-high dark sandstone boulder that had been burped up by the towering mountain behind it. Papin said it'd likely been lying right there for thousands of years just waiting to be theirs. "Their rock" was three-quarters of a mile from the hotel and the last frontier before the mountains climbed in majestic earnest.

Champagne Castle Hotel sprawled before him. Home. He knew every square inch of its manicured glory—neat tennis court; pristine bowling green; sparkling swimming pool; undulating manicured lawns; the many covered verandas with slate floors where guests lolled on lawn chairs. From where he lay, the white *rondavels* that were the guests' one-bedroom, one-bathroom accommodations were just little white dots spilling from the hotel across the lawns, linked by meandering, jigsaw-like slate paths.

Mom said it was a mystery to her why guests came some two

hundred miles and up a mountain to live in a hut the size of the servants' quarters built onto the back of their own lavish homes.

Dad's voice was filled with love when he warbled his made-up song listing what the lucky guests enjoyed at the hotel, and always ending with "and the most majestic mountains in all the worrrrrrrrld." And then he twirled Mom and dipped her till she giggled.

Dad reminded Jock of a packet of slap chips. Crispy on the outside and soft within. The very highest compliment in Jock's book of favorite things. The thought brought on hunger pains.

If Papin was there, they could get Thabo to make them sandwiches and ride off, Jock on Beauty, his favorite of the twenty hotel horses, and Papin on the horse most needing exercise, to find new places to discover. There was never time enough for all the adventures that were ready to be had.

*Where is Papin?*

Two weeks ago, when Jock came home from school for his bimonthly weekend, there was no sight of Papin or the horses as dad pulled the old Chevy into the parking lot. Their absence was like a bullet-speed soccer ball headed for the goal but landing in his gut. It sucked the wind right out of him.

Their ritual usually continued after the inevitable welcome-home fuss from his mother and a "hi" to Nicholas, Billy Pillay and whoever else gathered. Papin held out Beauty's reins to him from atop the horse he was riding, and off they'd gallop to explore hills and dales, streams and valleys, crags and cliffs, or find a ready game of barefoot soccer with the off-duty staff on their makeshift soccer field.

But none of these were fun to do when you were on your own. And here he sat, alone, confused, disappointed and betrayed by the continued absence of his friend. All anyone would say was Papin was "away on Zulu business." *Gollaga-inja!*

Jock was more Zulu than anything else! Zulu business was his business. But nobody was talking.

Jock's mother delighted in Papin's absence. It meant Jock hung around the hotel more and wasn't "out gallivanting with the Zulus," and perhaps the worst consequence of his friend's disappearance was that his mother forced him to play with the guest kids.

Guest kids. No use getting to know them. They'd just leave in three weeks.

Their games were just stupid. Even in the swimming pool, they felt the need to find "Marco Polo," whoever the hell he was. They were city kids. They knew the board game Snakes and Ladders but nothing at all about real snakes. Not one guest kid spoke or understood Zulu. It was pure torture.

Second day home, with four glorious weeks of December school holidays to look forward to and no Papin to share this huge event. Pissed off, he jumped off the rock and ambled back to the hotel, lost and aimless.

Jock slipped into a nondescript door marked "Staff Only" just to the left of the hotel bar. He sat on one of the booze boxes and gazed at the bar occupants through the tinted window. Jock could see the bar's activities clear as day, while dad, Bekah—dad's Zulu helper—and the lone guest sitting opposite on a barstool saw only their own reflections. Jock was invisible.

Being able to observe, eavesdrop and not be seen was one of his and Papin's favorite things to do. Since that bar on hotel property only served men and bar stewards who delivered drinks throughout the property, they learned all sorts of manly things. Best were some new swear words Jock could brandish about at school.

But not even spying was much fun without Papin.

Bekah was carefully spooning green olives with red centers into a silver bowl, then stabbing them with toothpicks.

"How's your stay been so far, Mr. Retief?" Dad asked the man sitting on the barstool facing Jock.

"Excellent as usual," said the man before he took a long sip of beer shandy from his frosted mug.

"Glad to see your boy and the black boy are no longer roaming around together all the time. The guests call them 'Zebra' behind your back, you know." Retief leaned back to gauge Dad's response. Jock had known many a telltale in his school hell. Here was a grown one.

Dad denied Retief the satisfaction of a reaction and merely lifted an eyebrow, but it wasn't enough to stop his shit-stirring.

"Zebra," Retief stated. "You get it? You can't tell where the white boy ends and the black boy begins." He grinned at his cleverness.

"Actually, the only reason they're *not* together is because Papin is away on Zulu business."

"*Zulu business*? What kind of nonsense business is that?"

"Important business to the Zulus, which is as important as your business to you, Mr. Retief."

*That blasted Zulu Business again.*

"Ag, no man. Your thinking is too liberal, David. People don't like liberal ..."

"Mr. Retief," Dad continued calmly, but Jock knew that face. It meant Dad was controlling his anger. "Does the boys being together in any way mar your view of the magnificent mountains? Or heat the cool waters of the pool? Or interfere with your fine dining? It can't possibly deter you on the tennis court, because you've become a master player."

Jock heard thick sarcasm and held his breath, but seeing pride flush Mr. Retief's face, Jock realized what Nicholas said was true. If you flattered people at the end of an insult, they'd only remember the compliment. They'd heard Nicholas, from this very position, tell Bekah the white man's weakness was his vanity.

Dad found Retief's vanity. Retief looked at himself in the bar's backboard mirror for ten long seconds before he said, "Ah. Thanks. I try. Now that you mention it, I'm moving up to tennis A league when I get back to Jo'burg." He smiled, trying to look shy, but his false modesty couldn't even fool an eight-and-a-bit-year-old boy, let alone his father.

"This is my third holiday here. Call me Japie, please." Retief smiled at dad. "I meant this place is so idyllic, it shouldn't be spoiled by mixing the races right under one's nose. *You* know what I mean."

"No clue what you mean, Japie," said Dad. He grabbed the sharp knife and the lemon Bekah was slicing and began chopping away furiously.

Dad continued without looking up from making the lemon suffer in slices: "That 'black boy,' as you call him, has been solely responsible for keeping my son safe in this treacherous environment for nearly five years."

Retief said quickly, "I'm just sharing what I see and hear from other guests. As a regular, I don't want you to be blindsided. And, let's face it, the pair *are* always together. But I suppose in this remote setting, anything goes."

Silence followed but for Dad's knife thwacking on the chopping board.

"I hear you built a school for the black kids on hotel grounds a while ago," said Retief.

"I did." Dad wasn't giving an inch more than he had to.

Retief finally erupted. "What the hell's the point, man? Those blokes don't want our Western culture. They're happy as they are. Hope to hell you don't send your kid to that black school; he needs a *real* education."

Jock wanted to scream through the glass. "Ha! Bet Papin's

smarter than you, old fart!" But that would mean exposing his and Papin's best lookout.

But then Dad sliced open the tip of his finger and saved them both from saying what they dare not.

Blood oozed as dad wrapped his digit in a serviette, rinsed the lemon and pushed the board and knife back to Bekah. Retief never knew death touched his shoulder.

The sliced finger must have calmed dad because he said: "You know, Japie, if helping the children around here learn to read and write is 'unacceptable' to some, I can live with that. But tell me again, does this school which you can't see from any hotel or rondavel window have any bearing on your comfort or the way you're entertained?"

"No, but I just think ..." Japie began, but Dad had had enough.

"If that's all it takes to irk those who complain, Japie, then they needn't come back. But I will share this with you. I am beyond pleased with the man my boy is likely to become because of his black friend. I wish I could have had a friend like Papin. Now! How about I pour you a stiff pre-pre-lunch whiskey on the rocks and you tell me all about your hike today. Did you have fun?"

And wisely, Jock hightailed it out of their secret lookout.

On his way to their rock, Jock thanked the ancestors Papin was not there to hear Mr. Retief's words. Papin seemed touchy about stuff like that these days.

Though he didn't understand it all, Retief's disapproval of their friendship was clear.

"'Zebra'? I kind of like that. Papin and I are so close, we're able to confuse the enemy and make them so dizzy, they can't harm us. Together, we can even chase away a lion." Now that part was safe to tell his friend.

Jock surveyed the scene from atop their rock. He'd once thought his life in a mountain hotel was everyone's life. Now, because of shitty boarding school, he understood his rare privilege. He thanked the ancestors with particular humility. *Gollagainja!* Speaking to the Zulu long dead reminded him of his best friend's abandonment.

He took the long route back to their rock so he wouldn't be seen. The four hotel dogs frolicked on the lawn. Two were play-fighting over a stick; Bonzo trotted off to see which guest would slip him the corner of a delicate cucumber sandwich; and Tripod, still Jock's favorite, stood stock still on his three legs, nose in the air. Jock smiled, wondering if his baboon-scarred, much-loved dog was sniffing to find his young master.

Tripod was a perfect subject for a Mind Brownie Moment. *Kah-chick* went Jock's imaginary camera, and his recently added attachments worked overtime to add color and smell, feelings and sounds.

He'd learned, when he'd re-discovered the swirling mist of loneliness years ago, the possibility of never seeing something again was reason enough to consciously use his mental camera to photograph every little thing that made him happy. That way he could see, feel, hear and be moved by these memories whenever he wished.

On the weekend Papin was a no-show, one of the guests had a brown, box-like thing attached to his right eyeball and glued to his hand and cheek. Dad asked the guy to show it off for them.

Jock was frankly relieved the glue came off easily as the guy removed the camera from his face. He explained the workings of his grown-up toy, delighted someone was interested. Information poured from his mouth, and fascinated, he and Dad leaned in to see how it worked. Dad seemed to understand just fine, and Jock was able to give his long-used remembering-instrument a name—'Mind Brownie.'

But it's what the camera owner said last that enhanced Jock's world.

"Every second here, there's a new scene that's picture-worthy. I have to capture not just the image but *every single nuance*"—the camera man paused, and the silence was so intriguing, they'd leaned in farther, and the Mind Brownie owner finished—"so I can remember it forever. See?" The man pointed his Mind Brownie and pulled the trigger at the magnificent band of rock that looked like The Sphynx. "As I take this, I can smell the delicious dinner being prepared. I can hear your wife playing the piano and, just like that, I've added nuance."

New Aunts. Just what he needed to improve his already top-notch, imaginary Mind Brownie.

New Aunts would add smells and tastes and feelings and stuff too! "All I have to do is attach New Aunts to my Mind Brownie, and I'll make even the most normal things spectacular enough to keep them forever."

Dad said earlier in the day, he loved the smell of newly waxed wood floors. Jock sniffed the air, inhaling the Cobra polish, pungent with pine, sunshine and beeswax.

"That's a perfect New Aunts," Jock said absently.

""Nuance? That's a big word for you, Jock!" Dad said, eyes wide with surprise.

Jock grinned, flushing with pride. Imagine! He'd impressed his dad with a word! Exploring his newly acquired New Aunts feature was the only thing that kept him going during Papin's absence. Later he'd go down to the stable and groom Beauty, and his mental recording equipment would be put to excellent use. Hay, neighs, a wet horse nose, and brown eyes more loving than even Mom's would prove to be excellent material.

He "moved" his Mind Brownie from Tripod down the valley to the *kraal.*

The Zulu homestead was positioned on a little hill a twenty-minute walk from the hotel. The circular area was protected by a primitive wooden fence within which a couple of animal pens had their own fences. *Kah-chick.* The camera captured the beehive-shaped grass huts hugging the inside perimeter of the kraal. His New Aunts added the smell of flowers from the bottle brush tree at the gate and caught the feeling of wonder he felt each time he was allowed to enter. Wow!

Jock heard a shrill whistle and looked down toward the hotel. Billy Pillay, the guests' favorite wine steward, who thought himself the world's next great magician, stood on the distinct line where perfect lawn ended and wilderness began.

The only communication device available—the whistle—rang loud and piercing as Billy wildly waved his arms, knowing Jock was out there somewhere.

Jock grinned and effortlessly scaled down their rock, his bare feet hardened by years of leaping over stones, boulders and crags in his path, like a rock rabbit.

As soon as Jock was in earshot, Billy shouted, "Quickly! Suh needs you in the bar." The Indian chap puffed up sizably with the importance of his task.

The usual hustle and bustle were in full swing as Jock entered the bar.

There was Papin! Jock's joy at seeing his friend was quickly overpowered by confusion. He was back and yet he didn't come to their rock?

Dad, with Billy's help, was loading drinks onto wine stewards' silver trays for delivery to verandas, lawns and lounges.

Dad spoke without looking up. "Jock, Papin asked permission for you to attend a ceremony at the kraal tonight."

Oh, no! Dad must have found out Jock was a frequent visitor

to the Zulu homestead. His bum smarted in anticipation of feeling the consequences of disobeying his father. Ouch!

But when nothing happened, Jock mustered his courage and looked up at Dad. He was smiling.

Smiling?

"Your first Zulu ceremony ..." Thank the ancestors Dad was unaware of how many he'd already attended, albeit from the periphery. Then the words sunk in, and Jock couldn't help but look at Papin for confirmation. His friend nodded, his smile a dazzle of white. Jock felt the stirrings of excitement.

"... A big event in Papin's life. He really wants you there. It's going to be a hell of a job keeping your whereabouts secret from your mother." He worked as he talked. "When she asks about you before dinner, I'll tell her I gave permission for you two to have a sunset picnic."

Jock was speechless, and all he got in explanation, from a brief glance at Papin, was another giant grin.

After he placed four gin and tonics onto the tray, Dad said, "And later, when she looks for you during the dancing, I'll tell her Billy Pillay's teaching you magic."

Billy's face lit up like a Christmas tree on the sands of the Kalahari Desert. "SUH! Did I tell you I have a new magic trick? You will be surprised what a very clever trick it is."

Dad's response was the usual, "Billy, what *will* surprise me is if you get any trick right. Just don't make my liquor disappear or there'll be hell to pay."

"Suh. I look so very, very forward to teaching little Suh more than the fundamentals of magic this evening."

"It's a cover, Billy. Just a cover. It's your night off, so you magically disappear before anybody sees you're not teaching this little bugger your terrible tricks, okay?"

"Good idea, suh." Billy picked up his tray and twirled it on splayed fingertips as he left the bar.

Dad continued: "Papin, Nicholas will make sure you have an ox at the kraal for the occasion. You boys can help haul it, plus a sack of *mealie meal.* Jock, go and make a quick fuss of your mother. Mention your evening "plans." I'll reinforce them, and then don't let anyone report where you really are. And for God's sake, get to bed before she looks for you, you hear me? Otherwise, my boy, we'll both be locked in the laundry with Constance for a fortnight."

Quite speechless, Jock looked from his dad to Papin and back several times until his dad said, "Now get the hell out of here, you two."

But Jock was rooted in shocked delight. "I'm allowed to lie?" Boy! Two presents in one day?

"Only today. No more lying after today. And it's just a white lie," Dad managed before a wine steward needed him.

Jock was elated with the revelation that white people got one day to lie. Maybe Zulus got to lie too—maybe even for more than a day. He'd surely also qualify for those lies. He hoped so, since after today, his white lie would be all used up.

Later, as their horses grazed nearby, Jock was sprawled over the rock and Papin sat in his usual position—long legs bent, knees tucked close to his chest, hands linked in front of his shins.

They only spoke Zulu to each other. It was Jock's first language, the one he dreamed in, even after nearly three years of English school. And all because Papin owned his formative years and when he was home, Papin was close to him as often as possible.

Gazing out toward his kraal, a shocking statement tumbled from Papin's lips: "I wasn't here, Tsotsi, because I was becoming a man."

Jock's eyes grew big. "How do you do that? Can I also?"

Papin laughed. "It's a Zulu tradition that happens when a boy is thirteen, Tsotsi."

"I am Zulu because of you, right?"

"Right. But you are Zulu in your head and white on your body. The white part would be very angry if you became a Zulu man." Papin laughed—but not freely like he always did.

Jock was not laughing. "But that's what I want."

"No, Tsotsi. Your world will always be different from mine." Papin's face took on a strange new look Jock didn't understand.

Jock scrunched up his face. It would be so much simpler if he was altogether Zulu.

Words tumbled out of Papin's mouth with little of his usual expression. Jock felt Papin wasn't talking to him at all but rather reliving the time he was away.

Here was a boy who looked the same as his best friend but who Jock feared had been replaced by a different man.

"By Zulu law, it was time for me to become a man. I went alone into the bush and built myself a hut from branches and reeds I wove together as my father had taught me. I had no machete, only a fighting stick and a pot."

Jock wanted visceral details, but when he leaned in to ask, Papin seemed not to know he was even there but continued spewing up information. Jock felt he was on the outside looking in. A weird sensation to feel when that someone was the most important person in your world.

"I stripped naked, burned my boy clothes and covered myself with clay I found in the marsh. My mud dried and fell off and was repacked many times before *Sangoma* arrived."

Jock's feeling of separation was quickly replaced by fear, and he shivered in spite of the sun's warmth. He knew all about the revered, terrifying, all-seeing Sangoma. He had supreme power and could talk to Zulu ancestors and glean extraordinary information not even available in the *Sunday Times*.

Jock had never seen Sangoma up close because he and Papin only watched Zulu ceremonies from the outskirts of the kraal when Sangoma was in attendance.

Getting close to the revered Sangoma was strictly off-limits, according to both chiefs in Jock's world.

The many kraals across the hills, escarpments, valleys and mountains of the vast Drakensberg range all had their own chiefs, as well as medicine men and women, but there was only one Sangoma, who administered spiritual guidance and advice to all the region's kraals.

Sangoma was so revered, he was only called upon for the most dire circumstances and seldom made an in-person appearance. Runners were dispatched to receive council on behalf of those in need when the mighty Sangoma—for any undisclosed reason—was indisposed.

When they first came to the hotel, his mom called Sangoma "witch doctor," and his dad scolded her gently. "Renee, we need to bow reverently to the great man and call him 'Sangoma.' He's as important to our mountain world as the Queen of England is to the rest of the world."

Jock didn't know how a queen got involved, but Sangoma impressed Dad. That was *really* something.

Jock felt the little hairs on the back of his neck prickle and rise as a vision of the ogre sitting opposite his best friend loomed large. "Sangoma arrived to see *you?*"

Papin nodded matter-of-factly. "Sangoma was already covered in clay. He wore skins with many magic oracles that dangled and clanged and tinkled and an ox bladder on his head, so I knew this was an important occasion."

Ox bladder? Enough to prompt Jock to switch off his Mind Brownie.

Papin continued: "His seeing instruments rattled in his cupped hands. He blew and spit into the 'cup,' shook them silly.

Then, with great flourish, he threw the many strange pieces on the dirt floor. Dead bones, stones and animal teeth lay in groups and by themselves."

"You sure they were animal, not human teeth?" Jock's eyes were about to pop out.

Papin gave him a dirty look.

"What did the bones say?" Jock's chest pumped like the wheels of a train a long way from the station.

"They told of my struggle. They also spoke of you."

Jock was more frightened than impressed. "Sangoma knows *me*?"

"Tsotsi!" Papin was impatient. "Sangoma knows everyone living and dead. No more interruptions."

Jock did his best to be invisible.

"Sangoma told me I will eventually find patience, but I have to teach you to be a good Zulu because your life depends on my instruction."

"Did he say I would become an important Zulu too?" Jock couldn't help himself.

All Jock got was a look of dismissal before Papin continued. "He made me light a fire in the hut and boil water from the stream in the clay pot. Then he took out the blade."

"Blade?" Jock's eyes were as big as a *nagapie*. So much for his invisibility.

"I watched steel go orange as sunset on a cloudless night. Then Sangoma placed a stone beneath my penis."

Jock recoiled in horror and rolled away, distancing himself from this dreadful news.

"When I awoke, Sangoma was gone. White *muti* sat on the edge of my penis. Where once there was loose skin was a large throbbing knob. I cried like a baby mauled by a hyena."

Jock was shocked by this revelation. Papin cry?

But the thought of a hyena's jaw clamped over any body part nearly brought tears to Jock's own eyes.

Imagine ... He cupped his privates with both hands and double-checked that his Mind Brownie and New Aunts were switched off.

Papin continued: "I opened my eyes, and a medicine woman from yonder kraal was examining me. She urinated on me ..."

"*Sis!*" yelled Jock in disgust and let go of his privates to clamp a hand over his mouth.

Papin disdainfully ignored the interruption. "Once the urine dried, she used a long white feather to remove every speck of dust. Out of her skin bag she took a small, carved, ivory box. Inside were two warrior ants."

Jock's skin crawled, and he pushed his hands together to tighten protection down there.

"She took out one ant and pushed on it till it opened its mandibles ..." And Papin's trance-like state shattered as he said, "Wait! I'll show you!" and jumped off their rock. Before Jock could figure out what was happening, Papin leaped back up with his hands cupped.

Sitting back down, he opened his hands, and an army ant quickly crawled out. Papin trapped it, and Jock leaned in to watch Papin take the ant by the head and squeeze the tiny head till its mouth opened.

"She moved the army ant, just like this one, to the side of my penis, where blood still oozed." In a split second, Papin's free hand grabbed the skin between Jock's thumb and index finger before he had time to resist.

"What?"

Papin moved the hand holding the open-mouthed army ant to Jock's trapped flesh and said, "Then she let go."

"Ouch! Eina! What?" yelled Jock as the ant's jaws locked down on either side of his loose skin.

"Shhh. Men don't scream for little ant bites. Only boys."

Jock clamped his mouth shut and held his arm by the wrist as the ant's body turned and writhed and dangled in fresh air.

"Just be glad I am not demonstrating on your penis," Papin said sternly.

He continued. "As the new pain came, she nipped off the ant's body." And Papin did just that, and Jock's eyes were huge as the ant's headless body dropped to the stone floor.

Gazing at his hand in horror, Jock saw the ant's head still there, little iron jaws still clamping the skin together like a staple.

"See how the head remains, sealing the wound?"

"*Gollaga-inja*. Will you take this thing out now?"

Papin reached over and pulled off the head.

Jock examined two holes in his flesh. "She did that ... down there?"

"Yebo. Both sides."

And with that, Jock moved to the very edge of the rock and clutched his family jewels tightly to ensure absolutely no more demonstrations could take place.

"Why?" was all Jock could muster from his almost fetal position.

"Ancient remedy. The dead head, like a pin, holds the skin together until it's healed and the head falls off. Then I slept."

Jock was speechless and curled his body into a tight ball.

"For two sunrises, my penis throbbed. I drank the rest of the boiled water. My aunt sent a boy with food. But hunger had left me and only thirst remained. I found *dagga* that the healer had left, and I chewed it. It took away some pain."

Jock sat bolt upright with this news. Papin chewed dagga? When his dad caught hotel workers smoking the wild weed that grew so freely, there was hell to pay. Boy! Never in his wildest dreams ...

"Then Chief came to tell me things a man should know," Papin continued importantly.

"What things?" asked Jock.

"How to welcome strangers and treat them respectfully until they prove unworthy; how to keep Zulu tradition through deed and retelling of ancient stories; consequences when ancestors are not properly respected; how to keep a cool head; how to treat a woman; how to settle disputes without blood; how all men are born upside down so we must learn through hardship and inner strife to plant our feet more firmly on the ground. I learned a thousand lessons over two days, more than I'll ever remember, but Chief said I'd remember when I had to. All the while, Chief and I inhaled more dagga than the Chief has years, Tsotsi."

Jock's head swirled with things he'd have to sift through later, but now it was important to Papin and so it was important to Jock.

Papin's smile, the first real one since that morning, revealed Jock's friend had returned intact, in spite of his horrendous ordeal. Jock's relief was humongous.

"It was nearly half a moon before my father came to fetch me. He brought my skins and made me burn down the hut that had sheltered me. When we walked into the kraal this morning, there was much noise and stomping and clapping and singing, and the preparations began for tonight."

"Tonight, the ceremony is just for you?" Could this day get any more exciting?

"For me and the others my age from all the kraals around who had their own recent boy-to-man experiences," said Papin as he stood. "Come. Let's go!"

Zulu business was still Jock's business. The world was back on its axis.

Papin surveyed his charge as the two carried a heavy crate of Castle Lager between them. This was their third trip from the hotel to the kraal with Inkosi's donations for the celebration. Tripod followed, back and forth, back and forth. What a dog!

"Boy! It's got to be an occasion," said Tsotsi, and his young face was alive with excitement, "when there's Castle Lager. It's not just a night; it's a festival."

Papin felt laughter bubble from his throat. Tsotsi had a way of tickling his funny bone, and for the first time since he was home, he felt more boy than man.

He wasn't sure about this man business. It felt like being trapped in Thabo-the-chef's pressure cooker. Being a boy meant uncomplicated freedom, and he envied his young friend that.

As they came closer, his kraal looked like a feverish anthill. Everyone went happily about their business. Kids swept steps of huts that hugged the inner kraal, and chattering Zulu women worked together stirring mighty pots over large fires as the older men did what they did best: sat on steps in groups, smoked, chatted and yelled instructions.

"I swear I can already taste the putu pap. My mouth's watering," said Tsotsi, and Papin had a vision of the boy grasping as much as he could of the maize meal with his fingers, then squishing it together and dipping all five digits deep into the onion and tomato gravy mixed with the rich drippings from the turning ox. Papin heard his own stomach rumble as he cast out thoughts of Jock's mother witnessing this "unmannered eating habit" the boy so enjoyed.

The newly skinned, gutted ox they helped carry from the grasslands earlier was being slathered in home-grown spice and patted none too gently by a dozen women for tenderizing.

Four *indunas* were in charge of impaling the beast with a long, sturdy, sharp branch the length of its torso, making easier the turning of the carcass over the fire every ten minutes. Papin was relieved the ox no longer resembled an animal but just a huge slab of meat. As brave and hardy as Tsotsi was, he was soft on animals, and the less it resembled an animal, the more appetizing it would be for his young friend.

Of all the information that had been drilled into him during his transition from boy to man, none was more shocking than the revelation that the only life he knew in these mountains was not how the real world worked, and they warned Papin would find that out the hard way.

He'd never considered leaving these mountains. Leaving Tsotsi. Leaving his new school. Leaving Inkosi—Tsotsi's father—who gave him nothing but kindness and money to have a good time with his son. But how else to fulfill his destiny?

It disturbed Papin most of all that a seed he had no use for had been planted. He shook his head violently to throw out such dark thoughts. Who wanted to be a man anyway!

Papin realized, now more than ever, he needed to see the world through Tsotsi's young eyes, to help hold on to some of that untarnished innocence.

"Tell me what you see. What you smell," Papin invited.

"I smell sweet and salty." Tsotsi licked his lips, and then his expressive face changed to disgust. "And horseshit." The boy grinned as he hauled up his side of the crate.

Papin laughed, a glorious release as the pressure cooker opened.

When it was time to assemble, Papin ushered Tsotsi to a well-sat-on, well-oiled branch of a liquid amber tree, right in front of the chief. Tsotsi's young face shone with the importance of sitting close to the chief when usually they had to hide from sight to watch ceremonies until all the revelers were too drunk to care.

Tsotsi leaned in. "Is it because you and Chief smoked dagga together we may sit so close to him?"

Papin smiled and nodded as he saw Tripod push himself between his young master's legs, demanding and receiving vigorous, loving pats.

The smell of rich juices from the roasting ox dripping into pots below heightened their hunger, and the four inches of drool at either end of Tripod's mouth shimmered in the festive light. Papin's tummy rumbled, and there was an answering rumble from Tsotsi's. They grinned at each other like only old friends can.

"TSOTSI ..." the chief shouted over the din.

Tsotsi turned and dropped his eyes respectfully. "Inkosi." In Zulu, anyone of importance was "Inkosi."

"Already three years you go to faraway school. And still Papin is only a one-color-zebra when Tsotsi is gone." Chief smiled, and there was but one visible tooth. He'd been appointed chief when Papin's father's father was a young man.

There it is again. *Zebra.* This time an endearment from one qualified to call them such. Papin had heard the name called in an unkind manner by guests for years now, but he'd never tell Tsotsi. He would not tarnish their closeness in any way.

"And I am always alone without my friend Papin"—Tsotsi's arms gestured broadly—"and all of my Zulu." And Papin felt a silly lump jump into his throat from nowhere.

"How many years do you have now?" Chief's eyes narrowed in question.

"I have eight and a bit, Inkosi."

"I bet three cows and my first wife, no matter the number of your years, yours is the only white face sitting close to a chief's in all of Zululand on this sixth day's night."

"And I am thankful, Inkosi," Tsotsi said, his face glowing as he bowed his head.

With Chief's attention elsewhere, Papin leaned in and whispered, "Then the rumors are true. Chief will bet on anything to lose his first, old wife!"

He was rewarded with a grin that matched his own.

D-DUM-DUM. *D-dum-dum. D-dum-dum.* The drums began, and Jock imagined his ears dancing with joy. The thought tickled him pink. His Mind Brownie and the New Aunts were in position.

*Kah-chick!*

There was no sound in the world—not in nature nor on vinyl records—as powerful and rhythmic as the sound of African drums. The deep bass cadence pulsed through Jock's feet and up his body until his mind was filled with pleasure, and in his chest, a happy giant pounded to get out and dance.

Raging fires inspired the moon to do better, and the grass huts, wearing tightly woven roofs, seemed to move to the rhythm as they encircled tonight's playground. The sky was navy, and though the fire's great light dimmed the stars, Jock's beloved mountains were outlined by the moon. Their magnificence and might gave him a cold shiver in the warmth.

The drums drummed faster as four maidens appeared and began dressing the chief in full regalia. Jock was hell-bent and determined to capture his first official kraal ceremony with his Mind Brownie and New Aunts. Already his memory had locked away a hundred perfect pictures, sounds, smells and feelings—with so much more to come. These rich, enhanced memories would serve up thousands of recaps to ease his loneliness when he was, once more, forced to leave this place of bliss.

Every moving part within the kraal, like those inside the well-oiled hotel generator making the hotel glow, powered up and came to life by Zulu energy alone.

Papin's mouth came close to Jock's ear to be heard over the drums. "Chief wears his revered leopard-skin cloak. It means it is a very important occasion."

*Kah-chick.* And Jock captured the big-cat ears perched on the top of Chief's head and the spotted pelt hanging either side of his old, leather-like face. Strips of the hide tied around his neck, and the rest of the animal's magnificent coat covered still-broad shoulders, then extended down Chief's back, the tail coming to rest three feet behind the high tree stump on which he sat.

A thousand light and dark images inked with mystery and intrigue and the sights, smells and sounds all bled into the night's splendor. *Kah-chick.*

*D-dum-dum. D-dum-dum. D-dum-dum.* Bare-breasted Zulu girls danced around one of the blazing fires, harmonizing in lilting voices and wearing traditional skirts made of beaded cotton strings. Seed rattles secured to their ankles beat in time with every downward step and kick.

Though bare black breasts were not unusual in this rural environment, Jock's New Aunts now demanded further understanding.

He asked Papin: "Why do you never see white *numbies*, but young Zulu ladies show theirs all the time?"

"You've seen Zulu numbies this way for four and more years. Is it that you're a man like me now, who considers such things? Or does white school force this question from you?"

"I'm using my New Aunts for more bounce to the ounce, more ..."

Papin interrupted with a cocked head and arched eyebrow "'New Aunts'? What's wrong with old aunts?"

"'New Aunts take ordinary things and add smell and touch and feelings and make them special enough for you to want to keep them in your head forever." Jock loved when called on to explain something to his friend. It rarely happened, except with sums from his school arithmetic book.

Jock's new and supreme knowledge of New Aunts clearly impressed Papin. That was something.

"Then let your New Aunts record tonight that these girls show off their numbies to potential husbands."

"Ewwwww." Jock worked on contorting his face to emphasize his disgust. Who would waste a Mind Brownie on girls?

"A would-be husband must see what he's getting before he has to pay with livestock to secure a wife." Papin looked so serious, it was Jock's turn to jab him with an elbow.

"*Gollaga-inja!* Bring back my friend, the boy! No talk of unimportant numbies! Let's rather think of new ways to steal Farmer Olivier's peaches and avoid a shotgun loaded with salt pellets pointed at us!" Jock could do with one of those sweet, swollen, stolen delights right now. His mouth watered like Tripod's.

The drummers beat harder on their drums and masked the rumbling of his tummy.

*D-dum-dum. D-dum-dum. D-dum-dum.* Jock could feel the bass rhythm come up through the earth into his bare soles again. Beats in two-three time boomed up his legs, his stomach, his chest and into his head. He felt free and unbound by space, time or place.

At boarding school, when the dark hollowness came in the dead of night and the mist of uncertainty and loneliness swirled, he willed those drums to take it away. Mostly they succeeded.

Jock took in the drummers. *Kah-chick.* Strips of animal fur were tied around their heads and arms. Skins hung around their waists and danced around long legs, keeping time.

They relentlessly hammered away at their instruments, which were hollowed-out tree trunks with goatskin, clean and stripped of hair, stretched over open ends. The beats became *Ra-*

*Rain-Rain. Ra-Rain-Rain,* and the hypnotic rhythm reminded him of rare time spent with his super-busy dad.

His heart clenched with love as he "saw" the trips into town together, just he and Dad in the family Chevy, going backwards up the S-bend to the hotel when torrential rain turned the dirt road to thick mud.

Dad said backwards was the only way up because their Chevy was a rear-wheel drive. The best part was Jock sometimes got to sit between his dad's legs and hold the wheel. Dad would talk to the car like it was another person on their trip. He felt a giggle well up inside him, and he reached down to find Tripod's ear for an enthusiastic scratch.

"Only the crazy and the lonely laugh with themselves, Tsotsi." Papin's voice infiltrated Jock's reverie.

"Which one am I?" asked Jock.

"Some of both," deadpanned Papin before he grinned, a smile so wide it made the kraal brighter still. Jock put out his hand and they shook, the Zulu way with an extra thumb twist.

Adolescent boys from this kraal and others within twenty miles sat wide-eyed on ox skins in the center of the kraal.

"Why aren't you with them?" Jock asked, pointing to the boys.

"In time," Papin said mysteriously.

Just behind the young men, elders sat on single hides or shields. Behind them, chief's first wife (no wonder he wanted to get rid of her —she was very old) and his revered mother sat on tree stumps of equal height that were draped in cheetah skin. Chief's three other wives sat to the side on skins that were once a small herd of impala. The rest of the Zulus sat on the ground or wherever they could, facing the chief. Visiting chiefs took their place on tree stumps behind the hosting chief—important but not as important tonight, Jock reckoned.

A maiden sat on her knees in front of the chief, her head

thrown back as she held the hollowed-out calabash to her mouth with both hands and drank deeply. She stood up, and the drums stopped.

"She's proving she can still stand so the beer has not been poisoned by *Tokoloshe*," Papin leaned in to explain. She bowed to Chief, then held the calabash out to him with both hands, averting her eyes. The crowd went wild along with the drums, but when Inkosi took the drinking vessel, all noise ceased abruptly. Chief drank deeply in the strange quiet.

The whole world held its breath as Inkosi swirled the beer in his mouth, then swallowed, eyes closed.

Seconds passed like hours.

When Chief let out a powerful moan of satisfaction and rubbed his stomach, the noise was as deafening as the silence.

# 4

# PRETTY BOY

*South West Africa/Angola, 1977*

BEFORE THE BEDFORD shivered to a stop, the bushman's face magically appeared on Lieut's left as if he'd done a lightning-quick dismount from the Olympic rings. The 1.2-meter-tall man of about twenty-eight looked like he'd just turned a hundred and ten. He jumped up and down with excitement.

Lieut never tired of trying to decipher the San language spoken by Bushmen. Constructed of clicks made with bursts of suction between tongue and palate, the language was as old and mysterious as Africa herself. But the little man's expressive body language and animated face were a dead giveaway.

Lieut hopped out of the truck and watched the little brown man sink easily to his haunches, scouring the dirt that looked much the same as it had for miles. Boesman rose suddenly and clicked away, shaking his head and pointing.

"Bring your bayonet, Neville. Boesman says there's a manmade disturbance," Lieut shouted.

In seconds, a tall 1.95 meter guy, a few years younger than Lieut's twenty-seven years, with a naughty, boyish face appeared beside him. His R1 rifle was slung over his shoulder and bayonet in hand.

"Little bugger knows his shit, man," marveled Neville as he inched forward behind Boesman, "but how the hell you understand him, Lieut, is a mystery to us all."

Without ceremony, the little man lay down, his weather-worn cheek flattened in the dirt as keen eyes surveyed a disturbance so slight, it was impossible to see close up, let alone from the ten meters away where Boesman had spotted man's intrusion.

Boesman blew on the light, dry twigs, then used a white feather to gently push them a half a meter away to reveal the manmade scar in the sand.

"Look at this, guys," Lieut said to the eight who stood behind him. "Terrs use the lightest foliage so they don't detonate their own landmine while covering it up. Boesman's smart enough to see through their attempt to conceal. See how the top soil's slightly darker than the rest? Little guy's a genius. Watch and learn, boys."

"Would that really have blown us up, Lieut?" Charl asked, horror marring dainty features.

Lieut balked when Charl was assigned to his squad. He had no hopes for this scrawny one with the girlish looks. But he'd been wrong. Pretty Boy had proved to be intensely dedicated to every task.

"To hell and gone, Charl. We would've lost men and many limbs between us. But don't worry too much—only Cairns, Boesman and I would have been goners. The rest of you? Just a few legs shorter or a handful of arms less handy. No big deal."

His men found new fondness for their limbs, and for some seconds, legs were patted and arms hugged. Good. He needed them to anticipate dire consequences. Otherwise, it was like a girl getting pregnant. It only happened to somebody else's girlfriend. Until ...

"War's no place for heroes. More scared you are, longer you'll stay alive." Lieut hoped the severity of his tone made an impression. He needed to scare the shit out of them.

Boesman continued his up-close quest, nose in the dirt.

"Donderse Boesman spotted that blerry thing from Jo'burg!" lamented Frikkie, the clown. Nods and grunts of agreement came from most, but a snorting guffaw erupted from Piet-Tire, who was Frikkie's greatest admirer and his audience of one. The two were from Dundee, a small town of mostly immigrant coal miners and hardworking Afrikaans farmers.

It never ceased to amaze Lieut that no matter how attractive or well-proportioned their meal, the two would mash it all together to look like a bowl of dishwater-colored slop and then collectively rave about its deliciousness. But the farm boys could shoot like nobody's business. No sniper instruction needed for them. They arrived for basic training already superbly skilled.

"Just watch and learn, *Rock Spiders*—get back as far's you can —but make sure you can see the work of these fine gents. You too, *Rooi Necks*," warned Lieut, using disparaging collective nouns for both his Afrikaans and English boys to show he had no bias.

"Can't we find a way to drive around the thing instead of going to a whole lot of trouble?" asked Tiny.

"Tiny, what if the next Bedford full of *roofies* don't have a Boesman as observant as ours? What if they don't see the disturbance?" Oh, boy. The trials of leading a pack.

"Kabooooooooooom!" said Nev.

"You've got to think of the guys behind you, boys. Just as we hope the guys in front will think of us," and he shouted, "Nev! Ready?"

Eight heads re-converged.

The naughty face next to him turned white as powdered sugar, and Lieut grabbed his own bayonet to demonstrate: "Use it like a mighty sword, Nev, and slowly, *ssslowly* insert the blade vertically into the sand on the very outside edge of the disturbance." Lieut watched sweat break out on Neville's forehead. "You can do this, Nev. You've got nerves of steel."

Neville's bayonet went into the ground slowly. "Good. Good. Excellent. Do you feel anything solid?"

"No." Neville's voice quivered slightly.

"Okay, now from the same edge, angle your bayonet slightly and push it into the ground." Neville glanced at Boesman. "Don't watch Boesman. He will shout when we all have to freeze. No sound, and you're doing well. Feel anything?"

"No." There was a drip of sweat dangling from the tip of Neville's nose. Even in fear and concentration, the guy looked like he was having a good time.

Again and again the exercise was repeated until Neville's face was a happy, wet mess.

"Holy shit, I hit something." Neville's eyes were the size of a pair of blowfish.

"Calm down, Nev. Slowly. Okay, Nev, now slowly take your bayonet back to the angle of your last penetration before you hit anything."

Lieut never took his eyes off Nev's face, trying to remotely navigate the man's brain to make his blade do as it was told.

"Now stand just like that. Don't move a hair, Nev," said Lieut. "Charl!"

The youngster stepped forward.

"Start scooping the sand behind the bayonet. Very, very, gently."

The slow process began as Boesman lay, cheek in the sand, watching each microscopic movement and guiding Nev and Charl with clicks and slight finger movements. He motioned

Neville's blade a tenth of a millimeter this way or that with merely the volume of his grunts and showed Charl when gentleness or forcefulness were needed to do his job.

Not an eyelash twitched in the gallery as Charl gently scooped away the sand like he was building a moat around an intricate, prize-winning sand castle on Durban beach.

At last, the lip of the land mine was exposed.

"Good, good, Charl. Okay, Nev, move the bayonet ninety degrees to your left and repeat the same process from the beginning: vertical penetration, then angle, angle again. When you hit, be sure to hit softly and back one step. Okay? Good."

Lieut turned his attention to Charl. "Pretty Boy, do your job."

Without a word, Charl continued to lightly scrape the area, further exposing the lethal object. At one delicately crucial point, Boesman—with a show of great reverence—allowed Charl to use his feather. The slow process repeated at 180 and 270 degrees. Once the killing instrument was fully revealed, Lieut said, "Nev. Pretty Boy. Take a breather."

Tension left their tightly wound bodies as Neville, Charl and their gallery of onlookers moved a good few paces away from the rusted metal disc that looked like an old flying saucer.

Lieut watched Boesman changing positions on the ground to view the land mine from every angle.

Lieut said, "Charl, I want you to push your hands gently under the mine from each side until your fingertips touch underneath." Lieut bent down inches above the device to demonstrate.

"Then I want you to *ssslowly* pick it up—it's going to be heavy, the heaviest thing you've ever carried—but you will do this, Charl. I believe in you. I want you to walk very, very carefully down the side of the hill for about eighty paces. Count those paces out loud as you go. And watch the ground two meters in front of you. Don't trip, otherwise I will have to write to your folks. Don't make me do that. I'm a lousy writer. Counting on you, Pretty Boy. Let's do it and get the hell out of here."

"Why me, Lieut?" Charl's eager face looked up, genuinely perplexed.

"Because you have the steadiest hands of all these idiots. Surgeon's hands. Now you and I will watch as the ladies run far away in the opposite direction and hide behind some rocks." Lieut waited until the nervous snickers died down. "Then we'll begin. I will watch and guide you every step of the way."

Once men had scattered to find cover, Charl's face was a study in concentration, his need to please almost tangible. *Poor little bastard. I hope the pressure doesn't screw him up for life. Nightmares. Spare him the nightmares.*

Lieut made sure his voice was deep and soft and calm. "Start now. Slowly. Slowly, Charl. Thaaat's it. I know it's heavy, but with each step it will get lighter. You can do this. And when you've done it, you've proved you can do anything at all. Imagine how many lives you'll save. What's your count, Charl?"

"Forty-one."

"Good. More than halfway there. You're saving the next load of our guys, Charl. Yes! Keep counting, Charl. All that matters is the next number, your next pace. And the next. You're nearly at eighty. Watch that ground ahead of you and keep counting your paces. Nearly there, Charl. Very, very, slowly. Imagine how light you'll feel when you put it down. Yes. Now. Slowly down, Charl. Put that killing bastard gently down and out of harm's way. So slowly ... so slowly. YES!"

Five minutes later, Lieut's eight soldiers and his invaluable tracker stood around the truck. They passed between them the large, precious canvas water container they'd detached from the hood of the Bedford. Thanks to forward momentum generating wind on water, they shared blessed cool water in the ungodly heat.

Lieut watched Neville's long arm flop down and around Boesman's neck and affectionately pull the little guy in so they could knock heads. "You saved our bacon; I think I love you."

Frikkie and Piet-Tire gave a warbly rendition of David Cassidy's hit.

Boesman's brown face crinkled into a million lines of pure pleasure. There was no need for interpretation.

Lieut pointed to the unlikely pairing of Nev and Boesman. "Mutt and Jeff are in love, guys. Let's give them some space."

Neville's voice was gruff. "Listen. I could French-kiss this little guy, Lieut. He saved our freaking lives, man." His voiced was choked.

"Hey, Nev, crying's allowed in my squad, but only after lights out, okay?" Lieut smiled, slapping the big goof's shoulder. "And guys, let's hear it for Charl, who was the bravest of the brave today. It took guts to carry that thing so far down the hill."

"Shit, Lieut. I thought I would piss my pants," confessed Charl quietly.

"I'm happy to hear it," said Lieut. "We don't need fearless heroes. But listen to me, Charl. You never have to prove your courage again. You'll always remember what you did today. No matter what life throws at you, you can beat it with your kind of backbone. You hear me?" and Lieut felt a damned lump threaten his throat.

*Charl, Cairns, Bennie the Bookworm, Penti—hell, none of us—had the chance to enjoy being newly grown up.*

"Nev, you've been here with me twice before; Boesman, four times. Pentifuckingford, Nev and I did basics together. Some of you were once new to me. No more. We're a team now. One I'm proud of. On behalf of this bitch of a bush war, I apologize for robbing you of your youth. I'm certain all of you could have misspent it very well."

His team nodded and chuckled, and Lieut continued, "But while we're here, let's kick arse!"

There was a metallic crackle from the truck, and Boesman jumped like he'd seen a ghost. Lieut gave the man a reassuring smile. "It's okay, Boesman. One day you'll get used to the radio. Nothing to be afraid of. There's no *Tokoloshe* here." But Lieut knew his words were empty. Tokoloshe—hell, trouble in any form—was always only a second away.

There was indeed *plenty* to be afraid of.

# 5

# SANGOMA

*Drakensberg Mountains, 1958*

The moon seemed to dance in time to the drums, but that was likely due to the three-day old, fermented beer Jock had gulped from the calabash as it passed him, doing the rounds. The fourth time the gourd was handed to him, Inkosi shook his head and stomped his *knobkerrie,* and Papin grabbed the vessel before Jock could take another sip.

Sizzling fat teased Jock's taste buds, and he felt ridiculously happy. He remembered his discussion with Papin on the rock and looked at his crotch to confirm all *his* business was still in order. Tripod licked his hand, and then the music and chatter stopped suddenly.

Tripod whimpered and pushed himself between Jock's legs.

When Jock's beer-befuddled eyes caught up with his brain, Sangoma seemed to suddenly appear.

The beer buzz didn't dilute the close-up of Sangoma. He was as scary as anything Jock had ever seen or conjured in his imagination. An ogre. Huge, dark and ominous. On his head he wore a pair of goat horns between which a blood-red mass hung. It seemed to pulse as Sangoma's glistening bulk moved.

"What's on his head?" Jock asked Papin.

"New goat bladder," Papin replied, and Jock felt bile build but swallowed hard before it arrived in his mouth. He was glad he'd not seen the demise of the poor goat. Watching even a housefly die was never fun for Jock, let alone the poor fly.

"What's around his neck?"

"Herbs, beads, animal claws and gifts from ancestors. They mean good luck and clear vision and strong ancestor guidance for him this night," Papin whispered back.

Jock wondered, since he was so close to them, if he should ask the ancestors politely for a kaleidoscope. It was the only thing he'd ever coveted that belonged to a guest kid. Hell, he'd even promise to wear it around his neck like Sangoma if that would make the obliging dead ones concede.

Strips of goatskin crossed over Sangoma's rotund, naked belly, which along with his chest was greased with goat fat, making it seem like a constantly moving, glossy mass. A cape made from a young lion's fleece was tied around his neck. His thick anklets were the tails of lions. In his hand, he held a wood staff with a thick knob on the end, his own knobkerrie. Around its base was a piece of leather to which a hundred small artifacts were tied—none of which Jock could decipher.

*That stick has its own personality. I wish my Mind Brownie was working.* But good sense prevailed through the haze. This scary being was nothing he should be using his Mind Brownie and New Aunts to remember.

The only proper high-backed chair Jock had ever seen in the kraal was carried in and placed next to Chief. It was covered by a magnificent lion's pelt, much larger than the young one worn by Sangoma.

As Sangoma settled into the scariest chair in the world, the huge lion's head—well preserved with mouth spread in a roar complete with raised pink tongue and teeth the size of dining-room butter knives—loomed above the horns suspending the gooey goat bladder.

The greasy troll settled his huge frame on the seat and moved his bare giant-feet on the lion's skin. The head of the mighty lion seemed to rise ominously behind Sangoma.

Jock jumped and felt the last of the beer-dizzy leave his head.

The lion moved again. The crowd let out a united quiver of fear as the massive beast came to life, its open mouth snarling, snout wrinkling in anger, eyes blazing, ears cocked and surrounded by the terrifying, wild, matted mane that moved from side to side while Sangoma sat, all-powerful and unafraid.

When Sangoma and the lion on which he seemed to ride lifted their ferocious head again, though the crowd's loud, frightened awe was the same, Jock realized the cleverly preserved beast's movement was thanks to brilliant manipulation of scary Sangoma's giant feet.

Billy Pillay was famously useless at getting any magic trick right. But Billy knew the theory behind the tricks and shared them with Jock, mostly to show off his vastly superior knowledge to save face when the trick flopped ... which it always did. Though Billy's sleight of hand was shit, his magic theory taught Jock how to look beyond what was easy to see.

Sangoma's "rising lion" was nothing but his own clever, foot-operated trickery.

Even with Jock being in on the lion ruse, Sangoma's great power was not at all diminished. Jock recognized this giant's importance in the eyes of his people gathered from kraals far and wide. His reverence was unquestionable, his might fierce and foreboding. And in spite of the illusion, Sangoma was scary enough to make Jock believe the great one could conjure up anything at all.

Jock asked the ancestors to be spared bumping into this giant, shiny apparition on a dark night. He reminded them of the kaleidoscope again for good measure since they were, Jock felt sure, still close enough to hear.

Then all the chiefs from all the kraals gathered around the medicine man.

Jock turned to Papin. "What're they doing?"

"Throwing the bones." Jock's arched eyebrow, copied expertly from his friend, forced Papin to explain. "By the way the 'bones' fall, Sangoma will be shown forthcoming difficulties for the various kraals, and he will advise elders how to prepare and deal with them."

It was all very complicated. "Like Sangoma threw the bones for you. Boy, those ancestors are busy," said Jock, impressed.

When these important men went back to their places of honor and the music and dancing resumed, an unsuspecting goat was led out into the center of the circle by Papin's father, Sponon. He was herdsman to both kraal and hotel.

The glistening giant was up and the crowd moved farther away as Sangoma approached the goat slowly. Then, with a lightning glint of steel, Sangoma slit the goat's unsuspecting throat. One of the wives held a wooden bowl to catch the blood as it pulsed from the poor animal's neck.

Jock felt desperately sad and thanked the ancestors his imaginary camera and New Aunts were not recording.

He hoped this goat was best friends with the last one, whose bladder was suspended between Sangoma's horns. Then at least neither would be without the other, because being left alone was a sad business.

As the goat slowly collapsed, Jock was ridiculously grateful someone was there to ease the poor animal to the ground, and Tripod got an extra hug.

"Don't worry, Tsotsi. The goat passed easily to a happy afterlife. It didn't feel a thing." Papin's tone was kind.

After washing their hands in bowls of water presented by the maidens, they tucked into the ox, putu and gravy. He'd never been so hungry, and Jock had to confess, it exceeded even Thabo the chef's finest concoctions. It was so delicious, his tongue had New Aunts of its own.

Tripod was happily gnawing on an ox rib while Jock managed to sneak in a few sips of brew without either Chief or Papin noticing. After dinner, once they'd all rinsed their mouths, the dancing and singing and drumming became more and more frenzied, and Sangoma sat on his ferocious pedestal overlooking the proceedings, the shining mucus of the drying goat bladder competing with the shimmer pulsing from his protruding belly.

The slaughtered goat was quickly skinned and gutted and now roasted on a spit for late night or early morning feasting.

Sangoma bellowed something that Jock missed by thinking about the poor goats.

Papin and his fighting stick moved into the circle the boys had created after rising from their ox-skin ground covers.

It occurred to Jock that his friend had given up a rare place in the circle with his peers to sit next to him. Jock felt ridiculously grateful for that kindness. He hoped that meant Papin had forgotten all the complicated man-business that had made him distant since his return.

Fifteen of them stood holding their sticks in a small circle around Sangoma. The revered one, towering over them, caused each to shrink a couple of inches when he waved his big knobkerrie in their direction. Sangoma chanted. It wasn't Zulu. Jock thought it had to be the ancestors using Sangoma as their talking instrument. The ogre splattered the young faces before him with goat's blood, and though well beyond the warm liquid's reach, Jock ducked.

Not a splutter was heard from the inner circle, and the outer circle of onlookers and Jock were awed into silence. There was neither bleat nor neigh nor moo nor oink. The hair on the back of Jock's neck rose. *This guy's so powerful, even the animals in their pens—way beyond the firelight—have been struck mute.*

With wild gesticulations from the wordless Sangoma, the teen boys knew what to do. They tossed their sticks outside their circle, and a maiden gathered them up as Chief entered the ring of new man-ship with a batch of blond, sturdy knobkerries. Jock swore he could smell the newly felled, newly carved wood as if the branch from which it came had just been ripped from a strong tree. His New Aunts served him well.

Maidens stood behind each boy-man on the outside of the circle, holding pointed oval shields, three feet in length and made of cow hide. Jock smiled. He knew the importance of the shield to Zulu. They were used as weapons to knock down the enemy, as camouflage to blend in and hide amongst a herd of cattle. They protected the holder from vicious blows, were used as a blanket for chilly nights, and worked like a charm as an umbrella.

Each newly minted man was presented with a new knobkerrie, a shield, and a private whispered word from Sangoma, which Jock suspected came from the ancestors.

Sangoma went into a trance for a bit, stomping and keening, and when the revered one came to, he gestured to Chief, who walked up to Papin. The other teenagers stepped back, melting into obscurity.

Chief raised Jock's friend's hand—the one that held his new, manly weapon—in the air.

"*Umanqoba*!" the proud Chief declared.

The crowd went wild, and the drums beat loud enough to be heard in Durban.

Pride sprung Jock into a standing position. His friend was the stick-fighting winner!

Then Sangoma lifted his stick. The simple gesture was all it took to command instant silence. Like a spell had been cast, people froze in position.

Sangoma gestured to Papin. Jock felt nervous as his friend walked toward the ogre.

"The ancestors have told me," Sangoma boomed, his arm around Jock's best friend, "that Papin Tshabalala, son of Sponon, will become a great Zulu."

People around him audibly gasped in surprise ... or maybe that was the sound of Jock's own shock?

"This new-man whose family name means 'shooting star' will become a famous leader. One whose name will be shared in stories around our fires and in our kraals for hundreds of years. But this I need you and you and you and you to promise me." Sangoma pointed with his adorned knobkerrie to a half a dozen people. When the knob was aimed at him, Jock shivered, and his head, like that of a frightened tortoise, tried to disappear.

Jock felt relief that Sangoma's eyes never found his own. He'd be called out by the all-knowing one for wasting the ancestors' time with his kaleidoscope request.

Thank the Lord the knobkerrie moved away as Sangoma continued: "You must never allow Papin to wear a big head, or he will be stripped of his promised destiny. Humility makes the true leader."

The scary one turned and faced Papin, who stood tall and seemingly unafraid. "Papin, today your journey to greatness begins, but expect to struggle along a difficult path to be worthy of becoming the man the ancestors expect."

Jock's mouth hung open. This was serious stuff.

How could his friend ever be the same after all this fuss?

Sangoma pushed Papin away and gestured for the gaiety to commence. Wild revelry followed as the crowd danced and drank and drummed.

Papin came straight back to sit with Jock on the liquid amber limb.

"So. Can you still be my friend?' Jock asked in dire seriousness.

Papin laughed, and Jock felt huge relief. Old Papin was back.

"Of course, Tsotsi. Without patience, I cannot become a great Zulu, and you are my teacher."

And the two laughed and laughed and sipped on the calabash as it passed them, doing the rounds.

When Jock looked again for Sangoma, he was gone. Disappeared ... lion skin, carved high-backed chair, and all. Jock wondered if the medicine man was the result of the beer or perhaps just a dream. Or was it a nightmare?

The next thing he remembered was seeing Tripod upside down from Papin's shoulder. He tried to pat his friend on the back, but his hand wouldn't cooperate. Imagine being carried to his room by a man who was just this morning a boy. *Eish.*

He tried to say, "Now that was more bang for the buck," but he heard it come out as "Nowshatswasmorebangforshebug." Papin responded with, "More bounce to the ounce."

Not too much later, the sun forced Jock's eyes open. Tripod was illegally on his bed, and the clothes and pillows which created the illusion he was fast asleep when his mother peeped in lay in a heap on the floor.

Fortunately, all this observation only necessitated eye movement, but even that felt like he was gripping bricks between his eyelashes. At the age of eight and a bit, Jock sported his first hangover.

He patted Tripod's head, though it cost him in dull pain, and was rewarded with a good dog-licking. He could only endure two licks because each felt like a leopard scraping off nine layers of skin with its tongue. Just pulling his hand away made Jock's head explode.

He hauled out his New Aunts to find the perfect remedy—fortunately that didn't take any actual movement—and he found a pristine white feather, which he willed to lightly stroke away and soothe the ache from his pounding forehead.

6

# FREEDOM AND THE FLY

*South West Africa/Angola, 1977*

LWAZI TWIRLED the snow-white feather he'd picked up on the path to the farmhouse. From his perch on the broad sill in the front room, he looked out through the bay windows to the pretty flower garden. He wondered childishly, if by one magical twirl, the feather could mute the screams of the farmer in the other room. Likely the farmer's stomach had just been spliced open.

He shivered as the feather spun, then he deliberately focused on the repeated attempts of a robber fly trying desperately to escape.

It returned to the same place on the glass each time, never learning from its mistakes. Just like his men. After every obstacle they encountered on their path of destruction, he'd laboriously teach the new cell he'd been commissioned to train how to overcome, strategize, and do better next time. But no matter what, they'd still charge in like raging bulls, single-minded, headstrong, superstitious.

He had to teach cell after cell, made up of Hereros, Ovambos, and the rare Xhosas—all with different beliefs and ideals—to work together for the greater good of his South Africa. And the hardest part was convincing the pacifists amongst them to affect the kind of horrific havoc that would eventually force change. Of course, being able to take whatever they wished from the farms they struck gave his men some good incentive.

He sighed. Tap, tap, tap. The fly continued its hopeless quest.

He tried to lift the window where the fly was buzzing up and down in frustration. But the pain held fast to the window. Stubborn. Refusing to budge.

Long ago, a man he trusted, a white man, recognized the restlessness and hunger for change churning in his young head, and the man shared some truths.

"The world beyond here is a treacherous one," the white man said. "The life of an African is cruel and hard, not free and uninhibited. You will have more limitations in that world than this, our hard-earned place of peace for all. Your beautiful culture will be stripped from you and you will be tainted by white man's avarice and anger, neither of which deserves a place in your eager soul."

The young Lwazi was quick to respond: "I have heard there is much money to be made by black men in Johannesburg." He dared not look into the white man's eyes lest the wisdom there would damper his naïve enthusiasm.

"Has this 'all-knowing' source of yours worked in the mines, or did he just hear about all the gold that was there for the taking?" The man's sarcasm was thick.

"He knows people ..." began Lwazi, but the white man was passionate and answered his own question.

"Working in the mines will not make you rich," said the white man, "rather it will make you double your long frame so you must duck for fourteen hours during each long day in stifling darkness. This black place will leave not just your body bent and lungs damaged, it will rob your soul of light, leaving you as useless as a coconut husk."

"Sir, I hear there are other ways to become rich and make a difference for my people."

"I will tell you how you make a difference. You learn from books and scholars but mostly from your mistakes. Study the mistakes of others. Strategize and plan and work hard and prove yourself to those who matter. It's the only way to elevate your position and make a difference in whatever direction you choose. Educationally you'll be well-equipped, but strive to always learn more because success only comes through knowledge and understanding; old philosophies and new; through calculation and contemplation. Fill your brain with challenges, face them and defeat them. Fill it with information that can lead, guide, advise and inform. Digging your own grave in a mine will not change anything. But education can change countries."

He had finally looked into the white man's eyes and saw truth. So he'd stayed. And he'd learned. And he knew as much as any other man of his color.

But it was Disappointment wearing an unexpected cloak that ultimately forced him to seek change, and it was Hurt and his brother-in-arms, Despair, who had finally lured him away ...

The farmer screamed in abysmal agony, and Lwazi knew the man's scrotum had just been removed. Not procedure, superstition.

Sometimes you had to let them take what they believed they needed.

He didn't belong here. Though he was as strong and as skilled as his best warriors, his strength was not in the trenches. He had no stomach for torture. He found it barbaric, but he understood the philosophy of being feared by the locals more than your opposition. If the African National Congress lost power over local tribes, they'd lose the end game —South African autonomy. These shows of abominable cruelty were as much for the local tribes as they were for their sworn enemies. Fear was the most powerful motivator.

And though he was told this position was only until he proved his strategic prowess, like so often happens when you're good at your job, he became too valuable to be promoted. Politics was where he could, where he *would* make a real difference, but this was the only way to get where his destiny lay.

He laid down the white feather on the windowsill and used long fingers to rub his face, forehead to chin, as if to wipe away the abomination he was forced to orchestrate.

He had to consider the overwhelming stench from the carnage his men caused was just another unpleasant odor on his path to victory. And yet he felt nauseous every time. Not because he was weak of stomach but because he was strong for humanity. All humanity. He hoped desperately he could convince a nation that every color counted when he got to where the ancestors intended.

The farmer's pleas for a reason why his family had been singled out became so frantic, it penetrated his fortified wall of resistance. He sighed and unwound his long frame and moved from the sun room into the midst of the bloodbath. He tried at all costs to avoid witnessing his men's cruelty, but he felt he owed this persistent, dying man—innocent but for his color—an explanation.

The rest were dead now, and the farmer's life was almost over. He forced himself to look nowhere but into the farmer's eyes. The man's surprisingly bright orbs were at once perplexed and wounded, angry and desperate for answers. Lwazi felt a pang of admiration for his stoic strength.

"You weren't singled out. You were just in the way. Your farm and consequently your family became the showcase for our intent."

The farmer's face showed surprise through his pain. "You speak good English." He croaked, then coughed loudly, and drops of blood landed on Lwazi's pristine shirt.

Lwazi spoke in Ovambo to one of his henchmen, who returned with a cup of water. Lwazi held the cup gently to the dying man's lips and let him drink. Lwazi would make an effort to delay his passing for a few more minutes to help him understand.

The farmer's eyes were wider and more alert. "Why. Why do you want to torture? To go to war?" The words were softly forced through bloodied lips, and eyes begged to understand.

"We don't want to, but we need to, to get what we want. We must show we are powerful enough to be feared, that we are a force that can no longer be ignored. This is our land as much as it is yours. Only the Bushman ... and, perhaps, so far north, the Ovambo ... are the real natives. Yet we blacks may not own land in our own country. Our livelihood is inadequate and our living conditions appalling, unsanitary and jeopardous. We have made you whites rich dying in your mines, and we've been abused as your servants. You and your family will help us prove we are no longer nonentities but a force for change to be reckoned with."

"Me ... okay. But my wife? My young children?" The farmer's words were labored and far apart.

"I am truly sorry." Lwazi felt true regret burn in his chest. Again. "But this tragedy is ultimately your government's fault. Your family is but a tableau of unnecessary pain for the police and military who will find you. They will see you were forced to watch your family die. They will witness our cruelty, and they will fear us. Only terror forces change. And the black men who hear of this will fear us more than they fear the white man's army and will follow us in our quest for equality. If your nationalist government gave us another way to get what's fair, your family would be alive and well, enjoying Sunday lunch. But there is no other way. No one will listen when we talk or reply when we ask, so we have to make them look by showing them something so obscene, they cannot look away. Destroying life goes against my grain with every fiber of my being, but I must for the greater good of my people."

Lwazi realized his last words were lost on the farmer, whose mouth was gaping in death. The once bright, curious eyes were lifeless.

He shouted an order, and his men grabbed anything they considered of value and stuffed it into pillowcases and sheets fashioned into carryalls and left the farmhouse.

Avoiding looking directly at the carnage, Lwazi deliberately placed his boot into the farmer's blood still pooling beneath his chair. He lifted his sticky boot and planted it firmly onto the vinyl floor, holding it there for a few seconds so he could adequately leave his blood-mark. All part of the strategy.

Just before he reached the front door, he turned back toward the window, where the robber fly continued its attempts at freedom. Its huge green eyes were forlorn with desperation and exhaustion and it barely hung on. The leader pulled up the window with all his might and suddenly his arms slacked and a crack of hot air gushed in where the window broke free from the resistant pane, mercifully diminishing the tangy smell of blood.

He cupped his hand to guide the tired fly to the opening, and what he did not look at in the kitchen flooded his vision. Vile regret bubbled in his esophagus. Shame on them or shame on us?

Close to the window gap, the fly tapped its head twice against the glass as if in thanks before it sailed through the opening and into the bright of day.

Lwazi watched the robber fly disappear from sight before he picked up the white feather and left the farmhouse for good.

# 7

# BALLS, MEERKATS AND POPCORN

*South West Africa/Angola Border, 1977*

THE BUMPY BEDFORD had become almost lulling, and Lieut thought about sitting alone last night, in the wind-blown braaivleis area used by the whole camp. There, guys from all battalions gathered to grill meat, sing, tell filthy, seldom funny jokes, laugh and generally decompress. Mercifully, all the outdoor revelers had called it quits, leaving him alone with the stars and the smell of sizzled fat and spilled beer still lingering in the hot night air. He lay down on a wooden bench, a boot each side of him as he studied the dark night sky. The depth of the Milky Way brought him peace, and he'd made a ridiculous wish on a shooting star. How could things ever be the same?

The brightness of this new day reflected Lieut's men's light-heartedness after the land mine incident. Oh, that every day turned out as well as the last!

"Bravo. This is HQ. Come in." The radio voice was steeped in static.

Lieut picked the mike. "HQ, this is Bravo. Receiving you loud and clear. Over."

"Bravo. Suspected terrorist at Pamula farm house. Believed to be Lwazi. Over. Grid reference to follow."

Lwazi. Cold-hearted leader and most notorious terrorist in this war. The worst of the worst. This wasn't the first time over the years Lieut and his teams had chased the elusive son of a bitch.

"Get ready for action, boys, Lwazi calls!" he shouted through the open plexiglass.

*This time I swear I'll get close enough to chop off the head of that poisonous Lwazi snake. Maybe then the army will leave me alone so I can get my life back.*

The Bedford lurched and bumped forward, Boesman's trusted feather dislodged itself from his waistband above, and Lieut stared, mesmerized, as it waltzed this way and that, this way and that, until it landed gently in the palm of his open hand.

That feather took away the angst of waiting for the farm's coordinates and made him think of their amazing Bushman, so integral to their safety.

Boesman was born prepared for the hardest possible life—it was part of his indigenous fiber. When finally, Lieut got to go home after a tour, Lieut always remembered poor Boesman did not go home. Yes, he was a nomad, so he didn't actually have a home, but his tribe was out there somewhere in the bush, missing him.

But whether he liked it or not, Boesman had no choice. He was the army's most valuable asset, as were the other Bushmen plucked from the land and immersed into the army for their brilliant tracking skills. Poor bastards.

Seven out of nine of his men were ill-prepared to see Lwazi's statements of war, but for the propaganda movies screened at training camps. *Poor buggers.* He was happy to have Nev back in his squad. Nev, Boesman and he were the only Lwazi-seasoned guys on this Bedford.

Not true. No one ever became used to Lwazi's special brand of terror.

Boesman's hand patted the air above the console while his head still protruded through the roof. "Slow down," Lieut said to Cairns, and when Boesman's hand balled into a fist, Lieut shouted, "Stop!"

Just then, static blew out of the radio and coordinates were delivered.

Typical that Boesman found it first.

Lieut picked up binoculars, opened the truck door and stood on the wide step.

Gazing through the magnifiers in the direction Boesman pointed, Lieut saw wispy smoke rise above the pinnacle of a hillock.

In remote areas, local farmers used multiparty phone lines to check on each other three or more times a day. If the ring didn't come, one of the neighboring farmers rushed the eight kilometers or more to check for abnormalities, which could usually be seen from the end of long driveways. They'd call the police, who alerted the army. The army was first at the crime scene to verify the particular brand of enemy, and police came later to clean up the mess.

Lieut jumped back in shouting "GO!" and Cairns floored the Bedford. The boys at the back careened like dominoes off the benches, but not even the thought of their comedic landings brought lightness to Lieut.

He opened the Perspex and placed his mouth close to the opening so they'd hear him loud and clear. "Guys, you've seen the propaganda movies during camps. You think you know how the Terrs make their mark. Film footage can't possibly prepare you for reality. It's horrendous—worse than your worst nightmare. The only way to handle what you're about to see is to convince yourself you're watching a movie. A movie so bad, you dismiss it for pure crap not worth remembering. As you leave the bughouse, forget it. If it comes back, tell yourself it was just a shitty movie you saw in the army. Nothing you want to see again. Believe me. It's the only thing that helps."

Silence followed as they bounced along the dirt road at a hell of a rate, thanks to the absence of large rock crags removed or smoothed by farmers' frequent usage. When they slowed to take the two well-worn private tracks leading to the burning farm, Cairns shook his head.

"Shit, I hate Terrs, Lieut. My auntie was in a Spar shop buying groceries. She didn't see a Coke tin lying in the bottom of her trolley. Kaboom! Bomb inside the Coke tin blew off her good leg."

"Holy shit, Cairns. That's bad, man," Lieut said as the smoldering farmhouse got closer. He saw Cairns go white. This would be the boy's initiation into war's carnage. He had to lighten the load. "Bad ad for Coke, Cairns. Bet your auntie's more of a Pepsi woman now."

Lieut was rewarded by Cairns's infectious laugh. When he'd recovered, Cairns said, "Boesman saw the smoke that far away? How does he do that, Lieut?"

"When you're alone in the bush, you train your eyes to find dinner from miles and miles away or you'll starve. His keen eyesight is one of the two most important reasons Boesman's here."

"What's the other reason?" asked Cairns.

Dammit. He'd not meant to say the last sentence out loud. Lieut ignored the question and pointed ahead. "Nearly there. Brace yourself, Cairns. This is not going to be easy."

Lieut would keep to himself as long as humanly possible that Boesman's main job once they'd left for the final attack was to carry their bodies back to the rendezvous, if it came to that.

Cairns stopped the truck. A barn burned. The farmhouse roof had collapsed over the garage from fire and still smoldered. Smoke twisted in a vortex from the gusts of wind blowing off the desert.

The main part of the house had escaped the licking flames. *Perhaps we're in time to save them.* Lieut jumped from the truck with Boesman before Cairns applied the brake.

His men poured out of the Bedford. Boesman took in the scene from every angle lying down, standing up and squatting. Neville, Charl, Frikkie, Piet-Tire and Cairns gathered first, their R1 rifles' safeties off. Tiny (who was anything but), gangly Penti-fuckingford and the skinny, bespectacled Benny Bookworm closed the circle next to Lieut.

As if to safeguard his sanity, Lieut's eyes were pulled toward a family of five meerkats standing in a long line, off the beaten track. Curious creatures by nature, and terrified of fire destroying their complex system of burrows, they stood bug-eyed on strong hind legs, small front paws together in front of their ribcages like they were knitting. Their bodies were still, but their heads moved this way and that to catch all the action. Lieut captured the image. That, along with those lions this morning, would work as his late-night escape.

Pistol in hand, Lieut led the way up the path, followed closely by Neville. Cairns, Tiny, Frikkie and Piet-Tire spread out, rifles at the ready. Charl and Penti moved backwards, covering their squad against incoming danger with their R1s. Benny, wearing his thick spectacles and his hand machine carbine, went back to the truck for a bird's-eye view so he could survey the surrounds and protect his squad inside. Lieut always kidded

Benny he had to have bloody good eyes to see through his thick glasses.

A black man lay naked on the front porch, his face in a pool of blood already beginning to congeal in the heat. Using his boot, Lieut gently rocked him over and onto his back. His testicles had been cut off. *Terrs. No question.*

"Why'd they kill one of their own, Lieut?" asked Penti.

"He's Shangaan or Xhosa or Ovambo. But he's not one of them. He serves the white man, so in Terrs' opinion, he must die violently to give warning to other natives that merely by serving us—the enemy—they deserve to perish in the worst way."

"Why his balls?" asked Frikkie, but Lieut was already entering through the open front door. The acrid metallic stench of fresh blood gripped the back of his throat, and he felt the bile of regret. *How could I have hoped these people would be spared? They deliberately left the worst of it un-charred for us to witness.*

"They're gone," said Nev.

*You're right! Physical danger's no longer an issue. But the head stuff? Now that shit's what really hurts.*

"Frikkie, Piet-Tire, to the truck. They're not here, but they're not long gone. Use those keen rock spider eyes and binoculars and help Benny find them," Lieut instructed.

The farmer sat slumped in a rocking chair on a once-cheerful, woven mat now stained dark with blood. His shirt was torn open, and his entrails sat grotesquely on his lap. His fly was down, and blood pooled around a shriveled phallus. Where once he had testicles was a severed mass. He was deliberately disemboweled first, Lieut surmised, so he could die slowly and watch his family being mutilated.

Two little girls under seven and close in age, prettily dressed in their church outfits—it was Sunday, after all—lay next to each other on the kitchen table, their matching frills stained dark pink. He couldn't bring himself to assess the cause of death. He'd leave that for the cops. The girls' mother was on the couch naked, legs spread, her body split from groin to goiter.

Boesman was on his haunches with his nose a millimeter from the carnage. Three of Lieut's brave ran outside to retch. Nev shook his head as tears streamed.

Lieut gave them sixty seconds, then shouted for their return.

"We're in the middle of a movie. Just do what I tell you. When we're done with this matinee, we'll get the fuck out of here, have popcorn and think of meerkats." He watched each of them grapple with the odd concept because God knew, he'd come up with this mental escape on the fly. Meerkats and popcorn? Well! Nothing made sense when faced with these real atrocities, so best he confused the shit out of them in their fantasies too.

Though he wanted to run and run and run, he needed to use this abomination to teach his soldiers to hate so they had no second thoughts when faced with the monsters responsible for this torturous carnage.

It was the only way they would all survive.

"Boesman?" Lieut asked.

The brown man looked up from studying the area around the rug, clicking, pointing and gesturing. Lieut nodded, suspicions confirmed.

He addressed his agonized team. "Boesman confirms Terrs' pattern and Lwazi's handiwork. Communist warfare in all its glory. These unsettled Africans believe we white people have stolen their land, and with Russia, China and Cuba's money and arms, coupled with African superstitions, they are a force to be reckoned with. What we have here, gentlemen, is a macabre, heavy-handed quadrangle of despicable horror and devastation."

He spoke very, very softly. "They've done this"—he paused as he gestured, forcing his men take in the slaughter and feeling like shit for doing so—"to show us, gentlemen, that we are vermin to them. Not human beings. Our families and all we hold dear are nothing but rats to be annihilated. They're posturing vile acts with our dead to demonstrate their hate and power to those of us who find them. By doing the unspeakable to white girls and women, they're showing how they detest the thought of us multiplying, so they're eliminating the bloodline."

Lieut watched his poor men glance reluctantly at the farmer's wife, slit from vagina to throat, but he had to continue the horror show. "And based on African superstition, taking the men's nuts will increase their might and virility. The abominable Lwazi is likely carrying them in his pocket as we speak."

Some of his guys looked at him, confused. Lieut said, "Lwazi. The smartest, most strategic terrorist bastard of them all. In five years, nobody's ever caught the motherfucker. Not even come close."

"How do you know it's him, Lieut?" asked Penti.

"Boesman knows his print. We've seen him on our missions before. Every boot print Boesman identifies that are not standard SADF issues are mostly Chinese-made. Some Russian. But Lwazi's brand of terror is marked by an indefinable print nobody can figure out."

"Why does Lwazi leave a deliberate footprint?" Charl asked.

"Because the bastard is so brazen, he uses that fucking print to rub our noses in his special brand of warning to the whites. He's sticking it to us in the worst way." He pointed to the vinyl floor. "It's as if Lwazi deliberately stood in the farmer's blood and used his perfect, unusual print to give us the finger."

A diatribe of English and Afrikaans swear words followed.

Penti asked, "Did you say Lwazi is likely carrying the black and white pair of balls in his pocket?"

Lieut nodded and immediately lost Penti and Charl as they hastened out the door with the urgent need to deliver their meager breakfast onto the well-tended lawn. Though he'd done his basic years before, Penti wasn't the sort you called up to defend the country if you had anyone else. This was his first tour after basic training. Poor bastard.

They were back, and Lieut continued, "And what's the farmer done to deserve this? He chose to work hard to buy this land; then he worked even harder to cultivate crops and raise cattle to sell to co-ops, who work hard to distribute to shops for hard-working city people to buy and feed their families. The Terrs want this land. They want us gone, and they'll go to any lengths to make sure we are extinguished for generations to come."

No one moved a muscle. Tiny, Lieut's biggest boy at six feet six and weighing in at a hefty 320 pounds of pure brawn, wiped his snotty nose on his sleeve. *Dammit, don't let his heart get as hard as his body.* With every fiber of his being, Lieut resented having to be the movie theater's miserable usher on behalf of this fucking war.

"They're animals!" shouted Tiny.

"No, Tiny! Animals have a code. These monsters do not," said Lieut and looked each of his men in the eye, then continued. "Are we going to let these fucking monsters win?"

"No. No, sir. No way," were the right answers at the wrong decibel.

"WHAT DID YOU SAY?" shouted Lieut, making them jump.

"NO, sir. NO."

"Look again if you must, boys. And again. Many times as it takes for you to understand the magnitude of evil our enemy possesses. And then, what I need from you is a certainty that you are all in. You have to be committed to do what we have to, to even this fight. Do you understand me, boys?"

"Yes, sir." "YES, sir." "YES! SIR."

When his men were furious and about to explode, Lieut said, "Okay, enough. Back to the truck. Send the others in. Then forget about this godforsaken movie and let's go and have popcorn and think about meerkats."

# 8

# GUARDS AND MEERKATS

*Champagne Castle Hotel, Drakensberg Mountains, South Africa, Easter 1959*

"PAPIN, you're wound up like a cheetah before it pounces," said Dad, and Jock wondered how Papin beat him to the kitchen this morning.

The five of them fit easily into the grocery pantry, the size of a double garage. Nicholas took up room enough for two. Shelves of different heights were stacked with cans of vegetables and fruit lined up like tin soldiers, bottles of oil, vinegar and such. Sacks of potatoes, flour, sugar and other bulk dry goods nestled onto bigger cubbyholes.

Nicholas. Every time Jock saw Nicholas, he felt a new surge of joy. He had no idea it was tenderness. The big man was as reliable as bacon at breakfast, and he'd more than once stepped in to calm his dad down when Jock was in trouble. All the waiters—even the Indian wine stewards—were afraid of Nicholas and did exactly as he bid. Nicholas didn't scare Jock. He was as much "home" to Jock as the mountains.

In the glare of the overhead lights, Jock smiled. You just had to look at head chef Thabo and his always-present smile forced your face to conform.

Thabo's Zulu birth name meant "happiness." Thabo and a smile were as common as Jock and bare feet. Dad said Thabo had the sunniest disposition. Jock wandered why Sangoma didn't heal Thabo of the Sunniest Disposition. Perhaps like some things, the sunniest part outweighed the "disposition" disease, so you let it be. At his ripe young age, Jock understood compromise.

Chef Thabo moved items around as needed for their first-in, first-out cycle to keep foodstuffs fresh. Mom planned three-meals-a-day menus three weeks before guests arrived.

Running a hotel two hours away from civilization and thousands of feet up a mountain needed more planning than the crowning of the queen, Dad said. Jock had no idea how a queen got involved.

Nicholas towered over them, pen and stock book in hand. A man of few words, when he spoke, others listened. Even white grownups listened to Nicholas, which in itself was a miracle, since whites didn't consider what blacks had to say important at all.

HA! Except Dad. But he was smarter than anybody.

In Jock's opinion, if old white ears listened to Zulus, they'd all be a hell of a lot cleverer and much happier. But then, Jock's opinion didn't count much either.

"Thirty-six tins of green beans," said Dad, glancing at Papin. Jock saw his friend still coiled for the spring, his bare toes twitching in readiness for his turn to speak.

Nicholas gave Papin a look, and Jock saw his friend's toes freeze mid-twitch.

"Are there any new cars in the parking lot this morning, Papin?" Dad asked, then continued without pause. "Thirty tins of peaches. Nicholas, let's put Peach Melba on the menu if we have enough ice cream."

"Still one red car, Inkosi. She doesn't belong to any of our guests." Papin's face and toes relaxed.

"You said they went up Sunset Trail very early five days ago?" Dad confirmed.

"Yes, Inkosi. Three mountain climbers," Papin answered.

Hikers and climbers often used the hotel's parking lot to leave their cars. Dad didn't mind. They slept in their own tents a decent distance from the hotel and came to the bar for a drink after their climb. Sometimes they even booked a room. Climbers stayed away for an average of five or six days as a rule and usually let Dad know how long they expected to be gone. It was another of Papin's jobs to take an inventory of non-guest cars.

As soon as Papin had delivered the message, the boys were off, stopping only to pick up four *koeksisters* steeped in syrup from Thabo and cajoling Mom to hand over two packets of Simba chips from the gift shop. Pockets were, as usual, stuffed with carrots for the day's adventure.

They galloped and trotted on Beauty and a colt Papin was training, all the way to the Grotto, where a hot spring constantly fed a big pond. The fascinating, unpredictable bubbles popped after their journey from the depths of the mountain. It was one of their many sacred places where they talked of nature and practiced throwing rocks sideways to skim the pond and bounce on the surface more than four times. They searched for skins that had been shed by various snakes, found a few and analyzed them. After the horses were treated with carrots, the boys found shelter in the nearby cave, and as they munched on their lunch, they studied the Bushmen paintings with stories different from the ones they knew so well closer to the hotel.

Later, once the horses were stabled and the sun threatened

to slip behind the first of the towering peaks, they raced to their rock.

High up, they absently watched a mob of meerkats at work and play about twenty feet away. Jock and Papin were part of the meerkats' mountain world, and the mob went about their business no matter what kind of odd human sounds emitted from atop the rock.

"Today's watchman is on the ball," said Jock, pointing to the guard loftily overlooking the meerkats' foraging turf. Papin said their territory likely spanned up to four and a half miles and consisted of tunnels with chambers of many levels, going down six feet deep.

The guard let out a low, constant peeping called "The Watchman's Song" to let his mob know all was well for the moment.

They relied on their watchman to do his job properly so they could do theirs, and he didn't disappoint. The rest of the critters calmly basked in the last of the sun, foraged for insects, termites or small lizards, or dug new tunnels with vicious, non-retractable claws on powerful toes.

As a falcon moved in for a closer look at his potential dinner, the guard let out a loud whistle, and in milliseconds, the mob of thirty strong was gone. Jock visualized them cramming into the closest bolt holes or special tunnels with wider openings, designed to hold a crowd of meerkats at once.

The boys focused on the bolt holes until a brave head peeked up and out. The falcon had moved off to find less vigilant prey.

Once the meerkats came out again and the guard "peep-peeped"—his assurance that the coast was clear—the vocal creatures went back to meerkat business, purring, squealing, murmuring and even spitting, clucking and growling.

"Show me a meerkat," said Papin, and Jock thought it would be more fun if he acted out the lesson of the day.

Jock stood with his legs apart, wider than his shoulders, knees slightly bent. He motioned with his hand behind him to show a tail being used as an anchor. Jock pulled his elbows into his chest and swiveled his head this way and that in spurts, taking in everything with focused concentration. He sneaked a peek at Papin, who was smiling from ear to ear.

"What color are you?" Papin tried to suppress his smile.

"My coat colors and markings adapt to what's around me," said Jock, his voice in time with his staccato head movements.

"And?"

"My stomach skin is thin and dark so I can lie on my back"—he demonstrated and was rewarded with a giggle from his friend—"and soak up the sun or ... I can flip over and cool myself on the always cold rock."

"Aren't you a clever little meerkat," Papin exclaimed, laughing so hard now, he was holding his stomach, but Jock held his meerkat pose, head spinning in bursts this way and that. Papin finally got out, "Tell me about those strange eyes of yours."

"My eyes have long horizontal pupils to give me a wide range of vision." Jock was watching Tripod on the hotel lawn trying to hump Bonzo while balancing on his only hind leg and, in his admiration for his dog's audacity, forgot his meerkat head movements for a couple of beats.

His master would have none of it. "Where has my meerkat gone?" Papin asked.

"I have a soft piece of skin, a membrane that covers my eyes so they don't get stuff in them when I dig," said Jock, getting bored but playing along so as not to annoy the still "new man." "And ears that close up to keep the sand out when I dig ... enough meerkats, please, Papin," Jock begged as he lay on his back to watch the mountains change from orange to red to purple to aubergine.

"And why did you meerkats do all that showing off?" asked Papin.

"Please, enough! Papin, I am meerkatted out!"

"Last one," promised Papin.

"To scare the other meerkat guys. Just like baboons, they pretend they're big stuff to scare off others trying to steal their homes. They don't want a war. They want the other guys to run away."

"Good. Always better to scare them off than to fight. These animals know the high cost of war. Many die. They must do everything they can *not* to go to war to keep their species multiplying. Zulu ancestors teach all of this ..."

"Boy! The chief sure told you some sad things when you were becoming a man. I think he spoiled your childhood." He sounded just like his dad but in Zulu.

Papin asked, "Are you Tsotsi or Inkosi?"

And soon both collapsed with laughter, and Jock was relieved his friend was still more boy than man.

They lay on their backs enjoying mild late-summer breezes and watching the colorful sunset sky turn deep indigo. Clusters of twinkling and static stars layered in swirls above them.

A shooting star lit up and sped through the ink sky. "Make a wish," Jock said as he watched the speeding bright orb and the stripe of shine following in its wake.

When the lofty show was over, Papin said, "A wish?" and began to laugh.

Jock bristled. He didn't like to be laughed at.

"While you were gone on your man thing before Christmas, I heard a guest say if you wished on a shooting star, your wish would come true."

"Don't be silly, Tsotsi. Next you'll tell me you believe in Tokoloshe."

Jock frowned. "You should believe. Your surname, Tshabalala, means 'shooting star.' The chief said so. You know, Papin, it was much easier when you were a boy. This new man is sometimes an ass."

"See the Southern Cross?" Papin said as if Jock's disappointed words held no merit, and he pointed at a bright constellation. "Remember if you are lost at night, Tsotsi, that is your direction to follow. If it's misty or rainy, just sit tight until you can see it, then the Southern Cross will lead you home."

After locking that information into his Mind Brownie vault, Jock stared into the banks of stars twinkling in their varying depths of brightness. Jock had learned that the sun was really a star in physical geography and was thrilled it was news to Papin. He supposed school was good for something.

"Don't be late for your mother," said Papin a second before Nicholas rang the bell for adult dining. A simple reminder devoid of mockery.

"Where will you have dinner?" Jock asked.

Papin shrugged. "Kraal. Compound. I don't care."

Later he sat with his mother at a table in the dining room, and their nightly ritual began.

"Elbows off the table, Jock ... sit up straight ... no, the flat knife's for fish ... don't butter your roll; put a pat of butter on the edge of your side plate ... good ..." On and on. Like these lessons in manners helped at boarding school, when the ravenous older boys drooled over your tired slice of tomato you hadn't yet touched.

His thoughts strayed to Papin, and he wondered where and what his friend was eating and suddenly felt guilty he was in the midst of a five-course meal.

# 9

# POPCORN AND MEERKATS

*South African Defense Force Camp,*
*South West Africa, 1977*

LITTLE WAS SAID on the trip back to Ondangwa. The camp housed about a thousand soldiers, airmen and para-bats. With its airstrip, planes and centurion tanks, the camp's infrastructure and essentials were managed by the largest division—the support company—which took care of logistics, food, water, fuels and necessary supplies. It was at least fifty miles from the next closest camp, called Oshikoto, which was the base for all the high-ranking officers.

They all lived and slept in fairly roomy six-man tents. Major Curry was the senior officer of the Armored Division, a lazy bastard who thought Lieut was his personal skivvy and whose tent he'd shared every time there was a call-up. Lieut, the major's adjunct—a quiet man—and the major had a decent amount of room to breathe in the six-man tent. Lieut, however, would give up all the spaciousness in a heartbeat for obscurity. He strongly suspected these close quarters were to blame for his frequent call-ups. To the major who made the call-up decisions, it was a hell of a lot easier to bring back a man who'd been taught to live "invisibly" with other boys in a dorm all his school life, than someone new who hadn't. When Lwazi reappeared, Lieut's name came up far too bloody easily.

Other squadrons were headed by sergeants. Few men with ambition joined the South African Defense Force. Permanent force officers were rare—most of the rank and file were made up of boys fresh out of high school. Some unlucky bastards like Lieut were noticed in spite of their goal of anonymity and were simply shit out of luck, because they had no option but to do as the government told.

Lieut opened the Perspex hatch to the back. "Prepare for some tank maneuvers," he said somberly, and his men were so shattered, they didn't even let out groans of resistance. It had been a long, hard, soul-destroying day, but nobody was about to get shut-eye after what they'd seen at the farmhouse.

Cairns' young face was disappointed as they passed the tents and belted toward where the twelve armored tanks were stored. Lieut watched him touch his picture of Cathy at least twice, a sure sign he needed calming.

The metal beasts stood solid and stoic and in precise military order. But like a new father in a room of screaming babies, Lieut always knew which one was his.

He felt a pang of regret, but what was the point? No one outside the army knew where he was, other than his father, who was sworn to secrecy. All his wife, his family, company and friends knew was that he was "fighting on the border." There was no date he could look forward to that would end this tour; calling home was just a once-a-month privilege, in spite of being the major's skivvy.

To say that his team flopped out of the Bedford with anything other than dread written in capital letters on their faces fiercely understated the lethargy and anger that brewed. Lieut understood.

"Nev, take her to the *braai* pit. Boys, stretch your legs and follow Nev and his hefty girlfriend. We'll meet you there."

As Neville maneuvered the armored tank out of formation, Cairns drove Lieut over to the braaivleis area, the only place in the camp to really let them get drunk and disorderly. Letting off steam was essential for survival.

His squad kicked their way into the braai picnic area, heads hanging, sullen and pissed off. Nev was still down in the tank. When the tank was ten meters from the rec area, Lieut threw his arm out and drew it back in invitation. "All aboard," he shouted and jumped onto the outside of the tank. Confused, the guys found places to jump up and stood on the metal brute, groping for something to hang on to. Well, all except Boesman, who stood six meters away, shaking his head and clicking furiously. *Stupid white people!* Lieut chuckled. Boesman was right!

"OK, Nev—make some circles," Lieut shouted down the hatch. The tank revved and turned right in a tight circle as the men held on for dear life. The army's version of a bucking bronco. Round and around went the tank, and soon his men were hooting and laughing while their beast of war danced like a merry-go-round at a carnival.

Frikkie nearly fell off three times while making obscene movements with his hips, and Piet-Tire came dangerously close to crumbling on the churning earth when too much laughter made his body go limp.

When the tank was half-submerged, Lieut yelled down to Nev in the driver's seat, "What do you see, Nev?"

"Dirt," came the reply.

"Now the other way, Nev," and the tank laboriously turned, spewing dirt up and out in the opposite direction.

Lieut looked at his boys. They were having fun. As soon as

the big hole was deep enough, they hauled metal ass out of the hole.

"Take her home, Nev," said Lieut as the tank revved hard to get out. "We'll wash her tomorrow when we're sober," he shouted to his boys. "Tiny, Frikkie, Pentifuckingford, catch a lift with Nev and bring back a tank tarp. Rest of us are waiting ... so hurry." They looked at him like he'd lost it.

When they came back, Lieut directed them to line the substantial tank-made hole with the tarp.

Rainwater was ferried from the water tanks until they had a swimming pool, army-style, too tempting to resist. Stripped quickly to shorts, all of them tumbled into the new toy—all except Boesman, who took himself off to the shade of a rare tree. Lieut took the truck and arrived back with five crates of beer and two huge cardboard boxes filled with popped popcorn and a salt shaker. At last, an advantage to being the major's skivvy.

His boys were high on atmosphere when he returned. "Come on in, Lieut—it's like the pool at the Carlton," Neville shouted.

Tiny was on his back, shooting water between the gaps in his teeth, the whale around which other fish maneuvered. Charl kept submerging long enough for Lieut to wonder if he needed water wings, and Frikkie was cleaning his armpits.

"Hey! It's not a bath, Frikkie. Wash your pits *before* you get in!" Lieut yelled as he hauled the beers out of the Bedford. He also delivered very rare venison and pap prepared by the chef at base and a calabash of African beer to Boesman under his chosen tree.

In spite of being in the braai area, where red meat usually sizzled in massive quantities, Lieut knew that after their day of carnage, cooking raw flesh was not an option for his team. So once he and his eight wet men sunned themselves on another large tarp covering the dusty ground, the popcorn hit the spot to quell their hunger. Boesman looked at them like they were the most dim-witted meerkats he'd ever seen and took himself off to the mess.

Downing beers would, for a time, assuage their gaping mental wounds. Whenever someone began to recall the horror of the day, Lieut—sober as a judge—shouted, "Meerkats!"

And so, it was that on that day, an extramural activity was created at the camp called, appropriately, "Popcorn and Meerkats."

# 10

# PAUL ANORAK

*Champagne Castle Hotel, 1960*

JOCK WAS NOT new to changing bedrooms.

His bedroom had become anywhere that couldn't be used or improved for guest accommodation. Frankly, he really didn't care where he slept, as long as he could no longer hear the bedroom whispers that'd so changed his life.

His new spot this Easter holiday was the storeroom next to reception. It was big enough for a single bed amongst all the office paraphernalia and gift shop stock. The threat of Dad's sjambok superseded Jock's desire to "sample" any of the gift shop's chocolates and other goodies.

Tripod was perfectly happy with the new arrangement. There was a bed. Jock was in it. Tripod had a preferred place for shut-eye.

"Inkosi! Inkosi!" The clock above the booking ledger showed 3 a.m. when Bekah's distant urgent call and frantic knocking killed sleep. Dressed in a second, Jock and Tripod joined Bekah the tea guy, with eyes the size of dinner plates, outside the family suite.

Next to him stood a young man in what Dad called an anorak and torn pants. In the light spilling from the family suite, dried and fresh blood covered every exposed part of Anorak's body.

"Paul," Anorak guy said, putting out his bloody hand, which Dad shook as he guided the young man into the hotel lounge.

Words tumbled from Paul Anorak, and Jock's eyes locked onto his clattering ivories. "Three of us in some-or-other gully after Monk's Cowl ... Russell's the climber. He knew ... Sorry ... all a bit of a blur. A snake bit Russell when he went down to the stream to fill the billy can. We hadn't erected our tents yet."

Dad's head bobbed up, caught Jock's eye and with a flip of his head reminded him of "the drill."

It wasn't the first time the mountain objected strongly to being climbed.

Bekah fled to make very sweet, hot tea, and Jock sprinted off for a blanket and one of the many first aid kits.

Even covered with the heavy blanket, Paul Anorak still forced his words through clashing teeth. Jock watched, ready to duck should one break off and launch from Paul's mouth like a bullet.

"We just sat on our tents out in the elements all night at an altitude of nearly 8,000 feet. We counted on Russell for everything. We were hopeless."

Damn, Jock knew he'd missed some vital information to tell Papin.

"When did you leave your camp?" asked Dad.

"About 5:30 a.m. yesterday. The map helped a bit, but the hotel kept disappearing as I walked and I was lost again." Paul's top and bottom ivories were like warring bull elephants.

"Holy mackerel. You were wandering, lost, for nearly twenty-two hours?" Dad asked. And in the silence as Paul sipped his hot tea, Dad shook his head as if confused. "A berg adder, you say ..."

"That's what Russ said. He knows snakes."

Jock also knew the snakes of the berg. They were as much part of their mountain existence as every peak visible from the hotel's veranda. He'd been taught early how to recognize snakes by color, size and temperament. He knew where they lived, what they ate and whether to ignore, circumvent, stand still or run uphill. And dealing with each snake's venom was as imperative to this hotel as advanced bookings.

When he was six, Jock was instructed on berg adder bites and learned their bite "shut down your organs." He'd asked how an adder bite could possibly be responsible for shutting down the organ his mom played for the guests in the family room. Papin laughed so hard he'd fallen off the chair in the scullery.

Paul Anorak had gone from talkative to silent, and Jock had missed out on all the good parts. But since everyone knew there were no known deaths from a berg adder, though it was scary as hell, Jock was relieved nobody was going to die.

Dad barked his orders: "Bekah, wake up eight of the strong outdoor team as well as Mandinsolo. Warmest clothes, work boots and in the bar in thirty minutes. Get Nicholas and Thabo." Jock saw the vein in Dad's neck pulsing. "Jock, get your mom in here to see if Paul needs the hospital. Take twenty pairs of socks, new batteries for nine torches, nine whistles and two dozen chocolates from the shop. Tell Mom later, so she can record it in the stock book."

Jock sprinted off, grateful he could visualize his dad's long list. Otherwise, his bum would be smarting for days.

He heard Dad say, "Paul, let Bekah know what you'd like to eat. While Renee's patching you up, I'll phone Natal Mountain Rescue."

He found Papin in the kitchen helping Thabo pack rucksacks with sandwiches and packets of sweet biscuits, biltong and nuts enough for eleven, in case the two stranded climbers could eat solids. They added two chocolate bars per pack from Jock's stash. Jock's arithmetic was good. He and Papin deserved a treat for later.

"Four days, eleven men, lots of food," Thabo said, smiling like this was a celebration.

In the bar, happy Zulu men pulled new socks over old ones, followed by boots. Food-filled rucksacks were stuffed to capacity with first aid kits and extra clothes.

It was just after 4:30 a.m. when the rescuers, with gear and a stretcher, gathered outside the scullery, which was as far as possible from where the guests slept.

Dad thought of guests before he thought of anyone or anything else. Jock knew his dad loved him best in the world. But only after the guests.

Eight of the hotel's strongest and Mandinsolo—the hotel's head guide, master climber and Jock's hero—stood in a horseshoe shape with Dad at the pinnacle of the curve. He cleared his throat and spoke in Zulu. Dad's kinship through his attempt at using their language was evident in the faces that watched him.

"Men, this will be a hard climb to find exactly where the two strays are camped. One by one, each of these gullies between Cathkin Peak, Monk's Cowl and Champagne Castle have to be explored until the climbers are found. There is no other way."

Jock looked at Paul Anorak, whose white face had turned ashen. *Imagine how I'd feel if Papin was lost ...*

Dad continued in English: "I send you on a very difficult life-saving mission. It's true the lost climbers are not our guests, but we can't stand by while others suffer. To do nothing would not do your ancestors—or mine—proud. Natal Rescue will be here in about three hours, so you won't be alone. Never take your whistles from around your necks. They are your only tools to keep in touch. If the mist is down, whistles will be the only way to find each other. Never separate in less than twos as you go up the ravines, in case someone gets injured. Whatever you do, listen to Mandinsolo. He knows these mountains better than all of our ancestors. Do your best. Nobody can ask more of you."

Jock saw no fear. Each face shone with pride and camaraderie. Jock glanced at his friend standing beside him and felt the very same as those brave Zulu men looked. Proud and safe with a friend he trusted.

*Kah-chick.* He captured this special moment of unity with his imaginary Mind Brownie. He knew it would comfort him endlessly when these Easter holidays were over.

In spite of their heavy loads, nine men walked tall and proud toward the mountains, flashlights bobbing in the darkness. Jock stood with the rest and watched till the lights in the darkness were but pinpricks.

Jock felt Dad's hand ruffle his hair. "What do you think, Jock?"

And Jock said what was in his heart. "I love being Zulu."

## 11

# A BABY AND A PRAYER

*Thirty Miles from Angola Border, 1977*

IN THE STRANGE light that lingers before the promise of dawn, Lieut woke up with a jolt as his chin hit the barrel of his gun. It was intentionally positioned to wake him if he nodded off in his sitting position. Why the hell bobbing lights slowly disappearing gave him an unusual peace, he had no idea, but they were gone as soon as his eyes focused.

He checked his guys in various positions of slumber in their sleeping bags, and Cairns's head and shoulders were visible above the Bedford. Good. Awake and alert. Using a leafy branch, Boesman was already raking over where he'd slept.

Tracking Terrs was an intense business, and though his boys needed their sleep, it was time. They quickly broke down the camp. Gear was packed and loaded, cigarette ends collected and spade used to cover their own excrement to avoid a telltale sign of their passage. Once all the white boys were in the Bedford, Boesman studied the scene and rearranged the site to ensure all evidence of their stay was wiped out.

Once in his usual lookout post, Boesman scoured the

surrounding area for abnormalities, found none and banged on the roof. Lieut and his men were out of there before first light.

There was no option but to use the main road to move more deeply into enemy territory. Five miles along, a troop of fifty-five-ton centurion tanks blocked the road, forcing travelers to stop.

Cairns asked, "Those are our guys. What are they doing, Lieut?"

"They're filtering out the locals from the terrorists. It's bloody difficult. The bad guys blend and merge. Go round and park behind one of the tanks," Lieut ordered.

"Man! Those 105-millimeter guns jutting out of army-green monsters would scare anyone shitless," said Cairns.

The boy wasn't wrong, but in this war, the army's goal was to scare the locals more than the terrorists could. That was no mean feat.

*The high cost of war.* That phrase took Lieut's mind away from the present to something long ago. He couldn't quite remember what the context was or where it had happened, yet the morning's feeling that all was right in the world came back for a serene second.

Ridiculous peace when he was in the midst of a vicious war.

"It's not fair on the locals," Cairns was saying.

Anger expunged Lieut's seconds of peace.

"These poor people. So badly affected by a war they have no part in. They've nothing to gain and everything to lose no matter who wins."

A tired old sedan, with peeling paint exposing three different colors, had been halted for inspection.

"Lieut, we could blow if that old junker is piled high with C4."

Lieut answered, "Lucky the thing is as holey as Swiss cheese. You can see right through it. You can't miss too much when there's only one seat in the old *chorrie*." He pointed. "Here is good. If I'm wrong and it does blow, tank'll protect us." He opened the Perspex partition and yelled: "Smoke break, boys."

As his men alighted from the Bedford, Lieut watched a corporal from the road-block contingent gesture with his rifle as he shouted into the old car, "Switch off and get out. All of yew. Ja, your wife an' baby also."

Four black men and a black woman holding a baby spilled out of the car. The men's shirts were frayed. The woman wore a traditional one-piece dress, the hem past her ankles. She held her baby swathed in a blanket. Lieut noticed she immediately separated from the men. He swore he could smell her fear as the hair on the back of his neck prickled. She must have felt his eyes on her, and she looked at Lieut briefly before her eyes darted away. She began swatting insects away from the baby's head.

Lieut watched a swarm of soldiers descend on the men and the car. They were completely ignoring the woman.

"Baby's got a ripe smell, apparently," Penti noted, and Lieut saw flies had amassed and created a dark halo around the baby's head.

"Tell Nev to get our boys behind the Bedford till I get back," Lieut shouted to Penti over his shoulder as he strode toward the woman, his voice getting louder as distance from Penti increased. "And tell him to bring me his bayonet."

Lieut passed by the corporal in charge of searching the car. Seeing Lieut's status, the officer straightened, saluted and said, "Can I help you, Captain?" Lieut had deliberately forgotten about his promotion and the new stars affixed to his shoulder epaulets a week ago. They meant nothing at all.

Lieut returned the salute and gestured with his thumb to the woman. "Either she really stinks or there's a problem with the *umtwana*. Mind if I check her out for you?" he asked.

"Hell no, Captain. Appreciate the help. Get you back on the

road sooner once they're all checked out." The corporal saluted once more.

As Lieut walked toward her, the woman put a finger to her lips. "Shh-shh," she cooed, rocking the babe in her arms.

Lieut shouted and gestured to the woman to put the baby down.

She started to sing a lullaby as if her baby's urgent needs made her deaf to Lieut's command. She sang and rocked the child.

"NOW!" Lieut shouted in Zulu. "Give me your baby."

She looked up. She was shaking with fear as she moved the bundle away from her body.

The baby's gray-colored head flopped backward awkwardly.

The woman dropped the baby, turned and ran.

Two soldiers chased her. Pulled her down.

Closing in on the baby, Nev, now behind him, said, "Fuck! The smell!"

Lieut cautiously nudged the infant with his foot. Nothing. He grabbed Nev's R1 rifle with bayonet attached. "Get back, Nev, back to the truck," Lieut shouted and then used the bayonet tip to very gently lift the blanket off the child.

The blanket was stained rust-colored with dried blood. The little boy's naked chest cavity was a mess. It had been cut open and hollowed out. "What the fu—?" Lieut heard behind him.

"You never see this before?" Lieut asked the soldier who'd appeared.

There was no reply as Lieut went down on his haunches beside the baby and sank his hand into the little boy's chest. He pulled out one hand grenade and felt three more hidden behind the tiny rib cage.

The answer from the soldier who stood behind him finally came—in the form of a not-so-dry heave.

A crowd of soldiers not involved in handcuffing the car's occupants gathered round.

"This little chest is big enough to hold four grenades that can be sneaked across the border while the nice Herero lady holds the 'sleeping' child in her arms." Lieut felt his own voice quiver with fury. "You see the horrendous things they make the locals do? This is terrorist warfare at its finest, soldiers."

"Captain, should I take out the grenades?" the corporal asked Lieut.

Lieut replaced the grenade and wrapped the little soul back in his blanket. "They're not our grenades, soldier. We don't know how stable they are. This little guy needs to be gently buried, as deep as possible with them inside him, just as they are."

"Vok, Captain. How cold can the Terrs be?" the young corporal asked of Lieut, of God. His face was wet with tears. Lieut understood. The first time was always the worst.

"Say a prayer for him, soldier, whether you believe or not. Pave this poor little mite's way to a better life. It has to be better than this one," Lieut said before he walked back to his men and the road block began to clear.

The high cost of war. He felt sick.

## 12

## BUSHMEN AND BATS

*Champagne Castle Hotel, Easter 1960*

"It's bloody inconsiderate of climbers to get bitten by a snake over Easter," Alone in the bar, Dad muttered to the bottles he was counting. The sun hit the mountains and bounced sharp brightness off the windows.

Jock found the understatement amusing in the face of the very real disaster that weighed heavily on everyone, and he stopped his grin in fear of a meeting with the sjambok. Dad and Mom worked harder than ever to give the guests lots to do. Schools closed for two weeks around Easter, and it was one of four peak times for Champagne Castle Hotel.

"Papin, you lead the horse-riding morning and midafternoon. Jock, you take the guests on the morning walk."

He could hardly believe his ears. *He was allowed to lead a walk?*

In the absence of the nine workers on the rescue mission and others filling in for them where needed, Jock became useful.

Some waiters were plucked from the dining room and now worked in the quarry to urgently repair a gargantuan pothole just before the S-bend. Nobody could get to or from the hotel until it was fixed.

"You two boys will be breakfast waiters before anything else!" Dad was in a mood.

It was quickly established Jock did not have many skills in this department, so he was relegated to delivering racks of toast to each white-clad table. Several times he narrowly missed bashing into his fellow waiters as they delivered steaming plates of eggs and bacon to guests who didn't appreciate the splatter of crumbs that followed Jock's enthusiastic toast delivery. Nicholas spent his time behind Jock, expertly coaxing crumbs to the edge of tables with a butter knife and into his open palm, subtly restoring the pristine order of things.

Well, okay, so he didn't cut it as a waiter, but Jock would show his dad he was quite capable of doing the morning walk, thank you very much!

When Dad walked into the dining room, tapping his spoon on a water glass, guests' huffs and puffs subsided.

"Folks, we abjectly apologize for the disruption of your usual service and routine. We've had to send up some of our guys to rescue a couple of climbers, one of whom was bitten by a snake. We don't know what shape he's in. Paul, the third climber, took twenty-three grueling hours to reach us for help. If you see Paul around the hotel, and you can't miss him—he's all banged up—give him a proverbial pat on the back, would you? But not too much enthusiasm. The guy's hurting enough already."

There were some mighty gasps and a smattering of nervous laughter before a dozen voices threw out questions: "Where were they?" "What kind of snake?"

Dad held up a hand, and the room went as silent as a night without drumbeats.

"That's all we know at this time. Renee and I ask you to bear with us if things aren't up to par —you'll find different staff doing different jobs, but it won't be for too long, and we'll do all we can to make your stay fun and memorable anyway. Please bear with us until all return safely."

Women put their hands over hearts; men shook their heads as if confirming Dad's decision; and soon the whole dining room stood, clapped and cheered as orange juice glasses and coffee cups collided in random toasting to "all the guys who're up the mountain."

"When will things around here be back to normal so we can get the attention we've paid for?" a hefty man with a thick beard and a thicker Afrikaans accent asked. Jock noticed he and his wife were the only ones still sitting.

"Hard to tell, Mr. Viljoen," Dad said. "We can't be sure where exactly the climbers are. Of course, we have no way to communicate with them, so there's no telling how long it will take the posse to find them. We also don't know their condition or what sort of help they'll need before they can get back. Just impossible to guess, but they have supplies for four days."

Everyone in the room sat back down.

"FOUR days? Why should you worry about them, man? They're not even your guests. Shouldn't you be worrying about us?" Viljoen's voice became louder as he half stood to show off his large, strong bulk.

Jock stomach knotted at the man's aggression, but his dad's voice was calm.

"Sir, you're right. They're not hotel guests but humans in jeopardy." Dad gestured to the whole room. "It's a lesson for us that these gorgeous mountains that so entice us can have deadly consequences if we challenge them. But if it were my son or yours out there, Mr. Viljoen, we'd want all hands on deck to get them out of their jam. I ask, Mr. Viljoen, that you embrace the consensus."

Jock's head snapped from his dad to the burly, hairy guy. The big man stood straighter, puffing out his chest, his face flushed purple with fury while his wife, her head down, tugged meekly on his sleeve.

Mr. Viljoen grabbed his wife's hand and pulled her through the dining room. At the door, he turned and shouted, "Don't expect me to pay my bill. Not with this lack of service. And start worrying more about your guests and minding your son who mixes with blacks all the time. Otherwise, Walsh, more people like me will refuse to pay their bills."

Jock's dad turned his back on the furious man, and the dining room crowd stood up and all started singing, "For he's a jolly good fellow ..."

As Mr. Viljoen and his meek wife disappeared, Jock felt as proud to be his father's son as he did to be Zulu.

He sought out Papin and saw him standing against the wall, four empty plates in his hand, and Jock saw in his best friend's eyes a fury he'd never seen before. He didn't have a chance to talk to Papin because his friend left to lead the early horse ride before breakfast was done.

Jock found his mom in the kitchen making sandwiches and packing fresh scones for his walk. *His walk!* Her eyes were wet. "Why are you crying, Mom?" he asked, confused.

"Your dad is my hero, Jock," she said softly.

"Mine too." He grinned up at her and saw her eyes crinkle at the corners. As she bent down, he ducked out of her way before her kiss landed. He loved her but didn't need kisses and stuff to be reminded he was still a boy.

As he rounded the corner of the meeting area for the walk, Jock saw a few of the guests already gathered. *His* walk. He felt a flush, and his chest, unbidden, puffed out, just like Mr. Viljoen. He quickly pushed his self-inflated air right out. He'd learned that morning if you puffed out your chest and thought yourself special, sooner or later, you'd look like a fool.

Still, he loved leading the guests as they set off to the Crystal Falls through the band of high gum trees. He wished Papin could see him. He'd be pleased, he felt sure. The heady smell of pine and mint and moss and honey made his stomach rumble, and he hoped his mom had dribbled honey over the melted butter on the soft inside of the scones.

Bekah's rucksack was filled with plastic cups and serviettes, tins of sandwiches laced with spreads and cold meats, and of course those scones, nestling on a fine layer of sugar-dust in the largest tin. Smaller tins held tea leaves and sugar cubes. A billy can—a large, empty, topless tin can with an unsophisticated wire handle—was attached by a shoelace to the outside of the rucksack. Inside the can was a brandy bottle with one third of the intended substance and the rest fresh milk. Brandy stopped milk from going sour. Jock knew for a fact, the more brandy, the more contented the guests.

The rucksack clinked and clunked on Bekah's back as the terrain became rougher.

"You okay, Bekah?" Jock asked in Zulu.

"Yebo, Tsotsi, very okay because I earn tips in the mountains. Nothing in the scullery."

Jock remembered he was in guide mode just in time as they came out of the fragrant tree line. He pointed and declared to his very own walkers: "There's the dam that gives the hotel its power." Jock felt the awe of his dad's magic as acutely as he had four years before. So Jock could follow the process of hydroelectric power, Dad had dragged his young self to the dam, and they'd walked the same path the water flowed: all the way from the dam and down the steep hill to the weir. Dad had talked away as if teaching himself, and though Jock didn't understand, he was with his dad. That was a huge something. Since then, he'd walked the flow and process alone many times, and each time felt his dad beside him, though of course, he was busy with the hotel. The very best part came that first day when it was almost dark. Dad had said, "Come, Jock. Let me show you how your dad single-handedly can make the world brighter."

Close together they sat on the lip of the ridge, and just as the sun's last pink-orange light switched off behind the mountains, Dad's water-driven generator switched on, and the hotel—a mile and a half down the valley—blazed with bright light.

A miracle created by Jock's dad. His hero.

Up and up, Jock and *his* guests walked and Bekah jingled, until the opening in the mass of rock was visible. From their vantage point, they could see the sunken forest on the "roof" of the cave flourishing. Below, moss gripped the edge of the cave—bright green, slippery and thick as the lounge carpet.

Jock ran ahead and stuck his head inside the cave, inhaling the pungent bat feces and wet stone. The smell took his young soul to old places.

Right there and then, Jock made his very first adult decision. Why not give the guests a little something more than just the Crystal Falls? Dad always said, "Give them more than they expect."

Jock turned to look for Bekah, and the whole walking group was looking at him. He felt a surge of power, but Mr. Viljoen's furious face intruded and the power quickly petered out.

Adult words sprang from his tongue: "Let's do something special today. Let's enjoy the Bushman Caves as well as the falls!" and Jock assumed the "Billy Pillay" position and in true "Ta-Da!" fashion, stepped back and held out his hand for excited guests to enter the cave.

He led them deeper toward the single shaft of light that saved the cave from thick darkness. It was but a small gap created a millennium before, Papin said, when the rocks fell just so, to make the cave.

Without fail, Jock was mesmerized by the specks of dust and

pollen that swirled in slow motion around the shaft of sunlight. He passed through the column of light and shivered, as he always did. It was as if going through the light cleansed you in some way and gave you the right to gaze upon the ancient history of life in these mountains.

Etched into and painted onto the rock was a massive wall of stories, waiting to be relived.

The quick intake of breath that came from the walkers didn't surprise Jock. It merely endorsed his own awe. He'd seen these Bushman paintings scores of times with Papin and they never got old.

The guests were drawn like magnets toward the rock wall, and Jock understood the strength of their pull toward the oldest picture book in all the world.

Though his friend was guiding the horse-riding tour, Papin's voice whispered in Jock's ear as if he was right beside him ...

SITTING TALL ON BEAUTY, Papin looked over his guests on the morning ride. All twenty horses from the hotel's stable had a guest astride them. The slower, lazy ones carried first-time riders, while the more experienced enjoyed the frisky horses. Luckily there was no need to corral these riders because they had no clue where they were going, so they paid attention. If they should wander off, the horses would lead them home.

He'd had time to think about the disparaging, demoralizing man in the dining room this morning. Was this the attitude of the whites his uncle spoke of? The insistence by those enamored with the Nationalist government on keeping the blacks separate from whites no matter what the circumstance?

This morning they were headed to Dingaan's Cave—so called because Dingaan, the great King Shaka's half-brother, who took part in murdering the king of the Zulus in 1828, was meant to have hidden in those Bushmen caves.

The terrain to the cave was grassy and wide for the easy mile-and-a-half trail ride from the hotel. He helped new riders dismount and showed them where to lead the horses to let them graze. Then, Papin led his entourage inside on foot to explore Dingaan's Cave.

The riders ooh'd and aah'd at the centuries-old depictions of mountain life. Papin squatted out of the way to oversee and ensure everyone was accounted for.

His uncle had visited last night. Just briefly while his father was tending the cattle, Uncle started again with his stories of the black man's injustice. With Uncle came discontent. He brought with him negative notions of a world Papin really didn't want to know about nor wished to contemplate. It was too crowded with the ugliness he'd only had a hint of in his world at the hotel. But then Mr. Viljoen's words proved his uncle was not imagining things. *Gollaga-inja.*

Both he and Tsotsi knew ugliness lurked because of their friendship. Sometimes he wanted to shout, "I'm being paid to be here, beside the boy!" But nobody knew he was paid to look after Tsotsi, least of all Tsotsi himself. The boy would feel betrayed. Truth was, Tsotsi *was* his friend. He loved him like a brother he never had. He enjoyed him far more than the Zulu boys his age. Tsotsi was a gift from the gods and the ancestors in so many, many ways. He was closer to that boy than anyone in his life. How dare that man, any man, sully their friendship?

Papin forced himself to swallow his bitterness as he thought of his charge leading his first hike. He smiled as he imagined Tsotsi leading the way confidently—as he should. He knew the mountains as well as Papin and would speak when he felt he had to.

That umtwana always made him smile. Well, mostly.

Papin gazed absently at the wall of bushman history the riders were absorbing, and he thought of the caves closer to the hotel where he and Tsotsi had spent many hours. As with all things, watching Tsotsi experiencing things for the first time made them exciting and new all over again for Papin.

When he'd introduced the wall of wonders to that umtwana, he'd never seen awe and wonder such as he'd found in Tsotsi's eyes.

Though only they two were in the cave, Papin had whispered to heighten the boy's awe:

*Where there is a stick-like figure, see a little brown man crouched low with bow and arrow poised? He's as close as any human can be to a wild animal without scaring it away. Wait! That little brown man is you, Tsotsi. In the next picture, you're loading your poison arrow into your bow, feeling tight control and harnessed tension of the hunter as you aim at the magnificent eland. In the next picture ... go on ... release that arrow ... it won't hurt the buck. There! All it felt was a little wasp-sting in its rump. This nerve poison will paralyze, but will not contaminate the whole animal. You will cut out the spot where the arrow strikes and throw it away, and the rest of the meat is fit to eat. You can already smell and taste the roasting game as you watch the eland moving away. You—the hunter—will follow the eland for miles and miles, days and days, until his body succumbs to the paralysis and he falters and can't go on. When at last he falls, you feel exhilaration and sadness. But then as he collapses and life seeps from his body, your tension releases and gratitude encases your heart. You are overcome with a deep sadness as you kneel over the magnificent animal you had to kill—not for the sake of seeing an animal perish, Tsotsi, and never for sport, but for sustenance—to keep your clan alive. And you, the hunter, raise your arms in the air and thank the animal gods for their great gift of bountiful food and clothing and weapons and medicine, all from one great beast. Food is life, Tsotsi, and the gods just gave life to you and yours.*

*See here how your helpers come. You and six of the strongest men in your clan carry the bounty back to your tribe. And then you're amongst your vibrant people—laughing and celebrating and dancing and drumming and telling stories—as your buck roasts over an open fire. You and your clan eat until your stomachs and your bums grow huge to keep you sustained through the harsh terrain that comes next on your nomadic travels, when only well-hidden berries, root, and bird eggs will keep you alive for months and months ...*

"Papin, what does this mean?" a guest asked, and Papin was up in a flash to explain one of the stick-like drawings.

Left at last to his own thoughts, he glanced down at the gift of white beads threaded with a length of sinew, hanging around his neck. He'd better take it off before Tsotsi saw the necklace and asked questions. If the boy knew how many isigcina sentliziyo or Zulu love letters Papin had been given by young maidens to show their interest, he'd never hear the end of it.

A ten-year-old boy was too young to appreciate the significance and magnitude of love tokens given by a bare breasted maiden to a fifteen-year-old man.

An age-old female activity and tradition, beads in varying shades of seven colors, each with their own meaning, were threaded into intricate geometric patterns. Girls and women made complex, colorful arm, wrist and ankle bands, necklaces and wildly elaborate pieces that covered from neck to shoulders for brides or heroes. Made of glass, clay, pods, ostrich eggshells and such, woven beads delivered candid messages of intimate intentions.

Beads were the language of love between women and men.

And it all started with a string of white beads to show a girl had a crush on a boy. Wearing the proffered gift, the boy showed he was pleased with her interest and wanted to further their relationship. And as the gifts became more colorful, so did their relationship, with passionate reds and promises of loyal blues ... until, before you knew it, you were betrothed.

That shocked Papin back to the consequences of his latest necklace.

Sure, he could have many wives in his traditional polygamous culture. Sure, he could have a life away from his kraal and still have his wives waiting for him without consequences of what he'd been up to. But wives, even girlfriends, were work. He had no time for foolishness, and he certainly had enough work. He had to learn about the world beyond his mountains if he was to fulfill his destiny. That was much more important than satisfying his body by breaking a young girl's heart.

A twinge of regret and disappointment poked at him for a minute as he removed the beads from his neck and shoved them in his pouch. Yes. She was ripe and lovely. And he must leave her alone for both their sakes.

His father said and Sangoma confirmed that for him to achieve the goals the ancestors intended, he had to learn patience. Perhaps, besides teaching Tsotsi, resisting temptation was his much harder lesson.

Jock bolted back to the present. He'd been hearing Papin's voice in his ear explaining the bushman paintings. So long ago but as fresh as this afternoon. Thank you, Mind Brownie and New Aunts.

The guests were oblivious to Jock's bushman experience infused with Papin's voice because they'd entered their own Bushman world. Jock knew that time disappeared here, and since he had to be responsible, he left them to join Bekah at the cave entrance.

"I see you, Tsotsi," said Bekah.

"I see you, Bekah," answered Jock.

They sat together in silence and watched the rock rabbits dodge in and out of burrows. A giant bearded vulture, more like an eagle than an undertaker with its golden plumage, swooped in for a better look at a young rock rabbit. All the while, boy and man checked the sun's position to ensure they were not there too long, otherwise all hell would break loose.

Jock's mind drifted and his Mind Brownie produced vivid pictures of his early days with Papin.

Papin ran everywhere, and Jock's four-year-old legs pumped double-time to keep up with the nine-year-old's much longer stride. Through the fields of grass they ran, where snakes slithered silently through the grass and duikers peeped shyly from thick undergrowth.

"What are those?" Jock asked, pointing to two bucks and a young one.

"Bush buck," Papin answered. "Don't scare them and don't stop. Respect all animals. If they're big and eat meat, respect them twice as much. Most of all, watch their movements. If they are threatening, act accordingly. Put your hands above your head to look taller and bigger than you are. Then back away slowly. They should stand their ground. Do this with any aggressive animal, even a rabid dog. If they still keep coming, run for the nearest tree. There are only three carnivorous animals in our whole country: lion, leopard, and cheetah. Only leopards can climb trees because they have one extra claw on each paw." And so, this became the way Jock learned all things, and he gulped in Papin's wisdoms like newly arrived guests did the fresh mountain air.

Papin refused to answer Jock in English, so he had to learn Zulu if he was to understand his new friend.

The first time the rock had become theirs, Papin leapt up and sat in that odd way of the Zulu, with knees pulled up to his chest, chin resting on his knees. Jock tried four times to scale it. He didn't think to ask for help, but Papin came halfway down, extended his hand, hoisted Jock up and immediately resumed his position. Jock tried the position gamely but unsuccessfully, so he draped himself over the rock on his stomach, which allowed him to take in the kaleidoscope of undulating colors and shapes that lay on nature's gorgeous tableau far below them.

Kaleidoscope. The ancestors still hadn't magically produced one for him, nor had his parents. He was bitterly disappointed, but Papin said the ancestors knew exactly what they were doing. When a boy was lucky enough to be surrounded by such ever-changing beauty, he didn't need a kaleidoscope; he just needed to open his eyes.

Papin talked little and laughed a lot. But Papin's ability to mimic said a thousand words. He impersonated the waiters and the guests to a tee, and his animal impressions were spot on.

Jock begged Papin to teach him. And the lessons began. They'd laugh at Jock's absurdity till their tummies hurt and until he got it right.

Jock loved not being made to talk. It felt like Christmas every morning he spent with Papin. His friend said when you didn't talk, nature spoke, and she was far more interesting.

When there were no kids around his own age he was made to play with, Papin would magically appear, and barefoot, they'd run as fast and as far as their legs could carry them away from the noise of the hotel. Neither would speak unless it was important and the mountains would get loud again and Jock would feel free and wild and joyful and he'd throw his head back and laugh because blissful happiness pushed its way out his heart and through his mouth. Soon Papin joined in. Their world was spectacular.

Once Papin taught him to ride, their perimeters of exploration increased and their adventures widened.

And they'd watch the sun setting behind the mountains and wait for Champagne Castle mountain ridge to turn red and orange and seem to shimmer.

"I heard a guest say a mountain is just a mountain and she'd wished her husband had taken her to the seaside," Jock said.

Papin's anger made his voice so low, Jock had to lean in to hear.

"These mountains are never 'just mountains,'" he snapped, and Jock jerked back, alarmed. "What do you hear?" Papin demanded, and Jock didn't know what was being asked of him.

When Jock was silent, Papin said impatiently, "They are alive. They speak! I hear water rushing from natural springs and into the dam so your hotel can light up the night sky. I feel warm because they are high enough to give the snow a place to go so we won't die of cold. Every day you and I see these nurturing mountains give food and shelter to animals large and small. This Dragon's Back is mighty and colorful and kind and nurturing and essential for a million creatures, and it gives freely to you and I so we might fill our minds with beauty and awe. No, Tsotsi. These mountains are never just mountains..."

"Come, Tsotsi, we must go for tea." Bekah nudged him back from his memories, and Jock jumped back to the present. *Shit.* He'd clean forgotten his important mission. Without thinking of anything but the burning consequences, he sprinted too fast into the cave, causing enough of a gust to upset up the cloud of bats hanging unseen from the cave's ceiling.

The first bat lost its footing and landed in an older lady's hair. She shrieked and swatted her head, screeched and ducked and beat her hair. The noise caused havoc. The rest of the colony's ultrasounds fell off kilter, and they flapped around trying to get reoriented.

They flew blindly, bashing into each other and into the frenzied, ducking, squealing guests. Jock tried in vain to direct the chaos and get the bats out of the cave, but the guests mistook his wild gestures for their direction, and Jock was almost trampled in their exit stampede.

Once outside and bat-free, the panicked guests calmed and were willingly coaxed by Jock's promise of a "nice cup of tea"—his mother's answer to death, birth and everything in between—to be enjoyed at the falls.

Jock knew it was more likely it was the hefty shot of brandy in the tea's milk they craved, to soothe bat-frayed nerves.

Later, after word of the "incident" at the Bushman Caves was leaked, Jock was in the master suite, gingerly pulling up his pants.

"The only good thing about your reckless behavior," Dad said as he carefully placed the sjambok back on top of the cupboard, "is some guests will make a big dent in their bar bill to still their bobbing heads. Imaginary bats will plague them for quite a while."

But as Jock prepared to leave the room, his bum throbbing and well whacked, Dad did what he always did after a lesson had been learned.

"Jock," he called quietly.

When Jock turned, he was rewarded by Dad's widest smile. "Other than the bat debacle, you did a hell of a good job today."

Those words managed to take away the worst of the sting in his pants.

13

# BOESMAN AND BULLY BEEF

*South West Africa/Angola Border, 1977*

"INTEL, this is Troop Two Seven en route to mission number eight. No sightings. All quiet. Out." Lieut placed the radio microphone back in its cradle and Boesman's bunched shoulders relaxed.

The last of the sun's fiery orb softened the bush veldt. The farther east they moved away from the Namib Desert, the greener the escarpment and the fatter the wildlife. It was nowhere near as lush as it should be, but the drought here was much less devastating. Water holes were easier to find. Lieut sensed the excitement of the animals lurking unseen in the bush. Sundown was hunting and drinking time. Animals would not let man and his foolishness get in the way.

Lieut said to nobody at all, "Smart animals drink in the middle of the day when the lions are too lazy to drink and too hot to hunt."

It was a perfect place to call it a day. Off the beaten track with running water nearby. Lieut shouted, "Benny Bookworm, go find us a good place to camp thirty meters from the water. We must set up before the sun goes down."

"Why thirty meters, Lieut?" asked Benny, pushing up his glasses.

"Firstly, crocs are unlikely to come out of the river that far. Secondly, we must sleep on the flat so we're not in the path of the drinking hole. Just like Nev and his Durban rugby misfits, nothing must come between animals and their pub!"

Benny chuckled. An uncomplicated sound that brought lightness of being.

"Go with him, Frikkie. Make sure there are no snake holes, anthills, termite mounds, and check there aren't thirty thousand hoof marks," Lieut shouted at their backs. "We also need a tree to camouflage the Bedford, preferably on a rise, so whoever's on guard duty has a three-sixty view from Boesman's perch. Piet's on first watch."

After reveling in a fantastic parade of wild game and thirty different species of birds that came to drink, Lieut and his seven lay in a circle of sleeping bags. Their legs were in, heads out, safeties off and guns at the ready. They relied on starlight. There was no luxury of a fire in the red zone. Most leaned on their elbows, eating dry rations. Piet's sleeping bag was empty, and Boesman sat cross-legged a few yards away, under a little bush.

"Shame, man. Boesman's one of us, Lieut—why can't he have a sleeping bag?" asked Tiny, the toughest oaf with the gentlest of hearts.

"His choice," said Lieut.

"Hey," said Frikkie, "you guys all think Boesman's such a big hero. But listen, man, Boesman's a kaffir, and for all we know, maybe he's on the Terrs' side."

Lieut's legs propelled him to his feet before his brain caught up. He used all the power behind his legendary rugby handle as

"Natal's Strong Prop" and lifted Frikkie off the ground by his collar.

Lieut's face was half an inch from Frikkie's very red one and his voice a menacing whisper. "Listen, you little bastard, and listen well. Without Boesman, you would be dead. I would rather have Boesman on my right than your sorry white ass. Don't you EVER use that bullshit propaganda and never, ever, ever use the 'kaffir' word again."

Only Frikkie's limp ankles still touched the ground. "You hear me, you little shit? Do you hear me?" He didn't know how many times Frikkie tried to nod, but only when his anger reverberated in his ears did Lieut let Frikkie go.

Frikkie crumpled to the ground as Lieut walked away.

You could have heard an owl hoot from the top of a beach spotlight on the Marine Parade in Durban two thousand miles away, thought Lieut as he calmly walked back to his sleeping bag, lay down and, propping himself on his elbow, continued eating his bully beef out of the can.

Silence. Lieut knew he had to be the one to break it. He needed a good enough reason.

The way Charl looked at Penti made Lieut think of Bonzo. That dog entertained guests by twisting his head this way and that, almost at right angles to his body, to try and understand what humans were saying. Charl was doing the same with Penti.

"Pentifuckingford? Why do you have a fucking in the middle of your name?" Lieut asked on Charl's behalf.

Lieut caught Nev's eye, and they couldn't keep it together. The two erupted in hysterical laughter. Lieut looked at Penti to make sure he could still laugh at himself and was relieved nothing had changed.

"Well," the gangly man began, and Lieut watched all of his guys lean forward—all except, of course, Boesman, totally unimpressed by soldiers' silliness, and Piet-Tire, who was on guard duty.

"I was at base camp with these two—" Pentifuckingford pointed to Lieut and Nev. "But ask Nev. He tells it better than me."

Neville stood up, his face naughtier than ever. "As all you *roofies* are aware, none of us know what the fuck we're doing or what's being asked of us during basic training. We're exhausted. We're confused. None more than poor Pentifuckingford here, who, prior to Sergeant Snyman, was only answerable to the chief accountant at Price Waterhouse. For an excellent bean counter with little need to impress anyone with his sporting or dancing skills, coordination was not a requirement. And as we once-roofies know, marching is what makes the army an army. *Links-leghs-links-leghs-links-leghs* ..." Nev slipped into Afrikaans and gave an on-the-spot demo to create the right atmosphere for the all too well remembered left-right-left-right-left army drill.

Lieut saw the men's faces shining with delight. Lieut could count on Nev's stories being funny as hell.

"So Lieut and I are doing our thing along with the other roofies, and all of a sudden, Sarge shouts: 'STOP! HALT!' Of course, after we'd all bashed into the backs of each other, we had to reshuffle into a single stripe."

The heads around the circle all nodded. No matter which particular sarge you'd encountered during basics, all had the same mentality and the same shtick.

Nev continued, "So we line up. Tired. Buggered. Ready to kill the son of a bitch who forced this come-to-Jesus moment when the drill was so nearly done. Sarge shouts again in Afrikaans as he points to Penti: 'What's your name, Soldier?' Lieut and I hear this squeak of a reply: 'Pentiford, Sergeant.' The sarge's face scrunches up, and he bellows, 'What the *vok* did you say?' Poor

Penti's voice is now barely a whisper. 'Pentiford, Sergeant.' By now Sarge's face is blue with rage—"

"WAIT, Nev!" shouted Penti. "You must tell the boys my voice goes up like a girl's when I'm nervous."

"Yes, sorry. So Penti the Soprano stands quivering, and Sarge shouts 'Roofie! What the vok is your name or do I have to squeeze it out of your long blerry worm-body?' Penti clears his throat for three minutes trying to make his balls drop down again, and he says a little louder, 'Pentiford, Sergeant.' Sarge's snout is touching Penti's nose. Sarge's face is indigo. 'Penti-Wie?' Sarge yells, and Dutchman spit lands all over Penti's face. 'Pentiford,' he squeaks, trying his best to make it louder, but it doesn't work."

Lieut, holding his own stomach, watched his men collapse with mirth.

Nev held the stage. "Sarge hits himself on the side of the head. 'Ah! Pentifuckingford! Why didn't you just say so? NOW! March for us, Pentifuckingford!' So Penti, once gangly, is now all muddled up, and for the life of him, Penti can't get opposites to work together. Sarge says, 'Nee, vok Pentifuckingford. Why does each arm only work with the same vokken leg on the same vokken side?'"

Neville pointed to the subject of the story. "This high nervous voice again: 'I don't know, Sergeant.' Then Sarge says, 'Well, you are going to get those donderse opposites to work right today, Boytjie!' 'Yes, sir,' squeaks Penti. Sarge again: 'You understand, Pentifuckingford, that these roofies will stand in a stripe at attention until you can show them how well you can UN-fuck up those long blerry limbs of yours, Pentifuckingford?'"

Nev turned. "Show them, Penti. Show them."

Penti got up slowly and walked normally toward where the

fire would have been. His first try was quite normal. "Don't show off now, Pentifuckingford," said Nev, and the crowd went wild. Soon enough, Penti lapsed into his drill-perfect awkwardness, and sure enough, right leg and right arm shot out together, and then the two left limbs had a go.

"Gentlemen, I give you ... Pentifuckingford," said Nev, the proud ringmaster presenting the gangly circus freak. It was the funniest sight they swore they'd ever seen. Their laughter egged Penti on until they lost Frikkie and Charl to the bushes before they wet themselves.

All was right again between him and his men, and now they knew what buttons to leave the hell alone.

Lieut called Tiny, and the big man looked over. Lieut pointed at Boesman and said, "Watch him." Lieut saw the heads of all of them turn.

Boesman finished his ration and reached for some dry grass, screwed it up and stuffed it into his right ear. Then he lay on his left side, leaning on his elbow with his head supported by the palm of his hand, covering his left ear.

"What the fu—?" Tiny gawked at Boesman.

"Little bugger's intent on keeping insects out of his ears. He'll sleep in that crazy position all night. If you've ever had an ant bite you inside your ear, you'll know what pain's all about. He's smart, Tiny. If Boesman does something, it's because he knows something you and I don't. That's why he's worth watching. He's proactive. His actions prevent as many consequences as his ancestors have taught him and his people over thousands and thousands of years. That makes him very freaking smart." Lieut chuckled softly as Boesman's slow purring began.

"Safeties on now," warned Lieut. "I don't want you young bastards shooting Boesman or Piet in your sleep." Nervous laughter. "When on guard duty, remember, this is what you do ..."

Lieut found a large, smooth rock, brought it to the center of their circle, covered it with his sleeping bag and positioned his rifle under his chin and said, "When sleep comes knocking and your head drops, the barrel will jolt you awake. Make sure your safeties are on, and just for you, Nev, remember to remove your bayonet before assuming this position."

When the laughter calmed down, Lieut watched as blessed sleep gnawed at bodies and his men slept. Lieut looked at them, his "kids." Though they were scant younger than him, he felt a hundred years old on days like these.

Without warning, he heard a voice he'd banned from his memory the day his world came to an end. Up to that time he'd had a Mind Brownie with New Aunts—a hungry combo that caught and held everything in three-dimensional Technicolor, better than the IMAX theater he'd read about in Ontario, Canada, with smells, and tastes and emotions. But then everything he'd ever believed in and trusted ended, and he'd had to lock away the memories of the good times along with the ones that broke him. It was called self-preservation.

Frankly, he didn't know if he was strong enough yet—eleven years later. And yet the persistent and familiar voice pushed its way in ... that of teacher to student: "In the darkness, just as you cannot see your enemies, they cannot see you. When you look into the darkness, you have to look in sections. Study each section. If it moves, there is something there. Watch the movement or change of color caused by movement and consider—is it a tree or a bush swaying in the wind? Is it an animal? Is it a person? You must study trees and animals and people in daylight so you recognize their shadow selves at night. And listen. Always listen more than you talk in life, but especially in the bush. When you listen to the night sounds, they will tell you if there is something you need to fear. The owl is your biggest friend. He usually finds the highest point on which to sit so his hoots can be heard by other owls, above the noise of the wild. When you're at ground level at night, the bush is filled with a million night-animal noises, as well as beetles, crickets and frogs. Sitting well above the noise, though you will hear the owl closest to you, his mate might be too far away for you to hear. But the owl will hear it and he'll answer, and when he does, you know that all is well. When the owl stops, there's a reason. There's a good chance your danger is coming from that owl who first stopped hooting. The animals of the night—nagapies, hyenas and jackals—hide when there are things to fear. Even insects sense danger, so their silence means danger to animals and possibly, danger to you. And if a flurry of birds takes off, then look to where they have left, not where they are going. Train your eyes. Find what the danger might be."

Lieut shook his head like a dog after retrieving a tennis ball from a river.

He held his ears and willed the voice to go away.

At last, his head was silent. He walked to the Bedford, camouflaged by a thorn tree, where his guard was on duty.

While they traveled, only Boesman's head protruded from the sunroof, but he was four feet and a smidge. At five feet eleven, Piet's head, shoulders and half his torso poked out of the sunroof, reminding Lieut of a meerkat guard. His head moved in staccato jerks, and he stretched his neck to ludicrous proportions before he moved his body to continue the 360 degrees of vigilance.

What a character. Lieut opened the Bedford door and heard "*VOK!*" from above.

"Chill, Roofie," said Lieut. "Remember what I taught you. Calmly create a big *O* between your hands, overlapping index fingers and thumbs. Focus on just that area and freeze. Close your eyes for five long seconds. Open and look through the same O. Has what you saw last time changed at all? If so, is it an animal? Look for the flick of ears. Focus on listening to just the sounds coming from there. Is it a person moving quickly? If you are in doubt, I'm twenty feet away. Hoot like an owl and I'll be right here."

"Ok, Lieut, but my owl might sound more like an ostrich." They laughed.

"That's okay, Piet. You're not trying to impress the owl, just alerting me." Lieut grinned.

Piet looked odd without his friend Frikkie. Lieut was so used to them being bound at the hip like conjoined twins. But there was no way to let Frikkie and Piet be on the same guard duty. He'd tried that. They'd sneaked up on Charl, snoring his head off, and poured a handful of sand into his open mouth. Charl had spluttered, spit and gagged while the two wallowed in their hilarity. As sharp as they were as marksmen, their observation skills dwindled to nonexistent with Frikkie's clowning and Piet's childlike appreciation.

He thought about Benny's question to him around the fire, "What's that scar on your arm, Lieut?" He'd asked, "Is it a croc bite? It's sure big enough!"

Lieut said, "It proves I'm half Zulu," and Benny had laughed at this absurdity, but unexpectedly, Lieut felt fresh anger and hurt emerge.

Charl started mewling and twitching. *Poor little bastard's still likely reliving the land mine.* He leaned over and shook the boy's leg to wake him just enough to end the dream. *I must keep them safe.*

Lieut knew real sleep would only come to him when they got back to camp. Sounds of the thriving wild with its many inhabitants would be cause enough for him to be woken by his nervous soldiers on guard duty for as long as they were in the bush. He just hoped to God the visitor from the past who'd invaded his head didn't come back in the wee hours. He was prepared for war but not the memories of happy times. He was odd, he knew. But life had made him so.

# 14

# BITCH SOCIETY, HARMONY AND MR. GOVERNMENT

*Champagne Castle Hotel, 1960*

AFTER TWO MORE DAYS AND still no sign of the rescue team, Jock discovered waiting was a bitch.

Desperate times called for desperate measures, and since there was no other warm, available body that knew the terrain as he did, Jock was able to redeem himself from his notoriety as the Pied Piper of Bats. He led two more, mercifully unremarkable morning walks, and the Bushman Cave was avoided like the plague.

His still-smarting bum was a constant reminder of how quickly quiet could become chaos.

Earlier he'd asked Dad if Papin could eat at their table in the dining room. His father had taken precious time to sit him down and give Jock the rare privilege of his full attention.

"Did Papin ask you to ask me this?" Dad's face was grave.

"No, Dad. But Papin's my best friend. It's not right that we have to eat in separate places when I am at the hotel. Why can't we eat together in the dining room?"

"Papin is Zulu, Jock. You are white."

"So?" asked Jock, but a stern look prompted: "I know, Dad."

"Do you see any other Zulus or Indians like Billy Pillay sitting in the dining room eating with the guests?"

"No, Dad. But there are snot-nosed kids eating in here all the time. Papin has more manners than all of them. Why, Dad?"

"Because the world is not always fair, Jock. Our unfair world made a rule that us white people have the privilege of being served by people of other colors."

"Who made up that rule, Dad?" Jock felt his face furrow in the same places as Dad's.

"Good question. The Nationalist government. Society."

"They're so important that even if the rules are unfair, people have to do what they say?"

"Yes, Jock. Society is the thing that dictates how we live so harmony can exist," his father said.

Now who the hell was Harmony? Jock shook his head to try and jiggle the confusion into sense. But nothing happened. He could eat at Papin's kraal. The Zulus didn't mind. He could eat with Papin anywhere on and off the property without fuss. All he wanted was to sit and eat with his best friend at his parents' hotel. Why was it so complicated?

"I've heard you say, 'Government's not listening.' So will you ask Harmony and Society if Papin and I can share a table?"

His dad smiled, which was unexpected. "Tell you what. I'll get Nicholas to set up a table in the kitchen just for you and Papin. For breakfast and lunch when you're not gallivanting. Dinners are your mother's time with you. We can't spoil that."

Jock felt ridiculously excited.

He itched to share this mammoth news all day but kept it in like an unopened gift you couldn't wait to give. Later, he and Papin sat on their rock, high above the flurry of the hotel. Two stories below, their horses grazed happily, and Jock's long-suppressed excitement could no longer be contained.

"Dad's going to set us up a table in the kitchen for you and me."

"Why?" asked Papin flatly, without looking at him.

"So we can eat together. I always have to eat breakfast in the dining room, and you eat in the kraal or the compound. I don't think that's fair. We should eat together when we're at the hotel."

"I don't care where I eat," said Papin, his voice devoid of emotion.

Jock physically recoiled in hurt and shock as far as the rock would allow.

He'd fought all three of them—bitch Society, Harmony and Mr. Government—all for Papin. And he didn't care.

Jock climbed down from the rock, mounted his horse, rode to the hotel, tied Beauty up to a tree, and went in search of his dad.

"Dad, don't worry about asking Mom and Nicholas about the kitchen table." He couldn't look into Dad's eyes because sure as hell, Dad would see stuff that had no business being in his young son's eyes.

"Why the change of heart?" Dad asked.

"Because Society and Harmony and Mr. Government messed things up for us long before I had the idea to share a table with my best friend."

Jock galloped off on Beauty, and for the first time in the only life he could remember, he chose not to find Papin.

After dark was the most looked-forward-to time of day for the adult guests, and his parents had to pull all sorts of magic out of their hats to entertain them every night. There were beetle drives, bingo sessions, singsongs featuring mom on the piano or organ, card nights, movie nights, table cricket, blow football and guessing games.

It was Saturday night. Those were the most special nights. Ladies dressed up in long dresses, and men's shoes were shined twice that day. The family room was cleared in part to create a dance floor. Sometimes there was even a live band. Tonight, there were records playing loud, which seemed to please the old people just as much as they jived and waltzed.

One record's worth of watching old people's antics was usually all it took before boredom pulled Jock's bare feet away from the gaiety and off to search for Papin.

But not tonight.

He ambled off to the back of the kitchen, where the off-duty staff gathered, smoking, laughing, poking fun, playing tricks on each other. So much more interesting than inside. Jock loved the free world without Society's rules, where Harmony was overjoyed and Mr. Government was nowhere to be found.

But not even that helped to ease the darkness of his disappointment, so he slipped away unnoticed and headed for the place that made him happiest.

But it was already occupied.

Papin had his back to the hotel, facing the dark mountains.

Without a word, Jock climbed onto the rock and sat in his usual place. He watched the light blazing from the hotel, painting the lawns greener than ever while people's elongated shadows danced across the grass. In the still of night, music and laughter traveled far.

He recognized the velvet voice of a singer his mom couldn't stop talking about.

"Elvis Presley." The sound of his own voice jolted him. He'd not intended to break the silence between them.

When the song was over, Papin said softly, "Darkness is your friend."

The last thing Jock needed tonight was a lesson. Even a Zulu one.

"But what about Tokoloshe? He makes himself visible at night," Jock challenged, referring to the evil little devil Africans believed caused havoc. Bricks were piled four high under bedposts in both the compound's quarters and in the kraal so the sleeper would be positioned well beyond the diminutive Tokoloshe's devious reach.

Papin ignored the boy's biting retort and said, "When you are eleven I will teach you how to conquer the darkness."

Jock reared back, wondering if Papin was in fact referring to the darkness he'd carried around with him all day. Their backs were facing each other—how could Papin know?

But then a shooting star blazed across the sky, and as Jock wished for a kaleidoscope, he kept one eye open and leaned back. He saw Papin the non-believer with eyes tightly shut, as if he too was making a wish.

And, just like that, darkness, disappointment, and the table in the kitchen disappeared.

DAY FOUR, and they were up at four thirty so they wouldn't miss anything. Surely today the rescue party would come down from the mountains? When they found Bekah preparing the early morning teas and coffees for room service, the scullery boy who'd become a man-turned-jack-of-all-trades was as excited as Bonzo finding a ham sandwich.

Bekah had spotted pinpricks of light bobbing above The Sphynx a few minutes before.

Though Jock longed to beat Bekah to the family suite to blab the news to Dad, it wasn't his to share. "Go tell Inkosi," said Jock. "We'll make tea and coffee."

Bekah looked to Papin for approval. Papin wore the invisible badge of being entrusted with the boss's son, so he enjoyed a vastly higher pecking order than most of the staff.

Papin nodded, and when the young man rushed away with

wings on his heels, Papin said proudly, "Today you are an excellent Zulu, Tsotsi."

And as they packed trays with China cups and teapots, Jock felt chuffed. There was no higher compliment.

The front veranda and porches were filling up with guests grabbing lawn chairs and spreading blankets on the neatly mowed grass to wait in excited anticipation of the great return. Some had binoculars. Paul Anorak had become the hotel celebrity. It was everyone's hope nine Champagne Castle workers, two climbers and the Natal rescuers would all make it down the mountain, ready to climb, serve or simply live another day.

"Boys!" Dad called to them. "Go and ask doc to drive his car to the delivery area."

It was all very puzzling, but they knew better than to ask. When they came back, they caught glimpses of the rescue team when they reached the bottom of The Sphynx and walked toward the Crystal Falls. They disappeared again for three long hours until they were next seen entering the top of the gum trees.

A guest asked loudly, "David, why is it taking them so long? We made it from Crystal Falls in a couple of hours on our walk."

Dad talked them through the men's probable journey. "Four days of ploughing through tough, unpredictable, uneven terrain—some of the most rugged in the world ... helping one weak man and the other in God knows what condition ... carrying a stretcher, lugging gear ... four fast-running streams in that last stretch ..."

Dad caught Jock's eye. "Jock, take buckets of warm water from the kitchen. Papin, fetch a pile of clean sheets from the laundry. Billy Pillay!" Dad yelled, and the Indian man appeared magically. "Get the rest of the first aid kits together. You three take everything to your mom's triage arrangement in the bar lounge—and guide the men in there as they arrive."

When it was likely the rescuers were on the last leg home, Dad, Doc, and Paul Anorak disappeared into the gumtrees to meet them. Damn. If only he was fifteen maybe he and Papin would have been invited.

An hour later, Paul Anorak and a Natal rescue guy came in first, supporting a new face between them—one of the climbers. He looked like a skeleton with thin, bruised skin pulled tight over his bones.

The guys got a hero's welcome. Paul and the new guy shrugged through the well-wishers as if in a trance and went straight to a newly arrived, older couple standing on the patio.

Jock watched, and the four of them disappeared into the adult lounge. Jock wondered why they didn't wait for climber number three.

Everyone craned their necks to look for the third man. Still nothing.

The banged-up, exhausted rescue team carrying supplies and rucksacks followed, as did Natal Mountain Rescue volunteers, but no Dad, no stretcher, no Doc, and no third climber.

The guys were beaten up and exhausted with cuts, bruises and open, bleeding blisters. The boys and Billy directed the banged-up bunch to Mom, who was busier than a meerkat guard.

Mandinsolo came toward Jock and Papin, pulling the once-new socks off his hands.

"You okay, Mandinsolo? Where's the third guy?" Jock asked his bleeding, exhausted hero. But Mandinsolo rushed off as if on a mission.

Jock saw people in the adult lounge and pulled at Papin's elbow. When they looked through the closed glass doors, they saw Paul Anorak, the new climber and the older couple. Otherwise, the lounge was empty.

It was an L-shaped room with two entrances. As so often

happened between Jock and Papin, there was no need for words, and together they headed for the opposite entrance.

As they entered, they heard Mom's voice, and both quickly hugged the wall. Though they knew she couldn't see them, they held their breath and didn't move a muscle.

"... Some tea and biscuits. Anything we can do to help, please ask." Mom didn't sound like her bubbly self. Why hadn't she just sent in a waiter?

A new voice. It sounded like an older man. "Thank you, Mrs. Walsh. You're all most gracious."

They sneaked farther in and positioned themselves on the floor as close as possible to where the "L" bent so they could hear everything discussed at the lone occupied table without being seen.

The same voice: "We want to know every single thing. It's the only way we will have closure." Papin and Jock looked at each other. Papin shrugged.

Paul Anorak started. "You know how Russ loved the mountains ... convinced us surfers to drag along ..."

Though English language and Jock were constantly at odds, Jock knew past tense meant someone—Russ —was old news. Why?

The older voice was choked up. "Mountains he loved, snakes he hated." A chuckle. A good sign. See? In English you were never quite sure. But Zulu? Nothing could be misconstrued. Jock let out his breath. All must be well.

"Russ spent his pocket money at Fitzsimons Snake Park talking to handlers, watching them milk snakes for antivenom, schooling himself, learning his enemy ..."

"He was known on varsity campus as the fearless climber with the snake phobia. He was an enigma." That had to be Climber 2's voice. There was soft laughter. Jock wondered if an enigma was similar to an enema—like Billy Pillay had in hospital when he swallowed a lock and key during what Dad called "Billy's regurgitation-trick phase."

Climber 2 was called Ray. He and Paul went into detail of their climb with Russ. Jock closed his eyes, following their every step over crags and up cliffs and through streams. Papin and he had explored every inch, unbeknownst to his parents, of course.

"Frankly, the next day is a bit of a blur," said Ray, and there was an eerie silence.

Paul Anorak jumped in. "I know we didn't take the direct route. Russ wanted to show off what he called 'The Grandest Scenery in the Drakensberg,' and when we finally got there, the two of us were spent. Fortunately, Russ said, 'You chaps set up camp. I'd like to have a look around.'"

Paul again: "The rucksacks that started off light became lead-filled to us amateurs, and Ray and I were thinking, 'It's all very magical, but when do we go back to the hotel for a beer?'"

That provoked a short moment of nervous laughter. Jock relaxed.

"We heard Russ shout," Ray said. "He was halfway up a low bank on the far side of the stream. 'I've been bitten.' We rushed to him and helped him back to where the tents still lay on the ground. Russ said, 'I was pulling myself up with a sapling, and I felt the bite in my left wrist.' Puncture marks were dangerously close to his artery."

Paul Anorak continued, "Russ said he'd caught a quick glimpse of the snake. He thought it was a berg adder."

Jock could see the berg adder in his mind's eye. He knew its venom hit the nervous system. It could take away your smell, your eyes would blur, and you'd even be blind for a while. You couldn't swallow and eventually you couldn't talk, and the worst was when it became hard to breathe. But the good thing was eventually those symptoms went away. You didn't die from a berg adder. It was a fact.

Ray interrupted Jock's thought and said, "Frankly, we were terrified. But Russ was fantastic. Calm as a cucumber."

Jock wondered how a cucumber could be anything *but* calm.

Ray went on: 'We spread the tents out as ground cover and followed Russ's instructions. He knew what to expect and what to do. In ten minutes, his legs collapsed. We applied a tourniquet to his upper arm. Paul made two cuts close to the wound. My hands were shaking. I wasn't up to the job. I rubbed Condy's crystals into the cuts."

"Ray made Russ proud." Paul's voice broke, and Jock was shocked to hear the young man gulping for air.

Jock stood up instinctively to help, but Papin pushed him back gently and shook his head.

Jock wanted to rush over and say, "It's okay. Berg adder bite won't ki—" But why was there so much crying? And where was Russ?

Fear seared its way from Jock's stomach to his throat. He looked at Papin in hopes of finding confirmation that the climbers were mistaken. It was only a berg adder.

His friend's eyes were kind but equally as perplexed.

Mom's voice. Jock and Papin pushed themselves farther into the wall, willing invisibility.

"... fresh pot of tea and scones ... David sent medicinal brandies ... rooms are ready." Mom's voice was gentle, and as he heard her leave, Jock felt a surge of love for her.

"We need the details. We must know everything. Don't spare us," the parents begged the two younger men, and as the four continued to dissect and share details Russ's parents were desperate for, Jock felt himself dip into a daze of detachment, but the most chilling words jarred him every time.

"... lost control of his bowels ... face became paralyzed ... couldn't talk or swallow ... two more injections—one in his stomach ..."

Papin stood up and cocked his head to indicate they should get the hell out of there. Jock shook his head, adamant. Papin reluctantly slid down the wall back to sitting position.

There was crying. Sobbing. Jock could feel each one's excruciating pain, their loss, their suffering and torment. But still he refused to move because the tiniest flicker of hope still burned. If it was indeed a berg adder, all these symptoms would fade and Russ would be okay.

Paul Anorak's voice, "Shots didn't help ... breathing labored, struggling to breathe. No voice or eye movement ... didn't slow Russ down ... he'd inhale then pound on his chest with his good arm—the bitten one was puffed and swelling bigger and bigger by the hour—and we'd take turns leaning on his chest to push out the air ... through the night."

Oh, boy. Jock's gut burned. Russ was mistaken. Face it, this was no berg adder bite.

He felt a mental slap that spun his head sideways. Everything he believed had been shattered.

Ray: "Bitterly cold....covered Russ with his one-man tent. Drizzle set in. One of us stayed with Russ, helping him breathe ... other went for wood and water ... small fire ... hot drinks saved us from freezing to death. Nurturing that fire in the rain ... harder than keeping our friend ventilated ..."

Paul: "Longest night of our lives ... started giving him mouth-to-mouth resuscitation."

Ray took over. "Dawn broke. Russ slipped into a deep coma ... watched over him till it was light. Neither of us had a clue how to find our way to the hotel. We drew sticks. I lost."

"We found a map in Russ's kit," said Paul. "Didn't mean much to either of us." Champagne Castle hotel was thirteen miles as the crow flies on that map, and Paul guided Russ's parents, his friend and the two boys through his long and arduous journey.

"What was happening back at the camp?" asked the older man.

"Two hours after Paul left, Russ passed away. Thank God he was unconscious most of that time." Ray's voice was raw.

Jock felt like he'd been bucked off a horse and landed on his chest. Now it was certain. Russ was dead from a berg adder bite.

He felt Papin's hand squeeze his shoulder, and when he glanced at his friend, he hated the pity he saw there.

He whispered, "Papin, it can't be—it was a berg adder! We know it's not possible. But now the guy is dead. How? Nothing's for sure anymore, Papin. Nothing makes sense."

And then Jock heard for the first time what happens when a loved one dies.

Abysmal human sounds enveloped him—desolate, haunting, dismal—and he understood the pain of loss. And his heart broke, and he begged his New Aunts not to record any of it.

He felt a drip of water on his knee and looked up to find the roof leak so he could tell Dad, then realized his own tears were flowing freely. He wiped at his face quickly and glanced at Papin. His friend nodded his head slowly, giving Jock permission to weep.

Mom was back. "More medicinal brandy ... a box of tissues ... chocolate...anything else?" Mom left. Lots of nose-blowing and a long silence.

The lady spoke. "How did you cope, Ray? It must have been horrific."

"It was. I have never felt so alone. Hemmed in by thick mist and the silence of great, brooding, unrelenting peaks. Beside me, the body of my friend. A day before, he was vital and excited..." And he went on to describe his desolation, his fear and his inability to do anything but wait, hope and then despair. "In some desperate part of my brain, I was hoping to gain enough strength to carry my friend home if Paul never came back." Ray's voice broke.

Jock was right there with Ray. He lived every moment of the misery and desolation all alone on that mountain, next to his dead friend.

He imagined Papin dead next to him. Panic the likes of which he'd never known—worse even than when his parents left him at boarding school that horrible Sunday nearly four years ago—made the dark mist swirl around him, the prickle of panic poking, prodding.

Papin's light punch on the upper arm was what he needed. He emerged from the spinning, claustrophobic mist. Papin was here. Alive. He was sublimely grateful.

Ray's voice: "The rest is a blur until I heard whistles. I thought I was dreaming. I shook my head first in disbelief and then adrenaline kicked in. I groped in Russ's kit for a whistle and blew until my lungs hurt. I was rewarded with a wonderment of whistles, and then they were around me, peeping through the mist. The most beautiful faces I've ever seen. Mandinsolo and seven of his men. I couldn't move. I just sat there with my head between my knees and wept. They were magnificent. Mandinsolo left one of the guys to direct the Rescue Club up to the correct ravine, and they arrived an hour later. They rested only about an hour, then we prepared for the return. They put Russ on the stretcher. They patched me up. I was a mess. They fed me, and we started down. They half-carried me most of the way. They'd worked so hard and carried Russ's stretcher over dangerous ground for all those hours, helped me when I couldn't help myself. They always stayed together. What an incredible team."

Mom's gentle voice: "Doc is ready for you.'

"Come with us to see our Russ," the older man invited his son's friends.

Papin shook Jock's foot, and his swift head jerk said they needed to get out of there.

Jock was empty and confused, but Papin pushed him out of the door gently and toward the veranda, just in time to see Dad tapping a spoon on a crystal glass for silence. The crowd was quick to quiet, eager for news.

Dad announced Russ was dead. He gave condolences to Russ's family and thanks to all the rescuers, and then he was quiet, allowing the shock to sink in. Then there were whimpers and tears.

Jock looked up at his dad just in time to see him wipe away a tear. It was the first time Jock had seen his father cry.

But greater than that shock was Dad was unashamed of doing so.

"Folks, Russ was a very experienced climber. His friends were exceptionally brave and fearless and did everything by the book for the type of snake Russ believed he was bitten by. If it was a berg adder it's the first death by that snake in recorded history. There's no feasible explanation. Paul and Ray and Russ's friends and family will never be the same. I daresay, nor will we."

His eyes sought out and found his rescuers. "You boys did a hell of a job. Now get some wholesome food in your bellies and a good few beers under your belts. There are cases out back with our thanks. But not too many." Dad smiled. "Rest and I'll see you back to work tomorrow. Natal Mountain Rescue blokes, please tell us what you need besides a good meal and a couple of rooms. Thank you for your tireless service."

Dad turned to the guests and said, "Your support and kindness during this long wait was deeply appreciated by us all. First and second drinks on the house tonight. We can all use them."

It was the only lie Jock would ever hear his father tell. His dad didn't drink.

So while the rest of the hotel drowned their sorrows, his dad would have to deal with Russell's death the hard way. With a cola tonic.

Jock and Papin found out Doc's car had been driven to the delivery area so Russell's body could be loaded without the guests being faced with the grim reality of the rescue.

Later, on their rock, Jock handed Papin one of the "extra" two slabs of chocolate that never found their way into rucksacks. Jock had kept them to celebrate the rescuers' safe return.

They each greedily took a bite of the thick double-milk chocolate. It tasted like newspaper. Jock's faced furrowed in disappointment.

"Today, nothing tastes good. Tomorrow it will taste like chocolate again," Papin promised.

## 15

# BAGPIPES AND BOARDING SCHOOL

*Ondangwa Camp, South West Africa, 1977*

ANOTHER LONG DAY in the bush and they were no closer to Lwazi. No amount of army-issue toothpaste could purge the sour taste in his mouth. Lwazi's trail had gone cold after the farmhouse. They would have to start again. Tomorrow.

It felt like the insides of his upper eyelids were lined with sandpaper, and grit wedged its way into every orifice. If only a shower could wash away what he'd seen today. Yesterday. The day before.

Their large camp was in a constant state of flux as regiments from all over the country came in, went on various missions, and then disappeared for good. It was the circle of army life. When Transvaal Scottish Regiment was posted at Ondangwa, they sent out a piper at sunrise and sunset to hail in and usher out each new day.

With *kos* in his belly, Lieut sat propped up, back against the trunk of a thorn tree, and let the discordant sounds of a tuning bagpipe push their way into the dark places. By sheer will, he was able to release everything but the anticipation of the haunting tune to come.

Mournful and moving, "Scotland the Brave" echoed through the camp from the highest koptjie. Men stopped what they were doing to listen, and a spell of quiet reverence settled over the whole of Ondangwa for a blessed five minutes.

Lieut softly sang the words to the last verse, dreaming of going home again, just like the song's lyrics promised. It wasn't the home he'd just come from that tugged at him but the home that was his early sanctuary, many lifetimes ago.

In the silence before the camp roared with appreciation, he found he was looking at his boots, and he wondered how in the world he'd ever managed to come to terms with having his feet restricted after being barefoot most days.

Boots. School shoes. The beginning of the end of life as he knew it.

*Champagne Castle Hotel, 1956-1957*

FROM THE TIME he was four, most of Jock's domestic information was gleaned from his bed in the family suite. It was from that bed, at the age of seven, he'd first heard the rumblings that would rob him of freedom.

His room was separate from his parents with a closed door between them, but thanks to Papin's expert training, his young ears were fined-tuned for nature's softest whispers. Listening to his parents, who thought he was asleep, was a breeze.

When he was six, his father imported a schoolmistress from Pietermaritzburg. According to his parents' late-night murmurs, his dad had lured Miss Evelroy with a small salary, free board and lodging and the promise of a year-round-holiday environment.

"What a cushy job. One boy in a school bungalow." His mother's voice.

"But she'll give us peace of mind. We can stop worrying. This will be our boy's education foundation. No more guilt because we can't teach him ourselves," said Dad. Just words. Jock quickly lost interest and fell into much more sensational Zulu dreams.

After Miss Evelroy arrived and a yet-to-be-updated rondavel was commissioned as the classroom, soft voices after midnight disappeared.

The "new regime" involved Jock being pushed into the classroom by 9:00 a.m. by whoever was doomed with that duty. By then, he and Papin had already scaled their choice of mountains in the Little Berg, ridden horses for three hours or swum in the Sterkspruit River.

These before-school adventures were the only way he was able to while away the hours in his bungalow-jail.

Imprisoned in a wooden desk-chair contraption, the humdrum of his young, well-intentioned tutor's voice became nothing but a mid-morning lullaby. Jock copied the writing on the blackboard but saw no need to listen or understand.

And while his eyes remained open, his brain traveled, blissfully unrestricted: contemplating with Papin how they could get the baby hawk back into its precarious cliff nest without leaving their human scent to prevent mother hawk disowning it; examining the fat puff adder's two-and-a-half-foot-long snakeskin shed on the contour path.

By mid-morning, the walls of the school bungalow moved in and his muscles twitched with inactivity. But the promise of Dad's sjambok, were he to flee, kept him locked in the wooden stocks. Thankfully, open windows let sights and smells of his real world in, to aid in his fantastical escape.

He'd hear the "whoosh" as one black eagle swooped down to flush out and force the *dassie* sunning herself on the rock to a more accessible angle. Then her lifelong eagle mate, wearing his magnificent coal-black plumage with white back and a broad *V* across his shoulders, would appear from a different angle and snatch up the confused *dassie.*

Prey safely in his lethal talons, the pair soared up together, and Jock swore he could hear the whistle through their wings with their speed of flight while seeming to move in slow motion. Papin said eagles were winged messengers from the ancestors. Boy! Those ancestors were everywhere.

Up, up, up toward the cliffs they rose, shouting victoriously, "Whaeeeee-whaeeee-heeeeeoh," and their shrieks echoed off rock faces and sounded like not just two, but an aerie of eagles, shouting news of their lunch to be enjoyed in a precarious nest. Papin told him if the eagle's prey was capable of defending itself or threatened to harm their chicks, they'd drop it from a dizzy height, then pick up and carry the broken carcass to the chicks for dinner.

... And a high-pitched tinkling bell.

The children's call to lunch. Twelve sharp and Nicholas's time to shine. White shirt, spotless jacket and a narrow tie that split his large belly in two.

The next twenty-five minutes, Jock's legs went from twitching to warming up for a marathon.

He clutched his satchel Mom insisted he carry, school books and packed mid-morning snack —like "real school," she said. He was ready to go by twelve thirty sharp, when Nicholas bashed the first of the six-note copper dinner gong. Grownups' lunch was ready to serve, and Jock and satchel shot out of the school hut at the speed of a cobra strike, completely ignoring Miss Evelroy's "Wait! I haven't finished ..." which was really just noisy air. There would be no consequences, Papin said. She wouldn't split on him. She'd have to admit she was in the wrong job. So Jock was safe and so was Miss Evelroy.

On the third day of this new school thing, as he rushed away from Miss Evelroy's exasperation, Papin climbed out of the bushes next to the window with his finger to his lips.

"What?" Jock asked, surprised.

"You learn. I learn," said Papin, smiling his thousand-watt smile. "Come. Let's eat, then show me your books." There started Papin's annoying habit of teaching himself to read. In English. What a waste of good play time.

Having plucked horse-salt crystals deeply lodged under their skin courtesy of the peach farmer's shotgun, Jock and Papin were still hungry and ambled into the kitchen in search of something more satisfying. Jock had taken a solid hit to his thigh that had melted under his skin and burnt like the blazes.

Nicholas caught him scratching.

"Were you two stealing peaches again?" Nicholas boomed.

"No ..." stumbled Jock.

"Don't even try. I know Farmer Olivier's marks of war. They are dotted all over your body like a leopard, Tsotsi. You're just lucky you're black, Papin, so I can't see your wounds too well."

They both looked down, worried they'd be turned in to Dad for one beating apiece. It certainly wouldn't be the first time.

"Why, boys?" Nicholas gestured broadly at the beautifully laid tables with shining cutlery, serviettes in the shape of swans and a shiny bowl of fresh fruit in season.

"But don't take from the tables. There's lots in the pantry." Nicholas waggled his long index finger close to Jock's nose. "And if that's not enough, your father has three orchids—which no one guards at all—where fruit hangs, longing to be picked. Why are you boys so stupid?" Nicholas implored, arms dramatically spread wide, palms up.

"It is not stupidity or greed, Induna," Papin said as he bowed slightly to show his respect, "but a lesson to Tsotsi that lunch must be earned." Papin was indeed fearless.

Nicholas's anger never came in front of Inkosi or the guests, but he didn't hold back from the two of them, and if the waiters stole, were cheeky or their service was slack, Nicholas's wrath-fueled words whipped them into a coma.

Jock took a step back, preparing for Nicholas's explosion.

Astonishingly, the big man threw his head back and roared with hilarity, setting in motion the jelly-like wobble that shook his entire body. "Seems to me, Papin, you can justify anything."

All was well in their world.

During their years of fun, about twice a year, Papin got serious. He'd point out how unprecedented veldt fires burned down perfectly healthy, centuries-old trees; how powerful, seemingly invincible animals became weak and broken because of a poacher's trap or a hunter's shotgun.

"Why do you show me such sadness?" Jock asked his friend.

"You must learn, Tsotsi, nothing lasts forever."

Jock wondered why he had to learn such ugly lessons.

A week later, Jock sat in the back of the Chevy, looking down at his new black shoes. And he understood.

Shoes. How he hated them. He was required, as were all guests, to wear shoes to dinner, but they never saw the light of day. No matter the weather, the sharpness of rocks or roughness of terrain, his feet were groomed by Mother Nature to take them on. They worked well as climbing crampons too. Dad said the two of them looked like monkeys with toes trained to scale cliffs. They wore Dad's words like badges of honor.

Shaka, the great King of the Zulus, made his warriors throw away their footwear a century or so before because they were a hindrance in battle. No self-respecting Zulu had worn shoes since, unless they were forced to conform.

Jock was a self-respecting Zulu, though his parents refused to accept it.

A week before, when midnight words were whispered in the family suite, he'd discovered the softer the words, the bigger the trouble.

"He's seven. How the hell did that happen? Where was I?" His dad sounded anguished. He was always so calm. Jock felt the prickle of alarm.

"We, David. Where were *we?* We were running a hotel, and neither of us had any idea how to ... we were trying to keep afloat ... learning, failing, re-learning, worrying, paying the bank, entertaining, juggling, balancing ..." His mother's untied balloon ran out of air.

"Is that any excuse, Renee, for neglecting our son?" his father asked sternly.

"We thought she'd teach him," his mother wailed.

Dad interrupted. "We were dead wrong. She wasn't strict enough. He's a tough little bugger—knows how to push someone push-able out of the way when he wants something. All he wants is to learn from Papin."

"Papin was your idea." Mom's voice was hard.

"Yes, dammit! He was. And I don't regret it for a minute. He's smart in ways no other kid will ever be. He can break a horse, shimmy up a tree, de-clog a weir, scale a sheer rock face, identify animal species by their sounds. He's a thinker, a doer. He's brave and kind, and he speaks ..."

"Zulu. He speaks Zulu, David. Like a native."

Silence. Scary silence.

His mother at last: "He's quiet around guests because, I suppose, he doesn't feel comfortable with his own language." She whined like a newborn puppy, and Jock's stomach began to ache.

"Renee, the kid knows how to navigate by starlight. He hears a sound that's just a sound to my ears and he'll say, 'Baby baboon's lost' or 'woodpecker's found his mate a home'—that's not a stupid kid, Renee. Dammit."

His dad was really angry. Jock needed the toilet.

"He's not stupid, just Zulu. He must become *English*." Mom ended in the way that really meant, "And that's that!"

"God. Imagine if I hadn't stopped him flashing past and asked him to write 'Today' on the hiker's list because Billy Pillay had left off the bloody word. When would we have known, for God's sake? So busy are we with other people's pleasures ..."

Silence was so much worse than whispers.

Then his mother's wail hit his ears like a nail being pounded in his head. "Tell me again what he said, just in case you misunderstood," she begged. At least the crying had stopped.

"He stared at me blankly—not at all embarrassed—and said, 'If you write it down like Miss Evelroy, I'll copy it.'" Dad's voice broke like someone had hands on his throat. In a few seconds, he carried on. "I thought I was expecting too much. 'Have you not learned to spell the word *today* yet?' He smiled at me—that bloody smile that makes my world all right—and he said, 'No, Dad, I can't spell, but I can copy anything.' And he didn't stop at that. He picked up the newspaper and handed it to me. 'And I can remember. Here. Read anything interesting and I'll show you.' God, Renee, he was proudly telling me of his progress when in fact our seven-year-old child is illiterate."

Apparently, that was a bad thing because there were no good sounds coming from the other room.

"Sad truth is, we can't let our son live the life he loves." Dad's voice, but it sure didn't sound like him.

And those shocking night-whispers resulted in him sitting in the back seat of the Chevy, with black shoes pulling leather together and strangling his *Gollaga-inja* sock-swaddled, hot feet.

The car roared to life, and Jock's heart dropped to his stomach. He looked up from the dastardly shoes and out of his side window. Papin's face looked like his felt. He wound down the glass partition separating them as fast as he could and leaned out, but as soon as Papin opened his mouth to speak, the Chevy started moving away.

Panic launched itself in his seven-year-old throat, and he sat, knees on the seat, leaning out the window as far as he could. The stupid tie-thing that was strangling him kept slapping Jock's face as Papin ran next to him, keeping up alongside the moving car.

Once they left the driveway and started on the steep decline, the dirt road didn't allow for an even ride. Unplanned potholes had to be quickly avoided by both car and running Papin, who had to be alert to get out of the way.

But Papin ran on in spite of the challenges, glancing through the open window every minute or so.

"Close the window, Jock," his mother shouted over the whoooooshing air. He deliberately ignored her, never taking eyes off his brave and determined friend. If it meant his dad stopped the car to give Jock a hiding for not having any ears, at least he'd get to see Papin's face for longer, and Papin could rest.

For a quarter of a mile, though some parts of the road were scary-narrow, Papin kept up with his open window. Only when the road widened and Dad pushed down the accelerator—harder than usual—did the Chevy distance itself from his friend enough to end Papin's marathon.

"Listen to your mother," said his father, and he did but then swiveled to watch out of the back window.

Papin slowed down and then stopped, and so did Jock's heart for a second. Papin was beaten. They both were.

But at least Papin got to stay home.

He waved and waved through the back window, but Papin was bent double, as if he had a stitch. The Chevy lunged around another corner, and Papin was gone, but Jock refused to turn around, just in case Papin came into view and found Jock wasn't waving. When the road swerved again, he was rewarded, but all he could see was Papin's back as he slowly trudged the miles back up to the hotel.

As the hole in Jock's gut got bigger and bigger, his best friend got smaller and smaller.

He begged his Mind Brownie never to replay the cruel divide created between Papin and the Chevy that day.

When they entered the red-brick school boarding school building for the first time, he could smell what was to come: dark, musty neglect and over-fried eggs.

There were walls without pictures and tables without flowers. He smelled bleach and floor wax. Long wooden picnic tables with chairs but no tablecloths and but one knife, one fork, one spoon and a paper serviette. Nicholas would not approve.

It was the first time he felt the thick mist again. Just two weeks ago before dinner, the lights started to flicker. Everyone else was busy, so Dad sent him to remove the debris from the pipe that rushed down the hill to drive the Pelton wheel for electricity. Dead frogs, crabs and sticks, sometimes dead snakes got snagged where the pipe narrowed to create a jet-type effect to drive the Pelton wheel, which drove the generator.

He'd been trained to fix the problem, and he ran the mile or so as twilight turned navy, then black. He cleaned out the debris, and just as he was ready to run back home, thick mist—like an unwanted, mystically moving gray blanket, wrapped itself around him. He was trapped, stuck, blind, and unable to move.

Papin had warned him never, ever to move in mist. "No matter how much you want to run away from it, you just can't. Running will make you trip, fall, or even die. You just have to wait it out."

Even the mist would be fine if Papin was right by his side,

but alone it was the scariest thing ever. He switched on his flashlight, but the thick, swirling mist looked alive. The light couldn't penetrate through the density and just reflected back into his eyes and confirmed he was trapped. All he could do was lean against the tiny hut that housed the generator and wait.

The thick, gray, restricting blanket churned around him and the air temperature changed all the time, like this living thing not only trapped but would soon smother and suffocate him.

It would be so easy to run.

Papin was having dinner at the compound. He didn't know Jock was here, and even if he did, he couldn't get to him. He, like Jock, would just have to sit and wait for the mist to pass.

In about half an hour—which felt like two days—the swirling blanket got thinner and thinner and then he could see. He ran home faster than the speed of a shooting star, all the while begging his Mind Brownie to lose any *kah-chick*ing it may have done during his ordeal. He never told anyone of his first real fear. Not even Papin.

That very night, he'd heard a guest call the sudden mist "as thick as pea soup." Jock swore off pea soup for life.

"Jock. Welcome. I'm your house master, Mr. Tomes. You will call me 'Sir,'" said a man with a ruddy, pleasant face, plopped on top of a neatly dressed body, who had somehow forced his way through the mist. He stuck out his hand. Jock felt his parents' eyes boring into him, so he shook the cold hand and said, "Thank you, Sir," as he'd been taught, though he was far from thankful. The mist swirled. Far enough away not to keep him from moving but close enough so he knew it was there and it could, in its own time, close around him so tight, he wouldn't be able to breathe.

Homesickness gnawed even while his parents were in sight. Papin. *What's Papin doing now? Tripod?*

The "tour" Sir proudly gave him brought no comfort. Rather the gray mist swirled and threatened to come closer.

It was all dark and old and unfamiliar. Downstairs had a kitchen, dining room and a gloomy "playroom" with benches and tables. These guys clearly knew nothing about playing. Windows were small and few and far between. Where was the light? Where was the sound of birds?

This "boarding school" wasn't for him. He'd learned his lesson. He had to get out before the mist closed in and he couldn't go anywhere. Trapped without Papin. He pushed through the swirling blanket to the front door. No one followed. He heard his voice shout, "Dad."

"Jock." His dad's voice was odd and wobbly.

Jock put his head down and ran through the threatening haze back toward his parents and stood as close to his dad as he dared, looked up at him and whispered, "I've learned my lesson. We can get back in the car now. I'll be good. I'll stay in the school bungalow with Miss Evelroy. I'll stay there all day if you want me to. Promise. I keep promises. You know that. Okay, Dad?"

His eyes, his heart, his very existence begged his dad to look at him, but he was studying something way above Jock's head. He looked at his mother. Maybe ... but her eyes were closed, and she was blowing her nose.

His parents were frozen Popsicles straight from the freezer. Unbending. Unmoving. Mute. Bastard Mist was moving closer, closer, making it hard to breathe. Why weren't they all high-tailing it to the Chevy? It was a long way home to Papin. To Tripod. Tripod would be so sad. Who would he sleep with? Who'd scratch him behind the ears? And Beauty ... he had to get away from the gray mist and take off the tight, hot, restricting black shoes. Quickly ...

"CAPTAIN?" Lieut opened his eyes with a start and to yet another pair of shoes. Boots. His eyes traveled up the legs and squinted to see the sergeant who'd take over the watch from him at midnight.

He looked at his watch: 5:30 p.m. Shit. His guard command started in thirty.

"Ah, Sergeant. What's your signal for your men tonight, so I can prep my guys for takeover?" Lieut asked, and the powerfully built sergeant saluted him.

Guard duty was a most contradictory post. If you weren't shit-scared, you were bored to death. If you were bored, you might fall asleep. Then you had good reason to be scared.

It was both Lieut's and Sergeant's job during their shifts to make sure men stayed awake and alert. But if you sneaked up on them, they might shoot you. The only safe way was to have a pre-discussed "distinctive" footfall or warning system the guards had in advance so they'd know who was approaching.

"I will hiccup, Captain." The sergeant smiled.

"Good. I'll drag a foot." Lieut jumped up and went off to brief his guards.

16

# THE SKINNY BITCH AND THE LIONS

*Champagne Castle, 1960, End of Easter Holidays*

After the "snake bite incident," as it came to be known, to cheer them all up, Beauty had a "date"—Mom's words—with stud Brutus the stallion, at Mr. Wright's farm. Beauty seemed to have a wonderful time, and Brutus confirmed she was every bit worthy of her name.

*Imagine if Beauty has a foal.* Jock's heart lurched, and his chest burned with excitement.

Dad knew he and Papin rode the horses hard but kindly, and he knew how much they both loved all the magnificent beasts, especially Beauty.

Since the Brutus episode, Dad insisted that in her new delicate state, Beauty should not be ridden, just exercised.

Jock was waiting for Papin's afternoon riding group to return. He waited on their rock, and dread—like ink on blotting paper —spread through him at the thought of returning to boarding school tomorrow.

"We will always be here for you. The hotel will always be

here for you. Papin. The horses. Billy Pillay. Even Tripod. Always." Dad's words. Jock's lifeline.

Sometimes at night, in the darkness, when the Mist threatened to close in on him, his world felt a baboon hair away from collapse. But Dad's promise would sustain him and the drums would dissipate the Mist until it eventually disappeared.

He closed his eyes and let the Drakensberg sun turn his closed eyelids red as the balm to his spirit that were Dad's words made returning to school less ominous. Then he concentrated on the solid, stable, familiar rock surface beneath him.

But the looming return to boarding school, no matter what tricks he used, always brought back that first day when he'd been abandoned by his parents and plunged into a world of rules, shoes and boys he had no need to know.

*Estcourt Boarding School, 1957,*
*First Day at Real School*

He looked out of the weather-worn window. Boys from about his age to twelve amused themselves in the dirt of the boarding school playground. It didn't even cross Jock's mind that all the boys were white; there was no other expectation.

Jock realized with a start he'd not seen a single black person since his parents had dragged him into this horrible place. That's what was wrong with it. No Zulus. Well, that, and so much else.

There were two groups of boys outside.

Papin said it was scientifically proven that South Africa had been inhabited for more than 100,000 years by the indigenous Koi Koi and San people known as Bushmen. The history of South Africa was a complex business, with Bantus migrating south from western and central Africa and European exploration in the thirteenth century in hopes of discovering an alternative route to the Silk Road. The Dutch East India Company established a trading post in Cape Town in 1652. European workers who settled became known as Free Burghers and later, Boers. When the British invaded the Cape in 1795, fed up, these Boers, who called themselves Afrikaners, led mass migrations known as the Great Trek and established settlements in the interior of South Africa. Discovery of gold and diamonds lured everyone from everywhere in the nineteenth century and led to new conflicts between Boer settlers and the British Empire, fighting mainly for control over the mining industry.

When the English defeated the Boers in the Anglo-Boer War in 1902, South Africa became a self-governing dominion of the British Empire, and the Union of South Africa was born.

It was all very complicated, but Papin summed it up for him.

"English and Afrikaans are still pissed off from the days of the Boer War they fought fifty years ago. They really don't like each other."

Jock deduced the English people thought they were posher than the Afrikaners. But in fairness, it seemed to Jock of the white people, Afrikaners were established well before the English. But it was really only the Bushmen who were entitled to this country, since when the earth was born, the Khoisan people were born at the same time. Papin said it was ironic that those original Koi Koi and San were nomads by nature and the *only* race who didn't want to own anything.

Such a confusing state of affairs, but Jock was happy to listen to the Papin in his head. Even if he didn't understand it all, it brought his friend closer.

His eyes focused through the glass out to the playground, and he saw two distinct groups—English on one side and

Afrikaners on the other. It was eye-opening and clear as the Sterkspruit stream that each preferred his own company.

Of course, he'd heard Afrikaans spoken now and then at the hotel, and his first- generation South African parents had, through the years, adopted some Afrikaans words into everyday speech, but the Afrikaans boys seldom spoke English. They were a tough-looking group of all ages, and they talked in their guttural language.

The English boys were mostly scrawny.

The brawny guys played marbles while the scrawny ones had a makeshift cricket match going. Jock thought of Billy Pillay, who'd taught him how to play the game, and a new pang of homesickness threatened to bring the Mist closer.

He was relieved to see everyone on the playground was shoeless, so he pulled off his own restrictors in a hurry and sped out into the fresh air.

A scuffle broke out in the yard just as he got there. He'd never seen white people fight before. Fascinated, he joined the side of the scrawny spectators.

A beefy Afrikaner, head and shoulders above the others, was the bullhorn for his group. *"Slat hom,* Gerrie. *Moer hom stukkend."*

The smallest of the English boys—though not the youngest—was apparently their mouthpiece. "Hit the Dutchman, Richie!" he yelled, and the smaller boys raised their fists in support.

The punches thrown in the makeshift ring mostly missed their target, so nobody was getting beaten to a pulp. Jock was quickly caught up and surprised himself when his own shout erupted. "Knock his teeth out!"

He felt someone looking at him. It was Beefy.

He shouted at Jock over the din of the scuffle, "Whaddu yew know, yew new little *Rooinek.*"

Though it was not a question, Jock threw back, "More than you."

Beefy crossed the solid line of separation, and in a flash, Jock felt a sharp pain in his jaw and was even more surprised when he felt himself going down. All he could think was, "Papin should have taught me to fight."

Beefy's knee was at eye level when Jock landed, and he punched out with both fists—one after the other.

Much to Jock's surprise, Beefy's knees must have buckled, because he joined him in the dirt. Beefy lost no time and put a solid lock around Jock's neck for too many seconds, and just when his inside air was all used up, the big guy let him go and punched him firmly in the nose at the same time Jock kicked out with all his might and connected with Beefy's balls.

Blood spewed. Papin would have been impressed. But the fact that Boet was down, holding his nuts and howling, would have ignited a ceremony at the kraal.

A scrum of bodies merged above Jock and Beefy, and the two warring factions merged because Richie and Gerrie's disappointing scuffle resulted in no blood at all.

A shrill whistle—which took Jock back to the mountains for a heartbreaking second—made the scrum scatter, and Jock saw Mr. Tomes standing over him.

Sir pointed to him and Beefy. "Jock. Boet. Cuts."

He'd never heard of such a thing. "Cuts?" He couldn't imagine it would be anything good, but he followed Beefy Boet's limping lead back inside the musty building. Jock's nose was well whacked and bleeding profusely, but that's what shirts were for. Beefy Boet was still holding on to his privates for dear life. Jock tried to grin, but it hurt like a bitch.

They followed Sir all the way to his office upstairs. Jock entered the small room after Boet, and the beefy one gave him a peculiar look.

Sir said, "You wait outside, Jock. It's not Boet's first time."

He did as he was bid and stood with his back against the office. Some English boys gathered close enough to talk to Jock but far enough away to distance themselves from trouble.

"Why're you not scared?" one asked.

Jock shrugged. He had no clue what was coming, but apparently it was scary enough to lure an audience. Billy Pillay would be so envious.

Sir's office door opened suddenly, and Beefy Boet came out. Jock thought, "He had the cheek to call *me* Red Neck. His face is the color of a beetroot."

"Jock," demanded Sir, and Jock went in and was told to shut the door.

"Not at my boarding school for more than ten minutes and here you are. Not a good way to start, young man. Bend down."

Seeing a reed-thin cane in Sir's hand, Jock understood.

The whistling sound of that thin cane coming down from above Sir's head to meet the resistance of his bum would stay with him forever. It seared like a red-hot poker, and he felt a sudden sadness for animals who were branded.

Another fierce whack and Jock managed not to utter a sound ... but wasn't sure how long he could bite his bottom lip without his tooth penetrating. And he didn't like the thought of Boet getting credit for that too.

He had no idea how many of these "cuts" were coming, so he stayed in a permanent brace for the impact of the next one.

Sir's voice came before the third whistle of the thin cane. "Two for a first offense. No more fighting. I won't tolerate fighting."

Jock was silent and frankly had no idea what was expected of him, so he kept bending.

"Stand up. You can go now."

He stood up, turned and walked toward the door.

Mr. Tomes said, "Say 'Thank you, Sir.'"

What the hell?

"Thank you, Sir," he mumbled, and before he reached the doorknob, his bum asked his brain why kindness didn't follow the beating like it always did at home. His brain reminded his bum that everything had changed.

As he walked through the door, the English boys all grinned. He was puzzled why this should be. Beefy Boet had stayed to watch him come out. Why? The big oaf-head turned abruptly and went downstairs. His waiting Afrikaans supporters cheered his arrival.

The dozen or so boarding school boys, mostly older than Jock, all started talking at once.

"Boet's furious cos Sir's cuts didn't make you cry."

"No one ever stands up to Boet."

Jock shrugged, more in confusion than indifference.

A loud bell sounded, and Jock saw one of the older boys ringing a huge silver bell as he walked through the halls, upstairs, and outside to the playground. Someone shouted, "Dinnertime!"

He followed the masses and found out stripes were a big thing in this awful new world.

They stood in stripes opposite each other, behind dining-room chairs at a long table. He didn't know what to do. Sir tapped his shoulder and pointed to an empty chair.

Jock stood behind the wooden chair and looked at the boys around the table. They all held their hands together in front of their chests, like meerkats but with palms together. Monkey see, monkey do. Jock went into meerkat mode. Sir called out a name, and an older English boy shut his eyes, bowed his head and said, "For what we are about to receive, may the Lord make us truly thankful."

They sat down to bone-colored plates with paper serviettes.

No knives and forks. Resting tiredly on the plate was a gray slice of cold ham, a half a tomato and a slice of buttered bread.

Jock couldn't believe his eyes. It was an odd starter.

Everyone wolfed down the food with Sir shouting to this one and that, "Mouth closed, DeWitt!" "Moyes, elbows off the table!" "Van Niekerk, slow down, you're not catching a train."

"Hey, new boy," Jock heard. When no one responded, he looked in the direction of the voice, and an older boy said, "If you don't want it, send it down."

Jock had no idea what was going on. The boy sitting next to him must have taken pity. "Aren't you hungry?" the boy asked.

Jock nodded. "Waiting for the main course and pudding."

The boy threw his head back, snorted and laughed so hard, he launched a half-chewed piece of tomato across the table.

Jock was stupefied. There was plain nothing funny about awful food.

When the boy stopped his roar, he took pity once more and said, "This is it. No main course"—he stopped to chortle again —"and definitely no pudding. That only comes once a week on the Saturday nights we have to spend at the boarding school. Eat up. It's all you'll get till morning."

"Really?" Jock had never known such a thing.

The boy smiled and nodded. "Man, you don't look like a half-wit, but you must be. You took on Boet Buis. Where do you come from? The moon?"

Strangely, Jock felt he wasn't being unkind, just curious.

Jock picked up the bread and took a bite. "I live up the mountain."

"Hut or a hotel?" the boy asked.

Jock slapped the floppy ham on the bread, hoping to improve the taste, but all he got was the likes of a salty sponge. But anything would do when you didn't know how hungry you were.

He swallowed before he could reply as he'd been taught.

The boy next to him was smiling when he said, "You just answered my question. You're hotel, not hut. What's your name?"

"Jock. Yours?" Starving, he took another bite and dared to speak with his mouth full.

"They call me Mac. I'll look out for you if you like."

"I don't need looking out for. But thanks, Mac." Jock was working on his tomato, much to the disappointment of the hungry guy a few chairs up.

Mac laughed again. It was the best sound he'd heard since he arrived. "You kind of proved that today. Hitting Boet. Getting cuts. Not crying."

Jock grinned at him and felt tomato pips push through his teeth. Nicholas would have had his hide for not eating properly. But Nicholas wasn't here. And his mother would have a fit, but she'd left him to fend for himself. He was doing just that.

Everyone thanked the Lord again for the bountiful food. Gollaga-inja. And white people thought Zulu customs were crazy!

After lights-out in the dark of the dormitory he shared with nine other boys, his bum hurt like a bitch and his nose throbbed, all thanks to Boet. There were two more dormitories down the corridor. His bed consisted of a mattress that had half the cushiness of the ones in the hotel compound, two sheets, a pillow and a well-worn blanket.

As soon as the lights were out, no one made a sound. Aches set in for Tripod. For Papin. He so badly wanted to cry, but he wouldn't. Ever. The mist swirled, threatening, coming closer. Though his Mind Brownie did not yet have a name, it blessedly immersed him into the memories of Papin's kraal during a celebration where the drumbeats were so loud, they blotted out everything else. He willed himself to stay right there amongst people he cared for, right next to Papin, until blessed exhaustion claimed him before the mist closed in.

Sleep was killed by the clanging bell, and Jock shot up, confused.

He looked around, and dread reentered the pit of his stomach. His dorm-dwellers were buzzing around their beds like bees around a thistle. What in the world?

Mac was sent to teach him how it was done.

Who knew making a bed required "hospital corners" and mighty precision? If it was less than perfect, Sir made you strip it and remake it till the corners were sharp enough to cut biltong. Where was Constance? If she was here, he'd hug her big, soft, sunlight-soap-smelling body into a coma—but only after she'd made his bed.

Everything had a place. An exactly folded towel onto which toothbrush and hairbrush had to line up in a very specific way, laid on the bed just so. Thanks to Mac, he passed that test.

Then they shuffled toward the passage and lined up in another stripe against the wall with the very towel and brushes they'd just lined up, waiting for their turn in the showers. Jock was dead last, thanks to his learning curve of morning duties. When the boy to his left passed him a tin of shoe polish and a cloth, he shook his head, leaned back and daydreamed of *nagapies* and falcons.

Sir loomed over him. "Why are you not polishing your shoes?"

"They're new, Sir. Wore them first time yesterday. They don't need polish."

"Every shoe needs a polish every day. Polish, boy, before I have to get the cane."

By the time it was Jock's turn for the shower, his face, hands, neck and pajamas were black, as was the wall along which he'd scooted to get to his turn in the bathroom.

For this apparently severe offense, Sir told him he'd get "lions" when he got home from school. As exciting as that sounded, by the look on Sir's face, he thought they might be man-eaters.

When at last he stepped into the shower, only icy needles of water remained, and each prick penetrating his skin reminded him he was not at home.

Breakfast was an icky plate of soggy gray porridge. Gray was a popular food color around here. It was the dawn of "Eat what's before you or go hungry," and the Lord was thanked for the gray matter before and after. *Gollaga-inja!* He swore he heard the ancestors laughing.

There was never a moment you weren't expected to do something. Spoon and bowl in the scullery. Another stripe was formed on the *stoep* for another inspection. In this awful world, if your tie was askew or straw basher crooked or shoes untied, you'd get cuts. Jock's bum tightened, and the skinny bitch who'd cut him yesterday smartly reminded him to observe and follow.

Their stripe (which Jock learned was called a "line") marched through the boarding school and school playgrounds. Playground? Jock's playground was five square miles, not these tiny one-hundred-yard-square spaces.

The line disintegrated when they stopped outside a large, one-story brick building.

Kids seemed to peel away to different rooms. Jock had no idea where to go and was strongly considering the shade of a nearby oak tree when a lady said, "Jock? This way."

She was Miss Dunn. A gangly lady who looked like a harmless daddy longlegs spider. She showed Jock to the same kind of table-chair contraption that'd boxed him in Evelroy's school bungalow. But this time there were twenty-three kids, all in their own jail.

They were around his own age, and there were girls too. He

learned not all kids stayed in the boarding school. Many were "day scholars." Lucky buggers!

June was an odd month to start school when school years ran from January to December. All the kids were a half a year ahead. Mind you, he was likely not at their level to begin with, so it was no small wonder chalk scribbles on the board made little sense to him.

"Open your books to page fifteen," said Miss Dunn.

Jock saw a book lying on his desk. He glanced around. Everyone had the same book. A drawing of a dog going down a set of stairs on the cover. It looked harmless, but he knew better. These books were the very things that caused him to be here. Far from home. Without Papin. He didn't want to touch it.

He welcomed in the drums and transported himself back to his Berg until the bell rang. It seemed school life was ruled by bells and *Gollaga-inja* books. When the classroom emptied out, he did another monkey see, monkey do, and picked up his satchel. But just before he reached the door, Miss Dunn pulled at his blazer.

"Jock, I hear you will need extra classes. Return to my class after lunch, and we'll begin to get you up to speed." It sounded like one of those boring car races Billy Pillay listened to on the radio, which might be better than anything else around here.

Lunch was a mighty disappointment, even worse than the breakfast letdown. One slice of cheese and next to it, a dollop of syrup and a slice of bread. That was it.

He'd hardly swallowed his last bite when Sir loomed over him.

"Off you go, back to Miss Dunn. Only when you have caught up to the rest of the standard will you be allowed to play after school. Except for every second Tuesday, when you go to town, and every second Friday, when you go home. Don't forget ... after Miss Dunn, it's back to me for lions," was what Jock heard.

On that first day, after Miss Dunn had been kind in explaining he was fathoms behind anyone else, he schlepped his new shoes through the dirt of the playgrounds because tomorrow he'd have to polish the buggers anyway.

He hoped the lions lived up to his expectations. He'd only seen a lion skin. It was humongous and scary, and he couldn't wait to see the real thing. He just hoped it wasn't in a cage. That was another thing wrong with this place. Not an animal in sight. Not even a rat-catching cat. Animals were smart creatures. Of *course,* they'd stay away from this place!

Sir was waiting for him.

Jock smiled for the first time in more than three days. "Where are the lions, Sir?" He didn't mind if they were man-eaters. He always had a way with animals and wasn't afraid at all.

"Come with me," said Sir and led the way to the playroom with a blackboard in it. These people had no idea.

"Sit," barked Sir. "Now read what it says there." He pointed to the board with the chalk scratch-marks.

"Please tell me what it says, Sir, and I will tell you back," said Jock in earnest. Where the hell were the lions?

"Good God! I see Miss Dunn has her work cut out for her. Okay, it says, 'I will only polish my shoes and not myself, not others, or my clothes, the floor or wall.'"

"Sir, what does this have to do with lions?" Jock was perplexed.

Sir never answered but put his hands together in meerkat style, lifted his head up to the ceiling and said, "God help me."

And then he gave Jock sheets and sheets of paper, a pencil, a sharpener, and asked Jock (and begged God) if he could count.

Jock was really put out. "Count? I can do sums like nobody's business." And Sir had another quiet word with God.

*Champagne Castle, 1960*

"Tsotsiiiiiiiiiiiiiiiiiiiiiiiiiiiiiiii," Papin called as he ran towards their rock and Tripod loped awkwardly to greet him from his usual position—overseeing his young master. Tsotsi waved like he hadn't seen his friend for fifteen years or more. Papin smiled from the inside out. *Gollaga-inja*. The boy would go back to school tomorrow. He hated that. Nothing felt the same without Tsotsi.

Once in position, Papin spared no details of the guests' ride. He knew how Tsotsi loved minutia. He filled his letters with specifics every week to help the boy's Mist disappear. It had taken two whole years at school for Tsotsi to finally share The Mist that plagued him, always close, when he was away from everything he knew and loved.

He wished he could go to boarding school in Tsotsi's place. Yes, to learn, but also to shield Tsotsi from all the things a young soul should not be forced to experience.

His uncle said Papin was unrealistically shielded here in the mountains. Knowing some of Tsotsi's boarding-school world made it clear his uncle was not wrong. The world beyond here was very, very different.

"What do you learn in history?" Papin asked, and Jock looked at him askance.

"Why do you bring up *Gollaga-inja* school now?" The boy was pissed off.

Papin smiled. "I am just interested. You see my uncle told me about things that have happened in South Africa I did not know. I didn't know if you learned such things at school. I am in search of the facts because you know my uncle exaggerates."

"What things?" Now the boy was interested.

"Have you heard of the African National Congress? It has been around since 1912."

"No. We learn about the Dark Ages and the Middle Ages. Well, some learn. I fly away with the birds of prey who soar outside the history teacher's window. When I feel a 'boink' on the head, his wooden duster has just connected, and I have to come back from my outside adventures." Tsotsi laughed, and Papin joined him. "What is this African national thing? Can I join? I am part Zulu!"

Papin smiled. "African National Congress. It's abbreviated to A.N.C and called 'ANC'. Its job is to bring all Africans together as one people to defend their rights and freedoms."

"Well, it's not working too well. No black person has rights or freedoms at my school."

"Uncle says there was a peaceful protest ..."

"What's that?"

"When there are no weapons and no fights, just lots and lots of people together showing the government they are unsatisfied and asking for change."

The boy was interested. Papin continued. "These people just the other day were peacefully asking the government to take away the green passbooks they are made to carry. The government force this Apartheid. It means separateness. Blacks and colored people must be separate to whites. The green pass makes the people feel branded. Like cattle."

"Mr. Government. That bastard," said Tsotsi angrily.

"Then the police just started shooting at them, Tsotsi. They had no weapons to defend themselves. Sixty-seven black, unarmed protesters died, and one hundred eighty men, women and children were wounded by those police. If what Uncle says is true, how ugly is this world?"

"Very," said the boy, and Papin at once felt bad he had

burdened Tsotsi with this heaviness when he had enough of his own right before returning to boarding school.

Well, perhaps it was hearsay and distorted by retelling. Yes, he'd seen a little of whites thinking they were better than anybody, but nobody that mattered treated him or anyone else that way.

Papin chastised himself for being so anxious to rid himself of this information churning inside him that he'd shared it with his best friend. Shame on him.

He jumped up and said, "Come, Tsotsi. The day won't wait for you. Eteemot spotted a leopard down the valley. Let's go! Show me how you can track animals." And they were off.

They bounded down, then walked past the hotel toward the hills linked by open, unspoiled, grassy fields. Tripod was tempted away by a guest and a piece of cold meat.

"What terrain is best for tracking?" asked Papin mid-run.

"Natural paths. Not well used," Tsotsi answered automatically.

"Where do animals rest?"

"In the shade. I start tracking from a shady spot under a tree or a bush."

"Show me who is the hardest animal to track, and tell me why."

"You are worse than Daddy Long Legs Dunn, Papin!"

Then Tsotsi bent over, his arms hanging limply at his sides. He swung them back and forth enthusiastically. He bowed his legs and walked forward unevenly before he ran sideways, almost skipping like a happy crab.

"So, you, baboon you, you changed the direction of your footprints, making you impossible to track!"

But his pupil was still in baboon mode. By the time Tsotsi got onto all fours with knuckles scraping the ground, Papin was doubled over.

WHILE JOCK CONCENTRATED on tracking under Papin's watchful eye, he forgot about history and Uncle and blackboard dusters and ugly riots where innocent people died and focused on finding the bushbuck.

As Jock followed the footprints, he marveled how no two animals had the same prints. Just like fingerprints and stripes on a zebra.

When he reached the short kikuyu grass, the print was easiest to see. Most of the front of the hoof was visible and slightly pushed back. "It's him, but he's been startled. Shame. He's afraid of something. Oh, no. Don't tell me he'll be eaten by that leopard."

Papin's reply came from behind him, and Jock jumped. He must have been following Jock for a while, checking his pupil's performance. "It's nature's way, Tsotsi. Eat or be eaten."

But Jock worried about that bushbuck and the leopard all night instead of enjoying Tripod on his bed.

The next day, when Dad drove the Chevy away with Jock in his *Gollaga-inja* black lace-up shoes riding shotgun, Papin ran next to the passenger side of the car as he did every time.

The day of separation never got easier for either of them, this Jock knew. It would be two long weeks before he would see Papin again. He was so much more than a best friend. Papin was Jock's Zulu self.

# 17

# THE WEIGHT OF A DAY

*Estcourt/Champagne Castle, 1957*

It was five days and twenty-one and a half hours since his parents left him. All alone. Jock learned twenty-four hours at a time, the weight of a day.

He found out there was no such thing as freedom in this overwhelming, demanding new world. Every minute of the day was accounted for. It was hell.

So much happened in his first week at boarding school. None of it was good.

You did as you were told when you were told, and you were told over and over again. Everything was done over and over the very same way, otherwise you got cuts.

Repetition was not something he understood. Every adventure, every meal, every day was different in the world Jock knew and loved.

He had but one mission: to get home to Papin. And Tripod. And Beauty.

On Tuesday, Jock found out, the boarding school inmates (what else could they be?) were expected to be hugely excited about a walk to Estcourt town with Sir. Jock had no desire to talk to other inmates. He just wanted to get this punishment over and get home.

There was animated chatter about spending their "tuck money" parents deposited in advance and left in Sir's care. Jock had no idea what they were on about, but he knew town, and he liked the idea of half a crown in his pocket.

Jock knew Estcourt. On very special days, he and his dad sang their way down the mountain to the bottle store in Estcourt to pick up the hotel booze and all the way up again. The hard liquor, as Dad called it, was sent by train from Durban and kept under lock and key in Estcourt station. Dad couldn't trust anyone else to pick it up. He said it was too tempting. The same for the "perishables" like chocolates and cigarettes Mom sold in the hotel gift shop.

It was the only real time they spent together, just him and Dad. He felt a pang where his heart should be, and the hollowness spread.

Estcourt was where you picked up hotel guests from the station, went for a haircut, had your car repaired or went to hospital—a metropolis, as far as Jock knew.

The town's one main street with its two traffic lights was a lively place that tugged his eyes in a dozen directions, filling some of the hollow spots in his tummy. It served as the main artery between Johannesburg and Durban, so cars came and went.

There was a two-story hotel, a feed store with an ever-changing trail of farmers trekking in and out. Jock had seen a hundred untethered dogs, a few domestic pigs, three goats and even a pygmy donkey coming and going over the years.

Jock reveled in the familiarity of the town. There was the post office, the chemist. His Mind Brownie recalled the day Billy Pillay tried to master another regurgitation trick. Boy! Billy's

Regurgitation Phase nearly killed him, but he never learned and he never quit. This time, the wine steward had attempted to swallow four razor blades on some fishing line.

Luckily, Billy's strangled cries echoed through the hotel corridor just before the first blade cut off his tonsils but after his tongue was sliced quite severely.

Dad and Mom were busy and it was after lunch, so Nicholas was entrusted with the sacred car keys, and the Chevy carted Jock, Papin and a blood-gurgling Billy as they wound their way toward town and the Estcourt pharmacy.

Dad gave instructions: "Nicholas, you take him to the chemist. Hospital's only for something broken or if you're dying. Billy Pillay doesn't qualify. In fact, with half a tongue, he might talk half as much. We can only hope. Be back before dinner. No dillydallying." Jock smiled for the first time in what felt like years as he smelled mercurochrome and saw the curved needle the chemist used to repair Billy's tongue. Billy's lisp lingered for quite a while but never slowed his chatter, much to Dad's disappointment.

Jock smelled town in all its glory: the heady yeast of broken beer bottles outside the hotel bar, spilled gasoline, curry, fried food, flowers and horse poop. Thoughts of Papin lovingly brushing Beauty turned the dull ache of loneliness into a sharp pain.

Thank the ancestors for the overpowering aroma of malt vinegar and deep-fried potatoes that made him forget. The pungent smell tickled the fine hairs in his nose and made his mouth water, and this became the first time he used his Mind Brownie in school hell.

Fortunately, the group of inmates felt the same aromatic pull, so he followed them where the pungent tang led.

Inside the Estcourt Café, he was introduced to slap chips (pronounced the Afrikaans way, "slup" chips). The Portuguese shopkeeper immersed a wire basket filled with raw potato wedges into deep, hot oil. They came out yellow, crusty, and sizzling and were scooped up and tossed into a whitish grease-proof packet.

The shopkeeper asked each customer across the counter the same question: "Salt and vinegar?" A nod would make him shake a big salt cellar upside down for three seconds. Then he'd pick up a Fanta bottle in which malt vinegar replaced orange soda and the steel cap, stabbed a dozen times, was bashed back onto the bottle. He upended the bottle, splashing the packet with gusto, until the buyer said, "Thanks!"

The Portuguese man scrunched the top of the packet and shook vigorously before it was handed over. All that shaking adds the magic, thought Jock.

By the time it was his turn at the counter, Jock knew exactly what to do.

And when at last he held his own packet and opened it slowly, a hot wave of vinegar hit him in the face and juices of anticipation filled his mouth.

As front teeth bit into the long chip—crunchy on the outside, soft within—Jock's mouth did the twist. This wasn't a snack. This was a ceremony for taste buds.

Too soon, he had only crumbs left. He watched one of the boarding school boys turn the packet inside out. Monkey see, monkey do. The piping hot, wet potato crusts had melted into the greaseproof paper, filling the creases.

Jock sucked those little clingy, delicious little bastards off the sides, then held the packet between his lips as he sat on the edge of the pavement and took off his shoes. Nothing could be truly enjoyed with shoes on. He sucked off the last of the vinegar and salt granules in unrestricted bliss.

"I'm Scotty," Jock heard.

He squinted up and saw a boy his own age with a freckled, smiling face.

"Jock," he said and licked the empty packet, just in case.

"Where're you from?" asked Scotty, sitting down uninvited.

"Champagne Castle Hotel."

Scotty chortled. "A hotel! That's pretty fancy."

Jock balled up his well-licked packet, aimed, threw and dunked it into a rubbish bin bolted into the pavement.

"Not fancy. Just where we live."

"I live on a nut farm, half a day away," said Scotty.

Visions of Billy Pillay falling into the pool while sprinkling in the chlorine in the early morning at least once a month played in his mind. "Most times, I live on one too," said Jock.

It took Scotty a split second longer than it would have taken Papin. But when he laughed, the wait was worth it. Scotty's hearty guffaw spilled out in three octaves. If that wasn't funny enough, he slapped his thigh while sucking in a huge breath for the next batch of three-note, laugh-hiccups to come.

Jock was riveted. He'd never seen such a thing.

He couldn't help it. It started at the core of his belly, and as hard as he tried to hold it there, it wormed its way up, his lungs forced it out through his mouth, and he heard the sound of his own laughter. Together, he and Scotty laughed and laughed, one giggling high, medium and low and slapping his thigh and the other rolling around on the pavement.

And for those minutes, Jock's hollowness disappeared.

"Yup," said Scotty, once they'd recovered. "That's pretty much what it is. Nutty. My mother's going through some change or other, and she throws plates at my father's head. Lucky her aim is bad. My sister loves boys, and she's always getting into trouble, so it's kind of a good thing I can get away from them for two weeks at a time."

"Two weeks?" Jock felt his heart drop. Two weeks could have been two years. Papin! Beauty! Tripod! *Gollaga-inja!*

"Oh, I forgot. You're new," said Scotty. "We go home for the weekend every other Friday."

Jock recalled mention of weekends between home visits when you were locked in the boarding school with shitty pudding as compensation. Buckets of hollowness returned.

"Not this Friday but next, we'll get to go home," Scotty said, watching four dark-skinned boys, who reminded Jock of the Zulus back home, play a game of one-bounce soccer with a tennis ball on the pavement. They were having fun. He wished he could join them.

"Then that's it? I don't have to come back?" Jock saw a faint glimmer of light.

"You always have to come back. Parents drop us back here on Sunday nights, every time a coconut." Scotty looked sorry to share this news.

"Always?" This was far worse than Jock had imagined.

"Ja. Except during holidays."

"What are ... when are holidays?"

"In six weeks, we get to stay home for two whole weeks with no school. This one's called Michaelmas holiday."

"And then?" Jock was more afraid of the answer than his Popsicle-stiff, unyielding parents leaving him in The Mist.

"At the end of each holiday, you get dropped back at boarding school on Sunday night. We get four holidays a year. Longest one's over Christmas—nearly four whole weeks. It goes like that every year till you're seventeen. If you fail your school year, then longer." It seemed the hopelessness of their situation hit Scotty at the same time it knocked Jock between the eyes.

"*Seventeen years old?*" Jock couldn't wrap his mind around the length of that. "You never go home to *stay*?" *Gollaga-inja!*

Scotty shook his head, smiled bleakly and tried to sound hopeful. "The holidays make up for it. Mostly."

But Scotty's chatter became a distant waterfall. Jock had to get home. A big green bus rolled in with Zulus and Sothos and Xhosas so crammed inside, many hung halfway out of the windows. The bus stopped. Jock saw a ladder that led to the roof of the bus on which tattered suitcases, a rusted bicycle and blankets stuffed with belongings were piled high and secured by rope.

"Where does that bus go?" Jock asked Scotty.

"To Loskop." Scotty was caught up in his investment—a deep-fried Russian sausage with thick batter.

"How often?"

"Twice a day, every morning, and it'll leave soon, once new travelers are on board."

"Saturdays too?" Jock asked, and Scotty nodded.

That green bus was all the incentive Jock needed to put Papin's bush skills to good use.

# 18

# INDUNA AND UBASI

*South West Africa, 1977*

LIEUT STARTED DRAGGING his leg a good fifteen feet away from where the private patrolled on guard duty.

His sergeant had warned him of the captain's dreamed-up footfall so the private would know the approaching figure was friend not foe. The young guy turned quickly, gun at the ready, before relief calmed his shiny face. Two hours was a bitching long time when your nerves were on edge. The private saluted.

"You doing okay, Private?" Lieut asked.

"Yes, Captain." He was still saluting.

"At ease, Private."

This bloody new rank. Too much fuss and no reward. He who Lieut had not dared think about for a decade whispered, "You can't fight evil disease with sweet medicine." How right Papin was. Sporting the three stars of a captain on his shoulder could never compensate for being in this war in the first place.

*Estcourt/Champagne, 1957*

It was Saturday, and they'd just been let out after breakfast to play. Jock knew he had until lunchtime to get as far away from hell as he could.

He was fast, he knew how to become "invisible," and he could duck and dive like no one else around. He needed all his skills as he casually walked through the playground, hands in the pockets of his after-school khaki shorts and shirt. He sauntered through the gate and through the schoolyard slowly, like he belonged there.

As soon as he left school property, he took off his shoes and socks and hid them in a tree hollow. He wiggled his toes. Free at last.

Then he ran like the wind.

Once he'd had the idea, on the way back to the boarding school after meeting Scotty, he used his Mind Brownie to memorize landmarks and gauge distances. He spent the rest of the week plotting his escape.

Papin said if you looked like you were on a mission, nobody questioned where you were going and just presumed you were allowed to be there. Papin's voice, louder in his head than it had been for days, made a smile stretch his mouth wide in excitement. Jock picked up his pace.

Papin's voice in his head continued: "If you run away from an animal, they think they have the upper hand. From watching the animals, you learn so much, Tsotsi. See how the duiker jumps high when he's happy and how the baboon picks at nits in the fur of the ones he loves when he's content? Animals can only show what they feel. Humans can show a face outside, but inside—their heart has a different face. You must always show the face you want others to see, because it's on that face or in that action they will judge you. If they don't know what's in your head, they can't figure out what to expect from you. This is your weapon for which they have no prepared defense."

At the time, Papin's words were just words. Now Jock understood.

As soon as the green bus rolled in, Jock's heart pounded, but he forced himself to stroll across the road. Kicking an empty can helped him seem unhurried and unworried—everything he wasn't. He aimed the can toward the bus, gave a hell of a kick, and ran after it as if it was just another day and he, just another kid in the street. Nothing unusual. While he angled and used the side of his foot to dribble the can like a soccer ball, he watched African folks boarding the bus. The Zulu driver was positioned on the roof of the bus, and passengers below hoisted up bicycles and suitcases to him which he roped in.

Once the driver was safely in his seat, seeing to boarding all passengers, an old Zulu man stealthily climbed the ladder as Jock watched and then lay flat, holding on to the roof carrier.

Jock lost no time at all. He was up the ladder in a flash, and he crawled toward the old man, who jumped with surprise but then grinned and patted the slice of bus-roof beside him.

Jock smiled his thanks, and man and boy lay side by side on their stomachs on the bus's green roof. All the way to Loskop, the two were as comfortable in their closeness as old friends but had no reason to say so during the bumpy ride.

Loskop was halfway to Champagne Castle Hotel. Its only reason for existence was that the Durban train detached a box car in Loskop, and a rural goods train going to Winterton picked it up. Loskop, with its one dirt road, became essential to mountain resorts and farmers as a depot to collect transported goods.

Segornie's, the general store, provided the odds and bobs the trains didn't offload that hoteliers and farmers might need urgently and would pay a little more for. It offered a plethora of delights, everything from putu pots to cough mixture; colorful cotton to planting ploughs; licorice to dining-room chairs.

But it was the post office on the dirt strip that was the major reason for Dad sending his farm tractor, which pulled an open trailer there every day. Hotel guest bookings were done by mail and were only confirmed once checks for deposits were received. Collecting the color-coded, green Champagne Castle Hotel canvas mail bag secured with a padlock meant new business, as was exchanging it for an identical bag with outgoing mail. No matter how expensive the goods that were to be hauled up the mountain, the mail was considered the most valuable of all.

As the scratch in the earth that was Loskop came into view from their rooftop perch, Jock felt irrepressibly happy. He was halfway home.

By the winter sun's position, he knew as well as he knew his own name that Eteemot and the outside crew would still be loading the trailer ...

*Wait! Being sent to boarding school showed me that whatever I know to be certain or true or forever can change in the softest night-whisper.*

He shivered.

As the bus turned the corner, Jock spotted Eteemot and his team. He felt the taut spring that was his body release, and the very first dose of gratitude filled his senses. Night-whispers be damned!

The bus began to slow, and Jock stood up, found his balance, then extended his hand to the old man to help him up. And still there was no need for words.

They were both down the ladder and off the bus in seconds, moving quickly behind a tree so the driver couldn't see them in his rearview mirrors. The old man held out his hand, and Jock took it as he smiled into the wise eyes, and they shook in the Zulu way.

"Where are you going, *Ubasi?*" Jock asked respectfully in Zulu.

The man looked surprised but answered, "El Mirador Hotel. My daughter works there."

Twenty miles was too many for an old man to walk uphill.

"Come. Follow me. I will find you a lift," said Jock and ran ahead, checking now and then to see whether the old man was following.

Eteemot, the tractor driver and chief of the outside staff, was carrying a box of cream soda from the large warehouse cage to the tractor trailer. He nearly dropped it when Jock whispered, "*Sawubona, Induna*" into his ear. More than words of politeness, *sawubona* carried the importance of recognizing the worth and dignity of that person.

The last thing Eteemot expected was to hear "I see you" from Inkosi's boy, so far from the hotel.

"Tsotsi!" Surprise and joy shone on the man's smiling face and he hoisted up the slipped crate. "Where've you been?" Eteemot asked.

"Stupid school," Jock answered. This morning was the first time he'd spoken or heard Zulu in six days. As the familiar language nurtured his ears, Jock found the great joy that comes when you've found something important you didn't know you'd lost. He felt happy for the first time in his forever.

"Papin. He so sad you go away," said Eteemot as he carefully placed the cream soda next to crates of beer. Jock jumped up to help load the rest of the boxes and shouted greetings to each of the outside staff.

"Everybody looks for Tsotsi," said one.

"Eish. But too much longing for Papin," said another, shaking his head.

Jock saw the old fellow walking up the hill.

"Eteemot? I met a good man on the bus. Can we give him a lift to El Mirador Hotel?" Jock asked.

"Yebo," the Ubasi agreed, and Jock motioned to the old man, still wending his way up.

Once drums of cooking oil were loaded along with bags of flour and sacks of horse cubes, the farm tractor pulled the rattling trailer over the dirt road to the only two manual petrol pumps in a thirty-mile radius, located outside Segornie's.

The Zulu with one pumping arm the size of the cartoonish Popeye the Sailor Man earned his wages by filling up the tractor and loose petrol cans. Then they were off. Jock and his new friend were nestled against the incoming mail sack after they'd stacked thick horse blankets under their bums—antidote to the lack of shock absorbers on the trailer. They climbed and climbed, and with every bump, Jock felt exhilaration as freedom coursed through his veins.

Eteemot and his second-in-command rode in the tractor, and the five Zulus on the back with Jock and Ubasi bantered with each other easily. Jock relished their sense of humor and their way of looking at the world. His world.

Dad said Eteemot and his crew were as important to the hotel as the entertainment and his mom's menu planning. "Without them, there would be no hotel. They fix broken sewerage pipes, whitewash bungalows and re-thatch roofs. But their biggest job is chipping sandstone from our quarry and repairing the roads so our guests can come and go."

At least twice a week in rainy season, the tractor and team were dispatched to pull guests' cars up the S-bend and safely to Champagne Castle Hotel. Dad said that job alone was worth their wages.

They stopped to let off Ubasi, who bowed to each of his new Zulu friends in thanks and then shook Jock's hand and said,

"Never before have I met a white Zulu. I am happy now I have. You do my nation proud."

Jock was chuffed.

Jock's excitement was bubbling over when at last they bounced up the entrance to the hotel lined with dogwood trees, around the verge of one of the undulating, manicured lawns and ... there was his dad. Jock felt a surge of joy.

Oh, boy! Dad had his hands on his hips. Not a good sign. But the sight of his dad annoyed was better than no sight at all.

Jock couldn't help himself. He stood and waved the tractor's oil rag as if he'd just won a car race, then jumped off before the trailer pulled up to the storeroom, out of guests' sight.

When he reached his dad, he hugged him around the waist. It was the first time since he was little that he'd shown his dad such affection. Hugging was not a manly thing to do, but today he didn't care. He hung on for as long as it took to get his dad to hug him back.

But Jock's delight was short-lived.

"Wait for me in my bedroom," Dad said after he'd cleared his throat.

Shit. The waiting was the worst part. *Gollaga-inja!*

Jock tried to think about anything but what was about to happen.

He would teach Papin his new word. "Shit" was the only good thing about the last six days. Shit and slap chips.

It had happened so many times, Jock knew the drill. He knelt on the floor, face down on the bottom edge of his parents' bed in the family suite. His bum twitched as he saw his dad stretch for the top of the cupboard.

Down came the sjambok.

Then came the worst part. The "talk."

"This is the last time you run away from school."

"Yes, Dad." Jock's voice was muffled because he'd pushed his face as far down as it would go into the mattress.

"This is it, Jock. Get used to it. You will stay at school and do your best. We've made arrangements for you to have after-school lessons to get you up to speed. School is now your job. But your home will always be here, waiting for you."

"And Papin?" He could barely hear his own voice bouncing off the mattress springs.

"Papin is your friend. He too will always be waiting." And though dad's voice was kind, Jock knew he couldn't delay the inevitable.

He steeled himself and thought of Tripod, who had wagged what was left of his rump into a coma when he found his young master. His dog's expressive disappointment pained his heart when Dad closed the door on his three-legged self to execute the inevitable punishment. He could handle what he knew was coming, but he couldn't handle Tripod's feeling of rejection.

Dad's clear upset at his unscheduled return was more painful to bear than the sjambok's three whips on his bum. They were different from Sir's cuts, and he surprised himself by being almost grateful for the sjambok's familiarity. Boy! Had he missed this place!

When the instrument of bad behavior was returned to the top of the cupboard, Jock stood but dared not leave the room. The reason for these burning consequences needed to be reiterated.

"Jock, you will never do this again." Dad's voice was quiet.

"No, sir, I won't." He looked his dad in the eyes, the way he was expected to.

Dad's face exploded in a mighty smile. "But I'm just hell-of-a glad you're home. Now go and have fun. You and Papin can sleep in the cave tonight."

Jock clean forgot his punishment and ran from the suite

toward the stables, Tripod in tow. He knew Papin would be there.

Papin's joy matched Jock's own, and they did their special handshake five times.

Beauty was happy to see him, and he brushed her till she shone.

Seeing Nicholas made Jock hungry. Not just for the divine food he lorded over but for the food Jock's soul so desperately needed. He was so happy. Each familiar, smiling face of the staff was a gift to him. Geez. Even the sight of Constance made him happy.

It took being forced to live without them for a whole week to learn how lucky he was. His dad said they'd always be here. He would have had ten cuts for that reassurance. Anything was bearable when you knew your bliss was waiting for you.

Billy Pillay pulled a confused chicken out of a full mealie sack to demonstrate his new trick. Of course, the chicken was more surprised than Jock, since the clucking could be heard long before the big reveal.

Thabo packed the boys a hamper of food fit for a week when it was just one rare night in the Bushman cave. The safe overhang was just fifteen minutes by horseback from the hotel.

"Boys!" the two turned in unison. Trouble already?

"Dad?"

"I want you two ready after breakfast tomorrow. Ask Thabo to pack for three."

"It's Sunday, Dad." Jock knew the weekends were a hectic time with new arrivals. Perhaps in the excitement, Dad forgot.

Dad winked. "For once, Jock, I don't give a damn. Your mother can handle it."

What in the world did he do to deserve such attention?

# 19

# RINKHALS AND PEELS

*Somewhere near Angola Border, 1977*

ANOTHER NIGHT IN THE BUSH. Lieut's boys were getting restless with inactivity, but at this hour, exhaustion overrode everything.

At 3:42 a.m., he tore off a strip of the dry, spicy, salted meat and let it rest on his tongue. He chewed the biltong or sucked if he was listening to something miles away, lest it be a threat to his boys. Saliva hurried in to celebrate the tang of wild game and spices in his mouth, and his taste buds had a party. At this hour! His biltong stash for his guys was plentiful. Even Boesman gave it a very Western "thumbs up." He smiled, pleased he'd found another perk to being Major Curry's tentmate.

The hours between midnight and dawn were when Tokoloshe crept in. Tokoloshe and his reactivated Mind Brownie and New Aunts made for a turbulent five hours.

Zebra. That's what they were. It was true Papin's Zulu teachings were always present here in the bush and in the bustling city where he worked. But to stop his anger and hurt, he forced himself to remember the unusual wisdoms as his own. The thought of the real source left a hole in what was left of his heart.

*How many conversations did Dad have about Papin and me with the guests I didn't overhear? Together all the time—being called "Zebra" was surely the best of what our friendship was called. Messieurs Retief and Viljoen were likely just two of many disapproving, non-returning guests. But Dad never took it out on the two of them. He was a man of conviction.*

*I'm twenty-seven. When I grow up, I want to be just like him.*

His father was the only one allowed to know how to get word to him when he was on these army missions and then only with life-or-death news. They'd only call Dad once Lieut was patched up or dead.

His biltong was nearly finished, and as much as he tried to resist going back too far, the door was already open a crack, and the dreaded hour made him weak ...

*Drakensberg, 1957*

THAT FIRST STOLEN night away from boarding school they'd watched thousands of bats exit the cave together and turn left—their instinctive direction.

"They'll be back once they satisfy themselves. They can eat up to a thousand insects an hour," Papin stated.

"I wonder who counted," Jock said, and they collapsed with laughter at the absurdity of it all.

They told their own versions of the Bushman stories etched and painted onto the cave wall a millennium ago. The flickering firelight fueled their imaginations, and spectacular tales of starvation and plentitude, defeat and victory, sadness and celebration were acted out. When flames became embers, full stomachs and too much fun tugged mercilessly at Jock's eyelids. The last thing he remembered was watching the millions of stars lighting up the mouth of the cave and the moon shone down the hole in the cave ceiling.

They woke at first light as the bats came roaring home. Tripod was under Jock's blanket and Bonzo under Papin's. Immense excitement rumbled in Jock's belly. The first whole day of his life he was to spend with his Dad. And Papin.

This was, without doubt, the best day of his life.

Dad had made sure the dogs were lured away to the scullery for a treat so they wouldn't follow. That was odd.

The three of them emerged from the giant gum trees about two miles from the hotel into high tufts of lush grass. A stream trickled nearby. It wasn't a place he and Papin had visited before, and he wondered why.

"Inkosi? Are we going to the place where horses are not allowed?" Papin's eyes popped out with concern, but Dad just winked.

It was all very mysterious, and Dad carried a pellet gun, upping the ante to the moon.

Jock couldn't contain himself. "Where we going, Dad?"

"Well, Papin's chief told me they need some new skins for his clan to wear at ceremonies. So, we're going to find some rinkhals."

"Really?" Papin's voice was incredulous, his eyes fit to burst out of wide lids, voice thick with disbelief.

Jock had a whole beehive in his stomach as he asked, "What's rinhkals?"

"It's a type of cobra that spits," Dad answered. "They like this spot. Lots of long grass, a downward slope so they can quickly slither away and avoid being lunch for hawks and eagles. I've never met a mongoose who doesn't fancy rinkhals for a meal at any time of day. These snakes are shy, and like most others, they won't bother you if you leave them alone."

A million frogs croaked, and Jock thought of the Drakensberg Boys Choir warming up before they sang to the guests a few weeks before.

"When did you have time to come here, Dad?"

Dad smiled. "Nicholas brought me when we first got here, to show me where it was they dreaded they would find you when you ran away. When Papin saved you."

"Why haven't you brought us here before, Dad?"

"There's a time for everything. This is that time."

Dad pointed to the patch of marshland that bled into the stream. "This is a snake predator's smorgasbord. Never ever bring the horses or the dogs here. It's far too dangerous for them."

A cricket orchestra was in full swing across the ravine.

"How do crickets make such a loud noise when their mouths are so small?" Jock wondered aloud.

Dad was quick to answer. "Bottom of the cricket's wing is covered with little teeth-like ridges. Top of the wing's a kind of scraper, so when they rub upper and lower parts together, they make a chirping sound called 'stridulating,'" Dad said. "Papin, what do you know about crickets?"

"I know, Inkosi, that when you get close to crickets, they shut up. Therefore, if you are not the one close to the crickets, then something or someone else is."

Dad laughed. It was a sound that warmed Jock's heart to the core. Real laughter. Everything his dad did was real. Dad would make an excellent Zulu.

"You're wise, Papin," Dad said and patted Papin's back. "Jock, the moral of the story is: Listen to the animals. They will tell you as much as you need to know."

Jock glanced at Papin. He was actually glowing from Dad's

compliment.

"If these snakes bite us, will we die?" Jock asked.

"Consider all snakes lethal until you know for sure. Rinkhals are a double threat ..."

Dad stopped suddenly, looking down at a little two-inch hole. "See? That's a rodent hole, but there could be a mother and up to thirty-five baby snakes down there." Jock jumped three feet away. Papin and Dad chuckled, and Dad continued, "They eat the rats and take over their holes. Rinkhals don't lay eggs like other snakes. They give birth to live babies."

Now that was something to consider in the dead of night in bunk three of nine. Jock turned off his Mind Brownie.

Papin's eyes were big as he shook his head. "Double trouble to horses."

"Right again, Papin, *and* to man. Rinkhals can accurately spit about seven feet. They aim at the eyes and can blind you. They also have lethal front fangs, which in a split second can sink into flesh, injecting you with venom that attacks your nerves and can kill you. We leave the buggers strictly alone. Except today. Today, we're supplying the kraal with new skins and you boys will learn something."

"Chief forbids us to come here. Now I understand why," said Papin.

A few slow paces later, Dad carefully placed his feet one in front of the other, as if testing his stance. "Looks like a decent spot. We need to be at least twenty feet away from our target."

Papin copied Dad's stance, and Jock followed. Dad handed the gun to Papin. "Feel its weight. Know your weapon."

Papin lifted it up and down and handed it to Jock, who did the same, then passed it back. Jock had never seen a gun before. Dad pulled a pellet out of his pocket, showed them, then, as if he was breaking the gun like a branch on his shin, it opened magically. He popped in the pellet, and in a snap, the gun was ready to fire.

"Don't move. Dead quiet. We wait." Dad raised the gun and squinted down the barrel.

None of the three moved a muscle for ... three days? Maybe it was just three minutes when a grayish-brown snake slithered out from underneath a rock. Dad's mouth opened, and he made an odd sound with his tongue, clicking it against his palate.

In a flash, the rinkhals jerked to full height, half its body off the ground, hood spread wide. The white bands marking its upper body seemed to get bigger by the second. Its black eyes latched onto Dad, and it pulled its head back.

But before the snake could spit, Dad pulled the trigger. The rinkhals' head flashed to the left and then dropped to the ground. Dead.

"Eish, Inkosi!" exclaimed Papin, clapping his hands.

"Dad, you're a pot shot." Jock's chest burst with pride.

Calmly Dad walked, gun in hand, toward his kill. They were both behind him as he bent down to look at the dead snake. Dad used the pellet gun barrel to flip the rinkhals over and onto its back.

"See this? Looks dead, right?"

Jock and Papin nodded vigorously, and Jock scooted back a good few feet. They laughed, but Dad said, "My boy's a clown, but he's not a fool. It's okay. This one surely is dead. But these little buggers are expert at faking their death. They lie on their backs, mouths open, tongues out to fool their prey into coming close ... then *zap!* They sink their fangs into flesh, and the hunter becomes the hunted."

Jock had no words. He looked at his friend and saw his own amazement there. He looked at his dad, then the snake and back at his dad. He caught Papin doing the same.

Their idol stood tall and said, "Real test is if I can do it again," and strode back to their spot.

They took up their waiting positions and were silent once more. Not long and another rinkhals reared its head above a long wheat-and-sage-colored trail of wild grass.

Dad seemed casual this time, aiming haphazardly at the extended hood of the rinkhals. As the pellet ejected at high speed, the reptile's tongue flashed out, ready to spit venom into the eyes of its enemy, but then it dropped like a stone.

Dead as a doorknob.

On closer examination of the second kill, Jock was speechless, as was Papin. Dad's pellet had hit squarely between the snake's lethal jaws, and he'd made it look so easy.

Dad started with a chuckle, which morphed into the kind of laugh that eventually makes you cry. Jock looked at Papin, and his face reflected Jock's confusion.

They waited patiently till Dad's laughter dried up, and at last he said: "Oh, boys. I wish I was as good a shot as it looks."

They waited breathlessly until he explained: "You see, I don't really have to aim. This dead snake and the last has nothing to do with my skill but everything to do with the snake's speed."

Jock held his breath.

"The rinkhals's eyes are so keen and its movement so lightning-fast, it watches the flight of the pellet and catches it in its mouth, killing it instantly. Its sharp reflexes are its own worst enemy," Dad said.

"Inkosi, you are not a pot shot?" asked Papin, a smile teasing the corners of his mouth.

"No, Papin." Dad laughed. "But the rinkhals is!"

Jock and Papin squealed with delight.

"Perhaps there is a Zulu proverb here, Papin?"

After a few minutes of concentration, Papin said, "Do not be like the rinkhals. Do not kill yourself with your own speed before your enemy has a chance to kill you."

Dad's eyes got big with surprise, and he smiled proudly at Papin. "Excellent, Papin. You're as smart as a whip. We can't let that intelligence go to waste."

Jock had no idea what was going on, but what he did know is that he'd never see a look of pride on Dad's face because of Jock's clever words. He'd just have to find another way.

"Now it's your turn, Papin. Then yours, Jock."

They each killed a rinkhals with Dad's gun. As chuffed as he was, Jock candidly told Papin that if the rinkhals was a tin can on a log, he'd have missed it by a foot or three.

"I don't want you two to ever come back here. There'll be no more killing. Jock, pass the tin from my rucksack. Okay, boys, now you must learn how to save someone bitten by or spat at by rinkhals."

Later, Dad said, "Collect the snakes, boys. Papin, tell Chief of your fine skill and let him put these, who died to teach us, to good use. And if you've learned nothing else today, boys, learn that hanging around with Nicholas will teach you amazing things."

"Dad," Jock asked, "can you teach us how to kill something that won't catch the bullet?"

"Hell, no. We're not hunters."

On their return, a mile away from the hotel, just as they came out of the gum trees, Dad spotted a greater double collared sunbird. Sighting such a shy bird was a rare treat, and they walked slowly with heads up, mesmerized by feathers the color of emeralds and rubies as they caught the sun.

Suddenly, a loud cry cut through the white noise of the bush.

Dad! He'd tripped over a sharp boulder. Blood gushed from a six-inch-long gash in his calf. Papin rushed to him and held the skin together as Jock opened the first aid kit.

Dad shouted, "Jock, pass the gauze. Good. Papin will keep pressure on this wound. I need you to run and fetch honey."

Jock's seven-year-old legs ran at top speed to the hotel kitchen. Thabo gave him a pot of honey and he fled back, thrilled to be useful. See? He didn't need words to impress his dad!

Panting, he got back to the offending rock and presented the jar.

"Not this honey, you clown. PEELS honey. Back you go," said Dad.

Peels honey?

And Jock ran as fast as his legs could carry him a mile there and back again, clasping the jar of Peels.

Much as he'd healed Tripod with axle grease three years before, Dad slathered mounds of Peels onto his wound, and though they limped home and Dad sported a bandage for a bit, the wound healed perfectly. Peels honey got all the credit. That Papin had to listen to Dad asking why the hell it took his boy so long, and Jock had to speed four miles to provide it, was of no consequence.

"Not this honey, you clown. PEELS honey," said exactly like Dad, became Jock and Papin's private joke and proved to be the perfect answer to almost anything. And they'd laugh till their bellies hurt or they fell off the rock. Whichever came first.

# 20

# TOKOLOSHE

*Near the Angola Border, 1977, Same Day*

LIEUTENANT JOCK WALSH's chin hit the barrel of his rifle, and he jumped.

Where the hell *was* he?

Ah ... He'd allowed himself to slip into his and Papin's world again. Now he'd opened the portal, it was just far too easy. He'd forgotten his world was such a magical place, in spite of boarding school.

School was the beginning of the end.

Sadness ripped through his gut as he tore off another piece of biltong with his front teeth and let it dangle from his mouth like a cigarette. The sun promised to peep over the horizon any second. He looked over to Penti, sticking high out of Boesman's hole like a firecracker—already ignited and ready to shoot high into the air.

Lately, even when he was awake, his mind filled with a thousand thrills he and Papin got up to. A Technicolor recall of them working the fireworks at the hotel to bring in the new year with explosions of fragmented color against the mountains' night cloak. Guests' cheers and oohs and aahs as burned fingers and charred hands were doused in wild aloe and quickly slipped into the pockets of their shorts, lest they were banned from executing the spectacular show again when warm December rolled into hot January.

An hour later, searing dust swirled around the bent fenders of the Bedford, creating small pockets of gritty sand that whirled through the passenger window and out the other side like a mini-sandstorm. The grains stung like a bitch, then sneaked into his mouth so when he clamped his jaws, it felt like he trapped boulders between his molars. Lieut would've killed for a cold beer.

Based on the morning's intel from HQ, they made their way off course to a remote village thirty miles south of the Angola border, close to where a rogue cell of terrorists had been reported. Some of the Terrs, Lieut knew, would still be in the village, hiding in plain sight among the village innocents, who wanted nothing more than to be left to live their simple lives.

Tiny had taken the wheel so Cairns could catch some serious Zee's in the back. How he could sleep like a baby while moving through enemy territory was a mystery to the rest of them.

Tiny was so big, his bulk reached from the driver's side and infringed on Boesman's territory in the middle. It amused Lieut no end that when Tiny came too close, the agile brown foot tipped with earth-hardened nails would kick ever so gently but hard enough to make the bulk more aware of its boundaries.

Tiny was a walking contradiction. He wore his heart on his face. There was no question what he was feeling, and it was mostly confusion. With a body that could stop a train, his smile was a show of relief that he wasn't in trouble, his befuddlement disappeared for an instant before his waning smile tapered into an apology. But when the huge man did something right and he knew it, like driving the Bedford, he grinned like the Cheshire Cat.

They rounded a hill, and the native village came in sight. Tiny slammed on the brakes, and the boys in the back careened from back to front with the closest of them knocking their heads on the Perspex window separating front from back. There was hell to pay. Tiny was cursed upside down. He looked like he wanted to weep, but Lieut slapped him on the back before he could shed a tear.

"Don't worry, Tiny, the girls need to be shaken up now and then. Keeps them on their toes." Lieut was rewarded with a grin the size of Durban Harbor. "Let's go!" Lieut shouted through the Perspex window.

When they'd found the best spot for the Bedford while they stormed the camp, and were gathering around for instructions, Tiny lit up a Lexington.

Lieut felt anger rise in his chest like sea water at high tide as he grabbed the cigarette, nipped off the hot end and pushed the dead end a hair away from Tiny's nose as he growled, "No smoking. How will we surprise them so they won't hide the Terrs if they can smell us coming? These people don't have cigarettes or batteries or radios or rock and roll. They can hear and smell us coming from miles away without Lucky Strike in the wind. Do you think your rations are put together haphazardly? No, girls. You're eating and shitting what won't smell foreign to a local. It's the only way not to advertise scores of miles in advance that we're on our way. Lighting up a machine-rolled cigarette will give us away in two puffs. You better hope you only had one."

Tiny quivered with shame and looked so sad, but there was no time to pussyfoot. These boys had to learn on the job and quickly, otherwise they were all dead.

Lieut continued in his soft growl, "From now till we get there, only hand signals. Cairns, you stay with the truck, eyes open at all times. No pissing! No smoking! No sleeping! Watch us with binoculars. Once we're in, drive the truck close as you can to the action." Cairns saluted and hung back.

"Benny Bookworm, when we get there, you take your mine detector and go around the huts. We're looking for a cache of weapons and ammo. Terrs recruit locals to make up their numbers. Usually, three or four men per village are 'convinced' into conviction. Terr propaganda appeals to hungry people, and in a long drought, there are too many of them. They're promised they'll inherit the farms they've helped annihilate. Arms for new recruits are delivered and buried until the men are trained and ready to join their revolt, or they could just be using this village as a pickup point for arms as needed by the Terrs. Arms usually come in a wooden box. We've found them mostly covered in a blanket and buried. So, Benny, look for strategic points close to a tree or a landmark—something that easily identifies where the cache is buried so new recruits or those re-arming can find them easily."

Benny saluted.

"Penti, use the other detector. Go in the opposite direction to Benny. Don't start your machines until we start ours for the chief. Understood?" His men nodded.

"Frikkie and Piet-Tire—you both speak passable Ovambo. Piet, you're with me, Frikkie with Nev." The two were unduly sober as they lifted straight hands to their heads in smart salute.

The farther they were from civilization, the more unsophisticated the people. Some places were so remote, they'd never been exposed to Zulu or any language other than their own version of Ovambo.

Lieut continued: "Boesman will be combing the place for anything else suspicious." Boesman clicked away.

"Tiny, you're the usual. As the enforcer, be firm, but don't be cruel. You hear me?" A crisp salute and a face filled with apology.

"Charl, you load those we find suspicious onto the truck. And keep a constant eye on them."

Lieut continued, "Boys, don't expect to recognize the Terrs among the locals. They'll merge into the kraal as soon as we move in." Lieut paused to make sure they were all paying attention. With all eyes on him, he said, "Above all, remember this. The locals are a thousand times more terrified of the Terrs than they are of us." The faces around him were intense, and he felt the adrenaline charge and knew his men were experiencing the same. "You know the drill. We'll stick to the plan as best we can. Let's go!"

In spite of their stealth, the villagers were gathered together defensively in the kraal center by the time they arrived.

Lieut conferred with Piet, who shouted in Ovambo, "Who is your Chief?"

The crowd separated to reveal a lean elder whose eyes were fastened on Lieut's pistol. Lieut continued to address the chief in English, and Piet followed with a passable Ovambo interpretation.

"Who among you is a misfit, Chief?"

"No one is a misfit here," answered the chief, the right side of his mouth twitching just enough for that to be a lie.

Lieut shook his head. He hated resorting to this, but it was inevitable. "Understand, Chief, we will hurt your people until we get information."

"I see you, Ubasi." The chief spoke directly to Lieut, knowing where the orders were coming from. "But when you leave, *they* will hurt us more if we give you information." Piet interpreted.

"Ah Chief, but the ancestors speak to us. You shall see we have spirits that guide us, and Tokoloshe comes to deliver our messages." Piet looked at Lieut, scratched his head, then translated.

At the mention of Tokoloshe, faces filled with fear and villagers huddled closer to their chief for protection.

Chief pushed them aside and stood tall. "Tokoloshe has been here many times without success. Our mats are high off the ground so that furious little demon cannot reach to rape our women and eat our children."

"Chief," Lieut said as he closed the gap between the leader and himself, "if you don't tell us who the men with guns are, the Tokoloshe will!" He spread his arms like an enthusiastic preacher calling to a higher power as he turned around slowly, shouting, "Tokoloshe, Tokoloshe, Tokoloshe!"

Like a tidal wave ebbing, the villagers backed away, their intake of breath audible as terror rushed in. Some screamed. A few women fainted.

Lieut handed his military hunting knife to the chief. "I will walk over there and turn my back to you." Lieut pointed to a clearing. "Bury this knife so all can see—except me and my men. Then I will have Tokoloshe find the knife."

As Lieut and Piet strode toward the clearing where Cairns was parking the truck, Lieut imagined Tiny using the butt of his rifle to gently nudge the reluctant chief into burying the knife. Nobody in their right mind resisted Tiny, even when they held a sharp blade.

Piet, Cairns and Lieut made a great show of *not* looking at the chief's chosen burial site for the knife. Nev and his boys would have done the same.

Then Neville shouted, "Okay, Lieut. It's buried. See if Tokoloshe can find it."

Lieut grabbed the last MD42 mine detector off the truck and carried it in front of him as he shouted, "Tokoloshe is inside this thing. He is our prisoner, but even so, sometimes he hurts people more than we want him to." Piet's translation caused pandemonium as the crowd backed farther away, gaping at the piece of machinery so foreign in their world. Many quivered; some keened to summon their ancestors.

Lieut understood how frightening it must be for these people unfamiliar with such metal wonders.

Their Tokoloshe, born of age-old retold stories, was short, mean and came out at night. By their logic, how angry would the already mean little devil be in the daytime, when squashed into a thick metal dish at the bottom of a long metal stick?

Lieut flipped on the power switch, and a low buzzing noise emitted. The soft sound caused monumental havoc. People tried to flee this way and that but were corralled by Lieut's men. They huddled, quivering, and Lieut felt bad that they had to take advantage of these simple people. But then he thought of the farms, and his resolve was back in spades.

"Tokoloshe, find my knife!" Lieut shouted in Ovambo and swept the detector just above the ground, left to right, right to left and back again as he moved forward, past the chief. People wailed. Lieut stopped, switched off his machine and put his hand to his ear. Silence. They heard two dueling buzzing machines softly in the distance. "Hear that? We have captured two more Tokoloshes in case we need them. For now, they just hover and wait." Piet translated, and a woman fainted. A few women began walking into the bush. Tiny was immediately behind them, gun cocked. Within twenty yards of the crowd, they stood four feet apart and urinated, then followed by Tiny, they filled in the gaps of the villagers' huddle.

Lieut knew Tiny would be talking about women standing up to pee for a long, long time.

Lieut and Piet and the machine continued on, and just a few paces northeast, the detector started to beep. More sounds of fear from the crowd as Lieut swept this way and that.

When volume and intensity of the beeps increased to a frenzy, Piet dropped to his knees and began digging. Rich earth went flying, and when Piet pulled the knife out of the hole by the blade, it was done with flair. Piet tilted the knife this way and that for the metal to catch the sun. Who knew he was such a showman? Piet was usually the audience!

"TOKOLOSHE! TOKOLOSHE! TOKOLOSHE!" The crowd's wail could be heard at base camp, thought Lieut, and forced the guilt from his conscience.

Lieut switched off his detector, but the faint buzzing of the machines maneuvering around the huts could still be heard.

When the crowd was silent, Lieut nodded to Piet, who translated, "Your chief will be standing far away. I will be asking him questions about each of you. You will be asked the identical question by my man. If your story matches the chief's, then you will pass the test, the Tokoloshe will sleep, and you will be safe."

The silence was eerie. Lieut continued, and Piet interpreted. "But if you are lying"— the pause elevated the tension another notch—"then Tokoloshe will SHOUT, and we will take you prisoner."

Lieut handed the mine detector to Nev, and he and Piet flanked the chief as they walked about thirty meters from the crowd and out of earshot while Nev and Frikkie selected the first of the villagers.

"Chief, it is my regret that we must scare your people so, but you gave us no choice." Piet translated, and the leader looked down at his feet.

They stopped and turned around to look at the man standing between Nev and Frikkie.

"Can you see your man from here, Chief?"

Chief nodded.

"He will answer my men's questions softly and then we will

ask you the same question. Please speak loudly when you answer my question, Chief."

Once Nev gave a nod, Lieut asked and Piet translated, "That man with my men. Who is he and what is his purpose?"

"Kagumbo Amepanda. Ovambo. He's an elder. Once an adviser," the chief said loudly.

Frikkie's thumb went up.

Lieut shouted, "Let him go. Next!"

And so it went, until the chief said of the man standing with Nev and Frikkie, "He is Bunga Kutako. Herero. Hunter."

"Negative, Lieut," shouted Frikkie. "Says he's a herdsman."

"See what Tokoloshe thinks," Lieut shouted back, and immediately Nev silently "swept" the man with the detector in the 'off' position for a bit, then surreptitiously flipped the on switch. *Buzzzzz.*

"Bundle and sack," Lieut instructed.

"Tokoloshe says he needs to be interrogated at base," Piet explained loudly.

In an instant, the man sprinted toward the brush. Frikkie and Tiny downed him quickly, and once his hands were tied behind his back, they led him onto the back of the truck, which had the canvas sides open so Charl could guard all the captured prisoners while Cairns continued his field watch.

By the time they'd finished, two Herero and four Ovambo men sat in the back of the Bedford with burlap sand sacks over their heads. Lieut had to stop Frikkie from only half-emptying the sand bags before heads were covered. "Once more, Frikkie, and I will do it to you," Lieut said and meant it.

Frankly, most of the men back there were likely innocent, but he couldn't take the chance, just as he couldn't leave their heads uncovered. The heat was deplorable, but if they were Terrs, memorizing the way to HQ at Indongwa could mean the army's intelligence hub was compromised and would be blown to hell. Lieut made sure Tiny was the one in charge of keeping them hydrated. It took two worries from Lieut's mind. They'd shy away from trying to overcome Tiny, and Tiny could be trusted to be gentle.

En route, Lieut opened the Perspex window and yelled into the back, "Warning you boys. You frighten them anymore, and I'll ask Tiny to give *you* the sand sack. And if it's you, Frikkie, I'll throw a rinkhals in with the sand, just to show you how shit the world is when you're the victim."

# 21

# NATURAL MIRACLE OR DISASTER?

*Champagne Castle Hotel, 1960*

PAPIN HAD the wings of seven hawks on his heels as euphoria flew him to the stables to check on Beauty.

He'd just had a heart to heart with Inkosi. The chief of the hotel always made time for Papin, though it was limited to a half dozen minutes at best. But today Inkosi took precious moments to open up a whole new world for Papin, igniting his elation.

Up till now, higher learning with books advanced enough to challenge him, as well as teaching kids at the hotel school, was just a pipe dream—as far as those pipes dreamed up for aqueducts in ancient Rome from Tsotsi's history book. But starting in the new year, Papin would be taught how to teach the younger kids at the hotel school. And the teacher would allow Papin to study Standards seven and eight in the same year, to fast-track his own education. He was indeed the luckiest Zulu since the dawn of time.

Beauty added to his joy as he stroked her lovingly. Just eleven months before, Tsotsi's beloved horse became pregnant after her visit with Mr. Wright's stud, Brutus. A true thoroughbred and retired racehorse.

As Beauty's belly grew, Mr. Wright's vet came in to check her and declared she was bearing twins. He advised even though she carried two foals, there was the slimmest of slim chances both would be born alive.

Papin's heart had lurched, then burned. Living twins had never happened to his father or his father's father—both dedicated horsemen—in a century. But not even this wonderful horse could be expected to do the impossible.

The vet suggested Inkosi allow him to terminate one of the embryos to make the other stronger.

Papin sensed Inkosi was heavy with indecision when he caught him walking up and down the stable, deep in thought, for three nights in a row. On the fourth day, he saw a sight that brought his worlds together and made him dispel all the niggles Uncle had planted under Papin's skin about the great divide between white and black people of South Africa.

It was indeed a rare thing to see an educated white man and a Zulu medicine man throwing the bones together behind the chicken coop to determine the best course of maternal action for a horse.

He never told Tsotsi he'd seen this unique conferencing. It was Inkosi and Sangoma's tale to tell, and they never did. But Inkosi received his answer, because when Tsotsi came home from boarding school, Inkosi called them both into the stable.

"Look how Beauty's tummy is growing with her foal," Inkosi said, tenderness clutching at every few words.

Tsotsi's face split with glee as he hugged the neck of his beloved horse. "Yes, Dad. I bet it will be a colt. Can we call him Dennis?"

"Sure, we can. His mother will have no objection." Inkosi

smiled as he stroked Beauty and continued, "Mr. Wright's vet tells me she may be carrying twins."

"Oh, Dad, twins! Imagine. Papin and I can break them in together and ride them together. They need never be apart."

Papin's heart stopped for a couple of seconds. Oh! The disappointment that could follow.

"Whoa! Listen to me, Jock," said Inkosi as he leant down and looked deep into the eyes of his son. "The vet also told me the chances of her taking both foals to term is very slim. He reckons we should have him terminate one of them now."

"What does that mean?" Tsotsi asked.

"He thinks it's best to stop one of the eggs from growing early, before it becomes a foal, so the other one can grow properly."

"Oh, *no,* Dad," the boy pleaded, "don't do that. Give Beauty a chance. She'd never disappoint us. She'll have two foals just to please you. Imagine, you'll have *two* new horses for the guests. That's just how she is."

Papin used his eyes to plead with Inkosi ... *Please be cautious with our boy's Beauty.*

"Well, it's a risk. Make no mistake. We could hurt Beauty by making the decision to keep both embryos, and we don't want that. We don't want to deprive one foal so the other can flourish, either. But we can't see inside her tummy to see what's going on. She'll need more help than we can give her, even with Sponon and Papin's great knowledge. The vet bills will cost us a fortune ..." Papin could feel Inkosi's stress.

Tsotsi's face contorted with the dilemma as if it was his choice to determine.

"I've talked to some very knowledgeable people," Inkosi said, and Papin recalled the two men he admired most, conferring over the bones, "and I think we should see how she does. Be prepared. If she isn't doing well, we'll have to terminate the other foal no matter how many months along she might be. Beauty comes first."

Tsotsi jumped with joy. Papin felt like jumping too. Beauty was Inkosi's priority.

Just that morning, he'd been shining up the glasses in the bar storeroom while Tsotsi was with his mother in the gift shop, when a local farmer popped into the bar for a drink after an errand. Inkosi and Bekah were preparing for the pre-lunch rush.

Papin was hidden by the one-way mirror.

"You'll lose your guests, man. South Africans can't stand seeing black and white so close together. You know they all call your boy and that Zulu 'Zebra' because the black and white are on top of each other all the time," said the farmer, his tone forcing an argument.

Inkosi never even lifted his eyes from the tots of whiskey he was counting. He just said softly, "Ah, 'Zebra.' It's the black that makes the white shine brighter and the white that gives the black emphasis and depth. The collective noun for zebra is 'dazzle.'" Inkosi wrote down the number of tots remaining in the Johnny Walker bottle, then looked into the eyes of the farmer. "If their colors are too dazzling for you, sir, well ... just look away, or find a different bar to drink in."

Inkosi waited for a response. None came.

"So, what would be your pleasure? The usual?"

The farmer nodded. Papin marveled at his hero—Inkosi's composure and his quick response. Then it hit Papin. His boss's response was a sure sign of great practice. He would bet this topic came up more than he would ever know. He wouldn't tell Tsotsi. This was something a man kept to himself.

Papin was amused by Tsotsi's warped concept of time as far as Beauty was concerned. She certainly looked fit to burst very early. From her ninth month, the younger lived in fear he'd miss the birth while away at boarding school. Papin supposed an eleven-month pregnancy to a going-on-ten-year-old was longer than a shoelace of licorice to a sugar ant.

Every few weeks, the vet would appear and listen with his stethoscope to Beauty's heartbeat and try to locate any others. He heard one strong heartbeat consistently. The other, slight to begin with, became hard to find. Without fancy testing, which Inkosi did not want to put Beauty through nor could afford, two heartbeats were never conclusive throughout her pregnancy.

Papin spent many nights talking to Beauty while Tsotsi was at school, asking her to tell him if she needed him to talk to Inkosi. But she never talked back. Papin believed it was a good sign. She seemed calm.

In Beauty's seventh month, his school's teacher had leant Papin some of her own books on philosophy, which had pulled him away from his ancestors and into new worlds. He immediately made amends and begged the wise dead for Beauty's health and Tsotsi's presence at the birth. He couldn't afford any malice or resentment from up there at a time like this.

Papin prepared himself to take in every single second so he could reenact the mammoth event and share it a thousand times, as was their custom when the younger missed a happening. No experience in either of their lives had ever been more important.

As her eleventh month approached, Tsotsi tried every trick in the book to keep from going back to boarding school. Blotting paper under the tongue to make him faint before his mother drove him down the mountain didn't work, nor did pleading and begging. The boy only came home ever second weekend. His chances of catching the birth were so very slim.

Beauty's stable was lined with fresh hay and readied for her long before she needed it. Papin's young horse boy was excelling, and Papin was relieved of all the shit jobs. Literally.

Finally, it was time. Beauty started pacing on Thursday

night. Tsotsi was due home late Friday. Papin put in a request for a consultation with Sangoma. It wasn't a simple matter. No! Such a message could only be dispatched via the chief of the kraal, who sent an induna—one of his teenage sons—to find Sangoma and beg an audience.

When Sangoma came, it was only after breakfast on Friday.

"Please, Sangoma. Make her slow down. Tsotsi has lived for nothing but this moment. It dare not come sooner than he can get here. My storytelling skills are good but not as good as living this miracle. Even if the second foal is dead, one being born from the horse he loves so much—well, not even the greatest storyteller can make that come to life. Make the ancestors understand the importance of holding back for my young friend, please."

Sangoma quickly lapsed into ancestor-communication mode, and Papin swore the horse's agitation waned. Beauty allowed Papin to scratch her long nose for an hour.

Panic surged through Papin. What were the chances of one foal *and* Beauty staying healthy when she had to muster the stamina to eject a stillborn foal as well? His blood ran cold, and he shivered.

It was a rare opportunity to witness the birth of a foal, let alone the vague chance of twins, and a couple of local farmers and a host of excited guests began gathering outside the stable. Mr. Wright, the stud's owner, was among them. Five past eleven.

Jock would be coming up the S-bend in six hours.

Six long, long hours.

He couldn't quite remember what he'd promised the ancestors if they held back the birth. He thought it might include that he and Tsotsi stop stealing peaches. He'd try and renegotiate after the birth.

Two hours later, peaches were the least of what he'd pay for Beauty's safety and just one healthy foal. And if they would—in their most esteemed wisdom—allow Beauty to wait until Tsotsi was there to deliver the live foal ... well, he'd go without sitting on their rock for a whole two months. It would be torture, but he would endure it.

The expensive vet arrived with gloves up to his shoulder and a box of tricks at 12:05 p.m. Papin couldn't help but feel resentment. This white man, a vet, on his turf. Who could know more about horses than Papin's father, Sponon, and himself? The white ways were sometimes a mystery, but he conceded the more attention Beauty had, the better for her.

Beauty became excessively agitated.

He couldn't help himself. "Sir?" Unable to make himself say "doctor," Papin pleaded. "Please help Beauty hang on for as long as she can so her young master can witness this birth."

"You're a horse boy. You should know better. The mare is what matters. She is already being pushed close to the edge of her endurance. There is no way we will give her more distress by delaying the process." The vet's tone was harsh.

Papin hung his head and felt shame burn his face. His love for Tsotsi had prompted an asinine question in front of a man he felt he had no use for.

His face kept aflame as shame turned to anger when the vet pushed and prodded at Beauty's bulging, sweating belly more than Papin felt necessary. *He's forcing this to happen sooner than it should. Let nature take her course.*

He glanced at the stable clock designed to keep the morning and afternoon guest rides on strict schedules.

Twenty-eight minutes past twelve. Time went by so slowly, and if that man pushed on Beauty's bulging stomach once more ...

Beauty was restless. She lay down, and her urine and manure seeped out without warning. Good training for his young horse boy.

1:02 p.m. *No! No! No! Beauty, get up!*

*Good girl!*

And then, at one forty-one, she was down again for a while. Up and down, up and down.

The animal doctor grinned when Inkosi's head appeared above the stall door. "She's getting ready," said the vet, like he was entirely responsible.

"Any inkling as to whether we have one or two live ones inside there?" asked Inkosi.

"There's a hell of a lot of movement in there, but I only hear one heartbeat. It's highly unlikely the other one will make it. I hope your son's not disappointed."

"He'll just be glad Beauty's safe. One foal would be a bonus," said Inkosi.

Beauty's tummy was stretched and looked fit to burst. She lay down and stayed there, and it was obvious her stomach was contracting in birth preparation.

It was 2:55 p.m. *Just two more hours, Beauty. Wait for him, please, girl, please.* He didn't care that the vet gave him a filthy look when he moved to her head. Beauty needed him. He'd glanced at Inkosi, who nodded ever so slightly as he smiled, so Papin sat on the hay next to her.

He whispered horse love words and stroked her wet neck. "Wait for him, Beauty," Papin whispered. "He needs to see your baby born. But please, don't wait if it will hurt you. Nobody wants you to hurt yourself. Tsotsi will understand if you have to push your only living baby out. It must be tight in there."

She got up again, and Papin thanked her profusely and concentrated hard to offer up humble thanks to the ancestors.

By four fifteen, she was down again, and her contractions were closer and closer together. As much as he wanted to, Papin could no longer wish waiting upon her. She needed to do what she needed to do to stop the stress on her body. "It's okay, girl.

Let it come. Tsotsi will understand. Let it come, Beauty. It's all right."

And she did. With a great push, a whitish membrane peeped from her rear.

"Here it comes," said the vet excitedly, as if he was doing the pushing.

Though many heads gazed over the stable half door, it was quiet as the mountains before a storm.

Instinct forced Papin on his haunches to leap to where the baby was pushing to get out, but his own father's warning stare from the corner of the stable stopped him in his tracks.

The vet pulled slowly and firmly on the protruding hoofs, and a pair of front knees emerged, protecting a head between them. Vet was quick to break the membrane, and the face of a beautiful brown foal emerged. After a few seconds, its nose lifted, and it took its first breath.

As the gasps from above the stable door subsided, Papin glanced at the clock. Fourteen minutes past five. *Gollaga-inja*. He'd posted one of the youngsters where Mrs. Inkosi parked her car. He was to run Tsotsi back to the stables without delay.

And then the rest of the foal slid out, swaddled in nature's slick coating.

"A colt," whispered the vet loudly as he broke open the membrane covering the rest of the foal.

Though Papin felt he could have done the job without the expensive price tag, he had to admit the guy was very thorough in his checking to see every inch of the young horse was in good shape, and then he concentrated his instruments on Beauty.

"He's a handsome devil," Inkosi said quietly to Sponon from behind the stall door, and Mr. Wright joined him. Papin grinned when he caught his father and his boss's eye.

Just then, Inkosi's face changed to sadness. "Wish to goodness that little bugger could have witnessed this," he said, and Papin felt just the same. If only.

Papin was in fact getting a little annoyed at the ancestors because it wouldn't be kind to let Tsotsi witness a dead foal rejected from its mother's body. He contemplated asking them to reverse his request for a time delay.

"We must see the dead foal before the placenta, otherwise Mama's in trouble," the vet warned quietly as he massaged Beauty's belly.

Beauty began her contractions again, and it scared them all, even Papin's horse-sure father and the vet. Her spasms were violent, as if she was really pushing to rid herself of that which her body had no use for. Papin really started to beg. "Please look after Beauty. Please, please look after Beauty. I'll do anything."

And he was just thinking about more sacrifices he could offer up when the newborn colt suddenly struggled to his wobbly feet. It was a breathtaking moment marred only by Tsotsi not being able to see it. But his legs quickly folded, and he went down, looking confused.

Beauty was resting before her next bout of pushes. She was the most obliging horse. She wanted them all to enjoy her colt before she once more needed their attention.

The colt gamely tried to stand on his spindly legs. Nearly ... nearly ... and another huge effort, and he was standing.

Papin was torn between the colt's first steps and Beauty's distress, which had restarted.

"Go to him, Papin." It was Inkosi's voice. He couldn't believe he was allowed the privilege.

Next to the colt, Papin made soft clicking noises. The little one looked vaguely in his direction. Papin felt a deep sense of love for this newborn as he stroked the long nose before the young legs collapsed again.

"Papin!"

The shout was Tsotsi's from a distance. He wanted to shout back but didn't want to upset the newborn, but Inkosi did it for him. "In here, Jock, quickly."

Inkosi opened the stall for his son, who looked at the colt. A beam as big as the moon in its first quarter spread across his face. "Beauty," he said quietly, "your baby is tall and strong." He gently stroked the foal, then at once went to sit next to Beauty's head. He kissed the side of her nose. "You did it, my girl. You're so clever."

Papin felt his heart contract as he watched boy and horse together.

"Papin? Where's the other one?" Tsotsi asked.

Papin was lost for words. He shook his head and shrugged his shoulders at the same time, and the vet said, "We don't know yet, son." He spoke softly, as they all did, to keep a calm environment for the birth. "She's contracting again, but I don't know if it's a stillborn or just a placenta."

"Oh, my Beauty, don't feel bad. It's okay. You did your best. You tried your hardest. We know. One is perfect. One is perfect," Tsotsi said as he stroked and soothed the horse.

Papin allowed himself a moment of pride, like a father witnessing an act of kindness performed by his child.

Papin moved to Beauty's udder and expressed her milk into a waiting bowl. He filled a syringe and handed it to Tsotsi, then Papin coaxed the foal closer to his mother's head. "You feed him. He's thirsty after his big push. He tried waiting for you," Papin said and smiled.

Tsotsi gently forced the tip of the syringe between the colt's tightly clamped gums.

"Okay, here comes something," said the vet.

Fear gripped Papin. Tsotsi should not see what was coming.

"You look after him, Tsotsi. Watch him. He is so precious," and as he spoke, Papin positioned his own body to shield Tsotsi's view so the boy would be able to concentrate on the new, vital foal.

Papin and his heavy heart watched for the release of the dead one, all the while stroking Beauty's neck, her nose, whispering to her.

The hooves in their yellowish membrane were forced out ... and then out came the head, protected between the knees.

The vet tore open the sheath, and they all held their breath in hope, but there was no sign of life.

Papin urged softly: "Keep feeding the colt, Tsotsi. Watch him carefully."

And then, the newest foal moved its head—just a fraction.

Papin felt a surge of hope but then dismissed it. It could have been a nudge from his mother's leg.

Then it happened again. A small gulp of air. It was so unexpected. So contrary to all odds, both the vet and Papin jumped, and in a split second, the vet went to check the foal's vitals as Papin moved out of the way for Tsotsi to get closer to the newborn. "Come quickly. It's breathing," Papin whispered to Tsotsi.

In a flash, the younger was next to the newest foal. "Look, Tsotsi, look. See how it moves its head. This is his third breath."

Papin went to the colt who needed attention and quickly gave the newborn another syringe of his mother's milk and made horse words that would encourage Beauty. He glanced up to the stable rafters. "Please do not let it die now, not after you've given the young one hope." And as if on cue, the rest of the thin body plopped out of its mother's womb.

The vet handed Papin another syringe, and he filled it and passed it to Tsotsi before he returned to nursing the colt.

"So weak." The vet shook his head.

*Please don't let it die. Please don't let it die.* The words helped keep Papin's panic hidden from his young friend.

He knew what was happening purely by Tsotsi's expressions. He wished he could be in two places at once, but the vet showed the younger how to gently feed the weak foal. The vet was right. Feeding might save it.

The vet pulled the rest of the membrane off the new foal's hindquarters, and he glanced at Papin, who joined him to help move the new one out of the way so Beauty could expel her placenta. It plopped out a minute later, just missing the hind legs of the weak one.

"He's a she," shouted Tsotsi, and all sorts of happy sounds came from the other side of the stall.

Papin looked to see how Beauty was doing. She was standing and her colt happily nursing. His heart was fit to explode.

"Beauty's doing exceptionally well," said the vet, glancing up at Inkosi, then to Papin. "We must get this baby girl up quickly. Standing will help her gain strength. Let's get her legs moving."

Vet took the front legs and Papin the hind ones, and they gently helped loosen her limbs. Papin started to beg again: *Please don't let her be lame. Please don't let her be lame ...*

Folding. Unfolding. Folding. Then, as they watched the weak one's ribs move up and down in short staccato breaths, miraculously the long legs began moving on their own.

Tsotsi's face was glowing with joy.

"Give her as much milk as she'll take, Tsotsi," Papin instructed.

Halfway through that vial of milk, the vet gestured to Papin, and they helped the young horse to her feet and held her there even though her legs were wobbly, then gently let her down.

"Let's give her a minute. Let's see if she'll try on her own. If she does, we'll know she'll survive."

One could hear a piece of straw rustle in the tense silence. Tsotsi ever so gently nuzzled her neck and stroked her long nose, but Papin motioned for him to let her be.

The first time she tried, she was just too weak. Papin could see Tsotsi ache to help her.

She tried again, then miraculously stood up for a second or two, long enough for all to see she could, before she flopped back down.

The now large audience hanging over Beauty's stall cheered and hooted.

Mr. Wright received pats on his back on behalf of his own clever stud, Brutus.

Beauty rose to the applause and nuzzled her firstborn, who was still standing.

The wobbly filly tried gamely to stand again and succeeded! Papin helped Tsotsi guide her toward her mother.

Papin felt his heart go soft as he watched the boy's gentleness, and gratitude coursed through his body. He'd deal with all he'd promised the ancestors later.

Tsotsi's face was filled with light and love as he said, "Look, Papin. She has a white arrow starting at her forehead, going all the way down between her eyes."

Sure enough, it was the only white part on her delicate but perfect brown body.

After mother and babies received shots from the vet and the elated crowd moved to the veranda, cigars and whiskey were called for in celebration of The Champagne Castle Miracle.

Only Inkosi, Tsotsi, Papin and his father, Sponon, remained with the horses.

"Jock, there is only one colt," Inkosi said. "I know you've had a name for him for some time. Remind me again?"

"Dennis, like Dennis the Menace in the Sunday comics." Tsotsi paused, then tilted his head. "Do you mean I can really have one of them, Dad? For my very own?" It was the first time the boy had glanced up from tending the weak foal. A true doting father. Papin's heart smiled first, then his mouth followed.

"Yes. Of course. He will stay here, and yes, sometimes the guests may have to ride him, but he is yours to worry about, love, take care of, and break in."

"Gee, Dad. You don't think Beauty would be upset?"

"By the time the young one is old enough to be ridden, she'll be relieved to have some peace from you riding her." Inkosi looked tenderly at his son.

"Can this one be mine, please, Dad?" he asked, stroking the skinny neck of the weak filly.

"And her name?" Inkosi asked.

"Same. Dennis," Tsotsi said matter-of-factly.

"But that's not a girl's name." Inkosi smiled.

"It's *my* girl's name," said Tsotsi. "Dennis." He was pleased with the sound.

"And your horse's name, Papin?" Inkosi asked him.

"I don't have a horse, Inkosi." He felt he should apologize for some reason.

"You got one this morning, Papin. A colt."

Papin's world stopped for a long second as the enormity of this gift penetrated his brain.

He felt his finger point to his own chest as he gazed in earnest at Inkosi, lest he'd misheard.

"What is your new colt's name, Papin?" Inkosi asked again, smiling.

He thought he was dreaming. A horse to call his own? Inkosi was giving him the exact same gift as he gave to his only son.

"Oh, Inkosi." He was struggling with getting words out. "Shaka. Shaka is the name of a king."

"And so," Inkosi said, his smile as broad as Papin had ever seen it, "World, may I present to you Shaka and Dennis. These boys will be responsible for looking after their own two natural wonders of the world. They pledge to groom them and break them, feed them, and most of all love them, and if they don't look after them, I shall take them back. Right, boys?" He looked at them both, and he watched Tsotsi's vigorous nod mirror his own.

It was the second time in Papin's life he'd cried. His first tears were caused by pain and loneliness in a self-made hut with the heads of army ants clamped on his penis. This time the tears came with overwhelming surprise, humility, deep gratitude and the unbridled joy of ownership. It was the first anything Papin had ever owned.

Because of his promise not to sit on the rock for two months, he and Tsotsi spent most of their time together with their new horses in the stable or out in the field.

Uncle came to visit from the city for a night, and Papin found an empty bed in the compound to avoid the kraal. His heart was thick with gratitude for this life. *His life.* He didn't want to be plagued by unsettling things in a fractured world he'd never seen. He would not think about hungry people without sanitation being exploited by greed. He would not dream of innocents being shot for simply asking for fair treatment. He covered his ears to shield them from Uncle's forceful way of making him feel he could one day make a difference on behalf of a nation.

He would block it all out because he had his best friend Tsotsi. His Hotel-Inkosi. And now his horse, Shaka.

He forced himself to consider his uncle a slow-creeping sac spider, appearing mostly at night with two pairs of legs going forward and two pairs going backward. When he sank his spider-fangs into you, it didn't hurt much and you'd no idea you'd been poisoned. Next morning, you'd see the bite marks. A day later a half-inch lesion would swell and ulcerate for four weeks. Unbearable pain and an oozing, ulcerating wound might eventually ease in a month, but the scar could remain for ten or more years.

How long had Uncle-Sac-Spider's deep bite been festering in

Papin's bloodstream? It would take a decade for his damaged tissue to heal.

As much as he knew every creature on earth had a purpose, he mentally positioned his fighting stick tip above the spider's black head and brought it down hard. He ground his imaginary stick into the split spider-head to ensure its demise, then turned away as eight randomly moving legs took their last ungainly step to nowhere.

# 22

# SIPHO, LUNCH AND BILLY PILLAY

*Estcourt School days, 1960-1962*

BOARDING SCHOOL, dormitory, playground, and classroom took on a repetitive daily grind that somehow pushed Jock through until he could have slap chips on Tuesdays and get home to Papin, Beauty and Dennis every second Friday.

Jock lived for Papin's letters. He could see Papin buying stamps from his mom in the shop that hid his closet bedroom, sitting in the stable after working out the twins, writing in his cursive handwriting, even better than Scotty's. It was Papin who always deserved to be at this "real" school, not he.

By the time the letters arrived, the news was old, but it was new to him, and it was the minuscule moments Papin captured that fueled Jock's Mind Brownie and New Aunts. The letters were his treasures, his Bushman Cave of familiar delights, a vivid movie of hotel happenings. Imagine making pictures with words! And in ENGLISH! Dad was right about Papin.

Ultimately, Papin's letters forced Jock to learn to read far quicker than Daddy Longlegs Dunn could. But he was fine with her taking all the credit for his improvement. Jock would copy a word or passage from the letter he couldn't decipher, then ask Scotty to interpret. He'd feel disloyal if he let Scotty read the whole letter to him. He couldn't let someone else into their world without Papin's permission.

He cherished those letters encased in neatly printed envelopes as much as the Afrikaans boys cherished their Bibles. The only difference was, Jock couldn't leave the letters next to his bed. He envied the Bible boys that privilege. He made sure to hide the treasures well back in his locker, the only private place in the entire boarding school. They grew to so many, he had to bring in a grown man's shoebox to hold them all. He couldn't take them home because they were at the boarding school to take *him* home. Papin's letters and his Mind Brownie made most things bearable.

In a very short time at school, Jock realized how differently native Africans were treated outside the hotel's environment. It was they who cleaned and washed and cooked and gardened, in and around school and the boarding school. But like ghosts, they were rarely sighted and quickly disappeared. The few times he saw an African on premises, he was thrilled and greeted them joyfully in Zulu. But they refused to make eye contact with him, let alone shout back the jaunty reply he was used to. He felt quite hurt and then realized Zulu or any other Bantu language was never heard on either boarding school or school premises.

But finding Sipho kept his Zulu sharp and his longing dull.

He met Sipho the day he was brought back to the boarding school after his first and only illegal escape.

As Jock crossed the big dining hall, he heard a soft, familiar song. He thought his Mind Brownie camera must be working overtime. Strains of a Zulu lullaby felt like cotton-wool dusting his ears, and the powerful pain in his chest he recognized as homesickness eased a smidgeon. The song continued softly and he was frantic to find the source.

In the game room, a wizened old Zulu in a trance mopped the floors, eyes closed as he sang. It was Constance who first sang the song to Jock in the hot hotel laundry, and he'd heard it many times since around the kraal, as mothers nursed or urged their young to sleep.

Jock's heart and his voice moved as one as he began to sing along.

He was home.

The old man's face changed from dreamy to afraid, and his baritone stopped abruptly.

"*Umfana.*" The old man addressed Jock as 'boy' and continued in Zulu, "How is it you speak Zulu?"

Jock smiled and answered respectfully, "My best friend is Zulu, Induna."

The old man's face was grave as he turned away. "Why do you taunt me? Let me be."

Jock was shocked at the man's reaction and rushed to assure him, "Induna, I am true. This white boy has one black friend who lives in the mountains with me, before this ... place. His name is Papin. He teaches me all things Zulu."

"Eish. It cannot be. It is not the way of the world." The old man shook his head back and forth, back and forth, refusing to meet Jock's eyes.

Jock stepped closer and held out his hand to shake. The man looked down and up again.

"Let me show you," said Jock, his hand still out-stretched.

The old man reluctantly put out his right hand, and Jock's right guided the elder's stiff one. Never taking his eyes off the man, Jock led the way, shaking like Westerners, then he folded his fingers around the old man's thumb and urged him to do the same. The induna's hand was at last less resistant, and Jock manipulated his hand back into another Western-style handshake. Jock was rewarded with a glorious, mostly toothless smile.

The old man extracted his hand hurriedly. "But a White-Zulu is not the way of the world, Umfana." His face fell into disappointment.

"It is the way of *my* world, Induna," Jock assured him.

"I have never in my many, many new moons on this bountiful earth known of such a thing," the old man said.

"What is your name, Induna? I am Tsotsi."

The old man's laugh was music to Jock's ears. "Tsotsi. That's not a good name unless it's said in kindness. I am Sipho." The old man smiled.

Footsteps on the creaky wooden floor threatened to come too close, and Sipho dipped his head to the floor and gripped the mop, his body catapult-tight.

Jock went to the door and looked out. "There is no one there. Why are you so frightened to speak your beautiful Zulu?" Jock asked.

"We are not to speak our African languages in front of the children. Only English and Afrikaans if we wish to keep jobs in towns and cities," said Sipho. "Now go, young white Zulu, and don't let anyone see you speak to me again. I am as invisible as the ancestors."

"But I hope not invisible like Tokoloshe," Jock said playfully and was rewarded with another smile.

He sought out Sipho again, and with Jock's nudge, they did the African handshake. But when Jock lingered to talk a while, the man's fear gathered like a thick rain cloud above them in the broom closet.

"What makes you so afraid, Sipho?"

"I am afraid of losing my job. I can take a beating or abuse, though not as well as I once could, but if I lose my job, those I support will suffer. Tsotsi, there are many who need a job as much as me. I am old, but I must be best, otherwise a younger man will take my place. And I am afraid for you too, Tsotsi, if you are caught being friend to me."

"But Sipho, I long for Zulu. What harm is there for us to speak—" he began, but Sipho interrupted, his face so stern, Jock backed away as if Sipho was physically pushing him out of the tiny closet.

"Yes, Zulu-Papin is your best friend. I hear you, Tsotsi. But hear me. This is not a place where you talk of this Zulu friend. This is your secret you share only with me. If the Afrikaners find out of your unusual friendship, they will show no mercy to your white self. They will taunt you and they will hurt you and they will call you names and they will piss on you and you will end up hating your Zulu-Papin because you were hurt in his name."

The shock of this information took Jock's breath away.

"But Sipho, it is not so in the mountains. It is my father who arranged this friendship."

"Then your father is one white man in three million others. Listen to me, Tsotsi. I am old, and I am very, very wise. Promise me on the ancestors of Papin, Zulu will stay in this broom cupboard." The old man's voice had a catch in it, and his eyes were wet.

AND SO SIPHO became Jock's necessary secret and vice versa. They shared African stories, and Jock learned some Xhosa because that was Sipho's given tongue. Just as English was an international language, Zulu was the tongue universally spoken and understood by most all the Southern African tribes.

Every time Jock went home, he'd ask for the employer discount at the hotel and buy Sipho something to bring back to the boarding school. The first year at boarding school, Jock used his Christmas money to buy Sipho a pair of white *takkies*.

Sipho wore the white lace-up tennis shoes with immense pride. They were a little big, but Jock's new old friend didn't mind. When at times Jock couldn't find Sipho and loneliness gnawed, he'd resort to reading Papin's letters twice a day just to get by.

Daddy Longlegs Dunn was a good old stick and really worked hard at getting Jock up to speed academically so he could be just another student. It took nearly a year of daily grind for two hours after school to catch up on all subjects—well, all except spelling. That was a lost cause with its exceptions, which seemed to exceed its rules. He'd rather learn geography.

Writing was another story. It was never neat enough, and thousands of lines of "I must learn to writer neater ... I must learn to write neater" failed to make any of his teachers' dreams a reality.

And when composition and—heaven forbid—essays became part of the daily grind, his teachers had no appreciation whatsoever for his very concise bullet points.

Fortunately, he had no need for pens or books to absorb and store the information he was interested in, and he knew more about earth science than his teacher. He was really good at geography, arithmetic and math, so he bartered his assets for those he desperately needed.

Mr. Tomes remained housemaster, and Jock continued all too often to be on the receiving end of his liberal corporal punishment. But Sir's cuts were nothing compared with that of a woman!

Jock discovered the headmistress had her own brand of punishment he had to endure during school hours. He'd never imagined a woman wielding a cane—and with such force!

Her sjambok hurt in a different way—a white-hot sword searing his bum with a thicker branding than Tomes's.

Jock recognized he was a practical person, and he hated fuss of any sort. So instead of waiting to be told by his teachers that he was to get cuts because he failed a spelling test or his performance was poor, he decided reporting directly to the principal cut down on the fuss.

"Mr. Walsh." Headmistress Emsley looked up over her reading glasses the first time he cut out the middle man. "Who sent you?"

"No one, Miss. I came on my own."

"What can I do for you, young man?"

"I came for cuts, Miss."

"If nobody sent you, why on earth are you coming for cuts?" she asked, glasses slipping farther south of her intelligent eyes.

"We have a spelling test today. I will fail. So best I get cuts now and get it over with."

Without waiting for her answer, he bent down.

"I'll give you one for your anticipated failed test and another for not trying," said the headmistress.

From his bent-over position, Jock said, "But, Miss, I hate spelling and will never do better because there are much more important things to remember. Even though I can't spell, everyone understands what I say. The way I spell words are the way I say them, and they make a lot more sense than those exceptions and stuff."

She must have known he believed his explanation with all his heart because she didn't add another cut for him being cheeky.

She gave him two on the rump and a note, which Scotty read secretly to Jock before he handed it over to the teacher. Scotty's three-note laugh-hiccups were almost worth the punishment. It said: "Jock Walsh has already had cuts for the test he likely would have failed. Make him do the test anyway." And then her fancy signature.

Jock swore his bum had The Sword seared in it by the time he was nine.

It seemed he had earned enough credibility on his very first day at the boarding school to let Boet Buis know he wouldn't be easily bullied. English and Afrikaans kids avoided each other like the plague in the boarding school playground and had little integration at school because they had separate classes taught in their own language. Most day students were English, and they lived in or close to town. Their parents were professionals—doctors, nurses, hairdressers, shopkeepers, bookkeepers, hotel owners and lawyers. The Afrikaners were mostly sons and daughters of farmers who lived too far away to be fetched and carried to school daily, like Jock and Scotty and another handful of English boys. That's why they were cooped up in boarding school.

Miss Emsley took no prisoners, and all were afraid of her mighty sword, so fighting was not an option between factions, even if it was sorely longed for, and there was always *kleilat* fighting.

A long thin branch of a wattle tree with lots of bend was the instrument of choice. There were parts of the boarding school grounds where wet clay was always found, far enough away not to be seen by Tomes. They would squash a palmful of clay into a ball and push it onto the end of the branch, pull the branch over their shoulder to maximize the thrust, then whip it forward, releasing the clay.

Though the numbers heavily favored the English at school, had they gone head-to-head with the Afrikaners, their odds of winning a kleilat fight would be dismally low. The Afrikaners were mostly sturdy giants of Dutch and German heritage with necks as thick as Scotty's thighs.

Scotty and Jock became friends. The nut farmer's son was easy to be around, his laugh was contagious, and they had a pact.

Scotty positioned himself behind Jock in English class for their purpose. He was an ace at the dreaded English. When Jock was called upon to read out loud in class, instead of being laughed at, he would rise and soundlessly mouth the words while Scotty read aloud behind him, using a lower register than his own voice. Scotty's ventriloquism could have earned him a spot as the Saturday night hotel entertainment. He was that good.

His fine reading skills were successfully traded for math homework Jock could do for Scotty in a flash.

The perfect arrangement. For six months. Then the common cold blew their ruse to bits. Jock sneezed loud enough to get Tripod excited thirty miles away... and Scotty kept reading.

He made his acquaintance with The Sword once more, but this time four cuts were in order and an extra whip for being a bad influence on his schoolmate.

Jock's teeth clamped down so hard on the end of his thumb to stop from crying out, he wore a navy-blue thumbnail much longer than the bum welts took to disappear. Luckily, Scotty only got two cuts for a first offense.

Scotty handled the ordeal poorly, because prior to his association with Jock, he'd never met a sjambok up close and personally, not even on the nut farm.

Jock was astounded by this. What a glorious world without consequences! Scotty assured him that skulking under the radar was equally painful because nobody recognized you when you did well either. Jock pondered that and figured just like science, for every action in life, there must be an equal and opposite reaction.

Leaving Emsley's office, Jock shielded Scotty from anyone

who might see his wet, red face. He felt like shit that he was the cause of Scotty's pain. Jock whisked him off to his favorite oak tree.

Jock felt in his pocket for his four favorite marbles and handed them over to a delighted Scotty, who stood on one foot and then another for twenty minutes in the shade. Lucky it was break. Later, to further heal the pain and ease his own conscience, Jock gave his friend a coveted cricket bat signed by a Springbok player who'd stayed at the hotel.

"I'll take cuts tomorrow if you have anything else *this* worthy," said Scotty, who remained standing for one and a half days and slept on his stomach without a covering for two nights.

The class went back to laughing at Jock struggling to read. He learned to live with it. He even played it up so the other kids thought he was a comedian with a dry sense of humor. His teacher did not, and he visited Miss Emsley more frequently.

Scotty and Jock traded school lessons over games of marbles in the boarding school playground, and the two practiced kleilat throwing, a favorite with the Boers and the only outlet the two factions had for their inherited (and not altogether understood) need for war.

Scotty's accuracy improved, and together they trained the other English boys so when kleilat fights were called for, the English were a bit more effective. But as hard as they tried to recruit a solid side at the boarding school, the English were always outnumbered three to one. Though the unspoken rule was to aim where clothes would cover any damage, when those little balls of clay hit, you knew it. Most participants sported dark bruises after a heated match, and that nobody lost an eye was a small miracle.

But better than slap chips, better than Scotty, was Sipho.

When every Monday morning Jock awoke to the obnoxious clanging of the bell, his stomach dropped. Another day without

Papin. Without Beauty. Without Tripod. Without mountains. Without Dad. He would ache as if he'd been punched by Boet—he had no other standard of punch—on the left side of his chest, and he knew what he had to do.

He'd make his bed and place his "ablution instruments" just so for Sir's inspection; polish shoes to shiny; race to be first in for the shower; and merely get wet under the dribble of the usually cold water.

All this haste to give him precious time before breakfast to dash downstairs and find Sipho, who was usually preparing for his day of cleaning.

Early on, the old man had asked, "Why is it you find me early two times between full moons, my son?'

"Because, Sipho, you make me feel closer to home. The first Monday after a home weekend is the worst. I miss Papin. But I find you, and my heart is easier. But on the second Monday, I know I will see him on Friday."

"Ah, it is difficult, Tsotsi," the man nodded, his expression sad and empathetic.

"I miss ..."

"Shh, shh. I know, son. Missing makes the heart very, very soft. I miss my family in Transkei. But I must work to feed my daughter and her young ones."

"But Sipho, it seems to me you need to be like the old men of the kraal. Wise and fat, sitting on the stoep, smoking, talking, laughing and watching the women work. Sometimes I wish my father was Zulu so he could relax and enjoy life and not work so hard. You work too hard, Sipho."

"My son, I have worked at this school since I was twelve, going home to Transkei only on holidays. First to marry and plant seed for a child. Then to see how much she grew in a year, every year. Now my wife is with ancestors. My child has children of her own, and her husband is a *real* tsotsi—not a Tsotsi like you—so I must make sure my daughter and her children eat."

"They are unfortunate. They cannot see you almost every day as I can," said Jock.

The old man smiled, and his face crinkled. "But it seems to me your white father has no time to enjoy you or your mother. So you see, my son, no matter what color we are, we all have to do what we all have to do. Only the doing is different."

The chatter of boys and girls bounding into the dining room changed Sipho's face to a worried wrinkle, and he whispered urgently, "*Go,* Tsotsi!"

Something to hope for, besides Papin's letters, was that Dad would have time to pick Jock up from the boarding school and take him for a Coke when he came to town to collect the liquor that came off the train. Sometimes he did. Sometimes he didn't. But hoping so made the days shorter.

They'd sit at one of the two tables at the Estcourt Café, and though it was early afternoon, Dad's plate would be laden with a beef pie and slap chips, all smothered in thick brown gravy lapping over the plate's ceramic edges. Jock opted most times for a packet of slap chips and a Coke float. Dad wouldn't let him suck the delectable crunchies off the grease-proof paper, so he sneaked it into his pocket for later.

The first time his dad called for him, Jock asked, "How come you've never fetched me before? I know you come into town every week."

His eyes were hot and burning, and his nose threatened to run, so he had to look down in case his dad saw.

"Jock, it wasn't that I didn't want to."

Jock looked up, and it was his dad who turned to look away.

"Your mother and I felt we should wait till you settled in before I disrupted your routine."

"You waited till I was *eight!*" Jock was incredulous. It was an eternity.

"We did what we thought was best for you. Being a parent doesn't always mean you're right. Just that you're trying your best without instructions."

And that was that. It was aired and addressed by them both; the resentment Jock felt was released; and Jock reckoned his dad's guilty feelings went away too.

As the years went on, their easy conversations were as comforting in their sameness as their menu choices.

"How's school?" Dad always asked.

"Fine. Did you see Papin? How's Beauty? The twins? Is my Dennis strong? How's Nicholas? Will you let Tripod sleep with you?"

"You must pull your socks up, Jock. School marks are the most important thing for a boy. Not sport or horse riding or rugby. Nothing ... nothing else matters when you are older."

"Can we worry about that when I'm older, Dad?"

"No. We have to worry now so you'll do what you must and there'll be no need to worry when you're older."

Beauty was always a strong topic, and Tripod got his share. Jock was so hungry for the nitty-gritty, he even asked after the chickens and the condition of the weir.

Dad smiled. "Ah, and Papin's training a new horse boy from the kraal. Your friend has school now too and takes hikers whenever we need him. He's busy."

"Why don't you let him take climbers up, Dad? He's as good as Mandinsolo."

"It would make Mandinsolo feel like his skill is being undermined and his importance threatened. I won't do that to him. Besides, the guests come back for Mandinsolo, Billy Pillay, the mountains, Nicholas and the rest," Dad said. The guests were fickle, and the order of popularity could change next week.

Jock would take a long swig of the creamy Coke and melted vanilla ice cream and change the subject to more silly things. "Please tell me what Billy Pillay did this week," he'd beg.

Inevitably, he'd hear the music that was his dad's hearty laugh. Jock knew Billy Pillay was Dad's laugh trigger, and there was an endless bucket of Billy antics to draw from.

"The clown thinks he's a guide now. He whispered to three families he was the best guide in the berg but he only did private walks for his most special guests. Of course, they deemed it a great privilege and gathered secretly before the scheduled walk. He told them if word got out that he was doing his private tours, he'd lose his job as a waiter. They were sworn to secrecy and their pockets were laced with large tips they would give Billy for jeopardizing his job to secretly delight them."

The two laughed so hard, Jock snorted Coke up his nose.

"When Billy and the guests were still missing at lunchtime, Nicholas had to strong-arm the bar stewards to find out what Billy was up to."

Jock, in pure fascination, leaned so far across the table, his bum slipped off the chair.

"We found out Sterkspruit Falls was the intended destination and sent out Mandinsolo, Bekah and Papin to find the poor buggers." Dad broke for a belly laugh, and father and son snorted and chortled and roared.

Once Dad caught his breath, he finished, "They limped in, bushwhacked and exhausted. They hadn't seen a drip of a waterfall."

By this time, Jock's laughter had pushed his bum in the opposite direction, with his head thrown over the back of his chair. His dad was in a similar state of hilarity, but he managed, "No tips for Billy at the end of that day and not even a whiff of a tip when they left for the season. Poor Billy will have to wait till next year, when their bad memories have turned their Billy experience into a whale of a time."

When they'd simmered down to chuckles, Dad continued, "If Billy Pillay didn't always have the very best intentions, I'd fire the bugger. In the meantime, I think I'll have Nicholas put up signs: 'Billy Pillay is a wine steward. An excellent wine steward. But he is NOT a tour guide. He is NOT a magician. Hotel management accepts no responsibility for anything other than Billy Pillay's drink-serving skills.'"

Every visit with his dad to the Estcourt Café was captured on his Mind Brownie, and the New Aunts added the extras and served him well in the weeks till the next time he had his dad all to himself. Spending those special hours with his hero was worth every long minute of bleak loneliness that followed the day's goodbyes.

# 23

## SNAKE MILKING

*Drakensberg, 1963*

If it was at all possible, Jock was more excited than he'd ever been to get home. He'd started a small business and, using his profits, had sights firmly set on his first purchase.

He'd asked his mom to pick him up at Segornie's. He told her Scotty's dad would drop him off there and save her an extra hour of driving. Truth is, he never asked anyone for anything unless it was in a fair exchange and had happily hitched a free ride on top of the green bus.

He made new friends on his illegal green-topped perch but couldn't offer anyone from the bus a ride home like he'd done last time. His mom would not approve.

Early on, Papin taught Jock to recognize what somebody expected of him. The goal was to strive not to disappoint. It meant nobody ever saw his true self. It also meant he was always on guard, but then again, he'd been at boarding school since he was seven. Being on guard was part of his existence. The only person who really knew Jock inside and out was Papin.

And it was time to show Papin how much he was appreciated. What better time than a birthday? And he knew just what would delight his friend.

Jock was comforted by the sign in the window. It was written in Zulu to attract the locals from the township close by. "Buy now with half down. Pay balance over six months."

The treasure was in a locked, glass case. It was *that* important. It lay just where they'd last seen it.

"Can I see that one, Mr. Segornie?" He pointed.

"That's an expensive watch, Jock. You looking for it for your birthday?"

"No, sir, Papin's birthday."

The shop owner whistled through his front teeth. "He'll have his socks knocked right off. Let's hope tsotsies don't steal it off him. It's a beauty. Everyone will want it."

Segornie handed Jock the watch. It was heavy. "TIMEX" was written under the glass. It was the most handsome watch Jock had ever seen. During the Easter holidays when he and Papin had caught the tractor to Segornie's, Papin saw the encased treasure and whistled.

"You have to be important to be allowed to wear that watch," Papin had said. He'd stayed looking into that glass case for as long as they were in the shop.

"Mr. Segornie, it's really steep for me. Any chance I can make a smaller down payment, then pay you every time I'm home?"

"One third now and I can give you nine months to pay me back. No excuses."

Jock put his hand in his blazer pocket. His heart was willing, but his brain wouldn't make his digits grip the envelope. The money he'd earned was the most he'd ever held.

"I have other customers. Do you or don't you want to buy your friend the best watch to be found anywhere between Jo'burg and Durbs?"

Papin was worth every penny. "Yes, sir, I do." Jock pulled out the tatty envelope and handed it over. "Mr. Segornie? Please don't tell my dad."

Segornie locked the glass case and said, "You come up short after nine months and I *will* tell your father."

Segornie knew that Jock's father would be furious he'd bought something he couldn't afford. Segornie's grand gesture had nothing to do with his good heart and everything to do with Jock's obvious and respectful fear of his father. He would have to go without slap chips if his business failed, but he would do anything not to let Segornie or his father down.

Safely on the bench seat of the Chevy with the watch in his school blazer pocket, Jock had a whole fleet of army ants in his pants.

"Sit still, for gosh sakes, Jock. You're more excited than ever. What's going on?"

"Mom, we'll break in the twins while I'm home this time, which means we'll get to ride them. I can't wait."

Later, as they sat on their rock, Papin and Jock shared their adventures with the young horses that day. Great storm clouds gathered, and though Papin knew each type by sight, Jock named them for him, courtesy of Mr. Low, the geography teacher.

After Jock's dinner with his mom, the cold weather drove the friends down the mountain to the kraal, where a huge fire blazed in the center and Zulus gathered informally, close to the blazing embers, sitting on mats, logs or skins. The chief and his wives were enjoying their own fire inside his large, intricately woven rondavel.

In their leader's absence, the beer flowed more freely outside, and no drums were needed to ignite singing and accompany dancing.

It was glorious, and Jock reveled in the very Zulu-ness of it all as he dipped his hand into the communal pot of *pap* being passed around.

"What are you boys up to?" They both turned sheepishly when Nicholas's voice boomed behind them, sure they must be guilty of something.

"Just sitting, enjoying being Zulu," said Jock defensively.

"I was sent to check on you." He pointed at Jock. "What will I tell your mother now I have smelled beer on your breath?"

"Oh, Nicholas, I take 'sociable sips' like Dad tells Mom to do. Tell Mom Papin and I are copying the bushman paintings onto paper for a school project. That should keep her still."

Jock thought it the perfect time to make his presentation to Papin and patted his shirt pocket to be sure the Timex was still there.

"Nicholas, can you stay awhile? I want you to be here for this." Jock's impulsive need to include Nicholas came from love, not practicality.

Nicholas pulled up a short tree stump, and when he sat, Jock thought he looked like a short-stemmed mushroom.

"What is it we three are gathered for?" Nicholas asked, taking the beer gourd from Papin and downing a hefty helping.

"It's not right that I have a birthday and get a gift and Papin doesn't. Since Papin and his father don't know when exactly he was born, I decided Papin's birthday would be on the twenty-seventh of July. Today!"

Nicholas chuckled, and his stomach moved up and down like a bouncing beach ball. "Ah, as you become more black, Tsotsi, Papin becomes more white."

The sips of beer acted like a truth serum, and Jock stopped just in time from revealing the real source of his newfound wealth. A boy had to be careful. "I saved my tuck money from school and got you ..." He fished into his pocket, and his hand came out clenched. "THIS!"

Jock opened his hand slowly and presented it—palm up—to his friend. The rolled gold watch and the goldish interlinking strap glinted in the firelight. Jock's Mind Brownie and his New Aunts were on overdrive as he captured Papin's shocked awe.

Papin closed and opened his eyes a couple of times as if testing to see if he was awake or dreaming. He shook his head to release any silly notions. But Jock was thrilled Papin couldn't keep his eyes off the shiny gift still in Jock's hand.

When he looked at Jock, his head turned in inquiry, Jock said, "It's yours, Papin. Happy birthday. Take it."

And Papin still wouldn't touch the watch.

"I cannot, Tsotsi. It costs too much. I might break it."

"It's yours, Papin. If it breaks, it breaks. Imagine the pleasure it will give you before that happens."

Jock lifted the watch so the face was visible in the firelight. "What's the time, Papin?" he asked, as he felt his cheeks bunch in pleasure.

"It's ten past nine." Papin grinned, still not daring a touch.

Nicholas, after another deep slug of beer, said suspiciously, "You should be the size of a matchstick with all the goodies you didn't eat at school for this gift, Tsotsi."

Jock regretted he'd begged Nicholas to join them. "Nicholas, I asked you to see this because I love you. I trust you. And my parents must not know how I spent their money. So please help us find a story that would be believable should my dad ask about Papin's watch."

As soon as the words tumbled out, Jock wanted to reach out, clasp them and shove them back into his mouth. Boy! Beer sure loosened the tongue.

"It is I who gave Papin this watch. It was from a Zulu chief who paid me for healing his daughter," deadpanned Nicholas.

Jock was both surprised Nicholas had agreed to his plea and impressed he'd come up with such a far-fetched excuse. He laughed and laughed, rolling on his back from side to side, his legs balled up. When he recovered, he said, "That's a good one, Nicholas."

To Jock's absolute amazement, Nicholas's face became as dark as thunder.

"What? You don't believe my powers are worth such reward?"

Jock sobered. "Nicholas, you are the best head waiter in the Drakensberg. Dad always says so. And besides Papin, you are my favorite Zulu and the kindest, most loyal friend ..."

Nicholas held up his hand, and Jock swallowed his last words. The big man looked at Papin, whose hand was still suspended, waiting to reach for the watch.

"Does this white boy know me?" Nicholas asked Papin as he stood up and loomed like a mountain over them.

Jock was shocked and hurt, quite frankly. What had he done to deserve Nicholas's contempt? He loved Nicholas.

Papin shook his head in violent denial as his hand dropped limply to his side.

"Of *course,* I know you, Nicholas. You're my champion." Jock was heartbroken and confused.

When Nicholas spoke to Jock, his voice changed so, it made Jock afraid.

But it was a voice he'd heard before, though he knew not when or where. "How do you think you got Dennis and Shaka? How do you think Tripod survived? How do you think we found you when you were four?"

Jock was stupefied. He knew he hadn't blinked for ages because the fire burned his eyes, but he dared not shut them for a millisecond lest he miss something else ... Tripod? Shaka? Dennis?

"Tell him, S— Tell him. It is time," Papin urged of the giant towering over them.

Jock ducked because he was sure the big man would not take kindly to such insolence, and he expected a hard slap coming Papin's way. By the sound of things, he might also be included in the blow.

Strangely, Papin's words acted like medicine, and the Nicholas Jock knew returned and sat back down on his stump.

Jock realized the entire revelry around the fire had ceased. All eyes were on Nicholas, and even the logs on the fire quieted to allow the giant to speak.

"I am Sangoma."

The big man's words hung like the indigo and purple dog-violet wildflowers of the Berg. Delicate. Rare. Quite unbelievable.

Jock never moved a muscle, his eyes fixed on this giant man he loved so well. The words he'd uttered were just words. Understanding was suspended somewhere between the fast-moving cumulus clouds and the bright moon.

"I am Sangoma," Nicholas said again, and as he did so, clarity hit Jock ten times as hard as Boet's blow to his jaw. But this time there was no pain, just solid, powerful understanding.

"YOU are Sangoma." Jock's ears were filled with the reverence of his own words, and he said it again in the way of a mighty revelation. And he felt an acute understanding as mysteries unraveled and acceptance washed over him in the form of relief.

"This Nicholas I love is also Sangoma." Jock put out his hand, and they shook the Zulu way. As they looked at each other and smiled, a thousand unsolved little puzzle pieces plopped into neatly vacant places in Jock's mind, completing an image once full of holes.

It all made sense, from the vague familiarity of the giant seer riding a snarling, ferocious "lion" who magically turned boys to men, to the "Champagne Castle Miracle of The Horse Twins" that people over a forty-mile radius still talked about.

It was only much later that night that Papin was able to accept his coveted and hugely unexpected eighteenth birthday gift and finally held the shiny treasure in his hand.

"WHAT TIME IS IT, PAPIN?" Jock asked as they brushed down a sweating Dennis and Shaka after a hard workout reintroducing bridles and saddles.

Nobody really cared because time was determined by Nicholas's bell and gong and when the sun went down or came up, but the question was important because it gave Papin the chance to gaze at his shiny present. Each time he did so, Jock felt thrilled.

Later, on their rock, Papin said, "This gift I wear because Sangoma healed a chief's daughter ... Tsotsi, how were you able to afford it?"

"I started a business at school."

"A business?" Papin was so impressed, he sat bolt upright. "How?"

"You know the boarding school was expanded—they took over the girls' section so now we senior boys stay in that section."

"Ha! Tsotsi is called a senior at thirteen?"

"I am in high school. Not sure how I got there, but I like the perks."

"And I am enjoying your high school books," Papin said with a grin.

"Makes one of us. We got big lockers—like skinny cupboards with locks, so nobody can mess with our stuff. I keep your letters in a shoebox in there."

"You don't read them and throw them away?" Papin's voice held surprise.

"Are you crazy? I read them whenever I am lonely for home." Jock was forced to pause with the weight and magnitude of what those letters meant to him.

"What of your business, Tsotsi?"

"Mr. Tomes is too busy worrying about the juniors to watch us closely, and he thinks by now we should know the drill. So, one Tuesday, Scotty and I found this shop door without windows that had a sign. It said "Fitzsimons."

"'Scotty.' Always 'Scotty,'" muttered Papin.

Jock ignored him. "I poked my head inside and asked what they were doing so far from Durban. Remember how Russ who died from a berg adder used to go to Fitzsimons Snake Park to watch how they handled snakes and milked their venom?"

Papin nodded.

"The guy said they were a collection depot for snake venom from the surrounding farmers. Fitzsimons buys venom and makes it into anti-snake bite serums, which they sell to hospitals and to the guys who make snake bite kits."

Papin said, "They have to get it from somewhere, and there will always be a fool who will risk being bitten and have to be treated with the venom he's just milked. Make sure you are not that fool, Tsotsi."

Jock grinned. "You taught me well, Papin. I am too snake-skilled to be that fool. So I said to the Fitzsimons guy, 'Would you buy from me if I brought you some venom?' The guy laughed and said, 'Hey, we'll pay *anyone* for venom. We can never have enough, and not many folks want to milk the buggers. No age limit required.' He told me the price per vial. He gave me a glass bottle that holds ten teaspoons, with a dropper in the lid. Said he'd pay me for every full vial."

"So that's probably five times milking a small adder," Papin calculated.

"Yes. There's a cluster of small ones in a rock bed near the boarding school. I don't want to keep more than one at time in case they get up to mischief." He grinned at Papin. These two knew what two could get up to. "I'll keep one for a couple of weeks or so, put him back and get another. No endless time in locker-jail for my snakes."

"Scotty has his own adder?" Papin asked.

"No! He's shit-scared of snakes. I just need quick money so am getting as much adder juice as I can while the need is great and the price is high. I use his locker for the second adder, and I get his stuff out for him when he needs it. He's too chicken to open his own with a live snake in it. It's not for long."

"What does Scotty's snake live in?" Papin the reptile policeman asked.

"I stole a cake tin from the school kitchen—they don't use them for cake, that's for sure—and poked holes in it."

"Maybe you could get a pair. A boy and girl. Keep them in just your locker."

"How do you know which is a boy and which a girl?" asked Jock.

"If one is lying on top of another and the one on top has a smile, that's a boy," Papin said, and they laughed and rolled and laughed and nearly fell off the rock.

When at last their funny bubbles subsided, Jock said, "Probably safest to have one at a time—but for now I have the two little guys for quick cash. I dared not steal another cake tin, so I had to use my shoebox that holds your letters, but they are under lock and key so they'll be safe, hidden under my play clothes. I punched holes in the shoebox lid, and four times a week I go hunting for crickets, grasshoppers and lizards to keep the little guys happy, and they have water in a jar lid. And grass. I put grass in so they don't feel bad."

Papin said nothing, so Jock added hastily, "They keep warm because the boarding school is heated."

Papin, satisfied with his treatment of the snakes, nodded approval as Jock continued, "One of the Afrikaans boys caught me feeding my snake. I told him if he told Boet, I would tell Mr. Tomes he had given me the snake. But just in case, I gave him a pound. Told him it wasn't hush money, just an Englishman making nice with an Afrikaner."

Papin slapped Jock on the back. "Ahh ... my Tsotsi is becoming a businessman. Shall I call you Mr. Tsotsi Segornie?"

They laughed some more and then chewed on the biltong they'd brought with them for lunch.

"Yes, please. And could you tell me the time, please?" asked Jock.

"Indeed, Mr. Tsotsi Segornie, sir, and it's half past three. Now tell me how you milk this adder," Papin said in his most teacherly voice.

"I hold my snake between thumb and middle finger with the index finger on top of the back of its head. I use the lip of the cup to gently force my snake's mouth wide open. I push the cup as far to the back of the snake's mouth as it will go. Then I pull it forward and slightly up very gently and slowly. It touches the poison sacs from behind. As I apply pressure to the sacs, venom is pushed through to the fangs and drips into the cup. I get about a teaspoonful at a time. I do it three times a week and get paid every second week when we go to town." Jock felt himself waiting for Papin's approval.

It finally came in a brief nod. "This birthday gift must have cost your poor snakes many teaspoons," said Papin as he held up his left arm, turning it to allow the Timex's gold hue to catch the light. "It is the finest gift anyone could ever receive, Tsotsi. Second only to a horse. I feel very, very lucky."

Just that morning, after breakfast when he and Papin were helping Dad haul out dead frogs and a few small snakes from the over-clogged weir, Dad said, "So Papin, where did you get that lovely Timex?"

Papin gaped at Jock in horror.

"You should ask Nicholas, Dad. He got it from a Zululand chief whose daughter was sick. He gave the watch to Sangoma as payment," Jock said, feeling superior in his knowledge of the real Nicholas.

"Aha! So now you know Nicholas is also Sangoma. Everyone kept it from you a long time. Mind you, nobody around here would have given Nicholas's secret away. There would be hell to pay." Dad smiled.

"It was more surprise than finding out Father Christmas didn't exist so long ago, but this time it was a good one." Jock felt elated. His secret was safe because of the ever-wise Sangoma. And Papin wore the best watch between Jo'burg and Durbs.

The last thing Jock remembered were Papin's words as he gazed at his watch the same way he looked at the male half of the Champagne Castle Miracle: "Thank you, Tsotsi Segornie, my friend the businessman. I will wear this gift as long as I am Papin Tshabalala."

And he dreamed of horses and watches and Sangoma and a night that would live in his heart forever.

## 24

# TRICKS AND FROGS

*Drakensberg Mountains, 1964*

IT WAS WINTER AGAIN, and Papin had owned his Timex for one whole year. Jock marveled the gift had not a single scratch and was as shiny as Shaka. Papin was the envy of Champagne.

During that year, Jock and Papin had been thoroughly entertained by Billy Pillay, who'd taken to sneaking tots of Cane Spirits. Seemed Billy believed his sleight of hand was at its best when he was making Cane disappear. If Dad found out, Billy would be out of a job.

Cane Spirits, made of sugarcane with a shocking forty percent alcohol content, was a popular drink that was both cheap and impossible to smell on one's breath. It also dramatically increased Billy Pillay's urge to perform his magic.

During the Easter holidays, while Papin was with his teacher down the valley, Jock was playing fetch on the grass with the dogs—far enough away not to be included but close enough to hear or see any interesting tidbits he could share when his friend returned.

Dad, still busy with the balance of the lunch guests, was yet to prowl, as was his after-lunch custom, looking for jobs for idle hands, including Papin's and his own. It was one of the reasons the friends steered clear of the hotel as much as possible.

Billy served a tray of Irish coffees to a table of four leaning back, heads turned up to catch the soft autumn sun.

"Would you fine people like me to flatter you with my disappearing scarf trick?" Billy asked as if he were offering a bowl of peanuts to enhance their drinking pleasure.

Jock watched the two couples lean in, interested. "By all means, 'flatter' us, Billy." The man smiled and glanced up and down the veranda. "The coast is clear."

Billy lost no time and whipped out a colorful, long, silk scarf, likely borrowed from the lost-and-found basket. He waved it around lavishly for full effect. It worked. The two other couples on the veranda and a few kids gathered around.

His showmanship went into full gear, and Billy's voice went up three volume notches. Jock noticed he deftly stepped to the side so there was no one behind him. Jock's magic training from Billy—such as it was—hadn't been in vain. He knew trick setup guaranteed ninety percent successful execution.

Billy declared to the piddly masses, "And not only will I make the scarf disappear, I will find one special card for ... you!" He pointed to a young kid, who was thrilled.

With great flourish, he stuffed the scarf in his right jacket pocket and pulled a loose pack of cards from the left.

"I want you, young suh, to pick the card you like best from the pack and hand it to me facedown. Without looking at your card, I will show the guests. Then still without looking, I'll pop the card back into the pack so I, The Great Billy Pillay, will have no clue what it is."

The boy nodded eagerly, and the first steps of the trick followed without incident. When Billy took the card from the boy, he added a touch of drama: "Don't forget the lovely scarf in my pocket."

As all eyes went to his left pocket, Jock noted, Billy quickly and deftly folded the corner of the card ever so slightly so when all eyes turned back, Billy was simply holding the card for all to see, with the crook of his index finger covering the new little corner-fold.

Looking deeply into each audience member's eyes, he said somberly, "Now the magic only works if I say nothing. Everything from now on, I will mime. Watch carefully."

Billy Pillay threw the pack of loose cards up in the air, and long before they landed haphazardly—some on the table, some on the slate floor—Billy turned around, his back to the eager faces befuddled by flying cards. There was no one behind to see Billy force the scarf into his wide-open mouth.

When he pivoted back to his waiting audience, he indicated—finger to lips—they should all be quiet, and with a flourish, he interwove his arms, fingers stiff and splayed, this way and that, causing major visual distraction as he searched for the corner-folded, "magic" card. Jock had to confess Billy had showmanship because everyone was looking at the peculiar man's spastic, fast-moving arms and not the cards.

The mess of card colors and pictures along with Billy's crazy snake-arms created an interlacing state of visual overload, cleverly preventing eyes on the card Billy searched for and quickly recovered.

Victorious, Billy Pillay stood, his thumb pressed down firmly across the telltale fold, and showed off the card the boy had chosen. There was an enthusiastic round of applause, but Billy put a finger to lips once more and slipped the cards into his wine steward's jacket pocket before anyone looked too closely.

Then he mimed a woman—pursed lips and all—wearing a scarf to remind them of his next show of brilliance.

The crowd shrugged in an exaggerated fashion, and the kids shouted, "Scarf! Where's the scarf?" He pulled the left pocket inside out, declaring its emptiness. Then, because change and the pack of cards was in his right, he pulled open the pocket, and each of his audience peeped in and nodded. Nothing there. The crowd went wild. All seven of them.

Enough noise, though, to drag Dad from whatever he was doing.

As Billy spotted his boss, his shock caused a massive intake of breath, forcing his mouth open, and the scarf—loaded as far back into his mouth as he'd dared to hide its billowing mass—was sucked deep into Billy's esophagus.

Jock was up and on the veranda in seconds to see if he could help, though there was no way he was going to touch the wet soggy mess Billy was frantically tugging from his open mouth. It seemed never-ending, and as it came out a half an inch at a time, slimy and disgusting...but still colorful. The poor guy choked and gagged. Guests' hands covered mouths in disgust as they backed away without taking their eyes off the train wreck that was Billy.

Dad shouted, "Billy, you bloody clown! Jock! Get Dr. Newcomb from the dining room."

Later, when Papin and Jock huddled around a fire in the bushman cave, Jock reenacted Billy's magic trick. He thought Papin would literally die laughing as he rolled on the dirt floor of the cave, holding his stomach.

When Jock "became" the doctor holding a tiny pair of ice tongs and straddling Billy, splayed on a veranda chair, mouth open, arms flailing desperately, sucking in tiny wisps of air through the scarf, Papin begged for mercy and made Jock stop.

Papin's hysterics subsided, and he motioned Jock to continue. Jock said, "Eventually, Dr. Newcomb managed to get all the chiffon from Billy's windpipe in time, and as you saw, he lived."

Papin spent his last giggle.

Then Jock delivered the punchline. "But there's no keeping that clown down. As the last of the soggy scarf was hauled out, he gagged and coughed and spat and his audience cringed. But Billy stood up, smiling weakly between coughs, and extended his hands out to accept his applause. When he bowed deeply, fifty-plus cards and all his waiter-change fell out of his pocket."

With that, Jock let loose his own mirth and joined Papin as they rolled around the cave at Billy's expense.

Billy sober was bad enough. But Billy with a few stolen shots of Cane became The Great Houdini in his own mind. He'd weave expertly between the tables, silver tray in hand, and as he bent down with guests' change, he'd say confidingly: "Billy Pillay is an excellent magician. Just ask and voilà! I amaze with my tricks."

After the scarf-suffocation-veranda disaster, the signs about Billy being an excellent wine steward but not a guide or a magician were resurrected and reposted, so the guests usually laughed off Billy's offers.

But he'd become worse in the three months. It was time Jock and Papin intervened, otherwise Billy would get into big trouble.

They hatched a plan with Nicholas for when Billy had a rare day off. They had to be early because it was suspected Billy hit the Cane long before lunch. They needed him sober. They found him in his bed in one of the dormitories of the compound and woke him with a start.

"Come quickly, Billy. Sangoma requests an audience with you," Jock said.

Billy's bloodshot eyes were huge. "Me?" He pointed to himself incredulously.

They scurried to ready him for his big meeting, which took

place behind the chicken coop, which Jock had learned was Sangoma's home base for consulting between mealtimes.

He also found out that when Nicholas the head waiter became Sangoma on the fly, though he was dressed as a head waiter without tie and jacket, his manner changed, his voice deepened, and his face morphed from the man Jock loved. He was as frightening as if he wore his lion pelt and held a bowl of warm goat's blood.

By the time they got to their rendezvous, Billy was quivering with fear, and the boys tried their best to up the ante. The more afraid he was, the more he'd take this intervention seriously.

Though Billy was Hindu, he'd been around Zulu folklore long enough to know it was nothing to be sneezed at. So influenced was he, he'd raised his bed as high as the Zulus' in case the short Tokoloshe had any inkling of threatening a sleeping Indian. He wasn't taking any chances.

"Sit!" boomed Sangoma, pointing to a prearranged stump half the size of his own.

Billy did so, and as the boys leaned against the wire coop, Jock saw Billy's legs shaking.

"Last night I had a dream, Billy Pillay." Sangoma conducted the consultation in English. Billy spoke just a smattering of Zulu.

Billy's eyes were the size of eagle eggs.

"The ancestors told me you are stealing Cane Spirits."

Billy's face had shame written all over it, and he sputtered and muttered and finally said, "Maybe once or twice, but mostly I buy it with my tips, Sangoma. Please tell the ancestors."

Jock felt sorry for him.

Sangoma made a great show of throwing the bones, and while the oracles were being received by The Wise One, though his bum was still sitting on the stump, Billy's legs took on a life of their own and started to bop like the teenagers did sometimes in the lounge.

"Ancestors say it doesn't matter how you get alcohol, steal or buy, the punishment is the same. You must stop, otherwise you will be very, very badly punished."

Despite the cold winter air, Billy was sweating as if he'd just climbed Monk's Cowl.

"But how can they see?"

"Billy Pillay. You know, I know, these boys know, everyone knows the ancestors see everything. My job as Sangoma is to warn people before disaster comes. Heed the ancestors' warning, Billy. This is very serious."

"Whatever you say, Sangoma." Billy looked almost relieved as he nodded vigorously and lifted his bum from the stump, ready to run for the hills.

Sangoma knew such a look and bellowed so loud, Billy's bum slapped back onto the stump. "Billy Pillay, if you have any doubt my words are true, look for a sign from the ancestors. Now go. Throw away your liquor, or the ancestors will send you a message directly, then—and hear me; hear the ancestors who warn you—you might never be the same again."

Billy jumped up on wobbly legs and turned to run, but Sangoma in his Nicholas voice called to him, and the accused turned his head to face the next blow. "And if I catch you with Cane in your blood in my dining room or my kitchen, I will tell Inkosi. That might just be worse even than what the ancestors have in store for you," Nicholas boomed.

As Papin and Jock walked back toward the hotel, well-dressed Nicholas between them, Bekah, Jack-of-all-trades, came running toward them.

"Quickly, there's trouble at Royal National."

"What?" asked Jock, feeling excitement stir.

"They've lost a climber. Need Champagne's help," said excited Bekah.

"Wonder if Dad will let us go?"

Bekah's grin started in Champagne and ended in Estcourt. "Inkosi said to find you so we three could join the team."

Jock looked at Papin, and they tore off, each to get his own rarely worn takkies and warm clothes. Over his shoulder, Jock shouted, "Bekah, tell them to wait for us."

The code between the five closest hotels was if they couldn't cope using their own resources in an emergency, they'd call on the other four to spare them as many staff as possible. A crew of nonessential workers would be sent out armed with extra-warm clothes, chocolate, blankets and whistles.

Jock knew it was a dire situation if they'd called for long-distance help. That he and Papin were allowed to go was better than Christmas. His adrenaline began to pump.

Three of the longtime guests, themselves climbers, were happy to offer assistance. They volunteered to drive the Champagne team and set off to Royal National Park Hotel, sixty miles away, in a couple of cars.

Mr. Barnes, sort of Dad's age, drove his Mercedes-Benz. Jock sat shotgun, with Papin and Bekah in the back. All three of them shared impressed looks at their posh ride, but it was Jock who said, "Boy, Mr. Barnes. I've never ridden in a Merc before."

"Well, enjoy the ride, boys!"

Mr. Barnes filled them in as soon as they were off hotel property. "Night before last, three hikers climbed up the Chain Ladder to watch the sunrise above the clouds on top of the mountain from the Amphitheatre."

Jock had visited the trail a couple of times with Papin and Mandinsolo. It was challenging and led through Royal Natal National Park, zigzagging through the mountains along steep cliffs. It took nearly three hours to reach The Chain Ladders.

That's what they were literally. Ladders made of chains. The first ladder went up vertically for about 145 feet and the second ladder another 70 feet. It was the easiest way up the immense rock wall to get to the vast plateau known as The Amphitheatre, where Tugela Falls, the second tallest waterfall in the world, pounded over the edge.

Mr. Barnes interrupted Jock's reverie. "New climbers! They didn't know the dangers of camping too close to the edge. It should be in a climbing handbook somewhere if common sense fails."

Jock thought how easily you could lose your way in thick cloud cover. It would be black as pitch, and if your tent flap wasn't facing the edge so you knew to walk left or right, you could easily misjudge and either get lost or fall down the mountain. And if Jock's nemesis Mist came a-calling, you wouldn't have a clue which way you were pointing. He shivered, though the heat was on in the Mercedes.

Mr. Barnes continued, "When the others woke up, eight more inches of snow covered the ground than when they'd gone to bed. There were no footprints to show which way the lost one had gone. They presumed their buddy had gone for a leak in the middle of the night and just disappeared."

"Whoa," Jock said.

Barnes said, "As soon as the mist lifted, after they'd searched for him, the remaining three descended and hiked to the hotel. Royal National called Mountain Rescue and dispatched their own posse straightaway. All day yesterday, no sign."

Papin said, "I hope he was not eaten by the mountain."

"Me too," said Jock.

Barnes continued, "They can't find him; snow's so thick up there now. Mountain Rescue called in a psychic. They are *that* desperate."

"A sidekick?" Jock pointed between himself and Papin, confused.

Mr. Barnes answered, "Psychic. A person who talks to spirits."

"Like Sangoma?" asked Papin.

Mr. Barnes chuckled. "Yes. Much like Sangoma." Sangoma was not a divine name given to Nicholas alone, rather a general term for a Zulu seer.

When they arrived at the Royal National Hotel, Mr. Barnes cleared his throat and avoided eye contact with them when he said, "The hotel has made room for the three of us drivers and Jock here." He cleared his throat. "The rest of the Champagne guys will spend the night in the cars. All good?"

"I will stay with Papin and Bekah," said Jock.

"There's a bed at the hotel for y—" the elder began.

"Thank you, Mr. Barnes. We will be fine. Which car do we sleep in?" asked Jock.

"You can sleep in mine if you'd like. Your dad made sure there are extra blankets for all, so you'll be warm. This hotel promised us all hot meals. Jock and I will go to the dining room, and the scullery is open for you guys." He gestured to Bekah and Papin.

Jock looked him straight in the eye and said, "No, thank you, sir. I'll enjoy being in the scullery with the guys."

Jock was used to being the only white face in a crowd. He had no longing to be anywhere else. All the white rescue parties were in the dining room, Zulus and Jock in the scullery. It was glorious to be immersed in their freedom with laughter and teasing and mountain talk. Far better than the elbows-off-the-table containment of the dining room.

Some of the other Zulu rescuers were doubling up at the hotel staff compound. Bekah, Papin, and Jock were envied for their luxurious accommodation. The three relished every moment. They could barely sleep with both the excitement and the smell of expensive leather.

At five the next morning, three of them and forty-three volunteers were gathered. Soon, the Mountain Rescue's four strapping men joined them and ... Mr. Palmer, Jock's history teacher.

What the hell was he doing here? Palmer looked nothing like a potential mountain climber.

It wasn't a surprise that in spite of all the people gathered, Palmer's eyes found Jock's and he said, "Mr. Walsh. Glad you could join us."

Jock smiled. "Hello, sir." He was always late for history because it came after English. The dreaded hour of the day when most of his cuts were earned.

History didn't excite Jock. He cared little about the Magna Carta or the works of Michelangelo so he switched on his mental Mind Brownie and joined Dennis, Papin and Shaka.

But Mr. Palmer was known to have eyes in the back of his head.

He'd be writing on the blackboard, his body language showing he was completely absorbed and concentrating, when all of a sudden, that chalk duster—made of heavy wood and a slither of felt—became a missile whizzing through the air, only stopping when it connected violently with the head of a non-attention-paying nitwit. It was a rough day when head and bum hurt at the same time. It happened quite often.

The lead Mountain Rescuer addressed the eager crowd in English. "Frankie's been missing two nights. The snow is thick; terrain, treacherous. Our search will be concentrated below the Amphitheatre wall. We don't know which way he walked or how far, but we think he fell down twenty-one stories. At this point, we're looking for a body."

He gestured to Mr. Palmer. "Harry Palmer is a psychic—for my Zulu friends, a Sangoma."

Jock felt the physical blow of shock push him back a few steps, and he shook his head. Mr. Palmer? A Sangoma like Nicholas? He couldn't believe it ... but then Palmer's sixth sense to determine which culprit should be nailed by his missile-duster's accuracy, suddenly made perfect sense.

Jock heard the noises of disbelief amongst the Zulus. "Eich! Not possible! Surely it cannot be!"

The Mountain Rescue leader continued. "He can see things we cannot. Mr. Palmer has proven himself countless times by helping the police find many bodies. Last night, he slept in the room where Frankie spent his last night before the climb. With him was a shirt Frankie wore the day they left on the hike. Mr. Palmer will do his best to find Frankie today."

Jock looked at Papin, whose eyes were wide, his head drawn back in apprehension. Bekah looked downright terrified at the thought of such important things being held in the hands of a white man. Jock empathized. A white Sangoma was enough to scare the shit out of anyone, even if he wasn't aiming blindly at your head ... and hitting it.

"And whites say Tokoloshe is rubbish," Papin whispered, and Jock realized it was disbelief his friend was experiencing. Understandably. Papin didn't sport lingering head-dings as Jock did.

The rescue leader looked at Jock. "You David Walsh's kid?"

"Yes, sir."

"How old?"

"Nearly fifteen, sir." Okay. It was a stretch.

"You're too young to accompany, son."

The entire Champagne Castle Hotel posse came to Jock's defense, protesting in Zulu and English.

"He is a white Zulu."

"He climbs like a guide."

Papin stepped forward. "Jock is a better climber than anyone. He will be a big help."

His best friend called him Jock. In that split second, he realized his friend was no longer a boy. He was nearly twenty, tall and quietly spoken. People took Papin seriously. Even white people. Jock was supremely proud of his friend, the man who had the last word.

Mountain Leader turned to Mr. Palmer. "It's your show, sir."

"Though he's not built like a runner, I watched him win the cross-country race at school. He wasn't even signed up. Afrikaans boy challenged him, and this boy won. Without shoes. Plays rugby like he was born to be a prop. Tough kid. Let him come," Palmer said.

After the leader gave his directive and groups were forming, Palmer walked up to Jock. "Good to see you wearing something on your feet, Walsh. Don't let me down."

"No, sir," Jock promised.

Palmer shouted to the leader, "These two are with me," and he pointed to Jock and Papin.

Jock grinned. He would take a blackboard duster every day for this privilege.

They set off in groups, all with long sticks fashioned from the surrounding trees the night before. Whistles were around necks; blankets, first aid kits, sandwiches in rucksacks; and Cadbury's chocolates in pockets.

Each climber, except Palmer, had a turn to carry the extra rucksack, which contained a heavy canvas tarp.

Getting to the bottom of the Amphitheatre was treacherous enough when you could see your footing. In snow, you were blind. You had to rely on feel. You had to test the rock you landed on with one foot to see if it was strong enough for your weight before you transferred the second foot. Slow going but

Jock was exhilarated and trying his hardest to live up to his team's vote of confidence.

Mr. Palmer's mountain skills were nonexistent, so there always had to be a leader whose footsteps he could follow to ensure his safety. Jock had the privilege of getting his share of being in the front. Leading was exhausting and needed to be traded off periodically. Every team member played a vital part, and Jock made sure he performed.

Once the full contingent reached the wall, half the teams went south and half north. They had to traverse the bottom of the rockface, which was steeply inclined at about eighty degrees. Each gully had to be searched, and there were many.

Using their roughly ten-foot sticks, they probed for anything that felt different than snow or rock. Jock saw Mr. Palmer holding his fingertips to his temples, not using his stick at all.

If their sticks made solid contact, it meant the snow was compacted below or it was pure rock, and they moved a foot farther, and so on. If one of the team felt a soft patch under the snow, the full team would converge and dig down until the cause of the softness was found—a rabbit caught in a rock having succumbed to icy conditions, a dense bush frozen before it lost all its leaves.

When Palmer used his whistle and put up his hand, the silence between the low sky and the high snow was so eerie, even the moments froze.

Jock's history teacher broke the silence, and it was strong and sure. "Dig here!"

All twenty-five gathered where Palmer stood, still pointing. Gloved hands started digging, flinging off the snow like dogs kicking up sand until behind them, a mini, white mountain appeared.

And then, there he was.

The body of Frankie was frozen stiff. Eyes and pants open.

Jock realized there wasn't a single Zulu in their midst, even Papin, who thought this white Sangoma would succeed. That he'd done so gave them the heebie-jeebies. He watched them turn their heads and move quickly away from the body, as far as they could—shaking their heads in shock, confusion and terror of the unknown. This Palmer, a *white* man, had switched on a spirit world—a mysterious world whites didn't talk about, and yet …

Palmer lifted his whistle to his mouth and blew three long, loud blasts. It was the prearranged sound they hoped would pierce the snow-packed silence so wherever the other teams were, they'd know Frankie had been found.

Three Durban mountain rescue guys and one of the drivers from the Champagne contingent lifted the stiff body up and out of the snow hole. Papin tugged at Jock's arm, forcing his face away from the action. Jock was relieved. He had no desire to gaze on this poor man. So cold. So dead. A dead body made all the worse for the Zulus because it was found mysteriously by a white Sangoma.

Once they covered Frankie's body with the tarp, the Zulus and Jock joined in to help. Jock mulled over the sadness of a life lost. It was hard to fathom how a person could be vital and climbing a mountain one minute, then dead and frozen the next. Mr. Palmer, as if reading Jock's mind, said, "This man died doing what he loved. Be pleased for him."

Jock had a vision of Frankie's open fly and wanted to say, "What? He loved peeing?" And immediately chastised himself for such a callous thought but felt morosely sad the man had died preparing to relieve himself. It hampered the dignity of his adventuresome death.

Guided by Mr. Palmer's team's consistent whistling, both teams converged at the point where they'd split up four hours before, and Jock and Papin shared a look of relief.

All fifty-one descended together, three at a time, taking turns to carry Frankie's body folded in the tarp. There were no footprints to follow. The falling snow had seen to that. They had to force a new and uncertain path over that perilous terrain. Those carrying Frankie's body were particularly at risk of falling because the carriers couldn't see the placement of their feet. One wrong move would cause a fall and an injury. But all the rescuers stayed together, passing off responsibility, and their descent was as slow as the slowest among them. Jock was relieved it wasn't him.

When they started the descent, a Zulu Royal National Hotel guide familiar with the terrain, as well as a Mountain Rescue guy, went ahead to find out from the hoteliers where the best place was to bring in Frankie's body so as not to upset the guests. Jock knew the drill from their own disaster.

Late that night, as soon as the two cars were nestled safely back under the huge pine trees in the Champagne Castle Hotel parking lot, a crowd of staff and guests surged to greet them. There was a frenzy of excitement and many questions.

Jock knew every Zulu rescuer present couldn't wait to tell their kin far and wide how, in spite of their odd Western ways, when they really needed a connection with the ancestors, the white man found their own Sangoma to do the job. Perhaps there was hope for white folks yet.

When they returned home and things quieted down, Papin and Jock were still too excited for sleep, so they went to the stables to check on Beauty and her miracles. While they brushed and patted, soothed and stroked the beloved horses, Jock and Papin relived every moment of their adventure. The highlight for Papin was sleeping in the Mercedes-Benz.

But then he said, "I did not know whites believed in spirits and ancestors." Papin's cheek rested against Shaka's as he spoke.

"Me neither," said Jock.

"Hmph. Nothing that Sangoma couldn't do."

"Maybe white Sangomas have to get a chance now and then to help them keep their skills sharp."

At that piece of wisdom, Papin nodded sagely, then sat down in the hay. "When you were at school, missionaries came to the kraal."

"Again! They've learned to book into the hotel so Dad can't chase them away. But he does tell them if they're trying to convert Zulus, they should be sensitive to whether they are welcome in the kraal or not," said Jock.

"I listened to them," said Papin. "When Chief with his advisors asked why they would want to be 'saved,' the missionaries said, 'So you can go to heaven. We believe in marriage to one wife under the laws of the church.' Chief laughed and laughed. 'One wife? Why would I give up my four ... now five wives—and the new one I intend—who work hard in the fields to cultivate, prepare and cook, make beer and see to my every need while I sit and consider the needs of my kraal? All to make your church happy, I must sit with just one wife who nags *me* to go to work?'"

Papin and Jock hooted at that one.

Papin continued, "Missionaries' eyes were big as nagapies, but Chief went on: 'And how can I have many children, all similar ages, who fill the kraal with laughter and hope? And how will I increase the kraal's wealth without my wives bearing daughters? What would my kraal do without suitors from other kraals who must pay big *labola* for a chief's daughters?'"

Papin took a breath and continued, "And, as if they hadn't been turned into white Zulus by then, Chief put the cherry on the ice cream. 'And why would I rely on just one God when I need many, as well as ancestors, to see to my kraal's many needs? My crops, my water supply, my cattle, my clan. Too much for one god, surely?'"

Jock finished for him, still chuckling: "And so they left, tails between their white legs?"

"Yes, indeed." Papin went quiet, and Jock accepted the silence.

After a while, Papin asked, "What is it you believe, Tsotsi?"

"I believe in Sangoma and in Palmer. Both are skilled. I look at the mountains, and I know someone is responsible for such might. I look at the animals, and I know somebody very clever made them. I look at us"—Jock's finger bounced between him and Papin—"and I see how our minds work and how our bodies function. Someone made us, and they were pretty damn smart. So yes, I think there is just one God. But I think there are spirits and ancestors too. I don't think it matters to that God what color you are or how good-looking." He chuckled. "Do you believe in Tokoloshe?" Jock had always wanted to know.

"Not Tokoloshe as such, but I believe in traditions. Tokoloshe is tradition. Zulus are people who work the land and call themselves 'People of the Heavens' so they have heaven and earth covered. They are simple and happy here in this kraal. No one else longs to understand things they don't know. But I do if I am to become a person of the world."

"I am simple and happy here. I don't think I want to be a person of the world like you."

"You are just a tsotsi," said Papin, and they grinned.

"I am a tsotsi who believes, above all else, in the power of Peels Honey," said Jock, and they did their crazy handshake, which added two fist bumps after the thumb clutches and an elbow touch before the final Western shake. Much more complex than Sipho's greeting. And then they planned Billy's "reminder from the ancestors" so he'd stay sober.

Next day, after lunch—usually a slow time for the wine stewards—the boys executed their Billy reform plan.

Billy was a coward, no question. He didn't attempt to pretend he was anything else. But though his fears were many, none were greater than that of frogs. They terrified him more than a black mamba, the most lethal snake of all.

The boys knew just where to find frogs, even in the snow. Just to the side of a sparsely used area of the veranda where water pooled and the lights above kept it from freezing, three small frogs were having a festival. Jock bent down and scooped up an unsuspecting frog, trapping it in cupped hands. He could feel the frog's middle expanding between his hands and thought of Nicholas.

Only guests, waiters and wine stewards were allowed in the guest lounge, no day visitors and certainly no kids whose parents owned the joint—Jock's strict father set the rules. Papin was safely watching from the look-see spot they'd claimed in advance.

Ensuring his dad was not around, Jock walked quickly toward Billy. When he saw Jock approach, the wine steward had guilt written all over his face. Jock smiled and leaned in to whisper in Billy's ear and simultaneously dropped the frog into Billy's right pocket, where he kept the change used for drink sales. "Billy, I see you are doing a fantastic job. The ancestors are proud."

Billy looked even more guilty than usual but smiled his thanks weakly as Jock hightailed it out of the lounge. He and Papin settled in to watch their plan unfold. It didn't take long.

"Hey Billy," one of the regular returning guests called, "come up with any new tricks lately?"

Billy beamed. It was not often anyone asked without Billy's heavy prompting.

"Well, suh. Would you like the disappearing hanky ..."

The man interrupted. "That involves a pot, a lid, and a hanky on fire, right?"

Billy's grin lit up the room. "You remembered, suh!"

"Well, I would, Billy. It was my hanky. Past tense intended." The man slapped his knee and chuckled. "Lucky it wasn't my favorite."

"Well, I can do a very fancy floating trick, but I will need props and Mr. Walsh's permission for such a gargantuan extravaganza, suh." Jock was impressed with Billy's vocabulary and wondered if Papin was coaching him.

Jock glanced at Papin. Waiting for the inevitable was exhilarating and scary all at once.

Billy put down three of the eight full glasses and two beer bottles from his silver tray and picked up two empties to take their place as the guest offered a pound note.

They watched with bated breath as Billy took the bank note from the guest and dipped his hand into his pocket for change.

Jock's teeth clenched just as Billy's shriek pierced the jovial atmosphere and he jerked his hand from his pocket, turning it over in a flash. When he saw the frog sitting on top of some coins in his palm, he screamed bloody murder and threw both hands in the air. As he did so, frog, coins and all the open bottles and full glasses from his loaded tray launched into the air.

The flying booze splattered the guests over four tables, and beer, ice, glasses and coins landed two tables over. The frog was sitting quietly on the tip of Billy's shoe, huffing and puffing in confusion.

When Billy spotted the frog, another scream filled the room, and Billy did a bizarre dance, lifting his own leg up past his hip and then jogging on the spot, knees almost as high as his armpits.

What a sight to see! The boys convulsed in hilarity at Billy's frog-dance.

Still screaming, Billy bolted out of the lounge, while a flurry of kids on their hands and knees plucked shiny coins from the carpet.

Jock and Papin's spines threatened to collapse as they laughed at the Billy-induced pandemonium.

A kid of about ten caught the frog, and Jock stopped laughing. Forgetting the trouble he'd get into, Jock ran to the lounge to rescue the poor frog.

He was taking it gently from the reluctant boy when Dad appeared at the doorway, his face ten shades of purple.

*Ohhh, shit!*

Nicholas stood in the lounge next to Dad. "What the hell are you doing?" Dad shouted at Jock.

"I was just rescuing the frog who was about to be squashed —or dissected—by that kid."

"Go to my private suite *now,* Jock."

Oh *shit.* A burning bum again.

"Can I just first put the frog somewhere safely outside, please, Dad?"

Nicholas positioned himself between Dad and Jock and said, "Inkosi, may we speak, please?"

Dad nodded, and Nicholas and Dad stepped ten feet away as Jock stood unmoving but for his chest expanding at the same speed as the frog cupped in his hands.

They walked back, and as they did so, Nicholas winked. Jock relaxed immediately.

"Take your frog and *voetsek* out of here," Dad instructed. Jock had never heard Dad use the vulgar Afrikaans word for "get out." But boy! Sangoma *was* a wizard!

"Thank you, Dad," Jock said as he scuttled out of that lounge at the speed of Beauty in full gallop before Dad changed his mind.

Once he'd returned the adventuresome frog to his friends in the puddle, Jock found Papin, well hidden from the aftermath of Billy's catastrophe, in the dog kennel on the veranda.

Once Papin had unfolded his long self from the small space, they went together to find Nicholas.

"Nicholas, how did you do it?" asked Jock, referring to Dad reversing his sentence of a beating.

"I told your father you just came in to save the frog from the naughty little boy who put it in Billy's pocket."

Jock couldn't believe his luck. Nicholas as Sangoma must have a host of black and white lies in his arsenal. "You're the best, Nicholas. Thank you."

"But the best part," said Nicholas, "I found Billy. He was shivering in the servants' bathroom. Crying. I felt sorry. But it was necessary. He saw me, and he started to cry more. 'Nicholas,' he said, 'the ancestors sent me a sign. Oh, Sangoma—I was a very, very bad man. I had Cane after they warned me. I couldn't help myself. They must have seen me.' He cried like a baby then, and I felt very, very sorry. I said, 'Well, now you know they are watching you, so you dare not do it again because they know how afraid you are of frogs. Next time it will be two frogs, and Billy, by the looks of you, one is quite enough.'"

Jock wanted to laugh and to cry. He looked at Papin, and he looked like Jock felt.

"We did a good thing," Nicholas assured them. "We saved Billy from losing his job. That would have been much, much scarier than a frog."

Billy became a teetotaler on that very day.

# 25

# PROPAGANDA AND ANOTHER ADDER

*Oshikoto Camp, South West Africa, 1977*

ONCE THE OVAMBO prisoners were handed over for interrogation and his boys had filled their bellies with *kos*, Lieut said, "Good news, boys. It's movie night!'

Lieut bet the groans could be heard as far as Windhoek. It was nobody's idea of fun, but the brass's goal was to keep their army pissed off and angry, and propaganda was their tuning tool.

"Dammit, we've lived it. Why must we watch it again?" asked Benny, and his team nodded in agreement.

"Hey, Benny. I'm with you," said Lieut. "But I don't make the rules. If it were up to me, there would be more cowards in the world. No need for war. But nobody asks me, so get your sorry ass and the bums of your ladies to the movies by nineteen hundred hours. It beats having to be on guard duty, so learn to appreciate luck when she visits." Lieut gave them each his most menacing glare. Man, sometimes he felt so old.

The army-style theater was a giant tent lined with rows of

chairs. A sheet, pulled tight and nailed to the wall, served as a movie screen. A projector was set up in the aisle, halfway to the exit flaps. Smoke from the moviegoers swirled like luminous lava lamps in the blue-gray funneled beam running from machine to screen.

A rugged middle-aged man in camo gear stomped back and forth on the half-meter-high stage. The sergeant major in any outfit was intimidating, built like a Bedford with a face scarred by desert sun and disappointment.

Piet-Tire whispered to Frikkie: "His *donderse* face is so lined, he looks like a bushman."

Frikkie whispered back, "Ja. Maybe if he eats somefing, his face will puff out like he's thirteen. And his arse will grow like a mantelpiece behind him. Somewhere to hang his Christmas stocking."

Lieut couldn't help but think of the San people. The Koi Koi were similar. Bushmen. They were nomads living for the journey, not the destination. Their bodies were designed to store food to use when none was to be had in their quest to wander the desert lands. When they ate, their loose skin filled in and their behinds stored sustenance for when food was nonexistent and their bodies in dire need. Mother Nature again. She was one phenomenal woman.

Odd noises were still coming out of Piet-Tire's nose as he tried to stifle the fit of giggles threatening to explode. Lieut sat behind these two on purpose. With both hands, he thwacked each above the ears, forcing two big heads to collide.

"Eina," they complained, rubbing the sides of their heads. Laurel and Hardy.

The sergeant major's voice boomed like the god of thunder. "By now, soldiers, you've all experienced the lengths our enemy will go to intimidate us. I would bet when we showed you footage of their evil during your basic training, you thought it was acted expertly using many bottles of tomato sauce. You all know now that was no exaggeration. The reason we gather again is to remind you to fight fire with fire. Because you see, soldiers, the human mind is a marvelous thing. It makes us forget what we've experienced to protect us. Few men talk about the horrors of war. You see, if they dwell on what they've seen and done, it'll drive them straight to the loony bin."

The thump of the big frame on the wooden platform pounded the message home, but Lieut knew he'd only just begun. "We in the army want you to forget. Absolutely. When you leave here, never think of this place again. But while you're here, I will make it my mission to remind you." He paused, and there was silence before he bellowed to the projectionist, "Let her rip."

Wobbly footage of a family frolicking on a beach had no sound, just the projector's whirr-whirr.

"This is the Johnson family. Sally is three, Mandy, five, and Cyril, ten. Father Jim and mother Pamela have a sheep farm a hundred kilometers or so from here. Jim's mother, Carol, lives with the family. This is their annual vacation to Cape Town."

The thunderous narration stopped as the Johnsons posed in their swimsuits, grandmother and all, with Jim the videographer trying to control the camera wobbling with the force of the sea wind. Grandma waved, looking coy, and the camera caught the giant, froth-tipped wave as it crashed. The youngest two and their grandmother were mercilessly knocked down, but Cyril and mom managed to outrun the surging surf.

They were having fun in spite of the angry sea, and they all converged again in a similar pose with Grandma facing the ocean. The family's meerkat guard, thought Lieut, before blank frames jumped over the screen as the end of the film released and spun free, flapping like the sound of applause.

"Jissus, it's like that donderse *Pollyanna* movie Poppie from the bakery made me watch! Poppie was *bakgat* ... but the movie! Where's vokken John Wayne?" asked Frikkie, and of course Piet's snorting followed.

The projectionist got busy loading another reel, and the thunder that was Sergeant Major's voice erupted again. "Nice happy family, hey?" he asked rhetorically. "Now watch and remember that as I speak, this could be happening to any number of people you know and love."

The large screen seemed to grow in size because of close-ups the camera had captured. A different farm but a similar scene. *Shit.* His boys were still raw from witnessing their atrocity; they didn't need this to open already gaping wounds.

Blood. Guts. Women sliced open. Farmer—this time strung up by his wrists from a Rhodesian teak beam in the living room —stomach sliced open ...

Lieut closed his eyes as others groaned and retched and ran from the tent. He thought of his mountains. Of the ancient Bushman "paintings," which were really stick figures come to life. Cool and well protected in a dark cave for thousands of years. Best comic books in all the world. Telling of life and celebration and hunting and hard times and hardships overcome. He concentrated on those figures so thin in art and so thick in depiction to block his mind from all this negativity intended to ignite hate.

During the two lifetimes he felt he'd lived in his twenty-seven years, he learned there were always two sides to a story. Nothing—not people nor groups nor governments nor situations—was ever just black or white. When all things were considered, every human action and reaction slotted somewhere in the midst of a trillion shades of gray, a place where no one was entirely blameless and no one was altogether to blame.

When respect-induced silence ran its course, Sergeant Major

said, "This is the work of the terrorist leader. We hear he goes by 'Lwazi.' He is more organized and more regimental than any of those who preceded him and therefore far, far more dangerous. He is strategic and informed. A loyal African National Congress member, he wants one thing and one thing only: to take over South Africa."

He drank from a glass holding a suspiciously whiskey-colored drink to wet his whistle and, Lieut suspected, take the edge off all he'd seen. "As you get closer to the Angolan border, aerial surveillance is almost impossible because of the thick vegetation. Aerial photography to measure the lay of the land is also limited because only the Ovambos and sparse farmers ever used this land before it became a war zone. There's never been a need to spend vast sums on accurate mapping. Sure, we have grid references, but they don't detail your battlefield terrain. Stay aware, stay alive, and report the terrain back to me. It's essential for our intel arsenal. We always need opposition who are willing to spill the beans. Captives are our best source of information. Intelligence will do their level best to get what we need from them to make our future missions easier."

Frikkie turned to Piet-Tire, but before he could tickle the latter's funny bone, Lieut lifted both hands quickly behind them, knowing their peripheral vision would send them an alert, and Frikkie swallowed the joke.

After the morbid hour, Lieut took his guys down to the braaivleis area. A few of the troops were already gathered, and one of them was playing a guitar and singing all the old *Boere musiek*.

"Hey, guys," shouted Nev once the last notes had been pushed out. "Can you play some Uriah Heep?"

But before the guitarist could reply, Benny shouted, "SNAKE!" and men scattered.

"Kill it!" someone shouted.

"Leave it alone." Lieut's own shout surprised him. The poor snake must have been happily swaying to the music when some enthusiastic soldier poked a stick in his hole.

A big adder. Lieut positioned himself and quickly trapped the snake's tail with his boot just as the reptile rose to strike. The snake's confusion at his immobilization helped to slow him just enough for Lieut to quickly grab its head with well-practiced fingers and walk it away from the braai area. Then he set it free.

"Hey, Lieut's a snake charmer, boys!" Nev shouted gleefully, and the guitar conjured up a mystical Indian melody as Frikkie and Tiny—doing Cleopatra no favors—moved heads left to right on stationary necks much to Piet-Tire's great enjoyment.

That night in his camp bed in the major's tent, Lieut thought how, in the middle of nowhere in a war zone, this bed was more comfortable than the springless mattress he'd spent eleven years trying to sleep on at boarding school.

The adder and the bed charged his all too recently active Mind Brownie and New Aunts, taking him back to his first business enterprise at Estcourt Primary, which kept his friends in gifts till he was well into high school.

*Estcourt Boarding School, 1965*

"LOOK." Jock gently forced the adder's wide, open mouth over the lip of the cup, and applied light pressure to the sacs behind the fangs. "Scotty, it's not hard. The key is holding the snake like this." He pointed with his nose to his fingers holding both sides of the snake's jaw.

"Shit, Jock. I'm the nuts guy. Not the snake guy. You need

nuts? I can supply. But freakin' snake venom? *Aikona!* No way in hell!" Scotty shook his head and took another step backward.

"Scotty, please, man. Fitzsimons is really low on juice. They are paying double right now. I'll be away on the tournament till Wednesday. This little chap needs milking twice between now and then. And don't forget ... this one likes frogs. He doesn't do crickets. I'll even give you fifty percent if you do this. That's a lot of dough, Scotty." Jock soothed the snake: "Good boy."

"Shit, man, I don't think so ..."

"Scotty, we'll train with him when he's fresh out of venom. All you need to learn is to hold his head properly, then you're away."

"What the hell is goin'—"

Boet Buis.

His big pink head was far enough away to avoid a stray drop of venom and close enough to witness the highly illegal bootlegging snake business Jock was conducting.

Boet's about-face was quick as a spitting rinkhals, and the passage pounded with his speed to find Tomes.

Jock carefully disengaged cup from leaking fangs as quickly as possible and whispered, "Run, Scotty. The other way. You don't need the flak for this."

He was just about to run the snake outside when Tomes and Boet came bounding down the passage. *Shit.* He didn't want to throw the snake back inside and risk hurting him. Sir would just make him open his locker anyway, and then he'd get into more shit for untidiness.

He stood holding the head because the fangs were still loaded—he couldn't afford a dead Boet, as tempting as that might be. The snake wrapped itself around Jock's arm.

Boet stood, his chest puffed out like Mr. Viljoen. "See, Sir, this *oke's* up to no good."

"I can see the problem, Mr. Buis. Its beady eyes are staring right at me." Tomes looked at Jock. "What would possess you to bring a poisonous snake onto boarding school premises, Mr. Walsh?"

"Just for the good of the Park's Board, Sir. They desperately need venom for anti-snake-bite serum. The goal here is to save lives, Sir."

"Aaaha. I see. What does your enterprise net you in cash for this saintly occupation?"

"Cash is not—" He caught the look from Tomes. "Comes in handy for Christmas money, Sir."

"Well, hear me well, Mr. Walsh. If there is ever a snake in this boarding school again, even if it wanders in to catch a rat, you will be expelled. No questions asked. Is that understood?"

"Yes, Sir."

"I'm afraid the Parks Board will have to live without your life-saving contribution from now on, Walsh."

"Yes, Sir."

"And after you've disposed of your little friend here, I will see you in my office."

"Thank you, Sir."

"Oh, no need to thank me, Mr. Walsh. Besides eight of the best from my cane, I'll ask your coach to commission your second to take your place in the rugby tournament in Pietermaritzburg since you won't be there. You'll be ...

"Oh, NO! Please, Sir," Jock implored.

But Tomes held up his hand. "You, Mr. Walsh, will be writing an essay on the merits of listening to your house master. And it better be good, flattering *and* legible. I have a feeling that will take you well into next term."

"But Sir, school rugby ..."

"Ja! Jy wil mos!" Boet chanted "You asked for it," as telltales often do.

"And Mr. Buis, splitting on your classmates—though appreciated—is not an attractive trait. You might want to consider that it doesn't make you a hero in my books. Gone with you both. See you soon, Mr. Walsh."

Jock reckoned while he was getting Tomes's best eight, he'd have to consider what to buy Sipho and Papin with the last of his stash. It might help take away some of the pain.

# 26

# TOURISTS AT THE WATER HOLE

*Bush Between Angola and South West Africa, 1977*

THE INTEL WAS as clear as a puddle of quicksand, but it was all they had.

The suspicious men they'd singled out in the Ovambo village and brought in had proved to be an important stream of information. How that was achieved, Lieut had absolutely no desire to know.

They described the man they called Lwazi, which matched previous intel from other farms. This Lwazi was a conundrum. Soft-spoken, he turned away in disgust yet allowed his men to rape, pillage, and plunder. One described him as a body whose humanity had been sucked out, leaving only a detached, empty husk, mobilized by quiet anger that generated an innate power. His men were organized and terrified of him. The locals found him more frightening than Sangoma attacked by an entire colony of wasps.

And no captive spilled the beans on Lwazi without making enviable note that he wore the best-looking boots in all of Africa.

The prisoners gave up where the guns were buried, and a retrieval team picked up a cache of fifty-two AKs plus boxes and boxes of ammo a mile north of the village they'd scared senseless. Lieut was able to justify his fear-instilling tactics as means to an end.

Armed with that very intel, Lieut and his boys were moving closer and closer to the blight that was Lwazi.

*If I can snuff out Lwazi, the army will let me be. They will leave me the fuck alone. Let me live my life without interruption. Stop throwing me into a violent world for chunks of months. Months I can't talk about. I can't escape. I don't even know what I'm fighting for. Lwazi must die for the death of the farmers. For the fear and abuse of the locals from both sides. Lwazi must die for my freedom.*

They were three days into their week of rations. Two days into their full-force tracking from the last sighting of the strange, telltale boots. And in less than a day, they'd cross the border into Angola.

Boesman was forward and center, nose to the ground, directing them way off the beaten track. Lieut dished out tracking tricks to his men as they went.

Lieut called to them: "In tall grass, every two feet or so, look for bunches that've been folded. The fold will show you the Terrs' direction. Concentrate on the lower grass. It faces the direction the foot went. Go low, boys."

"Said the actress to the bishops," said Nev, and when Piet-Tire nearly wet himself, Frikkie gave him a dirty look as if wishing he'd thought of the punchline.

Lieut continued, "Good one, Nev. In some instances, you need to deliberately make your own marks to retrace your steps. Breadcrumbs for those German kids."

Penti laughed. "You mean Hansel and Gretel?"

"If you want to name those buggers, do. To put on your own

stamp, turn your right toe out slightly, or use your heel when you change direction. That way you'll recognize your own print to find your way home or to misdirect the enemy."

Ten kilometers ago, they'd spent precious hours camouflaging the Bedford with brush and foliage to Boesman's high standard.

Since then, they'd been on foot, going through semi-bush in a line-ahead formation. Each pointed their weapon in a different direction. It was nerve-wracking and slow. Cairns had fingered his picture of Cathy so much, she'd become just a color swirl. Benny and Penti were debating complex calculations involving distance traveled and proximity to the enemy; Frikkie and Piet-Tire were expending pent-up energy looking through their telescopic sites for irregularities; and Charl was taking his job of leaving retraceable footprints to follow seriously.

The day was long, but the signs were clear. They were headed in the right direction.

The first quarter of the orange setting sun had already been gobbled up by the horizon, but his team had made full use of their sixteen-hour day.

They found a giant quiver tree with a thick trunk close to a water hole. The San used the smaller branches as quivers to carry their arrows.

They were close to the Etosha National Park, and water holes were fuller here, in spite of the drought. He looked forward to the spectacle of bountiful animals coming to drink. Good. They'd be distracted during downtime.

"Look up the tree, Piet-Tire. What are we looking for?" Lieut asked as they threw down their gear in the shade.

"Uh ... fruit?" asked Piet-Tire, and the rest roared.

"Okay, you clever bastards. Who knows? Not you, Nev." Lieut chuckled.

"To see if there are snakes," said Benny.

"Right you are, and don't forget the vine snake. That little shit looks just like a branch—it even "waves" in the wind, and there is no antivenom for those little bastards."

His team circled the tree and prodded branches with their bayonets.

"What else should you look for?" he asked.

With that, Boesman literally morphed into the shape of a leopard before their eyes. Baring the spots, he was the beast itself. He even climbed the tree like a leopard, then draped himself over a thick branch and showed them how he, the leopard, ate his prey.

"Aaaaaaaaaaaaaand Boesman wins the prize." Lieut laughed. "Okay, quickly get settled, boys. This is prime time at the water hole. We can't miss it."

A plethora of wild game came to drink after ten minutes of human quiet. Three zebras sauntered down confidently; a small herd of black-faced impala drank tentatively, darting eyes focused on the water for stealthy crocs, while they turned highly tuned ears this way and that in case hunting carnivores approached from the bank. A mother and baby giraffe spread front legs awkwardly and bent their knees to reach cool water. A pack of wild dogs worked together to guard the pack and have turns to drink. Two warthogs waddled toward the water, sturdy and comical. A lone bull elephant sauntered down and submerged his hot self into the water, using his agile trunk to bathe the highest parts of his giant gray body while his Africa-shaped ears beat against his head in pleasure.

Just fifty yards away, Lieut's boys were privy to the best game sighting any lucky tourist had ever paid big bucks to witness. The evening air was filled with the chatter, hoot and bark of monkeys frolicking and songs of a thousand birds as a hadedah announced himself loudly and kingfishers circled and dove. Five blue cranes walked slowly and deliberately to the water's edge, and eagles, hawks and falcons soared.

His boys had to stay dead quiet or the cacophony of nature's noises would stop. That Piet-Tire and Frikkie managed was testament to his squad's unique and privileged immersion into this animal world.

Well-watered, the game skittered or stalked or ambled off into dense bush to find herds, hide from predators or hunt while Lieut's team lay in a loose circle of sleeping bags, digging into tins of army food.

Choosing biltong instead, Lieut threw Tiny his tin of bully beef, and his big boy's Cheshire grin lit up the sky. Tiny's forced nicotine denial made him hungrier than ever.

"Did you guys know the Etosha Pan means 'Great White Place' in Ovambo and can be seen from space?" Benny asked rhetorically.

"Impressive," Lieut murmured.

"I remember the first from geography class and the second from NASA's radio broadcast." Benny grinned.

"Speaking of impressive, Lieut, you can name more birds than Frikkie's had chicks. Are you a closet ornithologist?" Nev asked.

"Orni? Sure. But not as orni as Cairns!" Lieut retorted, and boys bellowed and Cairns looked embarrassed.

"Seriously, how the hell do you know all this shit?" Nev persisted, his straight glare forcing an answer.

"My Zulu blood brother taught me," said Lieut and watched his men laugh till they hurt. Even Boesman was chuckling.

Lieut suspected Boesman understood every word but chose not to let on. Hell, the guy could be giving English lessons at a San bushman school somewhere, for all they knew. He chuckled at the thought.

Lieut stood and said, "Boesman, show these boys what you can do."

Boesman jumped up, his face beaming with excitement. Though his click-click-clicking made no sense to his audience, his pantomime actions were as clear as this starry night.

Boesman mimicked gemsbok, springbok, honey badger, aardvark, and spotted hyena. The Dundee boys nailed all the buck, but only Lieut came up with the honey badger.

"Yissus!" said Tiny. "It's like being at the drive-in."

Then Boesman, in his element, painted pictures with his hands, and without Lieut's help, his boys voiced the bushman's tale.

In the wet summer season, which they hadn't seen for a long while, the huge 7,725-kilometer pan became a lake once more, standing at about ten centimeters deep and drawing thousands of migrating flamingoes.

Boesman did a hilarious flamingo.

"I swear, boys, there are so many of them, they change the entire sky. From horizon to horizon, there's a beautiful, undulating pink."

When Boesman was spent, he sat down cross-legged and used his eye teeth to rip off a long, thin strip of biltong. Like Lieut, he preferred the non-army dinner alternative.

"Show the boys your ostrich, Lieut," Nev said.

"I'm not whipping out my ostrich, Nev. I'm the shy type. You show them yours. It's much better than mine anyway."

Lieut thought Piet-Tire was close to getting a hernia from his gut-wrenching laughter, and the others joined in with side-splitting chortles.

"Boys, Lieut does the best ostrich. Come on, Lieut!" Nev urged.

"Did you know an ostrich's eyes are bigger than its brain?" asked Pentifuckingford.

"Did you boys have an excess amount of bubble gum lately? All this 'Did you know' trivia off the Chappies wrapper ... or are you having a general-knowledge duel?" Lieut tried to change the subject.

"Come *on,* Lieut. Boys! Prepare to be impressed." Nev started soft-clapping and soft-chanting, "Lieut ... Lieut ... Lieut."

Lieut got up slowly, and his boys forgot where they were and started clapping and chanting, "Lieut ... Lieut... Lieut" with way too much gusto.

Boesman and Lieut reacted with loud "Shhhhhhhhhhs," fingers over mouths, and when all was quieter, Lieut stood, and in a millisecond, he heard Papin's voice. *To hide from animals or people, you must learn to imitate animals. Merging with a flock of ostriches will keep the enemy from seeing you. But first you must convince the ostriches to let you join them, so you must move just like them.*

Lieut grabbed two of their precious maps, one in each hand He pushed out his chest, shoulders back and extended his head out, chin first, even farther. He held an open map fanned out in each hand, pushed his arms behind his shoulders, took giant strides and ran like hell around their circle, maps flapping like powerful wings that could never take off.

His team's hysterics became worse because they were trying to be quiet at the same time. He'd never head so much snorting and hiccupping. He thought of his nut farm friend, Scotty.

Lieut rolled up the head of his sleeping bag, squashed his face into the makeshift cotton pillow and laughed hard and relatively silently. Relieved to find a way to release their madness, his boys followed suit, screaming laughter muffled by army-issue sleeping bags. When Lieut lifted his head, only the back of his team's heads were visible. Boesman's face was split with pleasure, and catching his eye, the bushman bowed his head and clapped hands together. Lieut was chuffed.

According to Boesman, they were distant enough from the enemy for their ruckus not to be a dead giveaway to the enemy camp. The loud noise of the wild would mask any manmade sounds both in his and Lwazi's camps, so though they had to be careful, it wasn't life and death.

He had conferred with Boesman and Neville after their earlier reconnaissance and agreed they were close enough to attack tomorrow.

Dawn would come too soon.

Two at a time, they guarded the camp. Only the Dundee boys, Tiny, and Boesman slept like babies when they weren't on guard duty.

Lieut's mind was crowded with plans for tomorrow's ambush. In that dreaded death-hour before first light, when the most abysmal fears crept in, he recalled the last time he felt this kind pressure to save another ...

*Sterkspruit Falls, Drakensberg, 1965*

THERE WAS no room on the path for them to ride their horses side by side, but with the twins' need to be near each other, Dennis's nose was just to the left of Shaka's tail. The overgrown path followed the winding hill and forced their horses dangerously close to the edge when the contour so dictated.

Jock looked up at the layers of massive mountains. They were the catchment area for all the rain and snow. During a cloud burst, the water cascaded down either side of the vast range and tore through the countryside, upending boulders and trees and eventually the two tributaries merged together into a mighty stream. Down it gushed, forcing its way over the edge of the gorge, spewing hundreds of gallons of water along with nature's debris caught in its great power.

Suddenly, Shaka reared up. Neighing loudly, his eyes wild and afraid, he shook his huge head from side to side, and as Jock glanced down, he saw a puff adder disappearing into the grass. Papin controlled his horse, urging him down with comforting clicks, patting him. But instead of calming down, Shaka bowed his head, then used it to lift his massive shoulders, driving him ever higher as he bucked with all his great might and stopped only when he was at right angles to the treacherous path. Jock watched in open-mouthed horror as Shaka's manic neighing and whinnying exceeded the roar of the falls and he watched, helpless, as Papin flew up, up, up through the air ... and over the ledge.

Jock's stomach clenched and his heart pounded in his throat as he jumped off his horse and pushed past a confused Shaka to get to the edge. Dennis would calm Shaka. He rushed to the edge to get to his best friend, his Zulu self.

He closed the short distance from path to ledge, shouting, "Papin! Papin!" His voice sounded like it came from Loskop, and panic echoed in his ears.

Ten feet from the ledge, he crouched down and leopard-crawled to the very edge of the precipice, desperately afraid of what he might or *worse, so much worse,* what he might not see.

*God, please don't let Papin be dead.*

As he gripped the ledge, two inches of the grass-covered lip gave way and fell into the abyss, down at least 130 feet. Jock jerked back his hands as reality wracked his body with naked terror.

Eyes closed, he forced his body toward the edge. "Papin, Papin!" he called.

"Yebo."

Papin's soft reply popped Jock's eyes wide open. *Thank you, God, ancestors, Mr. Palmer, Sangoma ...*

Papin's face emerged from the leaves and looked up at Jock.

"You okay?" Jock managed.

"Tree not strong." His friend's voice was barely audible.

Relief swelled through his body and forced words out of his mouth. "Stay still as you can! I will save you," he said glibly as he briefly took in the scene.

Papin stood on a flimsy-looking limb and hung on to a delicate branch above his head. Those two pathetic strongholds were all he had between him and certain, shattering death.

*"I will save you" ... how the f—?*

Jock inched away from the ledge, ran to Shaka to lead him farther down the path and out of the way. Clicking and cooing and stroking, he detached the stirrups from Papin's horse.

*Save Papin. Save Papin.*

Jock ran to Dennis next, whose eyes hadn't left him. She was relatively calm as he removed her stirrup farthest from the ledge. He looped all three stirrups together, creating a long, strong rope, secured by one stirrup attached to her saddle.

Damn. It wasn't long enough.

He called down in the abyss's direction, keeping his eyes closed. "Papin. You okay down there?"

When "Yebo" was the barely audible reply, Jock realized even the tiniest motion caused by talking could break flimsy boughs.

*Oh, God.*

He wasted not a single second. With the Papin mantra on his lips and in his head, he removed Shaka's saddle and retrieved the blanket underneath. Next, he quickly removed the reins. Taking in the filly's girth, he knew that was what he needed to make up the extra feet to be in range for Papin to reach him.

Back to Dennis. Jock attached the girth to the end of his stirrup-rope concoction and tied a knot to secure it.

*Save Papin. Save Papin.*

Jock attached Shaka's reins to the blanket and gently placed the horse blanket over Dennis's eyes. The leather reins held the blanket in place successfully, and Jock thought he might have taken his first breath since his friend disappeared. His horse trusted him. *God, I can't let Dennis or Papin down. They trust me.*

He took a deep, steadying breath and tossed the end of the long reins over the abyss in Papin's direction.

Jock twisted the girth and folded it double, then pulled it over his head and arms. When it was secured under his armpits, he shouted: "Papin, when you see my legs and you know you can grab onto them safely, say *Yebo.* When I'm in position, I will say *Grab.*"

He paused, casting his gaze to anyone up in the sky for courage in case there was anyone there who could help "We only have one chance to get it right, Papin. Dennis won't be fooled a second time."

With forced confidence—lest Dennis smelled his fear—Jock clucked and whispered, soothed and gently pulled his blindfolded horse close, closer, closest to the edge of the mighty drop.

Jock tested his contraption's strength.

*Save Papin* was his only thought as he gritted his teeth and lowered himself slowly down. Down. Down. Down ...

Suspended safely, thanks to Dennis's blind trust.

Jock opened his eyes only to look up. He was three feet from the top. He kept going. *Save Papin. Save Papin.*

"Yebo" whispered Papin.

Jock braced himself, grateful for his mountain-bred, rugby-trained legs.

"*Grab,*" he shouted. At once he felt the leaden weight that was his friend attach himself to his legs. He heard a *snap* below, and though he had no intention of looking down, he knew Papin's only link between life and death had just snapped off the tree and was dropping down, down, down into the gaping abyss of thirteen stories.

Papin's arms were locked tightly around Jock's waist, and Jock's legs, wrapped around Papin's torso. Both holding on for dear life.

Quickly Jock reached for the dangling reins attached to the blanket covering Dennis's eyes. He shouted to Papin, "*Brace.* Hard jerk coming," and a second later, he yanked the reins, pulling the blanket off his horse's head.

Looking up, Jock saw his beloved Dennis's reaction to her darkness being replaced by a death-drop scant inches from her nose. Her natural reaction was to bolt in reverse as quickly as she could, and her immense strength dragged the friends, bound together by their twins' equipment and their own determination, up-up-up and over the ledge from death to blessed safety.

How long they lay on their backs looking at the sky, Jock had no clue. They were safe. Papin was alive. Next to him. That's all that mattered.

Their release came in the form of laughter. Great wracking laughter that could so easily turn into sobs. But neither Jock nor Papin would ever allow that to happen.

When he was spent, Jock got himself up and went to take care of his horse.

He stroked her and petted her and begged her forgiveness. She nuzzled him, and he knew she'd do it again if he needed her to. He'd never loved her more.

Papin called, "You saved me, Tsotsi."

"Dennis was the brave one. She saved us both." Jock slipped her a horse cube and led her down to be with her twin. He calmed Shaka with words and hands and horse cubes, and having Dennis close immediately took away his lingering agitation.

He joined Papin on the grass, and staring up at the bluest of skies, Jock considered that neither unkind words from guests, nor peer pressure, nor Bitch Society, nor Mr. Government or distance between them could ever alter the fact that he was always here for Papin just as he knew Papin was always there for him.

# 27

# THE CUT LINE

*South West Africa/Angola 1977*

THE PINPRICK of light he'd been waiting for at last penetrated his half-closed lids. Today was the day they'd kill Lwazi. But first he had to rally his troops.

"Okay, boys. That was our last sleep before we cut off the head of the *boomslang*. Lwazi's days are numbered. Boesman's analyzed Lwazi's cell movements, habits and patterns. He reckons we are four kilometers as the crow flies from that *Gollaga-inja* piece of earth scum."

The tension around Lieut was as thick as a Kalahari dust storm.

"Radio intel was entirely unhelpful this morn, so we're on our own, guys. Make damn sure of where you are and where you're going. Make your own breadcrumbs you can follow home using the skills you've learned. Look back and take a mental photo of every tree and rock outcrop because that's what you'll look for. Don't rely on anyone but yourself. You may find yourself alone. This is one instance where being selfish will save your life. Piet! Tiny! I'm talking to you! Make your own markers you can follow home. Don't rely on anyone else."

Lieut unfolded the map and placed four stones to secure each corner. His finger drummed the spot where they sat. "And this, boys, is home. Right here." Lieut let that sink in. "This is where we regroup if we split up."

He considered each of his boys around him, and a rush of tenderness turned to anger. *How the hell did you fuckers make me responsible for these trusting men? How can I be relied on to keep them safe when there are so many unknowns?*

He shook his head, forcing out the uncertainty. Focus. "Is this map reliable? All we can do is hope. That's why, ladies, we have to be super smart today. If you're in a jam, consider what Boesman would do, then do it! And use your heads. It's your heads more than your guns that'll keep you alive."

All eyes were on him. *God help me keep them safe.* Lieut continued, "The border is less than a kilometer away. If you've never been through a cutline, this is how it's done."

"A cutline?" Charl's pretty face lost perfection in its confusion.

"It's fifty meters of bulldozer-cleared bush running between the two countries. Our side planted loads of land mines in that area to reduce the traffic from Angola into South West Africa. Now we have to conquer our own deliberately planted war weapons to safely cross into Angola."

"Holy shit, Lieut, how the vok do we do that?" asked Piet-Tire.

"With difficulty. But we will make it easy. You'll lead, with Frikkie. If you don't blow up, we'll follow you."

Loud laughter ensued as Piet-Tire jumped back three meters in terror. Lieut continued: "When we get to the cutline, Boesman will help us find where the first land mine is buried, then the second. Our army planted those mines and recorded the pattern for their installation. Once we have identified where the first and second mines are, we can predict the pattern. We will take a single file at a forty-five-degree angle northwest with a gap a man's length between us so only one of us bites the dust if something blows."

"Really? Piet-Tire will go first?" asked Benny, nervous as hell.

"Oh, Benny, so sorry. Of *course*, you can go first if you insist," Lieut joshed, and Benny took four bold steps back to distance himself from the dreadful news. "But I'd much rather you let me lead." Relieved laughter erupted until they saw Lieut was serious again. "But you must stand exactly in my footprints for safe passage. The sand is loose, so prints are easily visible. No bunching. When someone stops, we all stop." He paused to let that sink in.

"Once we cross, the map is even more vague. We'll split into two groups. One group will approach directly from the back. The other group will circle round and approach them from the front. I've told you before, only stupid white people walk in the heat of the day. It's while they rest and eat lunch that we stupid white people will attempt to trap them quietly and surprise the shit out of them as we open fire from both sides."

"Cool plan," said Tiny as he inverted a fat thumb that looked like a sausage ready for the *braai.*

Lieut's demeanor was somber. "Plan's as cool as it's going to get given what we have to go on. We really have an unknown reality to face. That's why I need each and every one of you to be on your A game. Work smart and quiet and be alert and watchful. No jokes. No farts." He looked pointedly at Frikkie and Piet. "No smoking" was for Tiny, and for Cairns: "No looking at Cathy. Do not take your eyes off the prize for one second. Okay?"

A mixed set of agreements ensued.

"Use the basic sign language Benny the Brain taught you because it's the only way we can communicate with each other once we're close. Use the skills Boesman taught you to blend into your surroundings. Don't do anything heroic. No dead heroes in my squad. I need to see each and every one of your ugly faces gathered right back here with Boesman tonight, slapping each other on the back because our squad is responsible for wiping out Lwazi. You hear me?

"Charl, Penti, and Frikkie, go with Nev. You four will approach the Terrs directly from the west—you will be the frontal attack. Piet-Tire, Tiny, Benny and Cairns, you come with me. We will be waiting, so when you—Nev's team—open fire from the west, the Terrs will retreat to the east and we'll nail them. This means our position, boys"—he looked pointedly at Piet-Tire, Frikkie and Tiny—"has to be secret. 'Stealth' will be our middle name. Intel says Lwazi has six Terrs with him. Do not underestimate them. This is their turf. They know it inside out. All we have going for us is the element of surprise. So let's make it work to its maximum effect. Also remember that if for some reason they see you before you see them, or you're being attacked, don't be a bloody hero. Retreat and take cover. Make every bullet count. If you get lost, Boesman will find you. I don't want you to put your life in jeopardy any more than you have to. Don't tell the brass, but if the only way to survive is to run, run like the fucking wind, do you hear me?"

Only the wind could be heard. Even the noisy birds were quiet.

"I want you to know it's been a pleasure, boys. Tiny! Remember this: You're as strong as an ox, and you could lift a Bedford if we need you to. Pentifuckingford, it's an honor to talk about you around a campfire. Cairns, you get the hell back to your Cathy. Piet-Tire and Frikkie, sorry I have to split you up, but together you're not nearly as hilarious as you think you are. But solo? You're both sharp, quick and accurate. That's what I need you to be. Benny, your smarts helped us get to this point.

Charl, your bravery is something else. But don't be brave today, okay?" Lieut looked at Charl, waiting for a nod. It came. "Nev, you're a beauty. I don't like doing this shit, but you make it bearable. I trust you like a brother. Thanks for being here. Boesman?" Lieut looked over to their tracker, and he clicked away, smiling broadly. "Okay." Lieut smiled. "Boesman says to cut the shit and get on with the job. So, let's do it, boys. Let's kill Lwazi!"

Nods were all he expected and received.

"We have three hours to get into our ambush position. That should give us enough time to take up our positions. Gentlemen, we fire our loaded guns collectively at thirteen-ten sharp. You good?"

"Thirteen-ten sharp," they replied in unison.

"And not a peep before then. Nev, let's sync our watches."

# 28

# THE LETTERS

*Estcourt/Champagne, early 1966*

FOR ONCE, Jock and Papin were aimless. It was Saturday of Jock's weekend at home, and it had rained since they left Estcourt on Friday.

The guests were content. Dad made sure they had tons of things to do and play when the weather was shitty. But if Jock wanted to be with Papin—about which there was no question—they had to find somewhere they could be together and out of the rain. Sure, they could amble inconspicuously around the hotel, but Papin couldn't join in the games—it was not allowed—and he and Papin couldn't sit at a table together in the game room and play drafts or cards. Of course, they could work together. Dad would be more than happy to find them a job, but that was the last thing they wanted to do.

In this deluge, their rock was out of the question, and even getting to the Bushman Cave would be unpleasant. The horses would have to spend the night in the pounding rain. They could go to Papin's kraal, but that meant sitting in a very confined hut with adults, so that plan was nixed.

Together they roamed the passages of the hotel, ducking, diving and avoiding being seen. Together, inside the hotel, they were only observers. Never participants.

Jock recognized that Papin, at twenty-one years old, was a powerhouse of knowledge, strength of character and wisdom, and he reckoned his Zulu friend was smarter academically than fifty percent of the adults in Dad's hotel and at least three times more intuitive than all of them.

And yet, here they were as Zebra, unwelcome outcasts.

Their meanderings kept them aware of all the indoor hotel happenings, and they were never short of interesting observations and reasons to laugh till their stomachs hurt.

Billy, sober as a judge, still touted his tricks but less flamboyantly. Nicholas ruled his staff with an invisible iron sjambok, but the mystery of the head waiter's secret sauce that kept everyone in line had been solved. There wasn't a soul in a hundred-mile radius who would dare piss off Nicholas the Sangoma. Ask Billy, who still sported a slight post-frog tremor.

There was always someone interesting they could spy on coming from the bar, which was open to men only and not limited to guests. Billy Pillay came trotting down the passage, tray in hand.

Jock whispered of Billy's odd gait: "He reminds me of a flamingo. Those bloody knees bend the wrong way. I swear!"

The two were stifling guffaws as Papin exaggerated Billy's walk when the bar door swung open at a hell of a lick.

Out came a hefty man taller than even Papin and twice as wide, with a shock of blond hair and a red face. He weaved down the passage, bashing one arm and then another against each wall.

Jock whispered to Papin, "I bet Dad cut off his supply."

As he passed them clinging to the wall, trying to become invisible, they reeled at the smell of booze. Papin snuck behind the drunk man to mimic him, and Jock almost gave the game away with hysterics erupting through his nose, since his mouth was clamped shut. Jock caught up to Papin just as the man spilled through the door and onto the hotel's side veranda.

They saw the man looking to the left, shaking his dizzy head, then squinting again to focus on someone in the distance. Then he bellowed, "Whoooa. What are you doing here?" He spoke in Afrikaans.

Curious to see what would happen next, Jock and Papin, no longer fearing the man would catch them, walked out of the same door, pretending they had their own mission. Their intention was to turn in the opposite direction, hide, then watch the inevitable show.

But as they walked outside, Jock glanced left, and he saw ... Boet Buis.

Boet's crimson face was wet with mucus and tears as he tried to grab the man's hand. "Pa, come home. Ma's crying." His father kept pulling his arms out of reach, quick even in his stupor.

"*Voetsek!*" Boet's father shouted at him. An ugly word used to chase away unwanted animals.

Jock was rooted to the spot. He couldn't move. He was caught up in a debasing scene he'd never before witnessed. A horror movie starring someone he knew.

"Please, Pa—you're drunk. We must go home. I specially came to fetch you," Boet pleaded. "I've been everywhere to find you."

Out of nowhere, the big man found his balance, reached his arm behind his shoulder, whipped it around and slapped his son hard with an open hand.

Boet reeled back, clutching his cheek, and fell to the ground. It was torture to watch Boet come up after the blow, sobbing, pulling at his father's jacket.

He had to be hurting in a thousand ways. Jock felt Boet's humiliation burn his own cheeks.

"No son of mine cries like a bloody baby," his father spat, pulling his arm away violently.

And then Boet saw them.

His eyes connected with Jock's. Caught in the veranda lights, Boet's great shame flared fire-engine red on his cheeks. But it quickly changed to flaming, dangerous anger.

It was pure fear that turned paralysis to flight as Jock led the way, running in the opposite direction of the domestic abuse and Boet's mortification.

Jock couldn't put the sight of Boet as victim out of his head. Damn his Mind Brownie and his New Aunts! He'd never seen such violence, such raw emotion, such humiliation. Jock swore off drink for good.

Sunday, when he returned to the boarding school, Jock could feel the tension every time Boet was in the same room. Thank the ancestors they didn't share the same dorm.

Jock had no intention of rubbing in Boet's shame. He pretended he'd never seen what he'd seen. He didn't even tell Scotty.

Jock reckoned it was all the head-hits Boet had grown up with that kept the guy from leaving this shithole. He didn't know for sure how old Boet was, but he'd been at school longer than anyone else.

The tension rose, and Jock knew, like the pressure cooker Thabo used for soups and stews, if it was filled too high, the gauge would let out some steam. But if the heat wasn't turned down right away, the fuffy valve – as his mother called the nozzle controlling the output of steam - would fly off and the whole shebang would explode.

As usual, first thing on Monday morning, Jock found Sipho, and they did their own handshake they'd come up with over the years. Sipho was really old and slow now. Frankly, Jock had no idea how he would have coped through all of these nine years in this mournful place without the wise old man's true Africanisms.

After he'd presented Sipho with a silver pouch that held Mine Captain tobacco bought at the hotel shop, Jock shared Boet's fiasco.

"It is why he is such a bully. A good way to cover up what he fears most. And the only way he knows how to live. Hit before you get hit." Sipho was as wise as Papin. Boy, Jock hoped some of *that* would rub off on him.

"I feel sorry for him, Sipho. What kind of life must he hide? It makes everything a lie."

"I believe that is the human way. We never want others to see what really ails us. We cover up our weaknesses by pretending we are strongest in the areas we are not."

Jock considered that profound statement. "Hmm. Maybe even we start to believe we are strong where we aren't. Maybe that makes us strong. Our misguided beliefs."

Sipho smiled his gorgeous broad, mostly toothless smile. "I have made an elder out of you, Tsotsi. So besides feeding my daughter and her nearly grown sons, my life is four times more worthwhile."

Jock felt ridiculously proud. Sharing blood with Papin had worked to bolster his Zulu-ness too!

Sipho's last words resonated, and Jock said, "Don't speak like you are getting ready to visit your old kraal with your ancestors, Sipho. The world would be a sorry place without you."

Sipho smiled sadly. "Only you and my daughter will know I have left this world, Tsotsi. Not even my grandsons I see so rarely will care."

Sipho's still fine-tuned ears must have heard something because he froze. "Go, Tsotsi. We will talk another time."

He only had a couple more days before he could go home again. He felt the usual stirrings of excitement and longing.

After school, Scotty said, "Are we joining the kleilat fight?"

"Does an elephant get drunk on marula fruit? What time?"

Scotty and Jock came prepared. Their kleilat sticks were carefully chosen, tested and approved. They'd practiced with the other English kleilat boys. They'd squeezed damp clay onto the ends of their sticks, coiled them back like taut bows stretching to capacity, and they let them rip! Clay blobs zinged to intended destinations. *Clunk. Clunk.* Sturdy tree trunks took the brunt of the wielded sticks' accuracy. Next targets would be Afrikaners.

Yes, they were ready. Well, ready to be beaten as usual.

And they weren't disappointed.

But this time, Boet used Jock as his lat-landing target to release his nigh-exploding pressure cooker. The bastard had violated the unwritten rules of kleilat fighting and had laced his clay with tiny stones, and they hurt like hell. Jock took the punishment. He retaliated with shots to Boet's chest and upper thighs so his humiliating lat-hits would be less noticeable. Circumstances required it.

But by the time Jock sported a blue, swollen cheekbone, three bumps on his forehead, a broken back tooth and one pebble-laced lat had narrowly missed his eye, he'd had enough.

He aimed for Boet's solar plexus and nailed it. Boet doubled over, and Jock got one hell of a fright. But Boet rose up even more pissed off and aimed a beauty at Jock. He went down, fair and square, with the wind knocked out of his chest.

There was no question the Afrikaners won. Again. And Jock sported very visible signs of Boet's vengeance. To make matters worse, because the fights had rendered such visible injuries, both ringleaders had to pay the price.

Jock and Boet each got six cuts. It took the rest of the week to get the clay out of his hair and ears and a further three days for the bruises on Jock's face to turn yellow.

The next weekend with Papin was, as usual, spectacular, and they rode their horses far and wide and picnicked on a basket of fresh feasts Thabo had packed them. Papin made a great fuss of Jock's bruises and broken tooth. Jock assured him he would take care of Boet himself when the time was right, though he did manage to rub in that he'd do that in spite of never being taught how to stick fight.

When Jock returned to the boarding school after his home weekend, the only thing he had to look forward to for two long weeks was finding Sipho on Monday morning. He'd run the hotel gift shop on Saturday, and with tuck money he'd saved—damn, he missed his snake money—he bought his old friend some Wilson's toffees and a packet of Sipho's favorite, Lucky Strike.

He went through the long and required morning routine as fast as a rinkhals's tongue to fit in a visit with Sipho. He dashed to unlock his locker and head out to check for trolling prefects and fished for the well-hidden Lucky's. He glanced up to where the ex-snake Veldskoen box now held Papin's letters. He missed taking care of his snakes, let alone the money. Bastard Boet.

Deep in thought, he pulled out the packet of Lucky's and was closing his locker door when Mr. Tomes's face appeared six inches from his own.

He nearly jumped out of his skin.

"Sir!" he all but shouted, slamming his back against his locker door. Papin's letters!

"What's that in your hand, Walsh?"

The Lucky Strikes! Shit! "Sir, these are not for me."

"Well, considering you need all the air you can gulp down to beat Durban High's rugby team next week, I would hope not. But you still have contraband on school premises."

"They are a gift for one of the staff, Sir."

"Frankly, Walsh, I don't care who they're intended for. I only care about the extent of the pain I must inflict to ensure you'll never do this again. With you, that's always a challenge."

Worse even than the cuts was that he didn't get to see Sipho that morning but was relieved he still had the Wilson's toffees to give his friend after rugby practice that afternoon.

Sure, it was uncomfortable sitting on a wooden contraption for seven hours fresh from six of Tomes' best, but fierce rugby practice would take his mind off his bum for three hours and then he could find Sipho.

The mop was propped up against the games room wall. Odd. Sipho's mop was his reason and his armor.

Jock went around to the broom closet. As he approached, he saw a blue uniform in an unmoving bundle on the floor.

Sipho! Jock bent down, heart in his throat. His old friend was bleeding from his nose and mouth. "Oh, God, Sipho, what happened?"

"Buis hit me," he slurred and flinched.

"Wha—? Why?"

"The letters came when you were at practice. I was mopping the floor when Big *Baas* was handing them out." Sipho's pain was clear.

"Wait. Try and sit up, Sipho. Let me go call the matron ..."

"NO! No matron. No fuss." Sipho's words were slurred by his quickly-swelling mouth.

Jock's fury started at his feet. "Bastard Buis. I will get hold of that big shit and—"

"NO! Aikona! Leave Buis, or you make it worse."

Jock rushed off to beg some aspirin from the matron for his

own "headache." He wet his facecloth and grabbed a cup of water. If Sipho was caught drinking from a plastic cup the students used, there'd be hell to pay. But Jock didn't give a shit, and the wrongness of society's pathetic superiority stung Jock like a hive of African bees.

Back in the closet, he helped Sipho to sit up, watched him take the aspirin, then gently wiped away the blood. Jock was relieved to see there was only a small gash where one of Sipho's few bottom teeth had penetrated his lower lip from the punch. But his old friend's face would ache for days. Bastard Boet.

"What happened?" Jock asked.

"Big Baas held a letter and called out your name. Boet said, 'He's at rugby. I will take it for him.'"

Jock felt alarm like a thousand needles pricking his veins. "Wait! *Boet* said he'd take *my* letter?"

Sipho cast his eyes down and nodded slightly.

"Where is the letter now?"

"When Boet was going up the stairs, I called him. 'Baas Boet, I can give letter to Baas Jock when he comes in. I will see him in the game room.'"

Jock felt his chest start to burn. Then his neck.

Sipho continued in English: "Boet said, 'Come. I want something in the broom closet. Come.' I look around. Nobody else. He call me, '*Kom. Kom*. I haven't got all day.' So I hurry. As I walk around the corner, Boet stand with big arms over door. He says, 'What, kaffir? You know the Englishman so well you give him his letter?' I say nothing, Tsotsi. He says, 'Tell me why it is better for you to give than me to give?' I say I was just trying to help. 'Tell me. Is he your friend?' I say, 'No. I just help you, Baas. Not him.' He says, 'I don't need your blerry help, kaffir. And never, ever talk to me again, you hear?' He says, 'Do you want me to report your insolence to the high-ups or do you want to taste my fist?' I say, 'Please, no report.' Then, Tsotsi, I don't remember. I just find myself on the floor with my mouth *eina* and my head thumping."

Jock forced himself to remain calm. "Sipho, please take your mop and only go where there are people. I will watch and make sure you get out of here safely when you leave. I'll be back."

He ran out and didn't have to search far for Boet. From inside, through the fogged window, Jock saw Boet in the middle of the playground. He'd upended an empty steel dustbin and was standing on it, four feet above the ground.

Boet held an envelope in one hand and an open letter in the other.

Jock's blood dropped to his feet.

There was a crowd of boys of all ages around the dustbin.

Boet read aloud, his Afrikaans accent thick, bastardizing the written words. His voice was high-pitched like the words were written by a girl.

"'Dennis is pining for you.' Ja, that Walsh must be a moffie if a boy is pining for him. 'Billy is not as funny as when you are here.'" Boet forced out an ugly laugh.

Not only had the blood from Jock's entire body gathered in his feet, it had turned to concrete, stopping his legs and feet from moving. The dreaded Mist was moving in. He was stuck in the doorway of the boarding school leading to the veranda. He just stood there. Immobile. Forced to listen to his letter from Papin being vomited up by misinterpretation. Though The Mist swirled and trapped his concrete feet, it wasn't thick enough to block the view of Papin's letter still waving in Boet's hand. From his trash pulpit, Papin's words—distorted and ugly—spewed from his mouth. "'Chief looks for you around the kraal fire. Come home soon ...' You hear that? You *hear* that? 'Your friend, Papin.' Papin is a kaffir name." And Boet switched to English. "And Jock Walsh, my friends, is a one hundred percent Kaffir Boetie. He was seen at his father's hotel, hanging around all-a time wif a much older kaffir. In a public place, *nogal.* What kind of a white boy is this? A Kaffir Boetie, I tell you!"

Boet, his putty-face evil and menacing, waved Papin's letter back and forth and continued his tirade in Afrikaans. "This is proof. Read for yourselves. Don't touch Jock Walsh. He's a Kaffir Boetie. He's contaminated!"

And Boet hocked up and spat on Papin's letter as his pedestal wobbled with the force of his contempt. Boet jumped down.

In that instant, Jock pushed through that fucking mist, concrete replaced by pounding blood as his legs found their might, and he flew over the veranda toward Boet. Before the big lug had a chance to react, Jock launched himself at the brute headfirst. But Boet was fueled by the power in his hand that was Papin's letter. He faltered and almost went down but kept his arm aloft and out of Jock's reach.

As Jock looked up at the letter, the lug propelled his southpaw and hit Jock on the same side of his jaw.

As it happened, he felt a stabbing pain in his already-damaged back tooth, and a piece of loose enamel twirled in his mouth as the iron taste of fresh blood fueled his fury.

Like a bull made angry with a dozen swords, Jock used his square frame, made for a rugby scrum, to charge the Dutchman with all his might.

Winded, Boet went down. Jock grabbed the letter and envelope and ran to his tree. He fished inside a hollow he shared with some critters and removed a box of matches. Without reading it, he set alight the letter which he'd been so looking forward to, his heart as heavy as the day he was dropped off at this detestable boarding school. He did the same to the envelope, burning every trace.

Instead of crying, which is really what he wanted to do, he sucked down his base instinct like he'd taught himself to do, and anger began to fester. At Boet, at his parents for putting him in this horrible place, at his friends for not coming to his aid, and mostly, at Papin.

He felt ashamed he'd forgotten Sipho. When he rushed back to check on his friend, the elder had left school for the day. He'd let Sipho down.

Then Jock did what he vowed he'd never do no matter what. He split on another human being.

"Sir." Jock knocked tentatively on Mr. Tomes's door.

"Come," said the voice of authority.

"Sir, Boet hit Sipho."

"Who?" Tomes looked blank.

"The janitor. Boet punched him in the mouth. Sir."

"Do you have proof?" Tomes had lost interest. Head down, he was reading something.

"Sipho ... the janitor told me, Sir."

Tomes actually laughed. "And you believe him?"

"He is more honorable than that fuc—"

Tomes held up his hand and sighed. "Stop! Before I have to sort out your language with a sjambok, Walsh."

Jock took a deep breath.

"Do you have proof of this so-called 'assault' other than the word of an old black man?"

"What kind of a world do we live in when that's not enough?" Jock asked, and he knew he'd suffer for the insolence of his tone. He added "Sir" for what it was worth.

At least Tomes stopped reading, and his tone was surprisingly passive. "When you're old, the memory goes. One forgets. He could have easily fallen. It happens, Walsh. You can't just blame somebody without proof."

Jock's words, angry as hell in his own ears, shouted before he could swallow them: "That's it? You don't care that a bully who screws with all the young kids and anyone else who's weaker than him actually drew blood from one of your staff? Sir."

Jock got a fright when Tomes rose so fast, his chair not only pushed back, it tipped over. "This will go no further. I am surprised you don't know this already, Walsh. In this environment, being a friend to anyone other than your own kind will do you *no* favors. Now get out of my sight."

Later, Jock took the Veldskoen shoebox holding all of Papin's letters to his tree.

He set fire first to the contents, three at a time, and then to the entire box.

Sure, he got cuts for starting a fire on school property, but Boet's despicable deed and Papin's words hurt him much, much more.

# 29

# TIME AND THE DRIED-UP RIVER

*Angola, 1977*

THEY MADE it through the cutline with an elephantine load of nervous tension and sweat but without incident. Boesman hung a khaki-colored bush hat in the tree, marking their position of entry, and hung another where they exited the cutline.

"Don't try to cross before you can see both hats and start where we end today. No matter how keen you are to touch South African soil, step slowly, deliberately. Be very careful, please. Remember what a shit writer I am and cut me some slack. I don't want your folks to think you had a monkey as a leader." The last thing he needed was for them to blow themselves up at the very end of their mission.

When they found an area thick with undergrowth, Boesman stopped.

Lieut said, "We're in Angola boys. Leave all equipment here. Boesman will camouflage it. When I say 'everything,' I mean mine detectors, gear, food. We take weapons, a pair of binoculars for each team, ammo and good sense. Everything else stays. Only Cathy gets to go, as well as your lucky tokens you can't live without and I can't see. Don't worry about this stuff here you're leaving. Boesman will take care of it. Whatever happens, you can rest assured, Boesman has our backs. Memorize where we left this morning. Think of yourselves going back the way we came, following your own German-kid breadcrumbs. Don't attempt to cross before you see both hats. Hats mean home, boys, and you know how to get there. You're well-equipped to make it back to the bush home we left this morning."

Once everyone had stacked their superfluous equipment, Lieut gestured for them to gather.

"Now we split up. Remember only one thing. In war, cowardice is perfectly acceptable as long as you're not endangering your fellow soldiers. Heroes are usually dead. I want to see all your ugly faces tonight on the other side of this cutline." He cleared his throat before he continued. Bastard lump.

"Nev, you go straight ahead, stay covered and wait till thirteen-hundred and ten, then open fire."

Neville nodded, and his boys followed behind him.

"Guys, let's go!" said Lieut, and he headed to the left.

Lieut reached the edge of what was shown on the map to be a slight decline but holy shit!

Before him lay a deep, wide and rugged gorge. How the f—? He crumpled the useless map and shoved it in his pocket. "Piece of shit." Likely the body of water had dried up in the years of drought, leaving a massive expanse of boulders.

"Okay, boys. We have to go down this side of the gorge and up the other side and get into position by thirteen-oh-nine. We have to run this gorge, not traverse it. Let's go."

Though Lieut hadn't climbed for a long, long time, he still had rugby legs, and it was even hard for him. Tiny struggled to balance over the massive rocks. Piet-Tire was fairly nimble, Cairns could keep up though he was slow, but Benny was his real problem child. His every step was tentative. A blind sand crane strutting over hot coals.

"Stay in single file and off the natural path. That's where land mines will be. I know you want to take Benny piggyback, Tiny, but you can't. Staying in front of him is what will help. Benny, walk where Tiny walks. That way you know it's safe."

Lieut glanced at his watch. Shit. Twelve-hundred and thirty-one. Time was being eaten up by the unexpected depth and breadth of the fucking gorge. He glanced back and saw how far Benny lagged and helpful Tiny was right there with him. They were only as fast as their slowest, and slow he could not afford. He'd be a man short, but he'd be a team short if he didn't do this. "Benny, can you track your way back to the regrouping area?" Lieut asked.

Benny pushed his thick, black glasses farther back on his nose, nodded and lost his balance.

"Go back and help Boesman do what's needed. He needs help. Go quickly. We'll manage. Go!"

As soon as Benny's back was turned in the direction of "home," Lieut said, "We waste no more time, boys. We don't walk over these rocks, we run."

The bottom of this hole in the earth was the resting place for giant boulders probably separated from the compacted sand cliffs when the rare but fierce rains came. It was a bitch to traverse.

"Tomorrow you can nurse your feet in the water hole. Now we run like the wind." Lieut glanced at his watch: twelve forty-three. They had so far to go.

He looked up at the hillock from the bottom of the deep gorge, and it seemed like the 11,000-foot mountains of his youth.

They were finally on the ascent. Head down, Lieut made sure his feet touched home, so Piet-Tire behind him, could take the same step confidently, as could Tiny and Cairns.

"Holy Poggenpoel," whispered Tiny loudly.

Lieut looked up as he heard "Fuck" spew from Piet-Tire.

A thick seam of dark gray rocks about ten meters high and eighty meters wide loomed across their horizon. Green moss covered the rocks, and the color blended into the short brush of the hillock, rendering it invisible till you got close. There was no way to scale the rock face without rock-climbing gear and time.

It took less than a second for Lieut to recover from the shock. "Scan for a gap in the rock face. Somewhere real grass is growing. We're about 110 meters from the rocks. Piet-Tire, use your eagle eyes. Cairns, binoculars and find that real grass. Quickly."

A precious thirty seconds later, Piet-Tire said, "I see a gap, about a man wide."

Lieut saw him point and headed there. "Piet! You beauty!" he whispered over his shoulder and changed course.

Twelve-hundred fifty-six. Fuck.

But at least he could see the top of the hillock. It was nicely lined with trees. They just had to get up through this gap and they might make the rendezvous on time.

"Piet-Tire. You're the quickest. Kick us some footholds as you go up. It'll make the going easier."

Piet climbed like a baboon, kicking holes into soft soil where boots could grip, testing the strength of the foliage to hang on to.

Piet-Tire's sterling job worked. Tiny was the most hesitant and the second-last to climb. "Tiny, I'm here to push from the bottom. Piet is at the top to help haul you up. No skill required. Look. Here ... here ... and here are the footholds Piet-Tire's made for your feet. Grab the plants Piet tested. The first hoist is the worst. Use my back." Lieut bent over, hands on knees. A bulldozer on top of a Datsun. Only his years as a prop holding up rugby scrums saved him from crumpling to the mossy ground from the heavy load.

"Stay behind me when I'm up," Lieut shouted, and his old

mountain skills came back, driven mostly by his watch. Thirteen-hundred and five.

Once clear of the rock face, they ran behind him at full speed, straight up in single file, off the path and heading for the trees.

They were twenty meters from the top.

Thirteen-hundred and ten. Fuck.

The firing started. Nev and his boys.

A rat-tat-tat of automatic weapons—Terrs firing in response. If nothing else, his team could provide an additional element of surprise in just five minutes. They were nearly at the top.

Tiny suddenly appeared on Lieut's left, running parallel with him.

In a nanosecond, he knew Tiny was just reacting to get there the fastest way to help his fellow soldiers.

Lieut shouted, "Get off the fucking path!"

# 30

## QUARRY STONES

*Champagne Castle, 1966*

It was the only weekend of his life Jock dreaded coming home.

Of course, he didn't want to be anywhere else in the world, but the weight of what he had to do was like carrying fifty pounds of quarry stones in each pocket.

As they drove up to the hotel, Papin was waiting on Shaka and holding out Dennis's reins for him as usual. The always welcome sight of his friend and his horse increased the weight of the quarry stones.

Jock had two weeks to think about the letter fiasco. It wasn't Papin's fault. Not by any means. How shocking he'd so quickly blamed the source and not the culprit. He felt ashamed, which made what he had to do that much harder.

He also missed the security of those precious letters in his locker and the chance to reread them when he needed, to take him home.

He'd discussed all this with Sipho, and his sage friend said it was the first time in Jock's life he really had to deal with the consequence of being a white boy who had a Zulu best friend.

"But Sipho, people have looked at Papin and me funny for years. It hasn't bothered us."

"You were left here in this boarding school because it bothered somebody," said Sipho gently.

"No. I am here because I couldn't read or write." Jock's reply was dogmatic. But as he lay for hours after lights-out on his hard dorm bed, he remembered how his banishment to the boarding school had coincided with him and Papin together first being nicknamed "Zebra." Perhaps Sipho was right.

He didn't know who he should hate—his father for succumbing to pressure from his sacred guests or that bitch Society and her buddy Government, who made up their own rules and fucked everything up for everybody.

Papin's grin was broad, and once Jock had hoisted himself up and onto Dennis's back, his friend's hand was out in readiness for their handshake. After a moment of hesitation, Jock grabbed Papin's hand, and as they shook and thumbed and elbowed, Jock knew that nothing would ever come between them. What others thought was not important. Not really.

As they galloped to their rock, Jock figuratively emptied his pockets of the heavy quarry stones he'd been dragging around for eleven days.

"Why are you angry? What happened at school?" Papin didn't miss a trick.

"I had another run-in with Buis. This time that same back tooth broke off at the base from clay from his lat. Bastard. I'll ask Tomes to let me go to the dentist next week. I don't want to make a fuss around here. You know my mother."

Saturday, the hotel was bustling with guests with energy to spare. Mandinsolo was booked with experienced climbers for an ambitious climb. Bekah had earned his place as a guide and was to lead seven guests on the Intunja river hike, so Jock and Papin were delegated to pick up the slack for the less ambitious.

Jock, Papin, Tse—the new teaboy—and twelve guests headed out after breakfast. Guests were excited since none of them had yet witnessed what was promised on the hotel brochure: "Astounding Cathkin Peak; the wonder of Crystal Falls; and the oddity of the rock formation that looks exactly like the Sphinx."

Jock and Papin had to curb their pace to allow guests to keep up as they worked their way through an avenue of blue gum trees and onto the side of The Little Berg.

The higher they went, the slower their hikers' pace. Not just because the going was rougher, but the grandeur of the peaks was worth capturing on film and in memory. Champagne Castle, Cathkin Peak, Sterkhorn, The Turret, Amphlets and, behind, The Dragon's Back. Besides the mountain majesty, there were nature's miracles: baboon families squabbling, picking nits from each other's hard-to-reach places, sharing fruit and frolicking on the outcrops along the narrow paths to the waterfall; hawks, falcons and eagles; dassies and meerkats; a rock rabbit family; a score of colorful songbirds. Even the huge red grasshoppers were spectacular enough to discuss over whiskey on the rocks or rum and Cokes before dinner.

Jock scooped a sun lizard off a rock and then another. He pinched their jaws open with two fingers, held them over each earlobe and released them. He made no fuss, and they hung from his ears for the longest time, till one of the women noticed them dangling and started to giggle. Jock's "bush earrings" created a wave of hilarity that lasted till one of the lizards lost interest, followed by the other. Jock hoped they'd find each other and start a new adventure.

They were about a hundred yards from the falls. The path narrowed, and the guests soon had to queue in single file to keep from slipping on loose gravel and stumbling too close to the edge. Tse's rucksack was laden with crockery and cutlery for their substantial picnic: scones, sandwiches, cake, biscuits, sugar cubes and tea leaves and, of course, the milk laced with brandy.

Jock heard the hikers suck in air, and oohs and aahs followed. The breathtaking beauty of the bottom of the Crystal Falls never got old. Sheets of water spilled in a rage over basalt rock, showing off and fanning out, spilling gallons and gallons at a time. Two-thirds of the long way down, the cascading water hit a rock outcrop and shot up in a million directions, catching the light filtering through the trees. An expensive firework display so brilliant it could illuminate the day. Then, on their way down, individual droplets seemed to suspend in midair for a millisecond, as if to grab your attention as they became multifaceted diamonds, pulsing with light before falling gently into nature's calm, crystalline pool.

As guests settled in the natural shade, reveling in the spectacular ambience, Tse lit a fire, then filled the billy can with azure water for tea.

Jock felt happy as the guests chatted amongst themselves. As always, Papin beside him added to that happiness ... and then he remembered the heavy quarry stones. Perhaps now was a good time to introduce the thought and then explain in detail later. His pockets would sure feel lighter.

He looked at Papin, sitting with his knees bent, arms linked around them. "Don't write to me at school anymore."

Papin's face was at first amused, and Jock dropped his eyes.

"Why?" Papin asked softly.

"Just don't, okay?" Jock couldn't look at Papin because tears —with which he had no experience—blinded him, and shame for lack of finding the right words added a hundred quarry stones to his pockets.

"I thought you liked my letters," Papin said flatly, and Jock felt his friend's confusion and hated himself for it.

"I did. I do."

A scream pierced the serene mountain air.

A guy in his mid-thirties clutched his ankle as a younger woman stood next to him, wringing her hands. He crashed to the ground before Jock and Papin could get to him. "Snake bite," Papin shouted, and Jock rushed to the rucksack, pulled out the snake-bite kit.

Jock opened the kit and grabbed the adder antivenom vial that was the antidote for all adder bites. "Does anyone have medical training?" he shouted.

No reply. He handed a new razor blade and tourniquet to Papin and shouted to Tse, "Leave the rucksack and go. Tell Inkosi snake bite and bring back the stretcher and whoever you can find."

Tse's young legs pumped away for help as Papin finished tying the tourniquet below the victim's knee.

The guy was going into shock. Jock took the syringe from the tin, turned the vial upside down, inserted the needle and pulled the plunger down, filling the tube. He flicked the air out of the tip of the syringe and handed it to Papin, who immediately injected the guy's leg.

Jock sat down next to the guy and looked up at the pretty young woman still wringing her hands. "What's his name?"

"Johan," she said and sat down next to Jock.

Jock shook him awake. "Johan, did you see the snake?"

Johan nodded.

"What did it look like?" Jock asked, but the man just continued moaning.

"Did it open its mouth very wide?" Jock pressed the guy, who, mid-moan, kept his mouth open and nodded, his eyes filled with stark terror.

"Was it fat?" Jock asked Johan, and he nodded.

"Likely a puff adder," he shouted to Papin over the raucous.

Papin had sliced through one of snake's puncture marks with the blade and was working on the second.

"What's happening?" the girl asked, clearly frightened.

"Johan's been bitten by what looks like a puff adder based on the wide puncture marks. It opened its mouth wide to nail poor Johan here. Its fangs are on hinges in the front, so it must open wide to let them spring out so they can bite. This snake strikes very, very quickly, but it's slow-moving. That's how Johan saw it." Jock rose and grabbed the brandy bottle filled with milk and handed it to Papin.

"What? He's taking a break to drink brandy while Johan suffers?" She was furious.

Papin's cheeks puffed out with the milk, which he swished around his mouth, then swallowed. "He's lining his stomach with milk. It might just prevent the poison he's about to suck out of your boyfriend from going through his stomach and into Papin's bloodstream." Jock could hear the edge in his voice.

"I'm sorry," she said.

"What's your name?" Jock asked.

"Calli."

"Okay, Calli. I want you to time fifteen minutes on your watch for me." She looked at her left hand, looked up and nodded. "Starting now," Jock instructed.

"Why?"

"We must try and slow down the poison from getting to his heart with the tourniquet, but we have to take it off periodically so the blood won't clot," Jock said as he moved to sit with his legs in a *V* so he could hold Johan's head with both hands.

He spoke to the victim sternly. "Johan, wake up. Wake up." He tapped one cheek and then another.

Johan's eyes blinked open, and as soon as awareness hit, his face was infused with terror.

"Johan, listen to me. Calli's right here ... see?" Jock turned the man's head to catch sight of his girl. "Now you have to be still, but you can't fall asleep. If you do, your muscles will relax, and poison will travel faster to your heart. Talk to Calli. Tell her what you like most about her."

Jock saw Papin was ready, and he held fast to Johan's head. Jock watched as Papin bowed his head and sucked with all his might to pull the poison from Johan's body and into his own mouth.

Papin spat out the mixture of blood and venom, bent his head down and did the same again. And again.

Jock was so busy watching Papin and considering each mouthful could mean his friend's own infection, he lost his firm grip of Johan's head. The man lifted his head in a moment of strength. He saw Papin sucking away and shouted, "What the fuck are you doing?"

Jock pulled his head back down and held it there. "Johan, listen to me. Papin has to suck out the poison from your wound or you could lose your leg. You may even die if we can't get it out. Do you understand me?"

In a split second, Johan pulled his good leg back to his knee and kicked out at full force. His tough mountain boot connected violently with Papin's face.

In disbelief, Jock watched Papin's head whip back from the force as Johan shouted, "No kaffir is going to suck my leg. I'd rather die."

Jock stood up quickly, picked up the brandy bottle and poured milk over Papin's injured lip, where the vicious boot had caught him. *God, ancestors, Sangoma, Mr. Palmer, please don't let the poison penetrate ... Please don't let the poison penetrate ...* He kept pouring the milk over Papin's lip in time with his mantra as fear burned through him. What if Papin ...

"Enough!" Papin's voice raged.

Jock went back and stood astride Johan's head, looking down

at him. "Papin was trying to save your miserable life, you stupid ass. Now you've messed up his mouth. Papin can't help you anymore. He can't suck out the poison."

"You do it, you little shit. You do it," Johan said to Jock.

"Can't," said Jock. "My tooth's broken. Poison will kill me."

"Fuuuuck!" shouted Johan. "Calli?"

She shook her head and lowered her eyes.

"Can anyone take over from Papin?" Jock asked, looking at each walker individually. Most avoided his eyes. Those his eyes met bulged in fear. "If you have broken teeth or open wounds, you cannot help. If you can, if you will, Papin and I will talk you through it. Papin's mouth is buggered now, thanks to him." Jock pointed to Johan. "So's mine. Also inflicted by an idiot."

Over Johan's wails, broken sentences spilled out from the hikers: "Can't. Need the dentist. Cold sore ..."

Calli said, "It's fifteen minutes."

Jock saw Papin rinsing his mouth out down at the pond, and Jock took off the tourniquet. "Time one and a half minutes please, Calli. Let me know when and I'll re-tie it."

When time was up and he was tying the tourniquet back on Johan's leg, Papin's voice came from above him. "I will start again," his friend said.

Jock jumped up. "No way in hell, Papin. You're at risk because of him." Jock stabbed the air in Johan's direction. "How will we stop the poison getting to your heart, Papin? With a tourniquet around your neck?"

"He could die, Tsotsi."

"As could you, and that would be much more of a loss to the world."

"What do you care?" Papin asked and walked away, but not before Jock saw the raw hurt in his friend's eyes. He hated himself. And Boet. And Johan. And Society.

A grim half an hour followed. Jock watched helplessly along

with the hikers, some of them in tears, others kicking stones, heads down as Johan—in and out of consciousness—intermittently hallucinated or wailed, "Please, I don't want to die. Somebody ... anybody ... help me."

Papin kept away from the crowd. He wouldn't even look Jock's way. Jock's head pounded with fury, and very quietly he whispered to the bastard who'd hurt his friend, "You did this to yourself. Now no one else can or will save you. You hurt the only man who could. Now we just have to hope Tse gets here soon. Keep awake. Scream if you must, but don't fall asleep."

When his fury subsided and fear replaced it, Jock held Johan's head to shake it when he lapsed into a coma. He urged Calli to talk to her boyfriend.

As he held the head that represented everything wrong in his world, Jock saw Papin walking around in a circle. Johan must have hurt and humiliated Papin to the quick, not to mention the physical pain this son of a bitch inflicted. With a jolt and a burning in his chest, Jock realized it was he, Papin's best friend, who'd hurt him more than any forceful Veldskoen could. And Jock cursed himself for allowing Boet to win.

Jock's dreaded Mist threatened to swirl around him, though the day was bright and clear. But it was the darkest day on earth as far as he and Papin were concerned. Nothing was worse than them being at odds. He had never felt so alone. Ever. That was saying something.

He couldn't leave Calli and Johan. If only Papin would come and sit down with him so he could explain what had happened. Then he'd understand. But Papin wouldn't even look at him and stayed at the water's edge, his back to everyone.

The bloody Mist of angst and loneliness knew just when to engulf him. All the mist would let him do was shake Johan's head or slap him into wakefulness. In what seemed like two months inside the threatening Mist, distant whistles meant help was close, and he forced his way through. Once free, he would look first for Papin. He was still at the water's edge, and Jock's view of his tense back made the dreaded Mist seem conquerable.

Jock nearly kissed Tse and the three strapping men from Eteemot's team with him. Papin joined in as they lifted Johan and placed him as gently as possible on the stretcher.

Jock said to Calli, "I am sorry I swore at him, but he would have been in a lot less danger if he'd let Papin do what he knows to do."

"I know. He's very anti-black. But aren't all South Africans?" Calli asked matter-of-factly.

Her shrugging acceptance of her boyfriend's ugliness hit him like her boyfriend's Veldskoen boot to Papin's jaw.

Jock was the exception, not the rule, and there was no place in Bitch Society for him. Or Papin. And no sacred place for two who were not only friends but extensions of each other.

That night, everyone in the hotel waited anxiously for the call from the hospital about Johan's condition. From their observation alcove, a perfect place for nonparticipants to see the action, Jock kept looking for Papin.

Where the hell *was* he? Papin had avoided Jock all the way back, and as soon as they were in sight of the hotel, Papin ran ahead and disappeared. Jock searched everywhere. He needed to be here because if that sorry, bigoted son-of-a-bitch lived or walked again, it was thanks to none other than Papin.

Jock left his spot and dashed into the bar, the adult lounge, the games room, kitchen, scullery, walk-in pantry, dog kennel ... no Papin. He got back to the alcove just in time to see Dad come in and mount the steps to the stage. "Folks, good news."

Jock looked around like a meerkat guard. Anxious. Alert.

Still no Papin.

"Johan is very swollen. He'll be in Estcourt hospital for a bit, but the staff there know what they're dealing with. And he'll get to keep his leg thanks to the training and quick thinking of our staff."

There was wild applause, and the guests all stood up. Jock felt a burning resentment. Not one of the bastards contributed to Johan's survival. His thumping heart pushed him from the alcove to the stage. He jumped up and stood next to his father.

"May I just say, if it wasn't for Papin—the only one of us who could help Johan—he would be dead."

"Hear, hear," shouted the still standing crowd as they lifted their glasses.

"To Papin," one guy shouted, and the rest joined in.

Jock waited till the noise died down. He sure as hell had something else to say.

But Dad's arm come across his torso, and he whispered, "Enough."

Jock wanted to scream and protest and call a spade a bloody shovel. Instead, he walked off the stage to find his lost friend.

He searched every square inch of the hotel grounds, the stables, their rock, the compound, the kraal. No Papin.

Sunday. No Papin. No one had seen him. Not even the chief or Sponon. Not even the stable boys. He retraced his steps from last night and even went up to the Bushman Cave, just in case. Nowhere.

He stole a sheet of Champagne Castle Hotel paper and an envelope meant for each rondavel's top left dresser drawer, right next to the Gideon Bible.

Jock wrote the first letter in his life. "Dear Papin, I am sorry I upset you about the letters. Boet Buis found one of your letters, and he read it aloud in the playground. All the kids—well, those brave enough—call me 'Kaffir Boetie' now. Well, it's true, I suppose—in the best sense of the word. I am your Zulu blood brother and proud of it. It's hard at school to be what I am in my heart—a Zulu. There is so much anger, and things are not fair. But fighting it alone is tough. I just want you to know I could never ever wish for a better friend or be more grateful to have some of your blood running through my veins. The best parts of my life are only best because you made them so. Your friend and blood brother, Tsotsi."

His mother was waiting to take him back to the boarding school. He licked the envelope and found Nicholas. "Please give this to Papin. I can't find him. Nobody can. Thanks, Nicholas." He turned as dreaded tears threatened, and as he swallowed them down, he felt Nicholas's big hand squeeze his shoulder.

It was the first time in ten years—except for when the boy became a man—Papin didn't run next to the car for two miles.

# 31

# THE SCAR

*Angola, 1977*

TINY!

The world exploded around him, and he went deaf.

Lieut watched his own rag-doll body fly high, high, higher into the air in slow motion. He surveyed the scene as if he had all the time in the world and watched in fascination as his unresisting body went down, down, down and finally crashed next to an outcrop of rocks.

He saw himself—or that which wasn't quite himself—with his leg at an awkward angle and his arm bent backward. Odd, he thought, and only then did his mind sync with his body and acute pain from dislocated joints and broken bones shrouded his clarity.

It was quiet. Had he blown his eardrums, or had the firing over the hill stopped?

Wait! He heard Zulu being spoken close by. *Where the hell am I? At the hotel?*

Through the ringing in his ears, he heard bursts from the AK47s close by and knew exactly where he was.

He waited for his own oblivion.

A shadow passed over his face. He tried to speak, but no words came out. Then it occurred to him. He had no good reason to beg for his life. None. So he wouldn't try.

He squinted to see his executioner. He'd make the bastard look him in the eye when he ended his life.

He couldn't see the face for the barrel of an AK pointing at him, but he heard the whiz of a bullet missing his ear by an eyelash. Just his luck. He found a killer with bad aim. He could be brain-dead with a perfectly functioning body. Now that would be shitty. Hmm. He'd seen his body. The chances of it being perfectly functional were slim.

The killer shouted to someone in the distance in Zulu: "Go ... go ... I will finish business here."

Lieut closed his eyes. Resigned. Just get it over with.

Then the eeriest feeling. He sensed more than felt something to his right. A snake? A scorpion? A sac spider?

He opened his eyes and tried to pull his arm away, but his mind wouldn't move his body parts. Damn. He could see ground level. No snake, spider or scorpion. His arm, unlike the left one, looked to be in working order, so it had the potential to work. The long, pink scar on his arm seemed to glint in the sun, winking at him.

YES! There was something ... A black hand gently laid a deerskin water bottle within Lieut's reach. The hand ... so close to him ... why did he feel no fear?

As the hand pushed the water-filled skin-bag closer, he saw the arm, and he went cold.

There was a straight scar running from wrist to elbow.

Identical to his, only not pink and white, but old beige hurt on black skin.

He must be imagining things. It couldn't be Papin ...

In that last moment, the pain of missing his best friend was far more excruciating than his distorted body, and just before darkness pulled him under, his only regret was hurting Papin ... his Zulu self. The only man, besides his dad, he admired most in the world.

## 32

## A NEW ADVENTURE

*Estcourt to Johannesburg, 1965*

PAPIN HAD NEVER BEFORE TRAVELED by train.

He'd also never had to stand so close to another human being.

"Packed in like sardines." He'd heard the expression and thought of the rectangular tin the size of his palm in which three dozen sardines squeezed tightly together. The only difference in this third-class carriage was he and his fellow sardines had multiplied and were all breathing the same stale air without being immersed in zesty tomato sauce.

But he was on an adventure.

On the Estcourt station platform, it was shocking to see the wide chasm that separated the different class passengers.

First-class passengers were all white-skinned and reeking of good fortune and good breeding in expensive clothes, with finely crafted monogrammed luggage (he thought he recognized two regular hotel guests). Second-class passengers—these whites, though moderately affluent, were never flashy (of these, he saw four families who came to Champagne Castle year after year). In third class, he counted twelve different Bantu languages spoken and saw a couple of disdainful-looking Indians and a handful of colored folks he found fascinating. He'd never seen a mixed-race person in his life.

His uncle's voice: "Coloreds will never be accepted by whites. Blacks shun them too, so they're forced to hover in limbo, and now they have created their own society."

What a concept, mixing black and white. Though he knew this phenomenon existed, he had to see the forbidden union of races to believe it. It was so beautiful, it stirred him.

He had plenty of time to observe, something at which he excelled, and the long train ride gave him both the time and the fodder to do so. He saw how people speaking the same language stayed together and didn't interact with other tribes, while the few Indians didn't socialize at all. He thought of the Afrikaans saying: "Soort soek soort." The English equivalent was "Birds of a feather flock together." Tsotsi's Afrikaans schoolbooks, barely opened by his friend, had finally come in useful.

Tsotsi. His friend?

His heart became heavy. Hurt stabbed it like a Zulu spear thrust in his heart and then turned. Everything they'd shared was shattered in five hateful, hurtful words.

*Don't write to me anymore.*

But really, it was many small incidents that had separated them in the last couple of years. Tsotsi's absence fractured their time together. Rugby. Rugby. Rugby. Tsotsi's love of and accomplishment in the sport took him far and wide playing away matches. On a couple of occasions, when Tsotsi was older, there were a few times—torturous for Papin (and he suspected just as hard for Tsotsi)—when the boy had been on a rugby trip when he should have been home with Papin.

When he was about fourteen, Tsotsi started bringing boarding school and sometimes rugby friends home with him to spend the holidays. That hurt Papin to the quick. He thought *he* was Jock's friend.

Sure, he joined the boys outside of the hotel. They all went riding and fishing and did some mountain climbing, but three wasn't the same as two. The visiting boys couldn't speak Zulu, so they used English, which Papin should have been glad of, to practice. But hearing Tsotsi speaking only English didn't feel right. They didn't go to their rock because there was only space for two. Tsotsi, he had to say, tried to include him, but he felt left out anyway. Alone.

But still he wrote his letters when his friend went back to school and would rather die than confess he felt left out. He never, in all the years, expected a letter in return. The letters became Papin's way of desperately bridging the ever-widening chasm that separated them.

When Tsotsi told him he no longer wanted him to write to him at school, the last gossamer thread that tied them together broke, and the gusting wind of life took one end one way and the other end, another. He knew he had to find his way in the world without his friend.

He'd realized Tsotsi could survive without Papin. Was the purpose of this adventure to prove Papin could survive without Tsotsi?

His father, Sponon, would be enraged at his sudden departure, and he didn't blame him. He should have explained. He should have said goodbye.

Shame burned his face when he thought of Inkosi's anger when they found him gone. His disappearance would leave a void in the overseeing of the stable, to guide walks and climbs and definitely in the school Inkosi had built.

He felt bad about all of it, and the hardest part was walking away from Shaka. He felt the prickle of hot liquid behind his eyes and clamped down his jaw.

He considered he was caught between two worlds. Too clever for his old world because of the books he'd been devouring for years and the debates he so enjoyed with his teacher. She was broad-minded and liberal and as hungry for mental challenge as he. She was always ready to throw down an intellectual gauntlet for him to ponder, and he'd take it up and their cerebral challenge was on. He considered her a friend, too. He'd also left her without notice. He swallowed another bitter mouthful of regret.

When Eteemot found Papin hiding between the mail sacks, he'd been furious and warned he would let Inkosi know he was running away.

"Why do you slip away like a jackal with a stolen chicken? Why do you leave these people who love you? And the boy who loves you like a brother? Why? Are you too good for all of us now that you know more than we, from stupid paper books? *Aikona*. You shame me, Papin. You will shame us all. You will make all Zulu less Zulu because of your selfishness. Adventure? Bah! I will not be party to helping a jackal escape."

"Eteemot, you must understand. I love them all. Tsotsi, Shaka, Inkosi, my father, and yes, I am a coward. I cannot face saying goodbye because I know they will make me stay. I have tried for a long, long time to say goodbye and go and find my own way, but I loved them too much. So I have to be the jackal. May the ancestors forgive me."

Papin begged him, promising on every ancestor he could name that he'd never reveal how he'd made his escape. He wouldn't ever label Eteemot a traitor. At Loskop, when loyal Eteemot refused to shake his hand in farewell, Papin felt like a vile turncoat.

By now they'd all suspect he'd abandoned them. Except Tsotsi. He was at school with no means of knowing he'd left for good. Papin's face flared up with shame.

But by the time Papin caught the next train from Estcourt, he'd consoled himself this adventure was what he'd earned by always serving others. His uncle said long ago Papin was destined to make a difference in people's lives. He intended to find out how, though he had no clue where or how to start.

Inkosi was not fond of Uncle. He was a troublemaker in everyone's eyes. Yet he'd opened Papin's own.

He would track him down once he'd had time to assess Johannesburg for himself. He didn't want to be reliant on anyone. This was *his* adventure.

He stood or sat on the floor most of the way from Estcourt to Johannesburg. A long ten-hour train ride. A better alternative to being squashed four-up on a two-seater wooden bench, breathing in other people's air.

All at once, panic beat like a frightened bird against his chest. Tsotsi was due home in two weeks unless he had a rugby game. Nobody would tell the boy Papin had gone. Not until he came home. He had the sudden urge to cry like a baby, and he ran his hand from his forehead down to his chin as if by doing so he could erase himself. Or at least his shame.

When at last the conductor's voice announced Johannesburg was the next stop, Papin pushed out all thoughts of regret and concentrated on the newness of the moment.

His adventure. *His.* He couldn't wait to leave the stuffy compartment's confines.

He was literally pushed off the train and onto the platform by the wave of bodies around him, all headed to the same exit. Having no preconceived plan, he stood still and was nearly knocked over as black people pushed their way past him. It certainly seemed they had a mission.

It reminded him he didn't.

The whites who alighted the train were but specks far down

the platform. They seemed in no hurry and disappeared off to what Papin presumed were private station exits.

First thing he did was check his Timex was safely in his kit bag. He dared not wear such an expensive, impressive temptation. A flash of Tsotsi presenting it to him with unadulterated joy made that spear of hurt stab him in the heart again.

He shrugged off his guilt, found his way into the street and ambled along, surprised by what he saw at every turn. Tall glass buildings—five times taller than Sterkspruit Falls. So many people on the streets. Most of them black, some airing rural customs in this urban jungle: women carrying pots on their heads and babies strapped with sheets to mothers' breasts; *real* tsotsies stealing pavement merchant's wares; and men shouting their conversations from one side of the tarred road to the other, as cars and trucks and fire engines and police cars whizzed by. It was chaos, but it sure was interesting.

As he entered the business section, it was only white people who carried briefcases and wore suits and drove cars. The black people wore uniforms of street sweepers and garbage collectors. Only black people sat on the pavement in rags, begging.

Every eighth person was white, and of those, only a couple threw a few cents into beggars' cups.

Not a single white person made eye contact with him, though he knew he was smiling. Mind you, the few blacks he saw didn't look at him either. He couldn't be bad to look at. He had, after all, buried a box *full* of white love-letter necklaces and bracelets he'd been given by the girls of his kraal and visitors from others. He'd never worn their gifts of intention in front of them. That would've been misleading. But keeping the woven treasures reminded him he could take a woman if he wanted to. Nubile girls stroked his ego, but they'd interfere with his ambition. Having one foot in western and another in Zulu culture was a tricky thing. Yes! He was sorely tempted by their attention, but the consequences of merely satisfying his base needs was not the answer.

He saw an attractive Xhosa girl dressed to the nines and gave her his most charming smile. She ignored him.

Had removing himself from the Drakensberg Mountains rendered him invisible? Perhaps obscurity was punishment for traitors.

He found a park and looked around for and found a café like the one in Estcourt.

He walked in, enjoying the smell of malt vinegar and hot oil. No one was inside.

"Out!" shouted the European shop owner. Papin turned to see who was behind him.

Not a soul, so he pointed to himself in inquiry.

The European nodded and flicked his finger a few times, yelling, "The other side. Enter other side." As if Papin was mentally inept.

Papin did as he was told, and sure enough, there was a line of black men queuing outside a smaller doorway that led to the back of the store. Above the door it said, "Nie Blanke/Non-Whites—Order Here."

*Uncle, you were right.* And yet seeing, feeling, smelling, watching the reality of it all sent shock waves through his body.

He wandered over to the park, chose a bench under a shady tree and began a festival for his senses. As he opened the package, the acidic vinegar hit him square in the face, but after a few seconds beyond the pang, he could smell greasy chips and heavily egg-dipped whitefish.

His mouth watered, and he pulled out the battered fish and opened his mouth for the first bite.

"Voetsek, dirty kaffir," said a white man in scraggly clothes standing before him.

His first thought was, *Inkosi does not allow that word,* then he thought, *This unkempt man must be joking.* Papin had donned his best clothes and wore his Swiss boots for the first time. He knew he looked sharp. This man, on the other hand, was likely what he'd heard called "white trash." A tramp, perhaps? Dirty, definitely.

Papin felt defiance burn through his veins, and he slowly, deliberately looked up at the tree and took that longed-for, slow bite of steaming whitefish.

The man stamped his feet like a three-year-old. "Yew dumb fool. Can't yew blerry read?" His English wore a thick Afrikaans accent, and he waggled his finger, pointing over Papin's left shoulder.

Papin chewed and glanced slowly over his shoulder as the man continued to stomp, his face becoming redder and redder as he shouted, "Look. Look. You want me to read it to you?"

On the slats of the utilitarian-green, wooden bench, "Whites Only" was stenciled —once upon a time in stark white, but it had been reduced to a weather-worn gray. Sadly, the message was the same.

"Get off my bench now, kaffir," the man shouted, and though some passing white heads turned, absolutely no one came to Papin's defense. Neither black nor white.

"It seems this happens often," thought Papin.

But good manners and following orders were ingrained in Papin, so he rose—slowly—took his old-but-new-to-him rugby kit bag, and he ambled off to find a peaceful place to relax. It was time to start really enjoying his adventure.

As he walked, he felt a pang of regret. This would never have happened at Champagne. Nobody would ever call him names. Tsotsi and Inkosi would see to that.

And then all he felt was desperately sad.

He gave up the notion of the bench and sat on the ground

under a tree. He'd barely finished his fish and but a few chips when he felt a strong hand grip his shoulder from behind.

He whirled round to see a short, white man in a policeman's uniform waving a stout wooden club above him.

"Geddup and gimme your pass," the man said.

His uncle had cautioned that in the city, your pass was your most valuable commodity. Without it, you were a persona non grata and would rot in jail. He stood, dug in his pocket and produced the small green book that held his photograph and work history and handed it to the policeman.

Holding the green book in one hand, the policeman looked stony-faced at the picture. Then, hanging his club over his arm, he used both hands to turn the book upside down as he chuckled, amusing himself. "It could be you. It could not. You all look the blerry same to me," the policeman said.

Papin was shocked. He'd never been treated by another human being this way. He didn't understand.

"Says here you are from Champagne Castle in The Berg. Now that sounds far too *donderse* posh for a kaffir. What are you doing here, boy?"

"I've come to work in the city, sir." He realized his English was so much better than the policeman's and wondered if that would be held against him. He figured it didn't matter. His blackness was enough to make this guy angry anyway.

"What work?" the policeman asked as he clutched Papin's green book to his chest possessively.

"My uncle has work for me," he lied. Well, it was a white lie really. He considered Tsotsi would lend him such a lie under the circumstances.

"What kind of work?" It was a demand rather than a question.

"Well, sir. I look after horses. I can kill snakes, climb mountains, teach ..."

The policeman opened his mouth, and hot, garlic air came out with his roar of laughter. "So are you going to join the circus or what, kaffir? Those skills aren't needed around here."

He looked at Papin from head to toe and continued, "No, man. We don't need the likes of a long slab like you in Jo'burg. Go back to your berg or go to the mines. They'll knock a foot or more off your shoulders."

He handed back Papin's pass. Papin tucked it in his back pocket and turned to walk away from this rude man.

"Where the hell you think you're going, kaffir?" the policeman yelled.

"I am going to find my uncle and start my job." Papin was done with the formalities, given the rude manner of this person.

"You watch yourself. You will be asked to show yore pass many times a day. Ten or more. Be sure you have yaw green book ready. An don't forget curfew. No kaffirs on the streets after nine, you hear?"

"Can I go now?" Papin asked.

"You insolent shit. You go when I say so. Giff your pass back." The policeman put out his hand.

Papin didn't move a muscle. He didn't trust this little Hitler.

"Giff it *now.*" He pulled a pair of handcuffs menacingly off his belt. "Or you get these."

Papin reached back for his passbook. The policeman snatched it from him.

"I'll keep it for now. When the next policeman asks for it, tell him Sergeant Elvis Presley has it."

Papin felt angst stir in his belly and repeated, "Sergeant Presley."

"Sergeant *Elvis* Presley, you hear me?"

Papin nodded. "Sergeant Elvis Presley."

"Good. Now bugger off." The policeman waved his arms wildly, club in one hand, passbook and handcuffs in the other.

"But my passbook ..." Papin was afraid for the first time on his adventure as his uncle's warning came back to him: *Passbook ... important commodity ... go to jail ... throw away the key ...* But the short policeman was off to harass another Zulu or Xhosa or Swazi or ... it didn't matter. Papin recognized as long as he was black, he would be guilty of something.

33

# ENTRAPMENT

*Estcourt Boarding School, 1966*

NOT DRUMS nor waterfalls nor Mind Brownie nor New Aunts could help Jock fall asleep that first Sunday back.

Where had Papin gone? He hoped Dad would come and pick him up on his trip to Estcourt so he could find out about his friend. He'd never known such worry or anxiety. He'd only discovered these two disturbing emotions after Boet found his letters. Bastard.

At 5:00 a.m. he was still awake. Anxious. Worried. Then he realized when Papin read his letter, it would explain everything. Papin was more than aware writing was pure torture for Jock, and the pain of his attempt at written explanation would surely absolve him of any hurt he'd caused. Then, once he got home, he'd have a whole weekend to explain in person what had happened. And Jock finally fell asleep.

He hurried through chores and checked on Sipho, whose lip was healing nicely. He felt bad he'd clean forgotten to bring the elder a treasure in the chaos that was his weekend. But Sipho didn't seem disappointed.

Jock and Scotty ambled to their lockers for their schoolbooks. It was earlier than usual.

Still worrying about Papin, Jock went to unlock the padlock on his locker and found it broken. Inside, his stuff was in even more disarray than usual. Some bastard was looking for something.

A snake plopped to the floor. It looked like a small adder. Scotty took off down the passage at the speed of a hummingbird as Jock grabbed the snake by its tail *just* as it posed to strike. Disoriented, the reptile forgot its mission, and Jock was able to grip the scaly head with his right hand, using skilled fingers to keep its mouth closed with pressure on the middle of the snake's head.

Scotty reappeared twenty paces away, and Jock whispered, "Bastard Buis is trying to get me expelled."

"I know. If you get caught with a snake, you're in deep shit. You think Buis put it in there?"

"Hasn't got the balls. Likely paid somebody to do it. Gotta get this guy to safety. Tell Sir loudly that I was on the toilet too long and have just gone to my locker so I might be late. Make sure Boet overhears you tell him that. See you at school."

Jock went out the side door, still holding the snake in safety mode till he set him down on the grass. Jock watched him slither away to safety for a few seconds, hurried inside, then deliberately sauntered back to his locker, whistling, as if all was well in his world.

Sure enough, Boet stood in front of Jock's locker, his face purple. Mr. Tomes was standing a few lockers down, trying to look inconspicuous.

Boet saw Jock, and spewing spittle, he shrieked, "Wharrid you do wif it, Kaffir Boetie?"

Jock put on a surprised face. "Boet? What are you doing at my locker, and why is the lock broken and the door open?"

"Where is it, you liddle bastard?"

Tomes appeared and butted in. "Calm down, Mr. Buis, and no name-calling. There is obviously no snake in Mr. Walsh's locker."

Jock planted a shocked look on his own face. "Snake? Sir! I would never have another snake in my locker. You warned me, Sir. I don't want to be expelled. Who tampered with my locker, Sir?"

Tomes said, "Glad we understand each other on the snake issue, Walsh. Buis? I need you to repair this locker before sundown. I will be inspecting it. And Buis? To my office after school for six of the best."

Jock smiled sweetly at Boet as he passed him.

He couldn't wait to tell Papin how he'd turned the tables. But he'd only just begun.

He had to suffer three more days of Boet calling him "Kaffir Boetie" and urging his posse and the English boys who were afraid of him to do the same.

Boet was the reason for every bit of shit: Sipho's beating; public humiliation; precious letters being destroyed; the quarry stones; his broken tooth preventing him from helping Papin; and worst of all, hurting Papin. And it was enough.

The only thing in his head that superseded his revenge-planning was the anxiety of not knowing how Papin was. Dad left word with Mr. Tomes that he would not have time to pick Jock up for an outing before he was due to come home. *Shit.* How else could he find out about Papin? No one was allowed to use the telephone at school. He simply had to wait.

Papin had taught him that only fools are impatient. So Jock tested out his Zulu skills and bided his time.

And then ... an opportunity presented itself.

## 34

## GARDENS AND BARS

*Egoli/Johannesburg, 1966*

*Warned you,* the voice of his uncle whispered.

And now Papin understood in no uncertain terms: If you were black and without a green passbook, your life was over.

In less than one full day in the City of Gold that was Johannesburg, he'd gone from excited to terrified as he witnessed intimidation and abuse—without provocation by the "authorities"—against men and women of his color ... or any color, other than white.

He hid in alleys and in bushes until night fell.

The oddest sight was watching a vibrant city swollen with noisy vendors, street workers, and commuters of every shade of brown and black disappear without a trace by 8:55 p.m.

9:00 p.m. A much less robust, less interesting scurry of white faces appeared as if Billy Pillay had mastered his first trick. This pale lot were allowed to talk and laugh and carry on till dawn if they so desired.

Papin shook his head and bits of bush poked at him. No

matter how hard they tried, they'd never be as riveting as the earlier crew.

He'd been forewarned. His teacher, in her wisdom, had called this the National Party's "Out of sight, out of mind move." The essential city workers and traders and craftsmen, who made up much of the flavor and ambience of the city and who kept it clean, were banished to their faraway, barren townships before nightfall.

This law, she said, was happily upheld by small-minded policemen filled with deep hatred and an equal measure of love for their pittance of authority.

He felt acute tension all around him. It was a volatile pyre just a spark away from a massive explosion.

*I should have listened to Inkosi. I should have come to see for myself before I burned my bridges at Champagne Castle.*

But it was too late now, and as the only black man on the street, he was the deaf young buck at the water hole who didn't hear his herd move off to safety. He was fast being approached by a crocodile coming out of the water on one side and a lion coming out of the grass on the other.

Ducking and diving out of sight, he found himself in an area of well-kept, modest homes, all with lush front lawns and flower bushes. How far had he walked? Where was he? He had no time for contemplation, so he found the wildest of the gardens and carefully draped his long form around the shrubs. In his dark clothing, he would be mostly undetectable as long as he lay still. He could handle the insects that used this garden as home. Luckily it was likely only small black snakes dared make claim to this well-tended turf. They were harmless and would stay away.

Blue plumbago, geraniums and snapdragons wafted around him in the cool night air and took him straight to the base of

Crystal Falls. How he wished he was home. With Tsotsi and Shaka.

The longing was fast replaced by raw hurt, and he found, regrettably, it was the bad experiences that burned your stomach and kept you awake, not the beautiful ones. So he vowed to let just the bitter memories keep him sharp and aware. He dared not let his guard slip. He dared not fall asleep.

But in truth, there were not enough of the lousy memories to effectively keep him going through the night, and soon thoughts of him and Tsotsi walking Shaka and Dennis through the crystalline water of Crystal Falls, or laughing in the Bushman Cave till their tummies ached, flowed in, unbidden.

It was the feeling of talking of everything and nothing and feeling safe, content and ridiculously happy that lulled him into an exhausted sleep between the geraniums.

He opened his eyes to an older white woman, her hands on her hips, and a policeman standing over him.

He shot up to his haunches, hands protecting his face instinctively.

"I came out to check if the frost had hurt my flowers, and I found this." She pointed to Papin. At least she spoke English.

"Well, well, well. What have we here? Give me your pass," said the policeman, and Papin sprang to his feet.

"I don't have it, sir," said Papin, and as words tumbled out, he felt the fear, like quicksand, sucking him under.

"Why not?"

"Sergeant Elvis Presley has it, sir," said Papin. As he did so, he had a flashback of sitting on their rock with Tsotsi and hearing a rich voice singing to them from the distant game room's turntable. The velvet voice flowed like liquid ambrosia and soothed his mind as Tsotsi said, "That's Elvis Presley."

*Gollaga-inja.*

"You think you're funny, boy?" spewed harshly from the

policeman's lips. "Put your hands behind your back. Let's go find your Sergeant Elvis Presley."

As the handcuffs snapped over his wrists, he was grateful Tsotsi's old kitbag was strapped to his back. At least he still had that. Inside, all his worldly possessions amounted to a Timex—once his most valuable inanimate possession, which became, less than a week ago, just a valuable timepiece, and most of his Tsotsi money earned, one way or another, for twelve years of friendship. *Gollaga-inja!*

But what did money matter without a passbook? What would become of him?

# 35

# DOWN AND OUT

*Estcourt Boarding School, 1966*

IT WAS PUDDING NIGHT—THE Saturday night of the weekend they did not go home. Jock always wondered which of the people who ran the place had succeeded in conning their conscience into believing any old sweet slop was enough compensation for staying in this shithole.

Once they'd said the second grace, Matron said, "Mr. Tomes is indisposed this evening. He won't be back till tomorrow. However, I will be covering. You over twelve boys know how to behave without supervision. I will be concentrating my time on the juniors, but if there is any issue, let me know."

Jock had followed Boet's movements for a good many days. He was oh-so-ready.

He knew Boet's routine was to go to the bathroom just before lights out. He was always the last to use the toilet. As Boet came through the door into the dark bathroom, Jock jumped up and threw an arm around his neck, squeezing with all his might. Boet was at a disadvantage in spite of his size, and Jock used that, slamming the big lug to the ground. While he was down, Jock quickly locked the bathroom door.

As Jock waited for Boet to get up, he stood, fists up, one foot in front of the other, bouncing, boxer-style. "Get up, you piece of shit. Get up and face me without standing on a dustbin. Without your little posse. Without your big mouth. Just you and your black heart. Up!"

Shocked and confused, Boet started to rise, and Jock kicked him in the ribs. He went down again.

Boet struggled to his feet. "You won't get away with this, you rooinek bastard. I'll see to it you get expelled. You can't do this while Sir's away." His whiny voice fueled Jock's anger all the more.

"What? You going to tell everyone I beat the shit out of you?" Jock asked, bouncing with his fists still up, protecting his face.

Boet had recovered. The evil smirk was evident in the light streaming in through the window. "Yew? Yew gonna beat the shit out of *me*? Go find a kaffir to play wif. I won't play wif you, kaffir boetie!" He turned, reaching to unlock the door.

"Don't you dare," Jock yelled, and as Boet turned, Jock dove between Boet and the door.

"Would you rather play with your drunken father, Boet? Huh? The one who beats you and makes you cry?"

Boet's face turned dark in the yellow light. His clenched fist lashed out at Jock's face, but Jock ducked, quick as a flash, and Boet shouted in pain as his fist connected with the solid wood door.

Jock's anger burned as he retaliated with a hard punch. Blood spurted from Boet's nose, and as he stumbled back, Jock changed positions, forcing Boet's back to the door and creating more room for his own maneuvering without waiting for Boet to recover. Jock's anger and hatred was balled up in the fist he smashed into Boet's nose again, and he felt Boet's bone move under his knuckles.

Boet put his hand up to his nose as tears of pain pushed through slit eyes and blood gushed from his nostrils. Jock took advantage of his confusion, taking him down again from behind in a choke hold.

Once Boet was down, Jock was beyond the point of no return. He had his takkies on in preparation for this very moment. He kicked Boet in the gut. "This is for Papin, you white son of a drunken bastard."

And again. "This one's for Sipho." Jock was sure the bastard wouldn't know who he meant. He'd never bothered to know Sipho's name. He kicked him in the kidneys.

And in his solar plexus. "This one is for me having to hurt my friend because of you, you bullying piece of snake shit."

And again. "This one's for Johan nearly dying, though he almost deserved to."

And once he'd got that out of his system, all the anger ebbed.

Just sadness remained.

Boet lay inert. Then he started to cough. Blood came up. Jock felt nothing but emptiness.

Only Boet starting to puke blood pushed Jock into action.

He put out his hand to Boet, lying on the floor in a pool of his own blood. Boet shook his head and looked away. Jock's hand was still there. Outstretched.

After a few long minutes, Boet took Jock's hand. Hauling up the big lug was harder than getting him to the ground.

Jock pushed his face into Boet's. "Now. Report me. Have me expelled. Or leave me alone. I have had enough of you," Jock warned.

Boet stood over the basin, blood dripping from his nose. Jock wadded up some toilet paper, wet it and gave it to Boet. "Put your head back and put this on the bridge of your nose."

Boet did as he was told. Jock took off his belt. "Okay. Lean on the basin so I can reach your nose." He studied his handiwork. "Hmm. Have to set it." He handed his belt to Boet.

Boet took it.

"It's going to hurt like a bitch. Bite down if you want to scream."

Boet placed the belt between his teeth. Jock bent his index and middle fingers and placed them gently on either side of Boet's nose as he said, "It'll be over ..." and he squeezed his fingers together quickly and in one movement pulled them down the bridge, aligning Boet's broken nose. Thank the Lord the walls were brick and the entrance door solid wood, because Boet's cry was loud enough to wake Matron in the next building, even with the belt in his mouth.

When he took back his belt, Jock reckoned the leather would disintegrate before the deep indentations of Boet's gravestone-like teeth disappeared.

Jock took off his shirt and used his school-required vest to clean up Boet's blood on the floor. "Go. Stand in the shower. I'll ferry Tomes's ice blocks to you, and by the time he gets back, new ones will be made so he'll be none the wiser. You need to keep the ice on your nose all night. I'll get aspirin from Matron for 'my headache.' She's used to those lately." Jock almost smiled.

"Why are you helping me?" Boet asked, looking at Jock via the mirror.

"Zulus say, 'Never leave an enemy behind.' I add, 'Particularly when he's bleeding evidence all over the bathroom.'" Jock grinned.

Jock was on his hands and knees, still mopping up Boet's blood, when he saw an outstretched hand in his peripheral vision.

Jock took the hand and shook it. His fury gone. His lust for blood satiated.

"Yew kicked my ass, Rooinek. Yew crazy? I'll never tell another living soul."

"Weekend's coming up. What will you tell your dad?" Jock asked, knowing full well his father would match Jock's punishment if it looked like Boet had come off second best in a fistfight.

"What can I say? Rugby's a violent sport." Boet grinned and then flinched.

"Well, nobody will hear it from me. As long as you stop calling me anything but 'Rooinek,' you will always be the scary Rock Spider everyone is afraid of."

"Deal," said Boet, and they shook again.

Jock couldn't wait to tell Papin how he'd finally nailed Boet, once and for all.

# 36

# JOHN VOSTER SQUARE

*Johannesburg, 1966*

John Vorster Square Police Headquarters loomed rectangular, uninteresting and eight stories skyward. Yet it was vastly more threatening than the thirty-story buildings in town.

Inside, Papin could smell fear. It permeated the air. Questions barked in bold authority elicited broken answers.

The policeman shoved Papin into a box and followed him in. It was small and made of steel, and he felt claustrophobia's knock get louder and louder as the doors closed.

The policeman punched a number that lit up, and if Papin still believed in Tokoloshe when the steel box began to rise, he'd have thought the little menace was showing off. His educated mind knew it must be a mechanical piece of engineering, and he'd look into exactly what it was when he could. In the meantime, when the button went from seven to eight, the doors opened mysteriously.

He was dragged in front of a burly officer who didn't bother to look up from his paperwork, which sprawled over an impressive piece of mahogany shaped into a desk.

Captor and prisoner stood in silence until the voice of the desk man bellowed without looking up: "Why are you bothering me, Constable?"

He spoke in Afrikaans and was answered in the same language.

"I think you will appreciate this kaffir's excuse for not having his pass, Sergeant."

Bushy eyebrows led the way, followed by a pair of tired eyes, then the rest—an older, white face, which tilted back to take in all of Papin's height.

The man leaned back on this chair, hands clasped together. "A Zulu, hey? What did you do? Steal a bicycle? Why are you wasting my time, Visser?"

"Sorry, Sergeant. But just ask him about his pass, Sergeant."

Annoyed, the sergeant propelled his torso back to his desk and picked up his pen. Head down again, he asked condescendingly, "Where's your pass?"

"I gave it to Sergeant Elvis Presley, sir, as I told this officer," Papin said respectfully, hoping this one could fathom it was indeed Papin who had been wronged.

The officer said nothing for nine fast heartbeats. Papin was counting.

Sergeant burst into uproarious laughter, and the arresting constable joined in.

Sergeant, between hiccups of mirth, got out, "Must be that son of a bitch Goosen again. Pulling the wool over these poor kaffirs' eyes."

At least this one sounded like he had a dash of empathy, so Papin let a little glimmer of hope light up his dire circumstance.

"Which township are you living in?" asked Sergeant.

"None, sir. I am from a kraal in the Drakensberg. I am looking for my uncle, Mr. Matheba."

"Beza Matheba?" Papin was too encouraged by his uncle

being well-known to realize the sergeant had lost the twinkle in his eyes.

"Yes," he said, smiling and hugely relieved. "Do you know him, sir?"

The sergeant's face changed. It became as dark as a thunderstorm cloud. "I know him well. I watched him going through that window over there," and he pointed to a window the size of four Swiss shoeboxes. Not the kind of window one could accidently fall from. And Sergeant stood and gestured to the constable for his club.

The club swung before Papin's eyes in a shallow arc, but in his wildest dreams, he never thought it would be heading for him.

Pain shot through his temple. The vast room went black, then varying shades of gray, as hurt ripped through his head and dizziness claimed him. He stumbled trying to keep his balance. The policemen laughed and clapped in time to Papin's wobbles as if he were the visiting dancer at a new kraal.

"Fucking Commie," said the sergeant, and Papin's reflexes were too slow from the first crack to his skull to stave off the club's blow to the other side of his head.

And his world went pitch-black.

Much later, when he was released onto the street, he realized the indiscriminate beatings, loud music and disorienting bright lights alternating with pitch blackness had not just broken his body, but during that indiscernible time in the cell below ground, they'd robbed him of ever again expecting the best.

His adventure had turned him into a pessimistic realist, and that pained him as much as his aching body.

# 37

# GONE!

*Champagne Castle, 1966*

JOCK ONLY HAD one foot in the Chevy when he asked, “Is Papin okay, Dad?”

“Nobody’s seen him. Don’t know where the hell he is.” Dad sounded hurt.

“But it’s been nearly two weeks. Surely somebody has heard from him or knows where he went?”

“Not a soul.”

“Did you talk to Chief? Wait ... Nicholas doesn’t know anything?”

Dad shook his head.

“That’s odd. Sangoma knows everything. If he’s gone, he had to get down the mountain somehow.” Jock’s mind grasped for anything that made sense.

“It’s not like him, that’s for sure. As angry as I am, I hope nothing’s happened to him,” Dad said.

With that new thought, Jock’s heart dropped to his restricting, shiny black shoes. Papin being hurt or wounded somewhere was worse than him being gone on purpose. Wait! What if the puff adder's venom had penetrated and ... *no!*

"Dad, he wouldn't miss teaching school. Has his teacher down the valley heard from him?"

Dad shook his head.

"Something's wrong, Dad. Something's dead wrong."

Dad was acting strange. Perhaps he was nearly as hurt as Jock at Papin's absence.

If his dad spoke again on the trip to the hotel, Jock didn't remember. His ears were filled with his own voice begging God, ancestors, Sangoma and Mr. Palmer for Papin to be waiting for him. When they arrived, he felt a hot rush of tears behind his eyes when there was no great, big, welcoming smile. No horses waiting. No Papin.

He managed to pull himself together, and his dad's stern voice penetrated his thoughts. "Don't you go off anywhere till you've said hello to your mother. And Jock?

"Dad?"

"Come after dinner. We need to talk."

His first stop was Nicholas. "Any chance the ancestors whispered where Papin might be to Sangoma?"

Nicholas shook his head, seeming not to trust himself to speak.

Jock also asked if there was any way Papin could be dead somewhere from traces of the poison, even though his own good sense knew that wouldn't happen since venom had an immediate effect. He felt helpless as Nicholas shook his head.

He sprinted to the kraal, the compound, all their haunts, the entire periphery, interrogating everyone he came across. Not a soul.

Jock had not even been to see Dennis and Beauty yet. He knew Shaka must be pining for his owner too. But he couldn't face the horses' confusion that surely matched his own.

He found himself walking down to the quarry, kicking rocks and thinking of the weight of those bloody stones that forced him to blurt out about the letters. No time to explain. What a terrible blow to his best friend.

He sat and watched Eteemot and his team working and singing as they hauled big pieces of stone up from the quarry, then bashed them into submission to fill the potholes in the hotel road. The song ended, and another began. The beauty of the melody, threaded with harmonies, made him more morose.

Damn this new anxiety. It must be something you were cursed with when you were old. He felt sixty-six. Where the hell was Papin? Oh God, it was all his fault. He saw his legs, like they were someone else's, bobbing up and down nervously. He thought of Billy Pillay and Sangoma at the chicken coop dealing with the drinking problem. Back when life was easy and anxiety was just a hard-to-spell word.

He picked up sandstone fragments and threw them away one by one to give his body something to do as he punished himself with thoughts of how he would have felt if he was Papin. Then he got mad and sad he didn't have a chance to tell Papin how he'd ended Boet's reign of terror.

He didn't even hear Eteemot come up to him.

"Tsotsi. *Klein Baas.*"

Jock almost smiled. Eteemot's names for Jock intoned he was nearly a young boss. "Eteemot," said Jock. "I see you."

"I did not want to." Eteemot's head hung in shame.

"What are you talking about?" Jock was confused.

"Papin asked me to take him to Loskop."

Jock's head jerked back reflexively. "When?" It didn't even sound like his own word.

"The Monday after the hiker was bitten." Eteemot dropped his head to his chest and then sat down on a rock close by.

"Why?" was all Jock could get out.

"He said he had to find his own way in the world."

"Why didn't you tell anyone, Eteemot? I've been worried sick. Everyone has." Jock felt anger burn his cheeks and close up his throat.

"Klein Baas, I found him trying to become invisible between the mail sacks." Suddenly Eteemot smiled. "How does a tall Zulu hide from me who knows my trailer so well? I did not want to take him. He begged me and begged me and swore he would never tell anyone I had been the one who drove him to his escape. Papin was broken, Klein Bass."

"Escape?" Jock shouted. "Escape? Why did he need to escape? He has ... had a good life here."

"He said he wanted to make a difference in the world. I do not know what that means." Eteemot apologized.

"He was making a difference in the world right here. Teaching kids. Learning. Being my friend. Loving Shaka."

Eteemot looked at his feet and said, "So sorry, Klein Baas. Papin felt he no longer belonged. That his usefulness here was spent."

"Why didn't he say goodbye?" *No!* He would not cry.

"He said he could not say goodbye to you, his father, Inkosi or Shaka—those he loved most—because each of you in your own way would make him stay."

"For two nights while he was waiting for you to go to Loskop, where did he stay?"

"He did not say, Klein Baas."

"Where was he headed?" asked Jock, feeling numb.

"He said nothing, and I feared to ask. I just dropped him at Loskop train. Klein Bass, I refused to shake his hand. I called him a jackal. He said I was right; he was a coward. I made a promise not to tell. But then I see you. I see you are broken. I had to tell you in case you thought Papin was dead."

"He might not be dead, but he's hurt. Maybe that's worse.

And it was me who hurt him," Jock said quietly. "His best friend hurt him. That's a terrible, terrible thing, Eteemot."

Jock saw The Mist, hovering, waiting to close in and smother him with guilt.

Eteemot broke the silence. "He stood for one and a half hours on the back. On the trailer, hanging on, speaking into my ear as I drove."

"Why did he not sit next to you on the tractor seat?"

"He said he was not worthy. And I didn't want to look at him, he was shaming me so. When I found him, he was crying. If you ever see him, don't tell him I told you. He stood behind me, talking in my ear all the time. Talk, talk, talk. I never knew Papin could say so much."

"What else did he say?" Jock was desperate for every word.

"He said he would miss you more than anyone. He said he was lost and only felt found when you were home. But you didn't need him anymore."

Jock clenched his jaw to stop from crying. He picked up a handful of dirt and a few sharp stones and closed his fist tightly. The sandstone bit into his hand, and it was a relief to feel a different kind of pain.

"What was he going to do?" Jock asked as The Mist swirled.

"He said he was going on an adventure and find a place where he belonged."

"He belongs *here*." Jock heard the wail in his voice and stopped himself by tossing the first handful and picking up another, which bit him in new places and took his mind off his need to weep. "Did he say he'd be back?" A sliver of hope surged through him.

"Aikona," said Eteemot as he shook his head.

The light that was hope died. It was instantly replaced by darkness deeper and darker than any he'd ever had to navigate.

"Thank you for telling me, Eteemot," Jock said, meaning it.

He knew for a Zulu to break a promise went against his grain. He felt the man's eyes upon him and looked at Eteemot and understood. "Nobody will ever know you took Papin down the mountain, Eteemot. You have my word."

"Thank you, Klein Baas." Eteemot had trouble getting out his words.

"Call me 'Tsotsi.' I don't deserve to be a 'Klein Baas.' I still have too much to learn." Jock got up, threw his handful of sand and stones away and dragged his feet up the hill of the quarry.

He had no idea where to go or what to do. Without Papin, nothing was worth doing. And he was gone. For good.

# 38

## 'DUBE' MEANS 'ZEBRA'

*Johannesburg and Soweto, 1966*

PAPIN ONLY FOUND out once he'd literally been kicked out of John Vorster Square that he was there for three days. He'd only been on his adventure for four.

His body ached, and he was thirsty and exhausted. It seemed each time he'd found merciful sleep in his windowless cell, a different guard woke him for yet another beating.

Again and again.

*Thanks for the good time, Uncle.* How Papin made it out alive, he had no idea. It pained him to squint up to the eighth floor with the only eye he could still open. How the hell did they manage to squeeze Uncle out of that window? *What did you do? What didn't you tell them?* Thinking was too painful. So was walking. So, even, was drinking blessed water that came from a factory-made steel fountain. Eish. Far from home. At home, a mile from anywhere, there was a place you could drink. Unspoiled waterfalls and streams where, as you lifted cool water to your mouth, you could see trout swimming over stony bottoms and hear Tsotsi's belly-laugh.

He stopped himself too late and realized the hurt he'd just suffered in a cell was nothing in comparison to the beating he'd received from his best friend in five words, "*Don't write to me anymore.*"

Five words that had the power to kick him viciously away from all he clung to and pierce his heart with a poison-tipped *assegai* or spear.

Since they were first uttered, a scant week ago, every recall of those five words painfully twisted the assegai—still lodged in his most vital organ—and destroyed yet another chamber of his heart.

Down the road was a dilapidated green bus marked "Nie Blanke." Non-Whites. Before he crossed the street, he carefully turned his throbbing head this way and that to check with his good eye, first for policemen and *then* for fast-moving traffic.,

The policeman who kicked him out of John Forster Square only gave him his passbook. He would never again see the kitbag with his carefully saved old pounds and new rand notes. His best clothes were gone. As was the finest watch between Jo'burg and Durban. But then again, it was just as well, because that shiny treasure had become a tarnished nail that bit into his wrist and affected his heart.

He heard his own voice in his ears: "Tsotsi. I will wear this as long as I am Papin Tshabalala."

It was very likely he was no longer who he once was.

He still had on his precious boots, and they'd left some coins in his pocket. Most importantly, he had his passbook.

The bus had a sign in the shape of a clock in the front window, showing when the driver would be back. He must have smiled because his face hurt like the devil and all because he was amused by the best way to cope with a dozen or more Bantu languages. The pain confirmed there was nothing here to smile about. His face felt as if one of those big, noisy rubbish trucks had ridden over it, reversed and done it again.

He peered inside the bus, hoisted his long and battered frame up and dropped all but his last coins in the metal box with the explicit illustrations for instructions. Halfway down the length of the bus, he found a window seat.

All he wanted was to be invisible. He wiped his nose, and his hand came away bloodied.

That blood in his hand sparked a rage in the pit of his gut he never knew he owned. It burned dark red and furious. But it was not long before exhaustion overcame his newly discovered hatred, and he fell sound asleep.

He awoke with a start, not knowing where he was but acutely aware of the fear burning in his chest. Fear was an unfamiliar feeling. Then the rage returned. When his one eye focused, he realized the bus was moving. As he watched the strange new world go by, he acknowledged he'd voluntarily immersed himself into this mess.

He had nowhere to go, nothing to look out for so he didn't miss the stop, so he let the momentum of the bus lull him back into oblivion.

The second time he awoke, an older black man sat next to him. The man smiled and tipped his hat. Papin, so grateful for the first genuine *Egoli* smile, returned the kindness and flinched.

*Gollaga-inja!* The pain of a smile.

The man next to him spoke, a hint of laughter in his voice. "I hear you speak the old Zulu, but I thought I looked more handsome than an ass of a dog. At least I did this morning. It's possible the day has jaded me."

The smiling man was dressed in an old gray suit and thin black tie worn over a yellowed shirt that was once white but had never had Constance's attention. The man was about his father's age but rounded by city living.

Trying to orient himself, Papin twisted his head to assess the others on the bus and let out an audible groan.

"You need a doctor, Papin."

In spite of the pain, Papin's head jerked reflexively. Suspicion was a new sensation. How did the man know his name?

"I was a friend of your uncle. Beza told me to expect you whenever the time came."

"But how? There are as many Zulus as flies in Egoli."

"I've been following you since you were kicked out of John Vorster Square." The man grinned and put out his hand. Papin took it, and the African handshake ensued. Papin's mind inevitably went back to Tsotsi, but he shut it down before the assegai turned.

"I am Bandile Dube," said the man. "My friends call me Bandi."

And all Papin heard was the man's surname.

Dube meant "zebra."

This world was full of irony.

"But still you do not tell me how you knew me by sight." Papin looked at the man, still not sure he should trust him.

Bandi's voice dropped several decibels. "Our organization has thousands of comrades who work in many buildings in Jo'burg. One of them—who others think is merely a janitor—found out who you were. Your uncle Beza was a well-known agitator for the rights of our people, and so you, Papin, are automatically accepted as a man to be trusted with our cause."

"Who did he agitate to get thrown out of the eighth-floor window at John Vorster Square?" Papin heard a caustic tone of his own he didn't recognize.

"Beza's enthusiasm got him into a lot of trouble," said Bandi.

Papin had nothing to say in response to that understatement. Best he never knew because his guilt box was already full.

Besides, Papin had paid the price for his uncle's deeds and knew his own name would already be on a roster for agitators when he'd not agitated at all.

"Tell me specifically of this cause. My uncle was long in riddles and proverbs but short on facts."

"Our aim is to wedge enough two-inch *doring bos* thorns between the bull elephant's toes. Hard to see, hard to get to and so very small in comparison, but if the thorns are placed in many places and they poke and prick long enough, they will eventually bring down the elephant. It won't die, but it will take notice and do something about it."

"My uncle, the thorn. You speak of the National Party's 'elephant'?"

Bandi's face lit up like Champagne Castle Hotel as sunset. "Exactly." He paused before continuing, "I am impressed you are so informed. But you said your uncle was unspecific ..."

"My uncle planted the seeds. His enthusiasm was marred by his slick nature. I was never sure what was true and what was imagined or at very least exaggerated. . But I foraged for information. And I had a teacher. A white woman with much wisdom and a wide vision," Papin answered.

"We have many sympathizers who are white and mostly English. Though only very few have courage enough to speak out."

"Perhaps it's not courage they lack but motivation. You see injustice and you abhor it, but your life is good, so you are not driven to change it." Papin surprised himself.

"Papin, you are wise beyond your years. And educated. Here in Egoli, you will see your book smarts brought to life in the vibrant colors only nature can produce. But be warned, there is no quick way books or money or strength in numbers can fix. You see, like after a hard rain, when the vivid, magical hues of nature have freed the air from man's pollution and stench, and we feel grateful, it's just for a minute. Because when we look beyond nature's cleansed, beautiful world, we see our long-harvested crops are no longer there. They've been washed away by that rain, and there will be nothing for us to store for winter." Bandi paused, sighed. "In our line of work, excitement can turn to devastation in a heartbeat. But we can't give up. Patience and the end game must push us onward."

"Bandi, you are a philosopher." Papin was impressed.

"You bring it out in me, young Zulu. Come. Ours is the next stop." Bandi pressed the bell above the seat.

Papin followed as Bandi wormed his way to the front of the bus. No plan. No money. What else was he to do?

As they walked the mile or so toward Bandi's home, Papin expected to keel over from pain and hunger more than once, but Bandi's arm was always there to catch him. The elder talked all the way, as if to give Papin something else to think about.

"We will soon be at my home in Soweto. It's our township we had to start from dirt without help when the government made us move a few years ago. I have a small house. I pay for it with money I earn driving a truck for the gold mine."

"You own a house?" Papin was prepared to be mightily impressed, but Bandi shook his head and smiled at the younger's naiveté.

"Oh, no, Papin. We blacks are not permitted to own property in South Africa."

Papin was shocked by this new information.

"My house is full, but we will make room for you. It was fuller when my wife was alive, but my three daughters manage to fill it with girlishness. When we arrive, I will send for the doctor. He is usually drunk, but we cannot be choosy in Soweto."

They came to a place that fascinated Papin, even in his state of dehydration and pain. This patched-together shantytown was nothing like anything he'd seen before. There were rows and rows of barely livable shacks made of cheap, rotting balsam or Coke and Fanta tins beaten into submission, or beer cans pounded with a big stone, patched together with cast-off nails, and bound by rope.

Very small, small, and medium-size children dashed and hid, cartwheeled and pushed what looked like outlines of cars made from old wire coat hangers. They chased dogs and chickens in the garbage-laden streets. There was no electricity and no running water. Certainly, by the smell of it, there were no sewage pipes or septic tanks.

"How do they live in such filth?" Papin asked, forgetting his own pain as he looked at theirs. And yet, they seemed happy, carefree.

"The children know no other way. The parents, though, have no choice. The pittance they earn as servants to whites or laborers under white supervisors is quickly spent on expensive transport to get to and from their jobs. There is nothing left for niceties and barely enough for food."

Papin felt miserable. Never in his life had he witnessed such degradation. *Please, Inkosi, take me back.*

"My house is just around the corner," said Bandi, but it was just a figure of speech because seeing around corners was impossible. Shacks were built so close together, they blocked all views of anything more than a few feet ahead.

"Welcome," said Bandi, doing a Billy Pillay by extending his arm toward a small red-brick building with a tar-paper roof. It looked like a mansion compared to the shacks yet would have been dwarfed by even the smallest guest rondavel at home.

Bandi unlocked an iron security gate, then opened a wooden door directly behind it, and they went inside the small area.

Three young girls somewhere near Tsotsi's age stood in a neat row, and Bandi introduced them proudly.

Inkosazana and Lulana were tall and seemed to be assessing Papin carefully as if he were something they were going to cook for dinner. He nodded and smiled but paid little attention as his eyes locked with the more petite girl called Ayanda, the oldest. Her eyes smiled beautifully.

"Sit, Papin. We will talk while Ayanda fetches the doctor, unless her feet are as frozen as her stare." Her father looked at her pointedly, and she rushed through the front door.

Lulana brought him a sweet drink, and he gulped it down gratefully, though it felt like razor blades with each swallow. Billy Pillay again.

He touched his throat, suspecting through the blur that was John Vorster Square that he'd been choked.

"You have already acquired many city battle-wounds, Papin. I was born in Jo'burg. All of us around here are used to being verbally abused, but we know how to avoid being beaten."

The second daughter brought Papin some gruel and a chunk of white bread. He apologized in advance for his manners. He'd never known hunger before.

"Your uncle bragged of you for many years. He believed you would grow into one of our cause's biggest assets. He said you are an excellent teacher and a born leader. Both skills are sorely needed in our quest to place those thorns between the elephant's toes." Bandi smiled at Papin, and the younger felt safe for the first time since he'd jumped aboard Eteemot's trailer.

"They—the authorities—said he jumped out of the window. But you've seen those John Vorster Square windows. No man on a suicide mission would choose to first ball himself up and then jump. There have been many 'suicides' from that building. Mysterious, isn't it?" Bandi asked rhetorically.

Ayanda bounced through the door, followed by a Xhosa

doctor with bloodshot eyes and a neat navy-blue, hard-leather bag with 'South African Airways' embossed on the side. Papin was amused how this first aid kit had found its own wings into Soweto.

The man checked him out, and though he was not as adept as Doc from the mountains, nor as skilled as the medicine woman in his first hut nor even the vet who aided in producing the twins, he seemed to know what to look for. He even managed to sew up three severe gashes, two on his face and a deep one on his back.

"Now you need a good wash for your stink and a half jack of brandy to help you forget how you got your damaged ribs and the other things that are broken and bruised," said the doctor as he flapped his hand around in the vague direction of Papin's face and upper body. "You're a strong young warrior."

Bandi handed over money, and the doctor disappeared.

He was directed behind the curtain by Ayanda. She had prepared a metal bowl with tepid water and next to it, some Lux soap and a washcloth.

When he came back through the curtain, Papin said, "Bandi, I cannot pay you. The police took all my money, except for this." He emptied his pocket, and only two silver and a few copper coins lay together on the low table.

"You will pay me back when you can. But first, I will get you a job with me at the mines."

Papin felt a rush of dread. Inkosi had vehemently warned him off the mines.

Bandi must have seen Papin's horror.

"Not in the mines themselves. You have too much potential for those pitch-black tunnels of death. No. I will find you a driving job like mine. You can drive?"

Papin nodded, though he'd only driven the tractor a handful of times. A vision came to him. He was talking to his much younger charge: "This is how you learn, Tsotsi." And he watched Tripod and then mimicked the dog's odd gait as he said, "Monkey see, monkey do." And their joined laughter rang clear in his head, but he shook it out of his head and said, "Yes, Bandi. I can drive."

# 39

# DEATH

*Later, Champagne Castle, 1966*

He watched Mom's face and felt her love. Had he been more aware, he'd have seen her wipe away tears while she prattled about her own hotel-world happenings. But he saw and heard none of it. He pushed decadent food around on his plate with a perfectly held knife and fork and with elbows off the table, but he only pretended to eat.

How could he enjoy something when he had, by all intents and purposes, banished his best friend into an unknown world?

As soon as he could, he ran, with Tripod in tow, to Dad's office to get whatever was coming over with. Unless Dad had something new to say about Papin's whereabouts, Jock had no strength for instructions on fixing the new weir or pumping gas for departing guests from the recently installed petrol pump near the car park.

"Ah, Jock. I wanted to talk to you before anyone else." Dad sounded odd. But then, everything sounded, tasted, smelled and looked odd.

"Papin?"

"No, no, nothing to do with Papin. Wherever he is, I hope he finds his peace. I saw his restlessness coming a few years ago when he asked me to stop paying him for looking after you."

Jock felt like Boet must have when his father slapped him down.

"Wha—? You paid him to be my friend?" No. This couldn't be. That would mean their friendship was one big fat lie. That was not possible. Papin was his best friend. He would never ... "And he accepted payment?" The words came out of Jock's mouth, but how? He thought his mouth still hung open in shock. "All these years? From when I was four years old? You *paid* him?"

"Well, it was a full-time job looking after you." Dad tried to smile but failed.

"I thought he just liked being with me."

"He surely did, but he and I had a business arrangement."

Jock couldn't stand any more. He got up, turned to run, but Dad's voice was sharp. "Stop. I haven't told you what I need to."

*Please, no more. Fuck the weir. Fuck the petrol pump.*

"Sit down, Jock."

Dad was nervous. Jock had never seen his father like this.

The enormity of his disappointment at being merely a commodity, a paid job to Papin, was devastating. How could Papin have been so two-faced? Pretending to be his best friend ... how could it all be a big fat lie?

"Jock. Sit down."

Well, whatever the reason he was sitting here, things couldn't get worse than the bombshell his father just dropped like an afterthought—a casual truth that changed the whole course of Jock's life in an instant, shattering the safety of his cocoon and all he believed to be true. He felt anger at his father for doing it and telling him about it. At Papin for accepting payment for something ... someone he pretended was his best friend. His blood brother.

Silence hung in the air like an overripe, bruised peach, ready to fall from Farmer Olivier's tree and crash to the dirt-tossed orchard floor, splitting in two.

"Your mom and I are getting divorced."

"Divorced? How? What? When?" The air had been sucked out of the room. It spun and he battled to breathe. "Why?"

"Sometimes even people who love each other need to live apart."

"But I will stay with you at the hotel, right, Dad?"

"Well, Jock ..." Dad fidgeted. Looked away.

This was *not* his father. This was *not* his hero. This man before him was fearful. A man of doubt and uncertainty. This man had to leave so his strong, stoic, determined, force-to-be-reckoned-with father could return and make things right.

He felt he had to quantify his worth to this mere wisp of his real father. "Dad, I'll be so helpful. I'll pump gas. I'll clean the weir. I'll tend the shop ... Why must Mom go, Dad? It's her hotel too."

"We're selling the hotel." Dad's voice was flat.

Jock must have misheard. He was imagining the worst because his state of mind demanded it. He shook his head and avoided looking at the father look-alike across the desk.

"NO!"

"It's true, Jock. It's already in the works."

There was no place for such a truth. None.

Aha! It was that fucking mist. The Mist could distort truth. He knew.

"Jock. Things change ..."

"You *promised* nothing would ever change. Papin would *always* be here. Nicholas would *always* be here. Billy Pillay. The horses. Nothing would change. You said so. It's the only thing I had to hold on to. You promised, Dad. You promised. Now Papin's gone and you're taking the rest away? Breaking a promise?" His words spat from his mouth.

Jock stared at his doppelganger-father.

The Mist would go, eventually, if he sat really still and didn't run. And all real things would fall back into place.

"It's a matter of economics, son. It was never intended to happen. Life changes sometimes and we have no control."

"Where will we ... where will I live?"

"We're still working all that out. Maybe with your mom in Durban."

"With Tripod?"

His dad nodded, but somehow, he felt no relief.

He shook his head. No! This weak version of the man he loved most in the world was just a trick of the dreaded Mist. He wouldn't listen.

And then his father stood over him. He knew it was indeed his father because he felt Dad's rare touch. Hand on shoulder.

"Jock, we have no option but to sell the hotel. There is no choice."

He shunned the always longed-for touch, stood, spun around and pushed himself against the desk, as far away as he could get from the messenger who was indeed his father. Trapped in the mist with The Truth.

No. NO. NO!

"You can't," he shouted. "You can't sell my home. What if Papin comes back and we're not here? What about Dennis and Beauty and Shaka? What about Nicholas? What about ... You can't, Dad. You just can't. And Tripod? And Billy? And ..."

But as he shouted, his father's face was crumbling and wet, and it told Jock in no uncertain terms that his life was over.

He had to run through The Mist to get away. He too had no

choice. If he fell and died, it would be better than staring truth in the face.

Run. Run. Run through the fucking mist.

And he did. All the way to the stable.

He hugged Beauty and Shaka, mounted Dennis and galloped as far away from the hotel as he could before his horse was spent.

And then he lay on her, his body bent from the waist, his torso and head on her bare back. The familiar smell of Dennis, the sturdiness of her body beneath, stabilized him.

But *his* body became possessed. It heaved and wracked and writhed. Peculiar, loud, mournful sobs started in his soul, moved to his heart and into his core, then pushed through his open mouth.

Jock Walsh allowed himself to cry for the very first time in his whole life.

# 40

# THE FINAL STAGE OF METAMORPHOSIS

*Soweto, 1966-1967*

In the six months that followed, Papin became quite adept at driving the truck to and from the mine to the processing plants where gold would be extracted. It was mindless, and the wages were dismal, but he was able to pay his way and buy groceries. Bandi was good company on the long bus rides to and from the mine, and Papin learned a lot about the African National Congress.

The policy of Apartheid, which directly translated means "Separateness," was so named when the National Party took power in 1948. In 1950, the population was classified by race, and the Group Areas Act was passed to segregate blacks and whites, to which the ANC responded with a campaign of civil disobedience led by Nelson Mandela.

In 1956, the ANC produced The Freedom Charter, which proposed South Africa belonged to all who lived there. It was quickly squashed by the government.

In 1957, the Union Jack no longer flew over South Africa, and in 1961, South Africa broke all ties with the crown and declared itself a republic, putting the Dutch founder of Cape Town—Jan van Riebeeck—on currency instead of England's king or queen.

After the notorious 1960 riots, news of which his uncle brought Papin, the ANC was banned and went underground. Continuing to organize secretly, they took up arms against the South African government in 1961.

In eighteen months, the ANC carried out two hundred acts of sabotage—thorns between the elephant's toes—but they were no match for the regime, which began using even harsher methods of repression. The death penalty for sabotage was passed, as was the permission for police to detain people for ninety days without trial. After the infamous Rivonia Trial, the ANC was all but destroyed. Some of the ANC leaders left the country; others left to undergo military training to learn how to fight for the country they loved.

The ANC was faced with the question of how to bring trained soldiers back into the country to continue the struggle. They campaigned for international support and assistance from the rest of the world. ANC membership was opened up to non-Africans.

All ANC members knew theirs would be a lifetime of struggle before anything was achieved, and Papin remembered Sangoma's wisdom delivered in a hut he'd built himself so long ago. "Impatience is a white man's privilege and a black man's curse." Because of the black man's patience, the ANC was still in existence and still fighting the oppression of the Nationalist Government. That big bull elephant found ways to enforce their abominable laws, making life as a black or brown person in South Africa nothing but a hardship.

Every day gave Papin more reasons to distrust the whites as he witnessed blacks being manipulated and downtrodden and mistreated and beaten by the self-proclaimed "superior" of the races.

And yet he had known supreme kindness and fairness and latitude from white people all his life ... well, until Egoli. Granted, all of the people he knew and loved were English. But in Egoli, some of the English were as bad as the Afrikaans, and surprisingly, a few Afrikaners he'd met were nicer than the English. Nothing, he realized, was ever just black or white, kind or unkind, good or bad.

At the end of his six-month anniversary as a driver for the mines, true hatred was delivered to him on a platter.

Bandi's girls were modern South African women in their late teens, early twenties. They dressed in western clothes and had no desire to become maids to serve spoiled white people, but they had to make a living. It was against the law for women to brew traditional beer, which had been an African staple for thousands of years.

However, since their father was a rebel in disguise, it was no surprise his daughters followed in his footsteps. Their home—more solid than most in Soweto—was the perfect brewing house because it could be locked up from tsotsies trying to steal the sought-after brew and the authorities looking to ban it.

Papin had moved out after his first two weeks' wages, and once the girls' plan was hatched, Bandi joined Papin in his small, makeshift hut so as not to interfere in the girls' budding business.

Liquor was not a poor man's pleasure, but South Africans—black, white and every color in between—were fond of drinking. It was the only national pastime enjoyed by all races. In Soweto, there were indeed many *shebeens,* as illegal drinking establishments were known. And if it was a matter of supply and demand, there was never enough of it to drown one's sorrows.

So the girls imported a distant aunt of their dead mother's from Eshowe and learned from her the ins and outs of brewing beer.

The little brick house was filled with big sacks of dry maize (corn), bottles of maize malt, the magic ingredient of local sorghum malt, and yeast, which were combined and fermented for days during the brewing process. Papin reckoned you could get drunk by merely walking past the house on a hot day, even with the windows closed. Papin teased, it was no wonder the girls were always smiling.

Papin found a very soft place in his heart for the petit Ayanda, and she and he would talk of his life in the mountains very often, sitting on Bandi's front stoep. She longed for the life from which he'd just "escaped."

"Tell me again about the real stars," she'd say, smiling as she gazed up, trying her best to see through low-hovering smoke and haze that was Soweto pollution.

"When Tsotsi and I lie on our rock, we can see not one layer of the Milky Way but three. Three ever-changing tiers. The close one, the one in the middle, and on a crystal-clear night, another behind it. Each band of stars goes from one horizon to the other. It's like a heavenly festival each night."

"Will you take me there, Papin, and let me sit on your and Tsotsi's rock?"

"Of course, I will, Ayanda. When I have found my path and can afford you, I will come back, claim you with a *labola* to make your father proud. I shall take you away and show you the real stars."

Papin congratulated himself on not having to borrow another of Tsotsi's white lies. He could show his Ayanda real stars from anywhere away from the cities. He would do all of those things, but he doubted he'd ever find the courage to return to Champagne Castle Hotel and the people he'd let down.

He wished he could promise her a future, but he had none, and his respect for her father stopped him from taking advantage of her in spite of the temptation she posed. It was indeed the biggest struggle he'd had in his life.

They both knew their time together was short. This was but a stepping stone for Papin.

"How will I know, if you are not here, that you will be thinking of me?" she'd whisper against his cheek, and his heart would leap like a springbok at her tone, sensual with longing.

"No matter where you are, just look up through man's dirty haze, my Ayanda, and find a star. No matter where I am, I will look up at the same time, find your single star and know you are with me as I am with you. And when you see a shooting star, you will know my wish is coming true and I am on my way to join you."

In the short months of their industry, the girls had a budding business. There were many young runners who delivered the beer for a reasonable take in plastic containers they'd begged, borrowed, stored or stolen. The girls were happy to use this distribution channel because the less they were actually seen with the beer, the less their chances of being caught by authorities. Brewing was, after all, a crime.

And make no mistake, the girls' profession was a competitive one. Beer brewers were cutthroat, but as long as they served only their turf—comprised of a few streets or sixty shanties—they were fairly sure they'd live to brew another day.

Virtually every night for the past six months, he and Bandi attended meetings after work for Papin to get to know the primary ANC players. Bandi explained it was imperative these important political chess masters could asses Papin's worth to the organization and decide where he would be of best use. Papin was due to leave for Mozambique in a week for militant training. Only leaving Ayanda marred his excitement.

After their long work day and the tedious bus ride home that Friday night, Papin and Bandi were looking forward to a gourd of the girls' beer, some pap and stew and good company on the stoep of Bandi's real home, the door firmly closed behind them to hide the brewery.

As they walked up the long narrow street, it was noisier than usual. Sure, it was Friday night, end of the work week, so beer consumption was high, but so was the girls' profit potential. Papin smiled. He couldn't wait to see Ayanda.

One of the runners ran up to them. "Quickly. Quickly. The beer ladies are in trouble," he shouted in Swazi.

Papin's city feet become mountain-goat hooves as he tore up the crowded street, dodging people, kids, dogs and chickens as he ran, his heart pounding with fear.

Miraculously, the boy was keeping up with him.

"What happened?" Papin asked.

"Police!"

He was thirty yards away. Three policeman held guns. Two black policemen were pounding on the door of Bandi's home, through the iron bars of the security gate.

"Open now!" they shouted in three languages. Afrikaans. English. Xhosa.

There was a small gap between Bandi and his next-door neighbor's house—a rare happenstance in these cramped quarters—and Papin saw the white policeman slip through the opening. Their house backed up to a trash collection station, so there was a rare common area behind the "brewhouse" spanning about fifty feet, used frequently by all to get to the giant dustbin.

Papin followed him, and fifteen yards away, the glow from many candles poured from the open back door, illuminating a body in flight. Ayanda. His Ayanda. She was close to reaching the trash bin. A few more feet and she could get lost in the chaos that was daily life in Soweto.

In a blur, Papin saw the white policeman lift his weapon in both hands and shout, "Stop or I shoot!"

Ayanda kept on running.

Papin shouted, "Stop, Ayanda. Stop!"

She must have heard his voice because she stopped and turned. Her hands were up.

But then a loud *pop*.

The smell of gunpowder burned the air, his nostrils, and a hole of fear in his heart. The world went into slow motion. He saw his Ayanda's arms fly out as her back arched, and she was looking at Papin with a surprised look on her beautiful face before her chest concaved from the impact. When the bullet exited her back, her head flew back. Disbelief and terror made each moment sluggish, drawn out, and his mind became a thick sea of molasses, collecting every dastardly detail of the horrors before him.

He would try and erase all but the look on her face when she saw him. There was nothing but unadulterated joy. But he'd always be haunted by her smile of sublime happiness crumpling in confusion as the deadly bullet did its damnable damage to her small body.

He heard his own strangled cry as he ran to his love and got there just as her body collapsed, so when his own knees gave in, he could shield her crash to the hard ground.

And there she lay, limp in his arms. "Ayanda, my love, it's all right. We will never be far apart. A star will forever unite us. Look for the brightest star in the sky and you will find me there, and I you."

Her face relaxed, and with her last vestige of strength, her eyes found his and her mouth lifted at the corners.

Her beautiful eyes closed. Her head became heavy as the last of life ebbed from her young, beautiful body. And yet he swore her lips still stretched ever so slightly in a smile.

He heard his own load roar. An alpha lion rendered powerless by the loss of his lioness.

With shattered heart and body soaked by the terror of the night, in the middle of this makeshift, unelectrified city, he gazed up through the hovering haze caused by a hundred thousand fires and managed to find a single star.

Then realization hit.

Ayanda was dead from a white man's bullet.

And he swore to avenge her death many, many times over.

And it was there, under that single star visible in Soweto, Papin Tshabalala of Champagne Castle became Lwazi, the cold-hearted, soulless anarchist and freedom fighter the South African government called "Terrorist."

# 41

# THE FLAWED VAULT

*Angola, 1977*

"NEVER LEAVE AN ENEMY BEHIND," Lwazi reminded his freedom fighters as they converged on the plateau above the gorge after the explosion.

Some of his own had fallen, taken by the enemy who'd surprised them. Two were dead, two had fled. But first things first.

He knew not how many were involved in their proposed ambush, but those who survived the blast must be obliterated. Had the mine not been detonated, he and his cell would have been slaughtered. Well planned, he had to concede, but for the unintended explosion.

He could see an enemy solider in one piece and watched his men empty rounds into the white boy, who was likely a hair away from dead already. Such wastefulness.

"Go down the valley. See if any others survived," he shouted to them, and they complied.

He felt more than saw something in his right peripheral

vision, behind an outcrop of rocks, and he walked over, ready to pull the trigger of his AK-47.

Lwazi—meaning "One of Great Knowledge," as he'd been christened by the ANC hierarchy—looked down at the broken soldier at his feet.

Surprise was so immense, he took a giant step back, as if he'd seen a ghost. He clutched his rifle closer to his chest ... to protect himself? Or to protect himself from using it?

God, the ancestors, Sangoma, Mr. Palmer ... his heart thudded against his ribcage.

It had been eleven years, four months and fourteen days. The body before him was contorted and the face obscured by spattered blood, yet it was like looking into his own soul. He had no need to look for further proof ... but he couldn't help himself.

There it was. A six-inch scar with raised pink flesh on the white arm.

"Nothing, Lwazi." One of his men's voices made him jump.

"Go, both of you. Find the others that ran away beyond our camp, but spare only fifteen minutes. Then meet me at the rendezvous in twenty." How did his voice sound so normal? So controlled, when surprise was buzzing and flailing through his very being?

"Go now! Shesha! I will finish business here." He watched his men go far enough away not to hinder him, and then, as if drawn back by instinct, he saw the man before him lift an eyelid.

There was but a glimmer of life left in the shattered body. Relief such as he'd never known, even when he was kicked out of John Vorster Square, flooded his consciousness.

Guilty, he shot off his AK-47.

*P-RRRRT!*

He needed time to think. To make sense of this ... this abomination that was war pitting people against people.

*No!* He must *not* remember.

Because to remember would make him soft. Make him lose focus. Make him feel. He hadn't felt since he'd last looked at that single, murky star. He couldn't afford feelings. They would muddy the water, as they always did. They were counting on him. He was ANC. His people had been finding new ways to fight for their land and their freedoms for sixty-five years.

He had seen for himself how every year it got worse for the South African black and colored people. The Afrikaner government's made-up laws continuously upped the ante for oppression, separation, hardships and lack of humane conditions for black and colored South Africans under the abominable banner that was Apartheid.

Nothing must stop him from his focus. Otherwise, eleven years of commitment to gaining freedom would be wasted. Not even his friend, his blood brother dying before him, must get in the way of his quest.

He'd long since abolished the weakness that was listening to his heart. Was there one left inside him? If so, he would have to rip it out and burn it. A heart had no place in war. Lwazi knew the liberty of millions depended on his fortitude.

But suddenly, he felt desperately sad—a sensation he'd long discarded—as his eyes focused on his beloved friend, broken by war, who lay at his feet. And then it was as if he couldn't help himself. His mind became bewitched, a gold Timex winding backward to the mountains. Back to times he'd deliberately suppressed and kept contained in a cold heart-cave, blocked by an impenetrable granite door.

How on earth had the granite shifted? One crack and he'd be done for.

*Champagne Castle Hotel, 1962*

"COME IN."

As Papin entered, he smelled the familiar leather of the old chair on which his hotel-chief sat. A hint of spicy cinnamon and a whiff of newly churned cream invaded his senses, and he looked down to see a half-eaten apple pie swimming in a puddle of melted ice cream.

It was month-end. Inkosi had to rush from dinner to finish the books before he led guests in the night's bingo game.

"You okay, Papin?" Inkosi asked.

"Yebo. Thank you, Inkosi. Can I see you?" he knew it was an odd phrase, but being there and actually being seen were two different things.

"Sit. Tell me." Inkosi put down his pen and interlaced his fingers, waiting.

"I no longer wish to be paid to be Tsotsi's friend." There. He'd said it.

"He's what ... twelve now? That makes you seventeen. He has a lot more growing up to do, Papin. I will need you to help him for many more years. Though I don't think he needs undue protection anymore—thanks to you—he can do with learning the many other things you can teach him. You are a good influence. Your teaching skills are inbred. Your knowledge of the land and nature is rich and lateral. I believe your life skills and most assuredly your education are helpful to Jock. And your Zuluisms will make a far better man come out of a boy."

"Thank you, Inkosi."

"It's me who should be thanking you. So why shouldn't I pay you for your good influence on my son?"

"Tsotsi is my friend, Inkosi. I should not be paid to be a friend. That comes from here." He beat his fist on the left side of his chest.

Papin watched as water filled Inkosi's eyes. A surprise as much to Inkosi as to himself, he reckoned.

He could see Inkosi was hatching a plan. As his fingers entwined, he rubbed palms together and stared, focusing on a point to the left of Papin's head.

"I think it's time. In the new school year, I want you to run the hotel school. Your teacher's salary will be substantial, but it will also cover all your other chores. Will that suit you, Papin?"

"Yebo, Inkosi." That was better. Then he wouldn't feel he was betraying his friend. Papin felt a rush of adrenaline. Head of the school. That would be something beyond his dreams.

"But how will I know what to teach them, Inkosi?"

"Miss Constable, the old spinster who lives five miles down the hill—you know her; she occasionally comes up for eggs—well, she's finally retired from teaching high school in Estcourt. I reckon she could do with extra income. Would you mind going ten miles down the hill on a Sunday afternoon when things are quiet here to get your student's lessons for the next week? Take Shaka ... or another if he is tired from guest rides. You know best. Miss Constable will teach you the upcoming lessons you will deliver, and the rest of the time, she'll teach you whatever you are most interested in. I shall pay her."

He felt his eyes widen, and excitement, like a joyful butterfly, beat its wings inside his belly. "Inkosi. I would *walk* ten miles every day for that privilege."

"Consider it done. Now I must finish the books."

# 42

# ZULU PROVERBS

*Champagne Castle Hotel, 1963*

TSOTSI'S TIME away from the hotel seemed to get longer and longer. Papin didn't know the meaning of resentment—there was no word for it in Zulu—but he could articulate it now because of the knowledge he'd gained at school. School was his biggest joy—well, after Tsotsi. And Shaka. And his shiny gold Timex.

Inkosi had taught him much over the years. Not intentionally but inadvertently. He studied Inkosi's ways of dealing with people. He modeled himself on Inkosi when he wanted to be at his best in modern society.

Just last week, Inkosi had called him into his office. He'd turned eighteen that day. A white celebration through and through that no one remembered when Tsotsi was away.

"Papin, I saw your uncle was visiting."

He was surprised. He'd ridden both Shaka and Dennis very early, then taught his pupils and marked their homework, so he hadn't yet been to the kraal. His Monday to Sunday were full, though when he was not learning or teaching, his often found his heart empty without Tsotsi. "I did not see him, Inkosi."

"How do you feel about him?" It was a strange question for Inkosi to ask.

"My father is not fond of my dead mother's brother. He does not like me to be in my uncle's presence." Papin hoped his answer, though steeped in avoidance, would satisfy Inkosi.

"And for good reason. That man's head is full of bees just smoked from their hives," said Inkosi. "Don't get any ideas about leaving us for Johannesburg, Papin. We need you here. You have a future in our hotel. And it's a rough world out there. It's not the City of Gold it promises to be."

He had no answer, so he remained silent.

"I saw Jock this week when I took him for lunch. He said it's your birthday soon. How many ... eighteen this year? Wait! What's the date? Ah! Twenty-seventh. Today is your birthday!" Inkosi smiled, and though Papin nodded and was about to answer, Inkosi blurted, "What size shoe do you wear?"

Papin used his hands a foot and some extra distance apart as an indicator. "This size, Inkosi."

"There." Inkosi pointed to a big box on the side of his desk. "A gift from a guest. Owns a boot manufacturing company in Switzerland. Damn fine pair but too big for me. If they fit you, they're yours, Papin. Try them on."

He was overwhelmed. Such a lavish material gift. He felt shy as he opened the box. The smell of leather prickled his nose hairs. A rich, wholesome smell, and there was another, unfamiliar scent—something, he imagined, that would preserve the leather for decades. They were magnificent and seemed to be machine-stitched. He couldn't imagine the size of the machine that could handle making these sturdy boots.

He prayed to the ancestors the boots would fit. He picked up the left boot and looked at Inkosi, who nodded and smiled, then he pushed his well-worn foot down into the new leather. It felt cold and cushy as he stood on it, and he knew his smile reflected his joy.

"It fits, Inkosi. It *fits!*" The excitement of possession he'd never understood in others spread through him, and he felt quite dizzy with not only the magnificent boots, which were to be his own, but the gesture of Inkosi giving them to him.

His first pair of shoes. Not counting the hotel-issued takkies, which he wore only when absolutely necessary.

Inkosi was beaming as broad as the ever-smiling chef Thabo as he came around his desk, knelt, then pushed his thumb down on the outside of the boot until it connected with Papin's big toe. Papin had no idea what was happening.

"Good! Gives you a good inch for your feet to grow before the boots get too small. Wear them well, Papin. Make each step you take in those boots purposeful."

Inkosi could have been a Zulu.

After he had made his gracious and grateful thanks known to Inkosi, Papin headed back to the kraal to find a suitable hiding place.

From a distance, his precious box under his arm, he saw his father and uncle sitting outside the hut and heard his father's voice in his ear, a variation of the same words each time uncle appeared.

"My son, I do not wish you to stand in the shade cast by that man. He is Tokoloshe. No reason to listen to his *nyagas*," his father warned.

And through the years, his uncle found ways to plant nuisances in his head. But each was erased by an act of kindness by Tsotsi, Inkosi and even the odd guest.

Comprising his world were Tsotsi; the endless Zulu wisdoms around him; the many fascinating animals and all of nature that changed constantly; the study of white people and their strange ways; and the plethora of books he had access to—including the hotel library, which he had Inkosi's permission to use. Now gloriously learning and teaching school. Papin's life was rich and abundant and fuller than he'd ever expected. There'd been no need to explore another world.

Before he entered the kraal, he hid his shoebox under a thicket, ready to be masterfully concealed when he had more time.

As he approached, he looked at his father, who nodded his permission, and Papin sat on the ground.

"I see you, Father. I see you, Uncle."

"Look at you, son of my dead sister. A full-grown man. Tall and strong. No more a young horse boy. A teacher. No. More than that. The head of a school!"

His uncle was a man who talked with an oiled tongue, but you couldn't help but listen to him. If you were to block your ears, that slick oil would still seep in and tickle your eardrums.

"Thank you, Uncle," Papin said respectfully.

"The ancestors wish you to come here for what purpose?" Father asked his uncle.

Papin knew Sponon's good nature was being challenged. The tone of his father's voice was sharp and hard like a steel blade you had no business messing with.

"Can I not come and see my family in the hills? You still speak of ancestors here. We don't think of them much in the city."

"Then the city must be a dangerous place," said his father flatly.

"The city is rampant with injustice. Black people who've lived in townships close to their domestic jobs for decades—fifty-seven thousand and more—plucked unwillingly from their homes and relocated by the government in trucks like cattle with their belongings, miles and miles from their jobs, to start again. Given nothing but a few square feet of dirt with a lot number. Expected to make their new home from nothing and still without running water, sanitation or electricity. Eish!"

Papin's father gestured around their kraal. "There is no running water, electricity or sanitation here either. Are we suffering?" he asked rhetorically.

Uncle took no heed. He just took a breath and continued. "Their old homes were bulldozed. It didn't matter if the houses were made of cardboard, repurposed aluminum tins, stone, bricks or cement. Gone. Obliterated, and with it, years of domesticity and memories demolished. All so the white man can build a suburb closer to town for his own convenience, with the blacks carted far enough away to not be a blight on the white man's state of bliss."

If what he said was true, it was understandable his uncle's words were filled with hate. Papin doubted it could be as bad as the elder made out. Uncle was known for his inclination to exaggerate as well as his endless quoting of Zulu proverbs.

"And—" his uncle began again, but his father raised up a firm hand.

"Enough! *No* more of your nyagas around this fire."

"I miss your mother's face around here." His uncle changed the subject slickly, addressing Papin.

"It has been sixteen years," Papin said. He had no memory of her and felt no loss. "Tell me the good things about the city, Uncle."

His usually passive father barked, "There are no good things about the city. Let it go, Papin, or you too will be banned from this fire."

"Ah, but my brother, the city has been good to me." Papin's uncle cleverly changed his tone and volume, looking directly at Sponon as if just seeking conversation.

"As the mountains have been good to my boy and me," said his father, unable to hide his irritation.

"I have found a place where my life can make a difference," Uncle Beza persisted.

Papin felt the stirrings of excitement in his belly. "How do I find such direction, Uncle?"

"No nonsense here," his father warned. "My boy's future is in these mountains. In this hotel."

"You know, my brother, we Zulus are not born to serve the white man. And they are certainly not our friends. If we no longer serve a purpose, they have no use for us," said Uncle.

"Perhaps in the city that is so, but not in our world. We work for a generous and kind man. He allows us to keep our culture but provides a means for Zulus who foolishly wish to explore Western culture. Though I do not approve of wrong ideas inside young heads, it shows this man's breadth of generosity. This is the best life for me and mine," his father said, looking pointedly at Papin.

"Yet he pays you less than you are worth, and you do more for him because you deem him kind. No! We must banish this acceptance of servitude. This thing that makes us less has to be squashed like a loathsome bug."

His father stood up abruptly, and Uncle stopped talking.

"Come, enough for one night. You will breakfast with us before you leave?" His father was clear this would not be a long visit.

"Where will you sleep tonight, son?" Sponon asked Papin.

"At the compound, Father."

"Thank you for your willingness to share your hut, Sponon. I will join you in a minute. I need first to enjoy the fresh mountain air," Uncle said.

"You won't find that in the city," his father promised, then said, "Straight to bed, son." There was warning in his voice.

But Papin paid no heed to his father's warning when he heard his uncle's urgent call halfway up the hill to the compound. Intrigue proved to be a wanton vixen.

"Come, nephew. Sit awhile and talk. Long enough for you to understand and short enough that your father does not miss me."

They'd sat down right there, and words tumbled from Uncle Beza's lips. "There must be rebellion and violence. It's the only way."

Papin was not a little alarmed by the inflammatory words that tumbled from Uncle's lips.

"You are educated. You go to school. You know as much as the white man from books, and you understand the heart of Zulu and other tribes. We will not rush. We will strike only when we have everything we need in place. When you bite indiscriminately, you end up eating your own tail. To succeed, we need men like you to teach other men to become as close as possible to the asset I see in you. There are riches to match my words. Not only in coin but in ways to remove this bigoted Afrikaner government and its preposterous, made-up laws that take away all our freedoms and treat us like we are a damning blight on a once-healthy crop of *mielies*. When you are ready, I will introduce you. You will go far, nephew. A Zulu born to rule. Like Shaka. I will be back, and we will talk again."

Uncle patted his back, and they shook hands the Zulu way. His parting words to Papin: "I've been waiting for you to become a man for eighteen years now. A chick that will grow into a rooster can be spotted the very day it hatches."

As his uncle ran back to his father's hut, the old Zulu saying "Do not leave your host's house throwing mud in his well" came to mind as the quiet breezes of Papin's mind blew this way and that until they become destructive winter gales.

# 43

## SHAKA'S PHILOSOPHY

*Angola, 1977*

*Never leave an enemy behind.* Yes! It was Zulu lore. It was Zulu law. It was good war strategy. But then, King Shaka was not faced with killing a blood brother he loved.

He knew what he had to do. He felt the course hairs of the springbok skin water flask that clipped to his Chinese-made belt. He wore and carried everything that spoke of the ANC's converged struggle for liberation and the communist countries backing them. He was a walking league of communistic nations. His attire and equipment merged African deerskin with Chinese-manufactured clothes bought with Cuban funds, and he held a Russian-made AK-47.

He looked at the face of the man who lay before him. It was as familiar as his own. He longed to look into the man's eyes. The eyes that hid nothing. But the man couldn't move his head. Perhaps it was just as well. He couldn't bear to see what disappointments lay in those orbs.

He laid the water bottle down as gently as he could and had a vision of placing the gift of healing at the feet of an ailing king.

He glanced again at the pink scar. It stood out on the boy ... the man's white skin, not in anger at being severed all those years ago but showing off. Proud of what it stood for.

An enormous gratitude opened his closed heart like a flower's awakening sped up by a time-lapse sequence. As he stood, gun in hand, hot tears streamed down his face.

This broken man at his feet knew all too well the Zulu law.

*Sterkspruit Falls, Champagne Castle, 1965*

DEATH. Papin had never contemplated it before. Now he wondered what he could possibly contribute to the ancestors with his life experiences. There was so much more for him to learn. And Tsotsi. His work with Tsotsi was not done. *No! Ancestors, I cannot die now. I've not yet lived.*

And then the terror kicked in, and Papin clung even tighter to weak, aching limbs of the fragile tree, not daring to watch Jock's rescue attempt. How would the boy find a way to save him? Papin was older. Wiser. And he was at a loss thinking of a way to save himself!

His mind reeled back, reminding him how he got there. Riding Shaka. Tsotsi behind him on Dennis. The footpath veering closer to the chasm created by the Sterkspruit falls. Just sixty feet ahead of them, great white waters tumbled over time-worn rocks and cascaded down, down fifteen stories or more. When the wall of liquid hit the bank of rocks at the bottom, the rainwater splintered, and droplets like shards scattered in a thousand directions.

Tight squeeze for two horses but he went ahead, closest to the drop. *Tsotsi must always be on the least dangerous side.* Then he felt foolish. The boy knew the mountains as well as he.

Tips of daring trees just ten feet below the ridge waved, showing how determined they were—even in their puniness—to grow up the side of an impossibly steep cliff. The loose sediment, eroded from the sheer rock by mist off the relentless falls, was their reason for existence. Nature had encouraged her seeds to grow and prosper over decades, and the tips of the trees strained upward to catch the life-giving sun.

He never saw it coming.

Suddenly his Shaka reared up and his body backward. He tried to rein Shaka in, but whatever caused his horse's fear came back to haunt the stallion while he was still on his hind legs, and he bucked again—higher and even more unexpected.

That's what did it.

Papin remembered watching his weightless body launch over the edge and hover over the abyss in suspended animation. Exquisite and exhilarating for the second before terror and gravity pulled him down ... down ... down ...

He heard himself scream over the rush of the falls, and he reached and reached and reached ...

"Papin. Papin!" He heard the desperate cry from far above, and he felt sorry he'd caused the boy such anxiety.

And then he realized he *heard*. He *felt*. He must be *alive*.

"Yebo," he answered. He dared not look down but felt a too-skinny branch beneath his feet. The ancestors must have known he was not ready to join them and had placed his feet on the strongest of the scrawny branches. He spread his legs to distribute his weight, and his toes gripped the bark with all their might, while his hands held fast to bunches of the delicate tree tips to help him stabilize.

He heard Tsotsi's attempt to talk to him, then there was nothing.

Papin felt like he did when Tsotsi was ripped from him to go back to school. So alone.

The slightest movement would cause this *Gollaga-inja* bough on which he stood to snap. Toes and fingers held fast with every muscle and tendon at full capacity. He asked, no, he begged the ancestors to reduce his weight by ninety percent so as not to challenge the ambitious but weak, odd-angled tree.

Tsotsi was checking on him again and when he answered he heard the bough that suspended him between life and death moan like an old woman with creaky bones.

He negotiated with the ancestors.

His nerves tightened and aching muscles twitched, defying their desperate need for stillness.

The bough swore at Papin, threatening to tear away from its mother tree because of its own strain and pain. He apologized and thanked the branch for its courage, but in doing so, he glanced down. It hit him like a hard slap. Any attempt at descent was impossible. It was way too far and too steep. That was not a possibility. He would die.

Whoa! His head spun as fear threatened to release his bowels. He clenched his bum, fingers, toes and jaw simultaneously, and they held on in spite of what his brain urged.

He willed himself to stay as still as possible.

He couldn't die. He had to raise Tsotsi properly. There was no one else who would, who could.

How could he save himself? The only way was up. But how?

He invited in the ancestors. Sangoma. Mr. Palmer. And concentrated with all his might to hear their advice.

They said he should think of the very best time in his life. There was no hesitation. The best time was when Shaka and Dennis were born and he got a horse to call his own. To train, to love and to cherish. Wait! What about the day he got his Timex from Tsotsi? Or the day he became head of the school and got to study under a brilliant teacher. A glorious day. What about the day he was given Swiss boots? His eighteenth birthday. And what about ...

A thousand recalls of his and Tsotsi's world surged through his head, and he realized every day with Tsotsi by his side was the best day of his life. Because of Tsotsi, he'd really lived.

He felt selfish begging for days on earth when his life had been so wonderful.

His boots. Inkosi told Tsotsi nothing of them and nor did he. He was saving them for when he went on his adventure. He couldn't tell Tsotsi his plan. It would destroy their present.

Inkosi had asked him why he didn't wear his new boots, and Papin said, "When something is so valuable to you, you must gaze upon it in appreciation until you can find a mission worthy of the wearing."

He thought of Inkosi's chuckle as he said affectionately, "You make every sentence into a Zulu proverb, Papin. My investment in your teacher is paying off a thousand-fold. Keep up the good work."

Tsotsi's voice coming from above brought him back, and his immediate recollection of his predicament made his legs go weak. Sheer force of will made his toes grip tighter around the branch.

Then the blur of waiting for '*Grab*' and Papin feared the mother-tree would cut ties with her weak offspring before Tsotsi was ready for him to jump.

But *"Grab!"* came. And Papin did, with the same blind faith it took to walk into the bush to find his manhood.

His arms locked tightly around Tsotsi's waist, and it occurred to him how much bigger and stronger he was than his nearly fifteen-year-old savior.

And strong legs locked behind his back like a vice.

In seconds they were forcibly jolted, but then they rose—quite miraculously—up, up, up, hanging onto each other for dear life until they were pulled over the edge of the ledge and onto solid earth and grass, still locked together. As soon as they rolled apart, Tsotsi disconnected himself from his ingenious contraption and sprang up to tend to his agitated horse, while Papin considered they were on the very grass where Tokoloshe had visited and caused all the ruckus.

Papin watched over the top of his head as his charge nuzzled Dennis's neck to say thank you. It was, of course, she who was responsible for pulling them to safety. But it was the boy's intelligence that made it happen.

Once he was sure his horse was calm, Tsotsi came back and lay on the grass next to him. On their backs, they both looked up at the bright blue cloudless sky. Safe. Together.

"Next time, get thrown off the safe side of your bloody horse. It'll be easier," Tsotsi said dryly.

Laughter became their release.

Before mirth had finished its bubbling, Tsotsi rose.

"You saved me, Tsotsi," Papin shouted and felt a big lump in his throat.

"Dennis was the brave one. She saved us both," said Tsotsi as he fished in his pocket and rewarded his horse with a carrot, then led her down close to Shaka and left them grazing contentedly together.

Tsotsi joined him on the grass again. There was nothing that needed to be said, but Papin allowed himself to feel the pride that comes when you know you've raised a child, or your tsotsi, well.

# 44

# BLOOD BROTHERS

*Champagne Castle Hotel, 1965*

PAPIN SHOOK WITH FEAR, but it was not the aftershock of trauma wracking his body. Rather the thought of what would happen if Inkosi found out Tsotsi put his own horse in such terrible danger.

Papin walked toward his father, who was tending the kraal's cattle.

"What is it, my son?"

"All is well, my father."

"Why then are your clothes torn? Surely if you dress like a hotel guest, you need to look like one in spite of your blackness?" His father had come to resent his education and his interest in Western culture. If Sponon had his way, Papin would still be wearing skins.

"It was a rough day, Father. Death whispered loud in my ear. But Tsotsi saved me."

His father's concern overrode his annoyance. "Tell me all, my son. I shall share Tsotsi's heroism with Chief."

Fear jolted through him. "Please no, Father, *no!* If Inkosi finds out that Tsotsi endangered his horse to save me, he will never be allowed to ride Dennis again."

"Tell me, son, and you have my word. I will make sure Tsotsi is protected. What are fathers for if not to protect the ones their loved ones' love?"

And so it was that the Chief, though he had but one tooth left, sported a lion cape that night, a gift from a visiting Zululand Chief who stayed for the night's hastily prepared festival. A young beast's pelt was all Chief needed because the years had robbed him of his once great height by buckling his legs and crumbling and curling his spine.

Tsotsi sat next to him on the log of the liquid amber tree they'd christened so long ago at their first official ceremony together, when Papin became a man.

Tonight, Papin wore a buckskin dyed blue, and Tsotsi wore a red one.

"What's with the skirts?" Tsotsi asked. Miraculously, Papin had managed to keep the reason for the occasion a secret from his friend.

"Red symbolizes your transformation."

His white nose, dusted with freckles, wrinkled. "Transformation?"

"Tonight is an important night. You shall see."

"What does your blue stand for?"

"Loyalty," Papin said, and though he saw Tsotsi's confusion, he dare not explain lest he let the cat out of the bag. He laughed. The English had such silly expressions.

Tsotsi jabbed him in the ribs. "Why are Shaka and Dennis in the kraal?"

Papin laughed. "Already you have had too much kefir beer. You are seeing things!"

Tsotsi shook his head like a wet dog. "To reconfigure my brain cells," he stated.

It amused Papin no end.

They'd washed their hands in bowls and feasted on two deer —it was too last-minute and quite impossible under the circumstances to request an ox from Inkosi, though the reason for celebration certainly warranted such mammoth effort. They'd washed out their mouths after the delicious feast, and all the while, the drums beat rhythmically, ceaselessly.

But all of a sudden, the tempo of the drums increased. The keening of the maidens began, and Papin felt stirrings of excitement and knew his friend felt them too, though he knew not why.

Chief rose from his place of honor, gourd in hand, and came to stand in front of Tsotsi. The younger looked guilty, thinking he'd underperformed in some way or overdone the drinking.

Chief drank deeply and then with both hands held his gourd out to the boy. Tsotsi glanced quickly at Papin for support. He nodded. The boy rose and took the gourd from the proffered hands of Chief and drank with gusto.

The drumbeats slowed to a three-four time and the volume decreased.

Chief began to chant in time to the beat, and everyone stood, even Sangoma, who had magically appeared, and each line Chief sang was repeated by his devoted subjects.

"Tonight's the night ... when a boy becomes a man ... and this man has our gratitude ... not only for saving our Zulu ... from certain death ... but for the loyalty and love he shows ... to his Zulu brother."

When Chief paused to grab the gourd back from Tsotsi so he could wet his parched vocal cords, the drums sped up, and the people danced with frenzy and abandon. Chief threw the empty vessel to the ground and was quickly proffered another by a nubile maiden.

Chief handed the half-finished gourd to Tsotsi and gestured

broadly. Tsotsi's face was infused with pleasure, and Papin was glad he had no notion of what was coming.

As the younger drank, the dancing stopped and drums quieted and Chief continued his chant: "Tonight we celebrate this Zulu, he who has become more brother than friend ... He who is young with old wisdom ... Short with tall courage... Strong with weak self-love ... And with a heart that bears a lion's courage."

Even insulated by beer, Tsotsi was shy in the midst of the attention. He did not like fuss. Another reason he was more Zulu than white. Papin knew the younger would have crawled under the liquid amber stump and pretended to be invisible if he could do so without provoking not only Chief's but Sangoma's wrath. Instead, the boy drank deeply from the gourd.

Chief put up a hand, and the celebration turned off. The drumbeats and keening and singing stopped.

Chief's voice sliced through the silence. "Tonight, we declare a union of body, mind and spirit." Papin stepped forward as he'd been schooled, then turned around to face Tsotsi.

Tsotsi's eyes held confusion in the firelight as an induna appeared on each side of Papin and took hold of an arm. The induna on his right held his arm tightly, palm up.

Chief continued "As Papin Tshabalala, son of Sponon ..."

Sangoma appeared, knife at the ready, reflecting in its shiny blade the fires around the kraal.

Papin never flinched as the lethal blade penetrated just above his wrist and sliced expertly and quickly through his skin, a cut so deep it was the ancestors themselves preventing his veins from splitting open. Up his arm the blade went, toward his elbow. A good six inches.

"*Gollaga-inja!* Holy shit," Tsotsi's shout boomed through the silence as he jumped up, ready to help his bleeding friend. Two indunas appeared at Tsotsi's side and held him in place.

Chief continued his speech and turned to his friend: "And Tsotsi-Jock, son of Inkosi David Walsh ..." And Tsotsi did not resist as Sangoma's knife did the same six inches of damage to his white arm. Papin was amazed Tsotsi was prepared to take the same pain without a fight and without knowing the reason for it.

This boy was prepared to go as far as he needed to experience what Papin was experiencing. Now that was confidence. That was commitment.

He was so brave. Papin felt proud.

Sangoma arranged them to face each other, then maneuvered them so their right, bleeding arms clasped each other, exactly where the cuts were made.

As his and Tsotsi's blood mingled, a maiden handed Sangoma banana leaves and long wild grass, and their arms were bound tightly together, so cut on cut, their blood could mingle.

Papin looked at Tsotsi and smiled. His young friend smiled back as broadly as he'd ever seen.

Chief called again for quiet and then announced in high volume: "Before our ancestors and our vast Zulu tribe, and in the name of all the great Zulus who came before us, I declare the joining of two hearts, two minds, two spirits and two bodies. You two are now and forever joined in strength, loyalty, and in blood."

Chief paused for effect, and there was silence once more but just long enough to make the last of his testament even more powerful. "Papin and Tsotsi, I declare you Zulu blood brothers."

The crowd went wild. The drums pulsed as fast as their beating hearts. He knew they beat at the same pace because their arms were still bound together, pounding out blood. Papin gestured for them to sit down, and they jointly, awkwardly did so.

"And before we dance in celebration of this great union, bring in Shaka and Dennis."

Tsotsi's face beamed with joy as the twins were led in. So great was his glee, he tried to go to his Dennis, but their well-sliced, well-bound arms made independent movement impossible, and they both smarted from the pain.

Papin watched Tsotsi gazing proudly at Shaka and Dennis being lavished with attention in the center of the kraal as all the Zulus as well as the Chief himself patted and rubbed them. In closing, a long story was delivered by Sangoma, who interpreted the ancestors' great thanks for their horses' courage.

Tsotsi's face was filled with light as he said, "Look, the twins are enjoying their first carrots blessed by the ancestors."

They grinned at each other. Papin had never felt so close to another human being as their blood mingled to herald their brotherhood.

# 45

# DEAD HEROES

*South West Africa, just south of the Angola Border, 1977*

HE FELT HARD, intermittent stabs to his closed eyelids. What the hell? He couldn't lift his arm to cover his eyes. He tried the other one and after a few attempts managed to pick it up, but shielding his eyes was easier said than done because his face hurt like a bastard.

He tried to open the one eye that worked, but his vision was blurred. Panic. He couldn't see a half-meter in front of him—it was all gray, and now his eyeballs were being stabbed. Was he blind? Had The Mist stopped its twenty-two years of threatening and was finally consuming him? Panic.

He closed his eyes and concentrated on taking a deep breath. One was all he could muster. It hurt like a bitch. But he could feel. That was a good thing. Ah! Raindrops the size of a five-cent piece were hitting his face like a BB gun. He slowly rolled his head to one side and opened his eyes. Thank God ... Sangoma ... the ancestors ... Mr. Palmer ...

He remembered Lwazi ...

Wait! It was *Papin* who stood over him. No! Couldn't be.

Impossible. It was his pent-up longing for his friend that caused this mind trick. He'd been hallucinating.

And yet ... their twin scars. Leaving him the water bottle so he'd survive the heat. Shouting for his terrorists to move on so he could "finish off the enemy" ... the burst of firepower whizzing past his ear. *Ha!* Couldn't be Papin. He'd never miss a shot.

Tiny.

Tiny tripped the land mine when the shooting started. He'd charged like an enraged bull onto the manmade path that Lieut had warned must be avoided at all costs. Poor bastard. Hurt tugged at his heart. No use looking for Tiny. That big fellow with the biggest heart was part of Angola forever. Perhaps Tiny—in his new role on high—had suggested the higher power send rain to water the parched earth and give life to nature in return for taking Tiny's. It's what he'd do. Tiny never thought of himself. That thinking brought Lieut solace.

With great effort and intense pain, he moved his head farther back and there, through the sheets of cascading rain, he saw Piet-Tire. Inert. Sprawled in death. Lieut had seen enough bodies to know.

How would he tell Frikkie his only audience member was no longer? He felt hot tears behind his rain-washed eyes as abysmal sadness overtook all else. The loss of a life with so much yet to give, not yet lived.

Nev? Penti? Charl the hero? His head hurt, as did his heart.

What the hell could have happened to his blood brother to turn into Lwazi? Why did Papin ... Lwazi spare him? You never left an enemy behind.

Cairns? Where the hell was Cairns? His picture of Cathy would be soggy by now. Rain would have washed all the color away. Cairns would be devastated. She was the link to his sanity. Oh God, no ... don't say the cluster mine took him too ... no!

He was still worried about Cathy's picture when his body painfully jolted him awake. Boesman's face was an inch from his own.

"Boesman?"

The hugest grin Lieut had ever seen split the brown man's face with joy, and wild clicking and hand-flicking began. Lieut looked up and saw trees. He was in their prearranged rendezvous point. How?

Lieut tried to sit up on his elbow, and that was a disaster. Pain shot through him like a hot poker branding his bone. He tried to move his leg. Well. One worked.

He managed to lift his head up to check out who else Boesman had rescued. Cairns was curled up in a sleeping bag. Relief. The boy would see his Cathy again.

Nev! His friend sat with his elbows on his knees. He was making repetitive patterns in the sand with a stick. The impish, always-happy face was gone.

"Nev," he tried to call, but it was nary a whisper. Boesman jumped up, stood over Nev and click-click-clicked away, pointing. Nev's smile was almost as broad as Boesman's as he hurried over, unscathed—at least on the outside.

"Man, you look like shit," said Nev, still smiling.

"How many here?" was all Lieut could get out.

"Six. Cairns only has a broken ankle. When Tiny blew—poor bastard—Cairns ran down the hill, tripped and fell over the steep rock face you guys had climbed, broke his ankle and tumbled into the undergrowth. He became mercifully invisible. It's what saved him."

Lieut got out, "Cathy will be pleased," but it hurt like a bastard.

Nev continued. "They shot Piet-Tire at close range, ten foot from you. How the hell you weren't shot ... Sorry about Piet."

He forced his mouth to make the words in his heart. "And Frikkie?"

Nev paused, and his face changed. "Frikkie and Penti ... fuck Lieut, gone, before your blast." Nev hung his head but not before Lieut realized it was shame that disfigured Nev's naughty, happy face.

"If Frikkie went, then you know Piet-Tire would have gone too. Better believe they're laughing their asses off up there, Nev. One would have been lonely without the other. Pentifucking-ford. He was a good one. It's war, Nev. Fucking war."

Nev continued. "And Charl? Now that pretty boy took your advice and ran like the wind when the fighting started. Climbed a tree. Became invisible and was quite safe because no dumb leopard would climb it, thorny as it was, and no Terr needed to check it because no enemy would be dumb enough to climb a bloody thorn tree. But it's what saved him. Terrs walked right under him. Boesman hauled him down covered in thorns, but he's still pretty." Nev grinned.

Lieut strained to look and saw his young hero, plastered with elephant dung or another of Boesman's natural remedies. Charl smiled and gave a casual salute from his sleeping bag.

"And you?" croaked Lieut.

"We managed to surprise them, even without you. We shot three of them to ribbons before they opened fire. I think it was Frikkie who did most of the damage. Then the bastards nailed Frikkie and Penti one after the other. I ran to them to see if I could fight from where they lay, just in case they were still alive and I could protect them, but then, BANG! The explosion from your position was the last thing we expected."

Nev paused. His eyes were pumping out tears, but he pushed

on. "I could have nailed all three of them in the back as they ran toward your explosion." He stopped suddenly.

Lieut said nothing. He just waited. It took a good few minutes before Nev said, "But I didn't, Lieut. I ran like a fucking fairy from a veldfire. I ran and ran and found a dry riverbed. I walked on the stones so as not to leave a trail. I had to go into the brush to hide, but when the coast was clear, I walked backwards in my own footsteps like you taught me. I was disoriented. Our maps were useless. God knows how Boesman found me. I am so ashamed." And Nev cried like a small boy, badly beaten.

Lieut didn't care that it hurt like a bastard to sit up. He had to. He did.

He used his good arm to shake his friend gently. "Nev. *Nev!* Listen to me. What did we always say? We'd never be dead heroes. You were alone. They would have nailed you. There was only one of you left to fight, my friend. You had no backup, and there were three of them. You did what I would have done. What anyone would have done. In my report, I'm going to tell them that you are traumatized. That way you won't have to come back here and lose your heart and your humanity and your sanity and your happy. You did fine, Nev. You did what you had to do."

"But Penti and Frikkie ..."

"Revenging them would have been your demise, Nev. Did Boesman say ..." Hearing his name, the little guy came close to Lieut and went down on his haunches.

Lieut used one hand and his facial expressions to ask after Penti and Frikkie. All Boesman had to do was shake his head slowly, eyes downcast.

"You see, Nev? Boesman says you couldn't have done anything. Be at peace, friend. No blame. You couldn't have helped them. And they didn't suffer."

Lieut wondered where he'd found the strength for the rush of words. Perhaps it was Tiny again. He smiled to himself and looked around. The semi-desert they'd left but a few days ago was now blooming. Flowers in a million colors and shapes hugged the landscape, transforming it into paradise. "Tiny, you've done a hell of a job, *Boytjie*!"

"What's that?" asked Nev, moving his ear close to Lieut's mouth, but Lieut just shook his head and asked a little louder: "How did we all get back?"

"Boesman," Nev said, and their bushman took the stage, miming the rescue. He showed Lieut how he'd taken two sleeping bags, used the knife in their kit and sliced open the bottoms. He'd searched for and found four thick branches and carefully removed all thorns. Benny had helped. Then they'd threaded the branches through the bags front to back, one on each side.

"Voilà!" said Nev. "Boesman and Benny made stretchers."

Lieut felt immense pride. He knew Boesman would never let them down. He only wished Frikkie and Piet, Tiny and Penti were here to testify to this savior's brilliance.

"By the time Boesman found me, he'd already hauled Charl back here over his shoulder and tended to him. Once he was treated and plastered with giraffe shit or whatever, we—stretcher team—hightailed it out to pick up you and Cairns. We only found Cairns by accident. We heard moaning deep in the bushes. No wonder he escaped fire."

Lieut put out his good arm, hand extended. Boesman took it, and they exchanged an African handshake—rather gently.

"Where are the ... other boys," Lieut asked.

"Under the tarp."

"Good. They'll get home before us, for their family's sake. But Tiny ..." Lieut stopped just in time to compose himself.

"Chopper will be here at sixteen hundred hours, Lieut. Bringing guys in to drive the Bedford back to camp. We'll be in

Ondangwa by seventeen hundred," Nev said, sounding more like himself.

Lieut lay back down. Every bone, every sinew, every muscle ached, but nothing ached more than his soul for the boys he'd lost.

Nev woke him up to ask: "How the hell did you avoid a final bullet with one of them on top of you?"

Lieut opened his eyes slowly. "I told you all." He paused, sleep tugging at his eyelids. Boesman had likely chewed a flower from the plethora available after the rains and made a potion to keep him sleeping till help came. "I'm a Zulu blood brother."

The last thing he remembered of that mission was Neville's chuckle.

# 46

# THE CHOPPER

*Champagne Castle Hotel, 20 September 1994*

JOCK'S EXHILARATION was just the same as when he and his dad navigated the S-bend in the rain. Backwards would always be his favorite way—young hands on the steering wheel and his bum wedged tightly between Dad's legs, the rearview mirror angled just so for them both to see behind them.

How he wished his Dad was around to witness this day.

The squeeze of his thigh flushed a warm sensation through him.

He glanced over, and she was there, where he hoped she'd always be. He couldn't wait to share his mountains with her. And the stars. She and the hotel had been a long time coming ... but they were both worth the wait.

His ever-present Mind Brownie and its attached New Aunts hadn't yet run out of battery, so how they managed to keep those bush war years dark was a mystery. Perhaps they'd listened to Sergeant Major in that smoky tent. If you remembered the war, you'd have to check yourself into the loony bin.

"It's even more gorgeous than I imagined," she said, and he heard the smile in her voice.

"We're home," said Jock, and he was happier than he'd been since just after he'd turned sixteen.

A ONE-AND-A-HALF-BY-TWO-METER PHOTOGRAPH of President Mandela in an elaborate glass-covered frame hung in the entrance. It was the first change he'd made in the two weeks he'd been back.

Just this morning, he'd heard the hotel's style referred to as "elegantly casual." It had certainly come a long way without the Walsh clan. That almost hurt him. But he'd vowed not to live in a state of regret.

There was no time to bugger around, as his father would say. This was a big day.

The first-ever black guest—a minister, no less—would be arriving to stay with them for three weeks. He'd no sooner finished the thought when he heard the chopper.

He shouted, "Red carpet rolled out?"

"Yebo, Inkosi," came the reply as the waiter, in his rush to see this historical arrival—and a chopper—nearly knocked over the pedestal holding a large black and white poster.

It shouted: "By popular demand, welcome back Billy Pillay. Famous Comic-Magician." Performance dates were listed underneath the picture of a dapper Indian man. Jock shook his head in wonder, smiling all the while.

He was still chuckling when he leaned on the frame of the open door and checked to see if there were any stains on his golf shirt. Heaven forbid. His wife would kill him. *Good.* Nothing obviously telltale he could see. He was safe.

The impressive aerial machine landed perfectly in the

nearest parking lot, which they'd had the guests clear of cars in anticipation in exchange for a free round of Amarula coffees. Everything and nothing had changed.

The security detail alighted first, very smart in ironed trousers and African shirts, shiny shoes and movie-star sunglasses. It was the nineties, and America had made her indelible mark on South Africa.

Minister of Education. He sure as hell hoped there wouldn't be a spelling test during the esteemed minister's stay. He chuckled to himself. With President Mandela at the helm, ministers were appointed left, right and center. Jock surmised it was payback to all longstanding ANC members who'd served the cause for years and years. Good for him. Reward was positive. God knew his South Africa could do with positivity.

He walked off the veranda and toward the entourage, flanked by his own team—new to him but not the hotel. Their excitement was quite infectious, though he was not one to be influenced.

"If it wasn't for President Mandela, this would never be possible," said the receptionist standing next to him.

"This is such an honor for us," said the new food and beverage manager, recently stolen from the *Elangeni*.

He glanced at them, impressed by their excitement and their willingness to accept President Mandela's new Rainbow Nation, where all colors were celebrated.

Jock was relieved. He really had no idea what he was buying into. The business broker made no guarantees of quality or mindset of the staff. All that drove him in his giant quest to reclaim this mountain paradise were memories and the need to get back to where he belonged. The only thing he had going for him was that he was his father's son.

That he found his inherited team to be diverse, dynamic and

progressive was as rosy as the flowering flora in the manicured beds.

They were twenty meters away when the newly minted Minister of Education alighted from the chopper. Tall.

Good. He was a Zulu. They were born leaders, and their ethics were of the highest caliber. This Rainbow Nation was starting off right!

Ten meters. They'd been briefed on protocol, and though his staff hung back, as host, Jock started toward the minister to welcome him, conscious of his limp for the first time in nearly twenty years.

The minister of education looked directly at him.

Jock stopped. So did his world.

So did the minister.

His head spun in time with his racing heart.

Could it really be?

As if he was watching his own dream, he saw himself push his legs forward and hold out a hand.

The tall minister grasped his proffered hand.

Their complicated handshake followed.

The minister said, "Glad to see you are well, Tsotsi."

And his reply reverberated in his head. "And all thanks to you, Minister Tshabalala, or may I still call you Papin?"

## 47

# THE LETTER

*Later: Champagne Castle Hotel perimeter,*
*20 September 1994*

TSOTSI AND PAPIN sat on their rock.

Their shoes and socks lay at the bottom of the great boulder they called their own. As usual, and in spite of his more than fifty years, Papin had his legs bent and close to his chest, arms hugging knees. Tsotsi had not been back to the rock since that fateful day in 1966. He struggled to climb up. His leg, severely damaged on the battlefield in Angola, had never regained its strength, and old, hard-earned rugby injuries were fulfilling their promise for his limbs to succumb to early arthritis.

"It's sure handy being a minister's tsotsi," he said as he stood on the back of one of the beefy security guys to reach the top of the rock he'd once leapt onto without thinking.

Papin drew a jar of Peels Honey from behind his back and handed it over with a grin. "After my surprise of finding you here, I went looking for this miracle cure. You won't be able to run as fast, so best you have a jar close by at all times."

"Peels," Tsotsi shouted with glee, like a boy. And they

laughed, and Tsotsi felt a lightness of being he hadn't since he was sixteen. He was indeed Tsotsi again.

In companionable silence, they listened to spring's symphony at sunset and gazed over the landscape they knew so well, while hadedahs called loudly and a hundred species of birds bid each other goodnight. It had been nearly three decades since they'd last sat like this.

The sun dipped farther and farther behind the mountain, and darkness turned the orange vista to red, purple, then indigo.

And the hotel lights came on.

He heard Papin's intake of breath match his own.

After a few minutes, Papin broke the silence. "Inkosi may be long gone, but his magic still works at sunset and sunrise."

"He was a great man." Tsotsi swallowed the lump in his throat. "Look at it, Papin. How it's grown. The hotel is three times its size. All our alcoves for observation have been reconfigured."

"If you ever need a partner ..."

Tsotsi's head turned sharply. "What was that? You have to speak up, Minister. A notorious terrorist—you may have heard of him, Lwazi? Well, that despicable, murdering, deplorable son of a bitch blasted my eardrums to hell and back some years ago. Bastard." Tsotsi heard the rush of rage—a decades-long visitor—force its way through his mouth.

He shook his reeling head.

The silence was long and electric. He glanced at Papin. In the twilight, luminous tears spilled down his sunken cheeks. Tsotsi said nothing. He superimposed images of his new wife over the ones that haunted him and waited for the rage to dim.

Minutes had passed, yet tears still poured from the minister's eyes.

Jock kept his eyes on his—and the bank's—old-new brightly

lit hotel and thought of his wife orchestrating the dinner without him. She was more than capable.

Without turning his head, Tsotsi's voice was barely a whisper. "Why did I never hear of Lwazi again after I encountered him?"

Papin stared ahead. "Lwazi realized in raw reality what war had made of him when he saw you ... damaged, shattered. Instead of killing you, Papin murdered Lwazi right there, and it was I, the more tortured, more regretful, more broken Papin who rose from that killing field."

Tsotsi watched guilt pass over his old friend's face as Papin roughly wiped his arm across his eyes. The new habit of passing his whole palm from forehead to chin followed. It seemed to take away his self-loathing. At least for a while.

Minutes later, Papin continued softly, "And I strove from that day forward to make a difference in positive ways."

Tsotsi felt a calm he'd lost a long time ago infuse his mind. When he spoke, it was with absolute sincerity. "I've no doubt at all you played a huge part in establishing our new Rainbow Nation. You've always had the means. And we've got a mighty leader."

Silence fell once more but for a family of baboons having an evening meeting a few hundred feet above them. A sound so familiar to them, it seemed to reinforce the enormity of two lost friends, blood brothers who found each other by accident after decades of being pulled by opposing forces. Accident or divine timing?

"Lwazi was a cold, detestable son of a bitch. I hope he never returns," Tsotsi said, vowing it was the last time he'd mention that dastardly name.

Papin nodded. "Lwazi was born to rid this body of the hate I'd accrued in a horribly unjust world. Seeing you so ... was a terrible shock. It pulled me back from the brink of my own madness. A madness born from all I had been forced to choreograph. I believed I could make a difference—perhaps because Sangoma told me so at thirteen—but I was made to prove my worth in the killing fields before I could be in a position to be heard. When you made me walk away from the war, I was surprised they kept me. But then my real work began."

"Thank God you are such a bad shot. Otherwise, we'd not be sitting here."

And they laughed because nobody shot more accurately than Papin. And they laughed and laughed and soon they didn't care four grown men were hovering at the bottom of a giant rock, arms outspread, lest their minister should roll off. It only made them hold tighter to their bellies.

Tsotsi glanced at the minister. He had the face of his Papin of old.

Papin's smile lit up the surroundings as he said, "I mean it! I will gladly be your silent partner. You won't have to run the place on a shoestring."

Tsotsi was silent, though his mind whirred and clonked like noisy, complicated machinery about to spit out a commodity of great pride.

"It's the only place I've ever called home," said Papin.

"It's my home too. I was lost without it. Dad sold it in 1966 when he and mom got divorced."

"Divorced?" Papin's face was wrought with confusion, then shock. "I'm so sorry."

"It happened right after you left, and the hotel was sold a month later." Tsotsi had stuck masking tape over his Mind Brownie during that time too. He knew the scars ran deeper than the long one on his arm, but he worked hard to make them invisible.

Papin continued, "That's terrible. The only reason I'm

smiling is because your Zulu's rusty. I thought you said your folks were discovered."

"And your English is still much better than mine." Jock smiled back.

"Where did you go?" Papin asked.

"Durban. A flat with my mom. Saw my dad often as I could."

"So difficult. How did you get Champagne back?"

Tsotsi felt the cool of the evening air on his cheeks and breathed in the glory of his mountains. "It was a long slog. It changed hands a few times, and I was never in a position to buy. Divorce for me too. Two kids I adore. Then I married my adventuresome girl. She recognized my heart lay buried in the Berg. We sold everything we had and waited for the right moment. It came, and the deed was transferred into my name just two weeks ago."

"Sorry to hear your life has been so turbulent." Papin's voice was soft and filled with remorse.

Tsotsi heard the hyenas barking above them. The hoot of an owl was answered by another, miles away.

"Well, I can't imagine yours has been smooth sailing," Jock said.

Their silence was companionable. Easy.

Tsotsi asked, "Do you have a family?"

Papin's head shook slowly. "No. No time."

"Well, it's not too late. And now you are so important, you'll have the ladies clamoring."

The face lost its newly captured, old Papin. "I found my woman shortly after I left here. And I lost her months later to a bullet from a white policeman's gun, when her hands were up in surrender. That's what sealed my fate and fueled the fire for the long, long fight."

"Life's a mean bitch. I am so sorry," he said, and he meant it. He knew then with absolute clarity that shaking off his many regrets would become easier from now onward. "Well, at least I helped prepare you for that long, long fight. I gave you many excellent years of patience training."

Papin chuckled softly and beckoned to one of his ever-present bodyguards, who handed him something. It was hard to tell what, since the indigo night sky had turned to ink-black blotched with gray from stagnant cumulous clouds on this windless night. The hotel lights were dimmer than usual, because the Sunday movie was on. Everything changes and everything stays the same. But suddenly, as if celebrating their reunion, a mere thousand stars pushed their way through the clouds and winked at them.

Papin said, "I always scorned you for wanting one of these because our life together was so colorful and interesting. There was no need for changing shapes in a man-made tube. But I think we both could have used one while we were away from this place. I know it's years too late, and you never need to look through it again because you're back. But it could be useful, if we should ever leave this rock, to help block out things in the world outside."

Tsotsi took the proffered box, opened it and howled with delight. "Where the hell did you find this thing?" He turned the object this way and that as unadulterated joy lit up his being.

"At Segornie's. I went down there this afternoon after I saw you, to get you something, and this was it. The old man's still there. Grumpy as ever."

Tsotsi turned the tube over and over in his hands, feeling its weight, its texture, its importance. He'd never held one in his hands before. He was four, seven, ten again. But now he owned one. His kaleidoscope. "Thank you, Papin," he said simply.

Papin spoke softly. "I had no idea you owned Champagne Castle hotel. I came only to heal my battered soul. To see my father. Sangoma in his new fancy kraal. No more dining room but Zulus visiting from far and wide to seek his council."

They both chuckled at the thought of the powerful Sangoma, their Nicholas.

"I came to recapture the peace. To remember. I never ever expected to find you here. When I saw you, it hit me. I knew as well as I know my name is Papin Tshabalala and nothing else that only together will we help erase the turbulent times we spent apart."

"Dad always loved the way you turned a phrase, Papin." He smiled at his old friend. "You're right, this kaleidoscope will come in handy if I ever have to leave this beloved place." He gestured broadly. "And it's going to be bloody useful when my still-charged Mind Brownie and New Aunts come up with things they shouldn't."

"Can I share it with you?" Papin asked.

"My kaleidoscope or my old-new home?"

"Both," said Papin.

"Those years we shared were the best of my life ..." He stopped short of what he wanted to say. But then he remembered his mantra. No Regrets. And he finished, "And then you ran away. Why?"

"I became too observant for my own good. I saw injustices, first small, then they became too big to handle," said Papin, "and then you shunned me once and for all."

"I never meant to," Jock said, then he had an epiphany. He'd forgotten, while he wallowed in his own misery caused by the shocking sequence of unexpected change that followed, that he'd hurt someone too. Papin. The avalanche started with hearing Papin was paid to be his friend; then the anguish of his best friend leaving him; then the crushing endurance of his parents' divorce; and worst of all, the hotel being sold and losing everything he loved.

Jock had forgotten that it was he who drove his friend down the mountain like a jackal because of his bad timing and inability to express himself.

"I am back where I belong," said Jock. After a long pause, he added, "And so are you."

Jock fished in his pocket and pulled out a tatty, yellowed envelope he'd unearthed from a hidden gap in their rock just this afternoon.

Twenty-eight years ago, when he'd retrieved the letter from Nicholas, he'd popped the letter in a glass jar, locked the lid with all his might, and buried it safely where only Papin would know where to look for it.

He held the envelope and looked his old friend in the eyes for the first time since their unexpected meeting that morning and said, "I left this for you when I went to boarding school that Sunday, after the puff adder hiking catastrophe. But you'd already run away."

Jock held the tired letter out to Papin.

"What is it, Tsotsi?" Papin looked apprehensive as he took the yellowed envelope with "Champagne Castle Hotel" embossed on the left-hand corner.

And he replied, "The only letter I've ever written."

# AFTERWORD

Thank you for reading *Zebra.* I hope you see why I fell in love with Jock and how Papin stole my heart.

If you enjoyed your soiree into my South African world, I think you'll be wowed by the charming Italian Pietro in *War Serenade.* Once a bon vivant opera singer and now a broken POW far from home, Pietro's waiting to die in a fortified South African camp run by a tyrant. But when he sees Iris, a fiery redhead, through the barbed wire and their eyes meet, they meld into each other's soul. She becomes his reason to live. A dangerous escape is concocted, and a death-defying love affair ensues ...

Roxanne St. Claire, *New York Times* bestselling author, called World War II historical romance *War Serenade* "A love story for the ages."

Both *War Serenade* and *Zebra* are inspired by true stories. Turn the page for an excerpt.

Go behind the scenes and read my musings at jillwallace.com ... and join CLUB UNTAMED.

CLUB UNTAMED is my Facebook reader group, where members get access to unseen outtakes of *War Serenade* and *Zebra* as well as works in progress, behind-the-scenes stories, first news and fun giveaways. In addition, beta readers, Advance Reader Copy recipients and a rootin' tootin' street team will be chosen from within CLUB UNTAMED. Just sign up for the newsletter at www.jillwallace.com, then join CLUB UNTAMED. I can't wait to see you there!

If you enjoyed *Zebra*, it would really mean the world to me if you went on to BookBub, Goodreads or your favorite reading site and left a review. Your positivity keeps me writing.

## EXCERPT FROM WAR SERENADE

Who, then, was she to judge this starving man bringing down a portly pigeon to roast over a fire?

The crowd roared with delicious anticipation.

She was amazed by the prisoner's gentleness as he reached for the bird while he clung to the wire for dear life with his other hand. Blood oozed from new lacerations as he manipulated the pigeon slowly through the razor edges, his own hand taking the pain, while gentle fingers encased the bird protectively.

Goodness! No wasted drop. They *were* hungry. She couldn't watch the poor bird's imminent demise, yet she couldn't look away.

He manipulated the pigeon from its lethal trap and held it above the fence while his other hand still gripped the wire, stopping him from falling three stories to a razor-sharp death.

She winced at the taste of blood and realized she'd bitten the inside of her cheek.

The man still held the bird firmly in one big hand. What a showman.

"Get it over with!" she wanted to shout. She'd learned to nip torture in the bud the hard way. *Don't be dramatic, Iris.* She heard her mother's voice but managed to ignore it as the fascinated guards lowered their guns, and the gleeful crowd was quiet. All eyes were raised up to the man on the wire.

He held up his hand as high as he dared without losing his balance.

"A sacrifice?" wondered Iris.

His tapered fingers opened. The pigeon froze. The prisoners were still and silent.

The bird took flight. Wobbly at first, likely overcome by its unexpected freedom, but mercifully, it caught the wind and soared away.

Free.

And then she understood: He freed the pigeon because he couldn't free himself.

Wild, angry "Boos" broke the silence. That was Italian she understood.

The man's face remained expressionless. He simply started his downward climb, and as he dropped his chin for a good look at where to secure his next footing ...

He found her eyes instead. His bleeding, bare foot remained suspended in midair.

And the world stopped, as did her heart, suspended in her chest. Then the blooming thing somersaulted. A great, big, double Boswell & Wilkie Circus high-wire dismount kind of somersault. Breathing wasn't important as his eyes penetrated her hidden, most private core, and seeing into his deepest self, she felt at once immediate recognition and the ache of long separation. Then joyous relief at the reunion, unfathomable understanding, and above all, deep, satisfying, all-consuming emotion she didn't understand. It pierced her heart like a long pin into a well-stuffed cushion.

"Get down now, or we shoot." Guns were cocked again, but the sound was far away, in another world. Another time.

From far away, she heard Dr. de Kleyn's insistent voice: "Let's go where it's safe. It's dangerous out here."

She blinked, breaking the connection and jolting her senses. She inhaled her first breath in what seemed like two days.

Before she turned away, Iris tried to find the bird savior's eyes again, but he was close to the barbed wire, so his concentration was on the careful placement of his naked foot. She felt empty. The doctor's last words echoed in her head, and the most profound thought hit her like a hammer: "Dangerous? I've never felt safer than I did just then," but she followed his white coat into the brick building.

Learn more about WAR SERENADE at jillwallace.com.

# AUTHOR'S NOTE

*Zebra* was not written with the intention of making a political statement. It is purely and simply a story about friendship. The only reason politics rears its ugly head is due to the times in which the novel is set. As much as I abhor politics, without the complexities of that time, there would be no *Zebra.*

Many of my friends who have known this story since it was a young screenplay fifteen years ago ask "What's true and what's fiction?"

Truth is, the Wallace family owned Champagne Castle Hotel for approximately 20 years.

Champagne Castle is where Athol grew up. It's where he was schooled in all things Zulu by Papin, a herd boy a few years older. He and Papin had incredible adventures together, and Athol, through this telling, pays homage to his first best friend, Papin.

If this was a true story or a memoir, Heather Scott nee Wallace (previously Fyfe) would be front and center. Heather is Athol's beloved sister. She's two years older and still visits the Drakensberg every year. As much as Heather has a right to be in anything remotely related to the Wallaces and Champagne

Castle, her story is not mine to tell. So, for fiction's sake, Jock became an only child.

If this was a memoir or true story, Athol's son, Terry D. Wallace, and daughter, Lesley R. Wallace Kimball, would be major characters.

Although there is a glossary with South Africanisms and some Zulu words, please cut me some slack if some words can't be verified. Though I own three Zulu dictionaries, they became door stoppers in the three years of this novel's making. Athol often insisted it *was* a word he and Papin used, and was sure of the meaning, so I resorted to phonetics. *Gollaga-inja!* I urge you to play along. Once you've read the book, you'll understand why I didn't have a hope in hell of getting the spelling out of my husband.

My Athol doesn't tell his own stories. It's one of the things that makes him all the more attractive to me. But as the book reflects, nothing is perfect ... so what most couples learn about their soul mates in two months took me thirty-four years to learn about my man.

Where fact ends and fiction begins must remain a mystery for the sake of the story. But safe to say, my Athol's experiences were lived, both in the mountains and in the Bush Wars of South Africa. Cultural, tracking and insightful African traditions taught to him by Papin made him indispensable to an army who paid no mind to how their need for his expertise affected his life and his heart.

Against his grain, his skills were used and abused in chunks of lost time over thirteen years in the South African Defense Force because of his intimate knowledge of the African culture.

This book is written about difficult times in the country Athol and I grew up in. A country we loved. We are and always will be, at heart, South African.

Thankfully, much has changed since the days in which this

book was set. Immense strides have diminished cultural chasms, and acceptance has nurtured this Rainbow Nation.

"But at least tell us about the ending?" my friends implore. "Did that *really* happen?"

And I say, "I took the liberty of writing a work of fiction, and in my perfect world, this is how the story ends."

# GLOSSARY

## A LOOSE COLLECTION OF SOUTH AFRICANISMS FOR READERS' REFERENCE

*During the early time period of this book, there were very few African words that were incorporated into the English and Afrikaans vocabulary. There was a definite attempt to keep languages pure and separate.*

*The modern South African spoken language is mostly English, peppered with words from Afrikaans, Zulu, Xhosa and many African languages, and also including European and Middle Eastern languages. Slang and Fanakalo are added for good measure.*

*Fanakalo is a conglomeration of languages created for the gold mines decades and decades ago to ease understanding between white mine-bosses and an assorted mass of many-tongued African laborers.*

**African** — Usually black-skinned and born on the continent of Africa, speaking a multitude of languages. African languages of South Africa include: Xhosa, Zulu, Ndebele, Pedi, Sotho, Swati, Tsonga, Tswana, Venḓa.

**Afrikaners** — Afrikaans-speaking people of South Africa, originally descended from the Dutch and Huguenot settlers of the 17th century.

**Aikona!** — Expresses shock or disbelief. Directly translated means "never," "not on your life."

**ANC** — African National Congress.

**Assegai** — Light spear or javelin made of wood with pointed iron tip.

**Baas** — Boss.

**Bakgat** — Wonderful.

**Beer shandy** — A tall glass of half beer, half Sprite.

**Blerry** — Afrikaans version of mild swear words "bloody" or "blooming," describing a noun.

**Boere musiek** — Old Afrikaans songs.

**Boytjie** — Term of endearment for boy/man.

**Braai** — Could be a shortened version of above or a verb — to braai or grill meat outdoors over a fire.

**Braaivleis** — Noun; South Africanism for BBQ.

**Bughouse** — A small-town movie theater.

**Cane, Cane Spirits** — A popular spirit distilled from sugar cane.

**Chorrie** — An old junky car.

**Dagga** — Marijuana.

**Donderse** — Not in polite use — adjective like "bloody" or "damned."

**Doring bos** — Thorn bush.

**Dustbin** — Trash can.

**Eich!** — Exclamation of dismay.

**Eina!** — Exclamation like "ouch!"

**Eland** — The largest of the South African antelopes.

**Elangeni** — Durban Beachfront hotel.

**Gollaga-inja** — Asshole of a dog.

**"Holy Poggenpoel"** — A made-up exclamation. Poggenpoel is an Afrikaans surname.

**Induna/s** — In this sense, leader and advisor.

**Inkosi** — Chief/king.

**Isigcina sentliziyo** — Zulu love messages made of beads.

**Jo'burg** — Slang for Johannesburg, aka Egoli — Place of Gold.

**Kaffir** — A racial epithet, akin to using the N-word in North America.

**Kaffir Boetie** — Literally, Kaffir brother. A derogatory term used to describe a white person who fraternized with a black person or sympathized with the cause of the black community.

**Kleilat fighting** — Typically a boys' game, played until the opposition quits from the pain of being pelted by wet clay.

**Knobkerrie** — A heavy wooden club with a knob on one end.

**Koeksisters** — Afrikaner confection: fried dough infused with syrup.

**Kom** — Come.

**Koptjie** — Hillock/small hill.

**Kos** — Food.

**Kraal** — Traditional African village.

**Labola** — A dowry. A custom of gifting cattle or goods to the parents of a girl to secure her hand in marriage.

**Mealie meal** — Coarse flour made of corn. Corn is known as "Mealies."

**Mnumzane** — Sir.

**Muti** — Medicine.

**Nagapie** — Nocturnal primate or bush baby.

**Numbies** — Slang for breasts.

**Nyagas** — Big trouble (as remembered). As in "He is full of nyagas" or "Nyagas is coming."

**Oke** — Guy.

**Putu pap** — Traditional maize porridge.

**Rock Spiders** — Derogatory name for Afrikaners used by the English. "Dutchman/men" used in same fashion.

**Rondavel** — Circular African dwelling with a thatched roof.

**Roofies** — New (green) army recruits.

**Rooi Necks** — Derogatory name for English-speaking South Africans, because the English usually have fair skin that burns red in the African sun. Also called "Sout Piels" because their penises dipped into the ocean on the long voyage from England to South Africa.

**Rubbish** — Used like "nonsense."

**SADF** — South African Defense Force.

**Sangoma** — Traditional Zulu diviner.

**Sawubona** — A Zulu greeting; means "Hello/I see you."

**Shebeens** — (Usually) illegal drinking establishments.

**Sis!** — Exclamation of disgust.

**Sjambok** — Long stiff whip, usually rhino or hippo hide.

**Slap chips** — Thick, soggy French fries smothered in salt and vinegar.

**"Slat hom. Moer hom stukkend"** — Afrikaans slang: "Hit him. Smash him up till he breaks."

**Takkie** — Tennis shoe.

**Tokoloshe** — In Zulu and Xhosa mythology, a dwarf-like sprite. A mischievous and evil spirit that can become invisible. Called upon by malevolent people to cause trouble for others.

**Trolley** — Shopping cart.

**Tsotsi** — Loosely translated as "thug" but in this book's context, "naughty little bugger."

**Ubasi** — Boss

**Umanqoba!** — Victor!

**Umfana** — A young man, not yet married.

**Umtwana** — Child/kid.

**Veldfire** — Wild bush fire.

**Veldskoen** — An outdoor ankle boot made with untanned hide and a rubber sole.

**Voetsek!** — Vulgar Afrikaans slang for "Go away" or "Get lost!"

**Vok** — Expletive for "Fuck!"

# ACKNOWLEDGMENTS

*Zebra* took me three years to write, just like *War Serenade.* It took a village to guide, goad and gear me up for launch.

Thank you, Debbie Shannon, bright, brilliant and accomplished Developmental Editor. In the midst of Covid, writing was a blissful escape until *Zebra's* complex timelines and four points of view overwhelmed me. Debbie caught me wallowing in confusion. "Send it to me," she said. I did. And there started a mentorship the likes of which I have never known. As *Zebra's* fairy godmother, Debbie tirelessly helped me shape him, make sense of him, bring out the best in him. She found his weaknesses and oftentimes slapped this author into submission (in the gentlest manner). She's held my writing hand over proverbial fire, forcing me to feel visceral emotions to share with my readers. I am sublimely, completely and absolutely indebted to Debbie for her investment of time, love, know-how, and her genuine wish to see *Zebra* succeed.

If this book is enjoyed by readers, it is in great part because of Debbie Shannon's unconditional love of it. And me. How grateful I am.

My thanks to my friend and author Muffy Berlyn, who helped me kick-start *Zebra* the novel.

My Virginia girls—thank you for many nights in Duck or Dallas or Hull or whereverthehell we were—listening to my script and rooting for Jock and Papin. 'Tis your excitement and love of the boys that kept me writing.

My SSCGs—wise, infinitely smart, intuitive, helpful beyond measure, always there in a crisis ... thank you so very, very much!

My Kacti (K.J. Pierce), my Kara Turey, my Megan Fuentes, Tobi Terrific, thank you all for helping me nurture *Zebra* and get him introduced to the world through website and social media.

Thank you, the irrepressible phenomenon that is Narelle Todd—Business Coach Extraordinaire! You graced me with your great patience, your underpay/over-deliver philosophy, and your brilliance.

Thank you, Ivette Griffith, who walked this walk with me and who never fails to publicly endorse my writing to all who enter her sanctuary. She blesses me..

My awesome, enthusiastic beta readers: Lorena Spensley (who read two versions, awesome LLL), Frank Giaramita, Beverley Wilcocks, Joni O'Connell, Debbie Clark, Betsy Galbraith, Brenda Morcom, Beth Barg, Darlene Hughes, Randy Hughes, Alana McIntosh, Andrew McIntosh, Kitty Low and Alasdair Low. Your feedback was immensely insightful. Thank you all so very much for your time and dedication to this book!

Thank you to my obliging ARC readers, Sandy O'Reilly, Chris Erickson, Lori Keen, Mallena Urban, Patty Mele and Veronica De Kleyn. So wonderful you volunteered to be early readers of *Zebra*.

My grateful thanks to two marvelous artists: Veronica Pins is an uber-talented South African artist who volunteered to create a map for *Zebra,* to give readers a visual perspective of distance within the story. Amazing jewelry artist Sandra Springs, of her own divine accord, dedicated one of her jewelry lines on Etsy to me and called it *The Zebra Collection*. Thank you for this great honor.

How privileged and grateful I am to have you both in my world!

Thank you, Heather and Neil Scott, for photos sent tirelessly in the mammoth quest to satisfy he who inspired *Zebra,* so the *perfect shot of Champagne* could be found for the cover. And whoever said many hands make light work was dead wrong. With two very different opinions to cater to, the cover took nearly as long to decide on as the book took to write. Thank you Sky Diary Productions, TJ Logan, and Dar Albert for your incredible patience and too many versions.

Thank you to my Club Untamed Readers Club, who let me infuse them with anticipation, some may say, ad nauseam. ;o) Thank you to my newsletter subscribers, who are equally tolerant and so sweetly allow me to share my musings.

Thank you to profound author and kindness personified, Kerry Evelyn, who took precious time during her short annual family vacation to wade through *Zebra*'s hundreds of pages in his final stages. Kerry in her inimitable way offered sound advice and encouragement as she does all things—with unconditional love and sincerity.

Grateful thanks to Holly S. Martin for her editor's eagle eye.

Thank you to my precious, priceless friends who constantly keep me on track with their positivity, their encouragement and their understanding of my desperate need to tell stories.

Thank you, my Besties—Alana McIntosh and Kitty Low—for always having my back.

Thank you, Chris Kridler. My editor. My last word. My compass. My heroine. I can honestly say, I cannot write a book without you and hope I never have to. You are always honest.

Always encouraging. Always true. Always right (damn)! I am desperately lucky to have you in my world.

Thank you, my husband. Without the incredible life you've lived, there would be no *Zebra*. Without your beautiful love, there would be no us. This joint book venture began as a tough journey ... a pushing of your pragmatism and a pulling of my imagination. At odds. But as we do all things, we worked it out. And I think I love you more because of it. I hope I've done you as proud as you deserve.

## ABOUT THE AUTHOR

Jill Wallace is a storyteller. Born and bred in South Africa, she's lived half her life in America. Just as it's hard to tell the roots from the branches of a baobab tree, Jill no longer knows where the South African ends and the American begins. She married her prince, helped raise two heart-children and lives too far from her granddaughters. Jill writes happily from the backyard of their home in the Space Coast of Florida, which she shares with her husband and two charming and delightful Aussie Shepherds. She believes in loyalty, dogs, kindness, dogs, long friendships, dogs, as well as the *great* power of chocolate and imagination. In any order.

Learn more and sign up for the Club Untamed newsletter at JillWallace.com.


facebook.com/jwallaceauthor

twitter.com/jwallaceauthor

instagram.com/jwallaceauthor

amazon.com/Jill-Wallace/e/B079ZBFZC3

pinterest.com/jillwallaceauthor

bookbub.com/authors/jill-wallace